two
HaLves

Book Two

Marta Szemik

MyLit Publishing

MyLit Publishing paperback 2nd edition, 2012

This book is a work of fiction. The names, characters, places, and
incidents are products of the author's imagination or have been used
fictitiously and are not to be constructed as real. Any resemblance to
persons, living or dead, actual events, locales or organizations is entirely
coincidental.

ISBN-978-0-9878772-1-5

To my parents who always support me,
Maya and Alex who zap my heart everyday,
and my loving husband.

PROLOGUE

Hundreds of miles—that's how far he ran each day. His feet should have been blistered, but they weren't. He should have been out of breath, but he didn't need to breathe. Exhaustion had set in years ago, but not from the running.

Where should I run next? What would be the best way to mislead the seekers?

Ekim imagined a map in his head of where he'd been. Black marked the roads he'd passed; red for those he needed to avoid; green for ones he could still use. The mental strain to keep the drawings organized exhausted him.

But running was his priority, the only constant in his life, and would be for a long time.

Almost twelve months had passed since Ekim's wife Saraphine died, since Sarah was born. He longed to see his daughter but didn't dare risk it.

Zigzagging across America, he retreated from the demons who concentrated their groups in the south. The seekers would think he returned to his kind and stop the chase—or so he hoped. Ekim has been a cold-blooded vampire since 1823, but with his judgment clear he was newly compassionate. Only when protecting his family did the ferocity and the viciousness come to the fore, necessary to preserve the human and vampire species.

He couldn't slow down. Sarah was turning one in a week. Seekers were still looking for her and William, Atram's one-year-old son. The decision to move Sarah to Pinedale was difficult, but he knew it was the right choice. Her aunt Helen would take care of her. She'd continue mixing the serums that kept Sarah hidden.

Atram, Ekim's best friend since the day they'd been turned, sent a telegram to the most northerly post office in each state once a month. Ekim stepped outside the building and pulled the paper from its envelope.

EVERYONE'S WELL. KIDS GETTING ALONG. HEART CONDITION GETTING WORSE. THEY'RE LEAVING IN TWO WEEKS.

Sarah and William couldn't get too close to each other. The children's heartbeats quickened uncontrollably when they laughed, turning the giggles into cries of pain. Thin veins appeared on their innocent, chubby faces. The electric shock between them when they touched was as quick and unpredictable as snapped fingers. They needed each other to fulfill their destiny, yet they couldn't be together.

How will they do it? How will they ever save both our kinds from extinction?

* * *

PINEDALE 150 MILES

The vampire read the road sign, then closed his eyes to picture his daughter's new home. A white picket fence of a red brick Georgian dwelling with white trim around the dormer windows and doors, a chimney protruding from the roof, and a lawn chair on the front porch. Ekim's only wish was to make a stopover.

"I can't," he whispered through clenched teeth. His stomach tightened, and the vampire bent to rest his hands on his knees for a moment. The pain wasn't physical but was still a torment.

How long before I can see my daughter for the first time?

I can't.

Ekim's path around Pinedale to reach the powerful witch Hannah had to confuse the seekers so they wouldn't know he avoided the town intentionally.

He sped up, running along the shadow of a railroad bridge, the forest looming on his left. The sweet fragrance of jasmine floated in the air reminding him of home. Inside, he could only hope Hannah would trust him and provide the protection Sarah needed. Was this too much hope for a vampire to have?

* * *

June 21, the longest day of the year. Ekim huddled in the shadow of a fir, wishing it was broad enough to cover his body. When his thoughts wandered, the sun singed the arms, and he'd have to shuffle another inch to avoid the scorching beams. Waiting since sunrise, he watched the fireball rolling across the blue sky. Moving his body with the tree's shade throughout the day, the vampire imagined sweat beading and running down his face, though he knew it wouldn't. He shifted his weight from one foot to the other, anxious. The sun almost touched the earth. Another two to three minutes.

Ekim looked to the west, his feet planted exactly in the spot he'd been told to be: 44.57N by 110.5W. To his left, the sun sank to touch the top of a hill. As the fiery orb collided with the mound of earth, its rays sprayed outward to fall across fields, hills, and valleys, bathing all life with an orange and yellow glow—everywhere except one area in the lee of the hill. He smiled. Its shade would lengthen, and he'd be able to escape the shadow of the fir toward it.

Now. He ran fast, ducking under branches, jumping over fallen pines. The faith he held onto inside didn't let him wonder whether Hannah would listen. Castall's promise that she would sufficed. After all, her husband was an influential warlock.

A noise in the bushes to the right kept Ekim alert as he sprinted. Something paralleled his route.

What else could move as fast as a vampire? A seeker? He inhaled, but the scent was unfamiliar. Ekim sensed another creature's tracking on the left and his fangs sprouted.

They stayed concealed until Ekim reached Hannah's hill before leaping from the bushes to block his way. They looked like vampires—their faces were similar in structure, their gestures familiar—but the smell of wet bear fur mixed with that of a wolf intrigued thim.

"What do you want?" the female shouted.

"I'm looking for Hannah," Ekim answered, careful not to give too much away. Anything he said could be used to find Sarah.

She kept her stern eyes on the vampire. "What do you want from her?"

The male stared, his brows furrowed, but although he looked toward Ekim, his piercing gaze concentrated on the forest at his back.

Something rustled branches and leaves behind Ekim, but he did not stir. He inhaled deeper, letting his acute senses work. Five grizzly bears, three wolves, six mountain lions, and two coyotes—all focused on the vampire. Four eagles circled overhead, their underbodies golden in the afterglow of the sun. The male murmured at the animals under his breath in a tongue Ekim did not recognize.

The mammals did not pose a threat to Ekim. He'd get a few scratches but could handle them. His mouth watered at the thought of some carnivore blood. He held back though, unsure of the two beings standing in front. Their bodies were well-defined, muscles taut without flexing, and Ekim wasn't the only one, he noted, who didn't break a sweat while running.

"My business is only for Hannah. Castall sent me." Ekim stood taller but lowered his shoulders and softened his eyes. He let his fangs retract.

A crunching sound accompanied subtle movement in the earth and brushes behind the two beings. Ekim smelled crushed rosemary and mint. Their arms were still crossed at their chests, and they did not twitch. An oval of grass in the hill moved a camouflaged door that swung open. A lady in her early fifties stepped out.

Hannah, Castall's witch wife.

"Kids, stand down. He's kin," she ordered, eyeing Ekim from top to bottom. She waved forward. "I'm Hannah. Come in, Ekim."

The male nodded and motioned with his arm toward the bushes at Ekim's back. The animals scattered into the darkening forest. Both "kids" stepped up beside Hannah, then parted to either side as the vampire followed her in.

Fresh basil and pepper joined the herbal aroma inside. The dwelling was larger than Ekim expected for the small hill concealing it.

"The outside's an illusion," Hannah said softly, as if he'd voiced his confusion. The witch's light and gentle voice did not match her size. Despite the weight she carried, she moved across the room with grace, her long skirt brushing the wooden floor as if she were dancing.

The air was warmer here than above ground, the dimmer light making it cozy. A small fireplace crackled on the back wall as steam hovered over a simmering pot hanging above the low flames.

"Have a seat, Ekim." She gestured toward an armchair against the opposite wall. Underneath her long sleeve, Ekim glimpsed a mark of three wavy lines on her wrist identical to Castall's on her wrist. The pair who greeted Ekim had taken up positions on either side of Hannah. She gestured to them next. "It's in their nature to be protective. Something that you're seeking, I gather—protection."

Ekim bowed, acknowledging Hannah's wisdom, and waited for her to speak again.

Hannah raised her thick eyebrows and dipped her head to look at him over her glasses. "Protection . . . These are my children, and I will protect them with my life." She gazed expectantly at Ekim.

"It's my child I need to protect, as well," he answered.

Hannah sat on a stool by the fireplace and threw a log into the pit before leaning forward to rest her elbows on her knees. With a pop, the settling fire spat two embers out on the floor. She picked them up with her bare hand and tossed them back into the growing flames.

"Castall said I could come to you for help. He gave me this to pass along." Cautious, Ekim lifted his hand toward the top of his long coat. The "kids" watched the movement closely. He pulled a white envelope from the inside breast pocket and handed it to Hannah. The initials *H.G.* were handwritten on the front, the back sealed with a wax stamp. "It should explain everything."

Hannah let a smile surface as she carefully opened the letter. The kids continued to glare at Ekim as she read. When she finished reading, she looked up. "Sarah and William are unique, like my children." She glanced lovingly at them. "The half-breeds can bring salvation to both humankind and vampires. Without them, the demons will win." Her eyes widened. "They will bring peace and balance to the underworld—but only together. When they learn who they are, they are to overthrow the demon lord. Together, they will be stronger than Aseret and his army." Her eyelids partially closed when she spoke. Her eyes moved from side to side; she was making a prediction.

Sliding from the stool, Hannah squatted beside a potted plant and scooped a fistful of dirt into her hand. She let it fall through her fingers down to the floor. Her eyes rolled back in their sockets, and her head tipped back. "You will be captured, Ekim. Do not fear. They will save you. You will be Sarah's only hope. Believe in what you feel." She paused. "Beware of Xela."

Then her head fell forward, and she looked up at the "kids" with her own eyes. "Your father's asking you to move to Pinedale immediately. You will be Sarah's secret guardians throughout her childhood and adolescence. You will be her friends and companions. You will protect her as if she were your blood." She rose and handed the letter to the girl at her side, who read it.

"Sarah's only one. How are they going to be her friends?" Ekim pointed hesitantly at the siblings.

The young woman looked up from the letter. "We assume whatever shape we need to be. We will befriend Sarah as children." Her gaze returned to the paper. "Your daughter has a difficult journey ahead. We will do everything that's asked of us and nothing less."

Ekim blinked rapidly, then wiped his eyes. The vampire features were gone from her face and her brother's. "Thank you," he said, taken aback by the sudden change.

"Our oath to you, Ekim, is to protect your daughter. She is destined to stop the extinction and bring balance. We will protect her with our lives," the young man promised, straightening his shoulders.

Ekim believed him. His hope restored, the vampire let out a long held breath.

"Ekim, you are part of the keeper's plan. Your family is part of their plan as well. You are therefore part of our family. You can expect the utmost faith and loyalty from Mira and Xander." Hannah pointed to the siblings. "They are stronger than many demons. They are wiser than most. You should stay away from Pinedale. Your scent is too familiar to the seekers. I'm surprised you've outrun them this long."

"Where should I go?" he asked.

The witch seemed to fall back into a trance. "Go back to the vampire territories. Spread the word that half-breeds will save their kind from demons. They should get ready for a battle." She opened her eyes and looked at him. "You should leave now. Take what you need from the forest."

Ekim wondered if she'd noticed how pale he was.

He pitied anyone who crossed Hannah's path. She was both a powerful witch and a mother with the fierce instincts of a lioness. A mother he wished Sarah had.

She tucked the letter into a leather-bound book on a side table. A mark identical to the one on Hannah's wrist was embossed on its cover, surrounded by colourful gems. Ekim smelled the centuries in the paper of its pages.

Unexpectedly, Hannah stepped forward and hugged the vampire, then turned on her heel and walked toward the invisible door. As she approached, the earthen wall cracked, opening to the outside.

"Thank you." Ekim bowed toward the siblings and Hannah before stepping through the door into the twilight. He had to move quickly to avoid capture but hesitated on the threshold before moving out into the woods and looked back.

Both siblings stared into a wall mirror. Their facial features changed. They ran their fingers across their face where the cheeks grew rosy, pudgy; the skin became smoother, younger, and softer; their noses shrank. The hair thinned and grew silky as eyes became blue, then brown, then green.

They were becoming toddlers.

CHAPTER 1

The sun had been up for an hour, but to me, it seemed like it had never set.

My stomach grumbled when the sweet smell of pancakes drizzled with warm maple syrup reached me. The hungry rumbles mingling with excitement felt like butterflies flapping their wings against the walls of my stomach. I hopped every second step on my way down to the kitchen. My heart thumped unevenly anticipating my freshman class trip.

"Good morning, Auntie!" I chirped.

Helen looked up at me and laughed. "'Morning, Sarah. All ready?"

"Yup. Did you sleep well?" I thought to ask.

"I did. And you?"

"Surfed a bit. Filled in another camping list." I waved the piece of paper, covered with scribbles and red checkmarks. This would be my first—and last—trip away from home.

Helen raised her brows. "Didn't think it was possible to find another list." She poured a glass of milk. In the warm kitchen air, drops of condensation formed on the outside of the glass. She pointed to the stack of dripping pancakes. "Breakfast's ready."

"Mmm, smells yummy! I bet it tastes even better." I sat at the round kitchen table and had the first bite in my mouth before Helen reminded me of the inevitable:

"Don't forget your other breakfast. Wouldn't want you to lose your colour on the trip." Helen never forgot what I hoped would disappear when morning came. It never did. It never would. And I couldn't blame her for what I was.

"I wish I *could* forget," I mumbled before filling my mouth. The thought of ending the lives of more guinea pigs disheartened me. I washed my mouthful of pancakes down with milk. "I guess it's better to do it here than in public."

"If you do have to fill up, make sure you're discreet," she cautioned.

"I won't have to." I was almost sure of that. It would take a rapid heartbeat, akin to a human heart attack, for me to run through the extra blood that would soon be flowing through my veins.

"Never say never," Helen said. It was one of her favourite sayings which I was beginning to use frequently. She leaned over behind my chair and hugged me. "Gonna miss you, hon. Please be careful."

I almost choked on the last bite I'd taken. "No worries, Auntie. What could possibly happen?" I rolled my eyes and shrugged before jokingly adding, "I'm sure I'll be the strongest one in the woods."

Thoughts of the dangers this graduations trip could present flashed through my mind. I wasn't afraid for me; I was afraid for those *around* me. I wanted my peers to go to high school. What if I lost control? What if the suppressed instincts surfaced? What if I hurt someone while trying to hide what I was?

I couldn't imagine wringing the neck of another human or sticking my fangs into their flesh to feed. Goosebumps covered my arms as I tried to forget the image. Helen had packed four extra serums to control the urge. Would it be enough? Secretly, I wished the serums could somehow be more potent.

"Sometimes things can happen that are beyond our control. I don't want you to do anything you'd regret later," Helen said.

"You mean like use my strength or speed."

"Or teeth," she teased. "Seriously, Sarah, you're everything to me. You have your entire life before you, and so much more to accomplish." She smoothed my hair behind my ears.

"I only want to be normal. I don't bring anything special to anyone in this town. No one would miss me if I was gone." I bit my tongue hard as soon as the last sentence slipped out.

"Don't say that, Sarah." Helen stroked the top of my head. "You— are—special," she said firmly. "I hope one day you'll realize it. Everyone has a purpose, and I'm sure you'll find yours."

"I'm sorry. I didn't mean it that way. I'd be so lost without you Auntie." I kissed her on the cheek and squeezed my arms around her. Getting Helen upset today was the last thing I wanted to do. She'd been so patient and understanding—the closest person to a mother I had ever known.

"I know." She wrapped her arms around me again and returned the kiss on my head. "Now get going before you miss the bus."

"I guess I'll just have to chase it." I laughed as I grabbed my new army backpack full of supplies and headed toward the door, halting on my way out to ask, "Oh! How is the stock doing?"

"Up!" she called, smiling about her ten-year-old investment in an emerging cosmetics company. "Don't forget the guinea pigs. They're out by the shed."

"Thank you!" I called, pulling the door closed.

"Oh, and Sarah! I packed an extra bug repellent in your side pocket."

Helen's last words rang in my ears as I took the first step on the warm air redolent of sweat and failed deodorant bus. Extra blood sloshed around inside me as I scanned the seats. Mira and Xander sat in the second row. I smiled, grateful for the two best friends I had in high school. I'd been home schooled until last year. Everyone had treated me like a toddler, ostracizing me in all imaginable ways, laughing constantly at my round-cheeked, childlike face and my small hands. Mira and Xander defended me. For some reason, others kept their distance from the siblings, the same way they now did with me.

We weren't brave enough (well, perhaps Xander was) to sit in the back with the cool kids. Even so, the catcalls came:

"Sarah, your kindergarten teacher called. They missed you on attendance."

"Xander doesn't have to climb the tree. He's as tall as one!"

"Let's declare a masquerade every day! Mira can hide her pimples that way!"

And these comments came from the nicer kids.

"Hi, guys!" I said to the siblings, dropping my knapsack in the first row.

Kneeling on the seat, I leaned over the back to face my friends. My limbs were not cooperating today; my arms waved in different directions and my thighs and calves tensed and relaxed periodically, all on their own. I felt like a chimpanzee on cocaine, except my narcotic this morning was adrenaline.

"Hey, Sarah, did you pack your bug spray?" Xander asked. He was like an older brother with occasional slips into father-like behaviour—not that I knew what that was like.

"Two full cans," I answered.

"Well, I have an extra one if you run out," he offered, winking at me. Xander was beginning to make me feel uncomfortable. The corners of his mouth were always up, showing off his white teeth. If I dropped something, he would pick it up. And the way he glanced at me from across the class all the time, grinning—awkward. Mira said it was a phase boys go through. I hoped it would pass soon, and I would have my friend back.

"What's going on at the back?" I focused on the last three rows. Although I could hear the electrifying discussion clearly, I still had to pretend to be clueless.

"They're talking about that bear attack again," Xander said. "Don't worry. If he comes back, I'll protect you." His smile faded. He wasn't joking.

"Xander, I'm sure if he comes by, I'll outrun you so he'll just have to settle for seconds."

Mira almost spit out the soda she was sipping. Bubbles formed around her nostrils.

"Ha. Ha," Xander said, his tone flat. "We'll see who gets the last laugh."

I glanced over at Mira as if to ask what's up with him? She shrugged.

"Turn around or you'll draw attention," he said, and just in time, too; I heard someone in the back say, "Freak," under her breath. I couldn't pinpoint who it was, but it didn't matter.

"Okay, okay." I slumped in the hot seat.

The trip to Shoshone National Park took just over two hours. It was a silent ride for the three of us, but a lot louder in the back. I heard everything that was being said, and I wished Mira and Xander had the same ability I had. How much fun would it be to be in on all the jokes? Thankfully, not another word was spoken about us.

* * *

The tents rose in the forest clearing before sunset. Four students were assigned to each one; Mira, Xander, and I were left to have our own. The three of us were like family so no one objected to our shelter being co-ed. Using half the can, I sprayed a solid coat of bug repellent all over my body.

It wasn't too long before the tall flames of a campfire danced within a circle of logs supporting students as we listened to Mr. Boyle's "scary" stories. I wondered how frightened my classmates would be if they knew what I was. The few stars in the sky did not provide enough light to find a clear path in the thick woods around us.

I had a harmonious link with nature and heard everything that went on in the forest. Three mice roamed their tunnels twenty yards away; a raccoon fifty yards to the east paused, perhaps contemplating when it would be safe enough to begin his nightly scavenging; a night owl on a frail branch on the third spruce to the right ruffled its feathers in preparation for a hunt. The noises teased my eardrums as nature wrapped itself around me. Finally I gave in, and my ears perked up, intent to hear sounds from the darker depths of the woods. The forest overpowered my mind.

My breathing quickened as I took in scents of the fresh green moss on the north side of the trees; the cool mist that blew from a nearby lake, carrying the scent of water lilies and algae; and in front of me, the over-sweet aroma of almost burnt toasted golden-brown marshmallows. I inhaled deeper, recognizing the sulphur of the Yellowstone geysers spitting steam and hot water. My heartbeat sped up even more. The pulse of nature—of life—pierced my skin, penetrating deep into my organs, giving me strength and vigour I hadn't thought possible. I absorbed the energy around me to enhance my senses.

The forest inhabitants knew what I was and kept their distance. My mouth watered when I thought about the sleeping elk three miles away. Would its blood thicken when it entered my mouth? My tongue slid across the inside of my upper lip when my gaze focused on someone's jugular. I swallowed in a dry throat as my eyes rose to the face of someone I'd dared to think of as a victim. The vampire instincts awoke.

Holding my head still, I peeked right, then left. All eyes were still on Mr. Boyle. I slid my right hand into the pocket of my shorts and wrapped my fingers around the familiar shape of the syringe. I'd done it so many times before to suppress my vampire side, no one would notice. I took the shot from the inside of my pocket. The serum spread through my body like cold water, cooling my veins. My breathing slowed, my heart rate steadied, and I heard Mr. Boyle concluding his story. Mira frowned at my audible sigh, then turned her attention back toward the fire.

The clouds above flowed to the east, and starlight shone brighter into the clearing. After an hour of jokes, songs, and laughter, and just as I was getting more comfortable in my human skin, Chris decided to be adventurous. "Who's brave enough to go on a hike?" he asked loudly.

Didn't he hear about that bear attack last week? It must be a ploy to get some one-on-one time with the girls.

"I don't think it's a good idea, Chris," said Ms. Wimsley, the other chaperone.

"Yeah, Chris, we all know what you want to do in the dark." Elizabeth sneered, zipping up her hoodie.

Chris's snide laugh was tinged with annoyance. "Oh, why don't you get ready for the next demonstration for women's rights, Elizabeth."

As they argued the reason behind Chris's urge to hike at night, I closed my eyes. A warm autumn breeze caressed my face. I stretched my arms lazily above my head, then froze when something tickled my palm. Tiny, hairy legs danced between my fingers—a spider. The revelation brought an overwhelming fear nearing panic. My inhale identified the arachnid as a tarantula—one immune to the three layers of bug repellent I'd sprayed on in the tent. With a scream, I flicked my hand, launching the monster from my wrist back into the darkness of the forest.

For some reason I lost consciousness, and I was now in a different place and time.

Mira, Xander, and I were in a dark underground cave surrounded by strange creatures with glowing orange eyes. The air was heavy and unmoving. Condensation collected on the rocky walls. I squeezed someone's warm hand. Our fingers intertwined, our heartbeats became synchronized. We were calm, despite the menacing situation. We were concentrating on—

"Sarah! Sarah!"

"Wake up, Sarah!"

"Is she okay?"

"Are you okay?"

"Sarah, take a deep breath." I recognized Mira's calm voice.

I opened my eyes and saw a dozen faces hovering over me. Another dozen voices whispered amongst themselves.

"What happened?" I asked. My head throbbed and when I touched the back of it, a bruised area swelled into a lump. "Ouch."

"Stay still." Xander placed his hands on my shoulders.

"You fainted," said Ms. Wimsley. "And you gave us quite a scare."

"Way to go, weirdo." Chris pushed through the crowd toward me. "Half the forest is gone because of your scream. We won't get to see any animals, man." He faked a disappointed moan.

Mira and Xander assumed a protective stance. Their shoulders looked broader, and I thought I'd heard a snarl.

I sat up to see Xander's profile as he stared at Chris from under his brows. "Shut up!" he growled with fury, his voice deepening to roar. He behaved like a creature himself.

Did anyone notice his incisor teeth gleaming just below his lips, even in the darkness? I could have sworn he'd grown a few inches, but perhaps it was the shadows and the flickering flames of the fire.

"Don't worry about him," Xander said. "If half the animals are gone, how come you're still here?" His attention returned to me, but his words were clearly meant for Chris. "Go to your tent and leave her be."

It wasn't a request, but an order; one no one would dare to defy.

Chris took a step back, spitting to the side, but fear and hatred painted his face.

"It's getting late. It's time to go to your tents," Ms. Wimsley interjected with forced authority. "Sarah, have some water. You must have fainted from all the excitement and dehydration." I guessed it was the best diagnosis she could think of under the pressure of teenage glares. She clapped her hands. "Chop, chop, kids. We have a busy day tomorrow. Everyone get ready for bed, and give her some breathing room." She turned to Mira. "Keep an eye out for Sarah overnight, will you? Make sure she gets plenty of fluids."

My throat tingled at that. I wished for fluids, but not the kind Ms. Wimsley had in mind.

The students' protests of "aww" and "no" echoed through the clearing to be muffled in the dark forest. We all crawled into our tents for the night. Xander took the right side, Mira chose the middle, and I took the left. We hung a glowing light stick from one of the ceiling supports, having no intention of sleeping.

"What happened to you?" Mira asked when we were settled.

I rolled on my side to face her. "I . . . I think I fainted," I fibbed, stalling. The memory of glowing orange eyes disturbed me enough to send chills down my back. Would the siblings think I was crazy if I told them what I'd seen? Would they dismiss my vision because I hit my head on the rock—the way I hoped they would?

The feeling of a dream being real was not new to me; I'd had them too often, and dreams this intense always became real—they foretold my future. Knowing what would happen wasn't so bad, but understanding a dream; that was another story. But this wasn't a dream. I fainted. Yet, the feeling of my vision coming true was identical to when I dreamt.

"Are you sure? Your eyes rolled back when you were out. Were you trying to see something?" Though she was obviously striving to sound casual, the muscles around her jaw and brow tightened.

"Well... I-I thought I saw you and Xander... But way in the future... With me," I stammered. I didn't know how much of my strange vision I should share.

Mira and Xander looked at each other, nodding imperceptibly. Xander couldn't hide his bright teeth, even in the dark, as his mouth curved into a wide grin. He slid into his sleeping bag. "It was only a small spider. You could have squashed it."

"It was a tarantula! I don't care how small it was, it creeped me out." My heartbeat picked up again at the memory. I rolled onto my back.

Mira smacked the back of her brother's head, hard enough that I heard the whack. He squirmed but didn't say anything. The intensity of the blow should have knocked him flying, but it didn't. She readjusted the thick band leather straps on her left wrist. Xander always wore an identical one.

"Calm down, Sarah. We know how afraid you are of insects," Mira said, still frowning at Xander. "It's not a big deal. It could have happened to anyone."

I didn't believe her. "I so didn't want to draw attention to myself," I said as I slipped further into my sleeping bag. Sliding deeper, I zipped it up to the end and tied the drawstring so only the oval of my face was exposed. With my eyelids lower I yawned loudly. They looked at me, surprised. Besides Helen, they were the only ones who knew how difficult it was to tire me out.

"We know. Don't worry, they should forget about it by morning." Mira zipped herself up.

"And if they don't, I'll introduce them to my biceps." Xander flexed his arms. Somehow I believed my skinny friend would fight anyone to defend me.

"Thanks, guys. I'm really tired," I lied. "Good night." I pressed my lips tightly together, ending the conversation, knowing I wouldn't sleep. My thoughts wandered to the vision and the horrific place I'd seen when I fainted.

The siblings didn't believe me, but Xander rolled his eyes without complaining. Mira's concerned gaze remained on me. It didn't matter how fake I was, they always understood. Guilt and shame invaded my thoughts, and I sunk into the sleeping bag. *I wish I could tell you the truth.* I sighed.

After half an hour of restless movements and giggling, the whispers of my classmates became lower and less frequent. The campsite fell quiet for the night. Breathing deepened, and snores broke the silence.

It would be a long night for me.

I waited until Xander's mouth sagged open and he started gurgling in the back of his throat. When the first drool streaked his chin, I crept out of the tent to stretch my aching muscles. They didn't really ache, but telling myself they did made me feel less like a half-breed.

The darkness didn't scare me. My night vision was perfect. I sat by the smouldering ashes in the fire pit, where the orange glow of the embers was as bright as the eyes of the strange creatures in my vision. Fear sent chills down my spine. What did the vision mean? Were the creatures real or a figment of my imagination? It felt real, almost as real as some of my dreams that have come true before.

Mira and Xander had been older; I guessed we would be in our early twenties. I sighed, resting my chin on my hand. Whose hand had I been holding so tightly? I touched my right palm as if I could still feel the softness and warmth of that other person.

My hand travelled to my chest to feel the beating of my heart. The rhythm was different from that in the vision. It wasn't right. It wasn't complete. I'd never thought about my heartbeat in such detail until now. Could it change one day to make me feel whole, and wanted?

The sounds of the night blurred together. Frozen by the memory of what I had seen, I sat by the fire. The six hours of darkness passed quickly and I hadn't noticed until now that the sun was beginning to rise. A breeze not yet strong enough to dispel the thick fog hovering above the grass brought a new scent. My nostrils flared, identifying its components: a hint of jasmine, rose, and lilac overlaying a sweet, woody musk that carried my mind to the shores of a nearby pond. I rose and followed the honey-like aroma. It was so sweet I almost floated across the undergrowth and grass as I focused on its siren song.

Just a few meters from the water, I found the source: a flower growing alone among the moss and short grasses. Its beauty captivated me; I stood frozen, like Medusa's victim. From a distance, it looked completely black. When I stepped closer, my nose only inches away, the navy blue and purple petals shimmered in the morning light. It was a blue orchid.

I pulled my eyes away from its iridescence to look around the pond for another, but there were none. The flower reached skyward, as if waiting to be found. Away from its humid habitat, the stem swayed in the gentle breeze. Its existence reminded me of my own. This orchid didn't fit into its surroundings, either, all lonesome by itself.

"What are you doing here?" I whispered. My breath left a warm trail in the cool air. I leaned in closer and saw an aura around its blossom, stem, and leaves. The twinkling light encapsulated the orchid like a shadowless lamp. "You are beautiful."

With my nose an inch from its center, I tapped a fragile petal. The sugary smell intensified, and the inhaled pollen settled on my lungs, then dispersed into my bloodstream. My eyes closed, and muscles flexed. I inhaled again. A rush of new strength and energy flew through my body.

Helen will be so happy! I examined the flower from each angle. "You should be an interesting one to work with." My fingers dug into the soil at the flower's base and I scooped its roots into my palms. "I'll take good care of you, I promise."

As I studied the orchid resting in my hands, a warm, odourous breath drifted across the left side of my face. I froze, feeling as if the blood was thickening around my spine. Something tickled my cheek, fur, as the beast leaned closer to sniff me. I dared not move, but I took a quick whiff. A black bear, trying to figure out what I was. The new treasure in my palms had so mesmerized me I hadn't heard it approach.

Still crouching, I slowly turned to face my opponent. A wave of adrenaline and something I didn't recognize built in my bloodstream.

The bear backed away, then raised his front paws to stand, preparing to attack. His head rose three to four feet higher than mine. I didn't move, focusing on the bear's muzzle and the scars around his nose and under his eyes, some still crusted. My gaze landed on a ripped but healed lower lip and his left half-missing ear.

I took a deep breath, inhaling the sweet fragrance that had placed me in this predicament. The scent travelled into my lungs and took over my veins. Time slowed; I watched the bear breathe in slow motion as it examined my crouched posture. It would only be a few seconds before its claws and teeth lashed out.

I considered fighting, but that would erase all the hard work I'd devoted to covering my true identity. Would I know how to fight? Besides, the serum from the previous night hadn't worn off yet; it diluted my strength—though I felt stronger than ever.

Fall down and play dead. No, fight back. Fall down and play dead . . . fight back . . . The two extremes battled in my head.

There was no room for error, no gray area.

I had nowhere to hide. There were no other options.

The indecision left my heart racing, and I absently counted the beats—280 per minute. Not normal for a human—but I wasn't human.

Blood rushed through my body at accelerated speed, and I knew my organs were using its energy too quickly. But the infused blood strengthened me, adding vigour to my joints and power to my limbs.

I can't lose control; I can't become a walking white corpse! With my next breath, my body responded as if of its own accord. My knees flexed, preparing for the bear to strike.

Then it occurred to me—I was not as afraid of the bear as I'd been of the tarantula. I feared my dark side was winning, and I knew the bear had no chance against me.

Run. I could run—fast.

But I didn't want to. I scowled at the bear from beneath my brows. Any control I pretended to have was lost, although I felt more in control than ever. Empowered, I shifted my weight forward. I felt I could take the bear down. Would his blood be thicker than a cougar's or would it be as revolting as a rat? Would it be more tart, or sweet? Would it strengthen me more than the vermin whose blood I was used to drinking? I licked my lips.

As the bear's paw came down, I shoved my arm in the centre of his chest. The bear flew back into a trunk of a tree. It shook its fur, refocused, and ran at full speed toward me.

I heard a loud two-toned roar behind me. The bear froze in its track, turned and ran back into the woods.

Crap. Is there a bigger bear behind me?

The roar was familiar, but I didn't let my guard down or let my smirk disappear. I slowly turned to welcome my new opponent, but onlty saw Mira and Xander, standing side by side, ten feet away, in the spot I expected the other bear to be.

My heart rate plummeted to seventy-five beats per minute, and I lost consciousness—this time for real.

* * *

"You're not supposed to be here!" Xander hissed through clenched teeth.

"She almost got attacked!" an unfamiliar voice said.

Semi-conscious, I couldn't open my eyes or recognize the voice.

"Leave, Eric. We can handle this," Mira said. Her voice fell to a whisper. "It's not your time."

"That's right, lover-boy, leave." Xander's voice had risen.

"Fine! But as soon as you can't take care of her, I'll be back." The strange voice shifted, as if its owner were looking down at me. "She'll be up in thirty seconds."

The wind picked up. My eyelids cracked open. I thought I saw purple sparks disappearing into the forest, but before I could focus on them, fresh water flooded my mouth and strong arms lifted me to sit upright. I coughed up the excess water, and it fountained out of my mouth.

Mira and Xander hovered over me.

"What happened? Where is the bear?" I panted.

"The bear ran away, and you fainted," Mira said calmly.

"Again," Xander added.

"Why did the bear run away? What did you guys do?" My gaze flew from Mira to Xander, then to Mira again.

"He saw Xander and got scared." Mira laughed. Although she was joking, I sensed some truth in what she said.

"But the growl? I thought there was another bear," I said.

Xander shrugged, looking innocent. "We didn't hear anything."

"Sarah, you were hyperventilating. And then you saw us. I think you fainted from relief and shock," Mira suggested.

"No, no, no. I'm sure I heard a growl. A two-toned growl. And who were you talking to?" I tried to remember the name I'd heard. My head throbbed. When Mira didn't answer, I looked to Xander. "How did you guys know where I was?"

Mira answered. "I woke up and you were gone. We waited a while, then came looking for you."

"Why did the bear run away? He was ready to attack." I furrowed hearing the annoyance in my voice as neither sibling was willing to share what they knew.

"Maybe he smelled you and decided there was something better to eat in the forest," Xander teased.

"No, he did the smelling before that," I insisted. "Something scared him. I heard a roar from where you guys were standing. I saw the fear in his eyes."

"Sarah, the bear reader."

"Xander, stop." Mira raised her hand as if to whack him but refrained. "Sarah, I don't know what scared the bear. We should be happy you're all right. Why would you go so far from camp?" She waited for an answer, but I didn't know what to say. She added, "You were holding this when you fainted." In her palms, Mira cupped the blue orchid.

She was trying to change the subject, and it worked. I smiled guiltily. "It's for Helen's store." My cheeks heated. Both my carelessness and this flower had put me in a dangerous situation.

"We should get back to the camp before anyone realizes we're gone. Let's keep this little adventure to ourselves," Mira said. I was more than happy to agree.

Xander frowned. "She's so pale. Are you sure she's ready to go back to camp?"

How pale am I? I pressed my palm to my face. *Do I still pass for a human? What if they find out?* My heart raced again, and I swallowed in a dry mouth, the reflex scratching my throat. "I'm fine. I just really need to go to the washroom. Will you guys wait for me here?" I lied and then pushed to my feet.

They looked at each other; something passed between them.

"I won't go far," I added, taking a few steps backward, toward the forest. I needed to replenish my veins, and the scent of a young hare called to me.

"Just be careful," Mira warned.

"If I see a bear, I'll scream," I assured them.

As I stepped into the forest and slipped among the close-growing trees, I heard Xander murmur under his breath, "I'm sure the bear won't be coming back."

"Shhh!" Mira hissed. "You've done enough damage today."

What was that about? My friends were behaving more mysteriously than ever. It's as if they're hiding something too. The hare stirred, and my ears perked up.

This would be the only time I would give in to the hunt for the next eight years.

CHAPTER 2

"Sarah, it's six!" Xander called up toward my second-floor window. He acted as my private alarm clock every morning when he jogged by my house and repeated his routine in the evening, close to sunset.

I swung my legs from under the rumpled duvet and shuffled across the thick carpet to peek outside with half-open eyes, then waved.

An empty syringe on the night table drew my gaze as I got dressed. Its serum controlled my traits and allowed me to sleep. Squeezing my eyes shut, I pressed my forefingers to my temples. My breath locked in my lungs as pressure built up in my head. Behind my eyelids, bright light zoomed across a thick, blood-red background. I jumped back, startled, and looked at my trembling hands. Finally, the rhythm of my pulse slowed, and I crossed my fingers, cracking them at the joints, hoping to regain control. The next exhale emptied my lungs and I felt my heartbeat adjust to that of a human.

"I'm out of here," I muttered, stumbling toward the washroom.

I was in the middle of the hall when I heard it. *Sarah.*

I froze.

Sarah.

The voice sounding in my head drew my eyes toward the stairs to the attic. I did what I thought anyone would if they heard their name being called from an empty room: my clunched fists whitened, I shrugged and hopped every second step upstairs. There was no door in the ceiling, and the open hole was draped with old sheets. I pushed them aside to uncover the entrance to the dusty loft.

Eye-level with the attic floor, I rose higher on my toes.

"Hello?" I peeked within. No answer. The last step squeaked as I put my weight on it. The air up here was stale, hot. Patches of morning sunlight filtered through the glass of the shaded dormers; lazily drifting dust motes floated in the light.

Sarah.

For the first time, I recognized Helen's ghostly voice. My aunt died in a car crash one year ago. Shivers ran up my arms. "There's no way . . ."

The dark end of the long room drew my gaze and I focused on the corner of Helen's old chest that stuck out from behind a full-length mirror. I tiptoed forward but stopped in front of the mirror. I shook my head, then leaned closer to the reflection and noticed my eyes twinkled with purplish stars. My breath made a round patch of steam on the surface. Stars . . . I closed my eyes, and when I opened them, the stars were gone.

Did I do something different with last night's mixture? I thought a moment, trying to remember the serum I took. My head hurt again.

Sarah.

"Okay, this is getting weird." I looked behind me, though the voice came from the chest in the corner. It wasn't large, but it rested atop a larger coffer. No person could fit there. The trunk screeched across the wooden floor as I pulled on the handle. Kneeling beside it, I wiped the dust from the lid with my hand. A swath of dark-stained wood revealed. The hinges squeaked as I lifted the cover, releasing an aroma I recognized—flowery yet musky. *So close to my blue orchid.*

I remembered the stranger who had picked up my hat yesterday morning when a gust of warm autumn air blew it off my head. *Coincidence?* My eyes flew open, and I shivered. "I don't think so." My voice echoed.

"Oh, Helen." I smiled, lifting the photos that topped the pile inside the chest—Helen's sneaky snapshots, some captured at home, and some from my camping trip. I held up a photo of her as a young woman. She sat in a low wooden chair in front of a log cabin nestled amidst the trunks of old trees, the vines draping the branches created a web of green mesh. Wildflowers in all shades of the rainbow covered the ground; other blooms scattered up the trees from the ground to the heavens. Dense and exotic, the vegetation was more than I'd seen in all of Pinedale. *Where was this taken?*

I rested my right elbow on my left arm while I chewed the tip of my thumb.

"Concentrate, Sarah, concentrate," I whispered, but I only felt tightness in my chest.

Setting the photos aside, I lifted the first of a dozen logbooks and turned its pages.

September 9, 1990: Today I bring Sarah home. It's with sadness and happiness that I come to Pinedale to settle with our angel.

I snapped shut the book as a lump formed in my throat. The remaining dust on the chest swirled in the still air. Helen's voice had rung in my ears as if she was the one reading the entry in my head.

Pushing the journals aside, I dug deeper into the chest. My hand touched on a rough shape, and I pulled out a ruby ring. The age-tarnished silver shone like copper in the dim light. It fit like it was custom made for my middle finger. I held up my palm, studying the ring and the emblem on its side of three wavy lines. The symbol was unfamiliar, and I wiggled my fingers, watching the angles of the diamond-cut red stone reflecting the light. After I took it off, its weight comfortable in my palm, I threaded the ring onto my silver necklace and tucked it inside the collar of my T-shirt. It rested intimately against my skin, like a cuddling kitten.

A sudden gust of wind blew open the attic window, and I leaped to my feet to close it. Something pulled at my gut, as if my stomach were attached to a hook at the end of a fishing line being reeled in. It hauled me back to the chest, and I saw a corner of paper protruding from its contents. I pulled out an envelope addressed in Helen's handwriting.

"Sarah Mitchell," I read. Chills trickled down my spine. I stared at the envelope, then ripped the shorter edge open and unfolded the letter inside.

Sarah,

If you get this letter, it means I'm no longer with you. If I'm not here, then you're no longer safe.

Your background has been kept secret for your safety. I always loved you as if you were my daughter. Your mother was my sister, Saraphine. She died after giving birth to you—but only so you could survive. Hunted by the seekers, your mother weakened. You were so hungry, Sarah. But do not blame yourself! His blood runs deep within your veins, and you could not stop the feeding. Neither could your mother.

You are who you are because of your parents. Their love for one another was strong; their differences could not stop your conception. You are a true miracle. Your father was a vampire and your mother human. You are a combination of your parent's best traits.

Please be careful. The vampire blood is strong—especially with you. Continue the serums! Find the right serum to turn you back to human! Otherwise the seekers will find you. The serum conceals you from them. Should your instincts become stronger, they will sense your presence.

I crumpled the paper in my hands.

"The seekers are hunting me?" The tension released from my throat. I stood still. Time stood still. Was this a dream? Would I wake up if I moved? My mouth opened, but I couldn't speak. The slowing beating of my heart reminded me to breathe, and the rhythm resumed its normal, human pace.

My hands shook as I stared at the letter. I wished could ask it questions, and that it could, in some magical way, start talking to me. Seconds passed. The sweat from my palms began to dampen the black ink, releasing its metallic odour.

Why hadn't Helen told me earlier? I'd always known what I was. The dark nature I denied had been buried for twenty one years. The last time I'd used it happened on my camping trip as a teen. My vampire emotions had been dormant, my sickening traits hidden.

Who were the seekers? Why did they chase my parents? How do I fit into all this?

"His blood runs deep within your veins." I shivered.

Mom. Was my dream of her a real memory?

I see her face, almost identical to mine, smiling lovingly. She secures my infant body in her arms, humming and softly hushing me to sleep. I satisfy the first hunger I feel as a baby and see her nightgown turn crimson. Her eyes lose their glow as tears trickle down. She places her right hand on her heart. "You will always be here." She taps her chest. "I love you," she whispers. I return her smile. She sighs and seems to go to sleep. I see a puddle of red liquid on the floor and the red imprints of my tiny palms on her cheeks, urging the eyes in the ashen face to open. They never do.

The dream always ended with me missing her more than ever. I'd wake up struggling to breathe, as if all the air had been sucked out of the room. I'd cry until sunrise.

A dump truck honked as it rumbled past outside. A tear rolled off my cheek. "I'm so sorry," I sobbed, releasing the pressure behind my eyes.

She died at the hands of the monster within me, the monster I despised, the monster created by my vampire father. The craving for blood, the uncontrollable hormonal impulses, revolting instincts and needs I'd suppressed—how were these "best traits"?

I'd never seen a vampire and didn't want to see one. They were not alive the way I was, and I never wanted to be one. I allowed the serum to spread through my body to control the needs and desires of this other side I wouldn't acknowledge. The serum changed the circadian rhythm of my days; it controlled my dreadful nature, my strength, my *thirst*.

"You're a true miracle."

Did she say that because vampire conception was impossible?

"But I was born from a human," I whispered. All I'd ever wanted was to be human. I just wanted to belong.

The tug at my heart made it skip a beat in argument, and I rushed to unfold the rest of the letter.

Find William—he's the only one who can help you. I hope you found the ring; keep it with you at all times. It always shows your true self. Protect it.

I wish I was here to explain more. I'm sorry.

Love always, Aunt Helen

"William," I whispered. *He's real. He's not just in my dreams!* Until today, I thought he was a figment of my imagination, because when I slept he was always there. . .

We sat in a corner booth at a dance club somewhere in New York City. I sipped on a Fuzzy Navel; William's favourite, a Bloody Caesar, set in front of him.

William took me by my shoulders. His touch sent electric shock waves through our bodies. The aches didn't stop us, and he stepped closer. William's turquoise eyes sparkled, both in the sunlight and at night. I saw my own identical pair reflected in his. I felt his breath on my face and concentrated on his strong jaw and lopsided smile.

Taking my hand, William gently kissed it and asked me to dance. We walked out on the parquet floor. Stepping behind me, William slid his arms around my waist. His shirt was open, and I felt his bare chest against my back, exposed in a Marilyn Monroe-style black halter dress that plunged to just above the swell of my buttocks.

Our heartbeats behaved. We moved slowly despite the fast rhythm of the music, building up endorphins that gave us power and control. With each touch, these changed to a natural aphrodisiac. Our being there was simple. We had to be together, as one.

In my dreams I'd known him since childhood, yet he seemed like an alien from another planet, visiting only when I slept. My hope to one day meet him turned to a quest, because now, I was certain he was real.

I glanced back to the letter.

Helen wanted me to find him. Now that I think about it, whenever I'd mentioned William from my dreams, the lines on her face had always creased up in approval.

And her warning about the serum—why would I stop taking it? The serum allowed me to sleep. Okay, so I had reduced the dose occasionally to stay awake at night to study, which had always displeased Helen. Now I knew why. It also kept me hidden from . . . the seekers.

My stomach clenched with hunger and I hefted the chest to carry it downstairs.

I set the wooden box of mementos on the table and pulled a bowl from the kitchen cupboard for cereal.

Since the kitchen was still dark, I looked out the window checking for trespassers. The sun's rim peeked through the golden-brown trees on the horizon. "What am I doing?" I said aloud. This was Pinedale, after all, one of those towns you could find on a map and know you could die from boredom. Yet for me, this town was ideal. No creatures from my dreams would ever think of coming here. It was home—my home.

I pulled the carton of milk from the fridge and checked its date. "Great. Expired two weeks ago. What the heck. It's not like it could kill me." The milk flowed in the bowl. White chunks splattered the table. A wet spot stained my khakis. *Crap!* I threw the empty carton into the sink. Sipping from the rim of the bowl, I made space for the cereal and then tipped in some Cheerios.

Helen would flip if she saw this! I set the box down and snagged the dish cloth to wipe the wooden table. Turning toward the mantel of the unused fireplace, I lifted a spoonful toward a small urn. "See, Auntie? I'm eating."

I swallowed the cereal, then took a sip from the bowl to wash it down. With my eyes closed, I let the flavours soak my taste buds. *Even spoiled milk is better than blood*, I lied to myself. Animal blood tasted almost like blended carrot and beet juice. My lips parted at the thought as I licked them over. The tugging at my arteries reminded me to fill my veins—a necessity I couldn't avoid if I wanted to keep my tawny complexion and heart beating.

I'm such a freak!

I left the empty bowl in the sink. My brain stormed for more answers, and I needed them now: even if I risked running into the demons from my dreams.

CHAPTER 3

I pulled out my backpack from under the hall table and frowned at a loose stitch along a patch covering a hole. Helen's chest barely fit into the pack. I threw two syringes and the serum on top of it, hoping William would come back when I napped.

Two weeks had passed since I'd last dreamt of William. Perversely, when the dreams stopped, I felt closer to him. I would turn my head to look across the street, expecting him to be there, but he wasn't. I'd wake up in the middle of the night and glimpse a shadow that disappeared. Only a scent of jasmine, rose, and lilac with a woody musk undercurrent would remain. I smelled William in my room, but he wasn't there.

A rustle from the living room drew my attention. Sunlight creeping in the hall window hit my eyes. I lowered my sunglasses from their usual hair accessory placement. *It's time.* The crate in the corner of the living room housed my meal. Inside, guinea pigs huddled under a pile of wood chips. One twist broke their necks, and I sucked them dry. A rush of new life swam through my veins but I stuck my tongue out in disgust, as if I'd eaten cooked liver with strained peas. It wasn't that it tasted bad—it tasted sweet yet sour. Sometimes I imagined a blend of sunshine and falling, stars in my mouth. But I refused to accept it. I had to make a face.

Sated, I grabbed a sweater and the backpack and walked out the double glass door into a warm autumn wind carrying the tantalizing aroma of baking pumpkin pies. Everyone in Pinedale baked on the weekend before Halloween, preparing for the annual bake sale in the town square.

I walked quicker than usual to my flower shop but had to stop when a gust of wind blew my hat off just like yesterday.

A stranger picked it up and held it out to me.

"Thank you," I said, accepting it. I hesitated, examining the familiar dimple in his chin. "Have we met before?"

"No." He dropped his head. The sharpness of his voice took me aback.

No, of course not. I nodded, ready to move, only to halt in mid-step, confused—curious. Not at his answer, but the familiar scent: floral and woodsy and musky. I turned to look at his back as he strode away, and confusion soothed into the same comfort I felt in my dreams. Yes, the tall stranger's build was similar to William's. I pushed my sunglasses up. His movements brisk but precise, the similarities were remarkable.

"Wi . . . William?" I whispered. *It can't be.*

William did not dress like a vagabond, I told myself. The hem of his long, worn coat was stained dark with mud. The black jeans soiled, and the untucked flannel shirt had been too casual. No, William's sleek style didn't reflect this homeless man's look. As a well-dressed buff in my dreams, William modelled a clean-shaven face, not what looked like two days' worth of stubble on this man's face.

Still, my heart skipped a beat. I clenched my fist to my chest, pressing it against a rhythm I did not recognize. My sucked in breath acknowledged the new pulse as I quickened my pace toward my store.

I bumped into someone and looked up at another stranger. "Oops, I'm sorry."

"It's Sarah, right?" the man said with confidence.

I stared at him like he was a movie star. Tall, with a fit body, the man posed like a model. Even a thick sweater and loose jeans couldn't hide his well-defined limbs. In a hurry, his cheeks blotched with red spots, and his chest rose and deflated in a quick rhythm. He studied me from behind his aviators, as if making sure he had the right person.

"Yes. Do I know you?" I asked.

His head skidded a fraction to the right, as if listening to something I couldn't hear. "No, I'm sorry." He moved his face closer to mine, holding his sunglasses with his fingertips. "I mistook you for someone else." A hint of purple sparked, reflecting from the lenses. He walked away. "What now?" I heard him mutter to himself.

"Wait—" I called, but he was gone, quicker than the vagabond.

This is going to be a strange day.

I resumed my trek along the narrow sidewalk, but I sometimes peeked over my shoulder, at the top of the two-storey buildings I passed, expecting to see someone looking at me from the roof. No one was there. My gaze shifted toward the windows but couldn't see anyone peeping. The deep and narrow alleys that ran between the brick buildings didn't scare me, but it felt like mysterious watchers would step out any minute.

No one emerged. *Nerves*, I thought, but a frisson swept through my body. Rushed, I did not stop until I reached the front of my store.

I admired the greenery behind the glass window. As I reached for the handle on the front door, my cell phone vibrated in my pocket. I pulled it out.

"Hi Mira!" I leaned back against the front window.

"Sarah!" She almost screamed.

I smiled. My upbeat friend could permanently engrave a grin on my face.

"Haven't heard from you in a while. Is everything okay?" There was tension in her voice. A while for Mira was anything over twenty-four hours.

"Yeah, why?" I ignored the fact that I'd bumped into two strangers in Pinedale this morning, "I had the weirdest feeling that you're going away somewhere without telling me."

"Me, going away? Ha!" I let out a sarcastic laugh.

"Weird, isn't it? I just thought, if you were leaving, you'd at least say goodbye."

"Mira, I don't think I'll ever leave this town." My jaw clenched at the sudden yearning to go away. "Or you," I added to ease her worry.

"Well, you know what I always say . . ."

"Never say never!" We both laughed. Around Mira, I felt as if I were still in my teens, acting goofy and odd.

"Meet me for dinner tonight?" she asked.

"Um, how about Saturday?" I tried, stalling, then quickly added, "I have a few orders to finish." The truth was, when alone with either of the siblings, I had a strong urge to tell them about my ability to foresee the future through my dreams, and about the real me. But I never did, too afraid to be shunned.

"That's way too long," she whined.

"Only four days," I adjusted my voice to a higher pitch.

"You know how many things can happen in four days?" she exclaimed.

"In Pinedale?" I snorted. "Oh, that's right—that black bear from our camping trip finally found your scent and came to get his revenge," I teased.

"Yes, you're so funny." She sniffed. "First of all, it's not my scent as much as Xander's he'd be looking for. And *now* I'm starting to hope he'd get you two confused."

"Okay, okay, let's do it Friday. I can't do it any earlier. Is Xander joining us?" I bit my lower lip. I enjoyed his company just as much as Mira's, but now that I knew the truth about William, I hoped I could finally muster enough courage to tell her about my dreams. She'd believe me. That's the kind of friend Mira was—she'd cry when I cried, laugh when I laughed, and believe the most doubtful truth if I said it was so. Only I never found the courage to spill all of my secrets.

"Of course he is. We'll meet you at The Grill, Friday at seven," she confirmed.

"Oh," I let disappointment slip.

"Unless you don't want him to be there?" I pictured Mira raising her eyebrows. I didn't find her questioning odd; the siblings were my best friends and came as a package deal. You simply couldn't be a friend with one and not the other.

"No, that's okay," I said.

"Don't be late, Sarah. I really need to talk to you."

"I'm never late."

"Never say never," she quipped.

"Hey, did you borrow my cream shirt?" I asked.

"Are you missing another one?"

"Yeah, I guess I've been busy lately. I'll have to check the laundry again."

"Let me know if you need help," she offered. "I'll see you Friday." She hung up before I found another excuse.

"See you Friday, Mira," I said to the phone. *Friday I'll tell her the truth. I'll just have to distract Xander with food. Yes. Food will keep him preoccupied.*

Tension tugged at my intestines. Chills ran up my spine. My confession would be one the siblings didn't expect.

I shoved the phone into my pocket and glanced across the street to Mrs. G's Natural Healings store. Mira's and Xander's mom owned it. Beyond the line of a shingled roof, the snow-capped peaks of the Grand Teton Mountains glistened in the morning sun. *A perfect ad image for her herb and natural medicine store.* In tune with nature, Mira and Xander would serve as the store's walking advertisements if people didn't keep their distance from them.

Sometimes they have reason to, I thought, remembering a time when I'd witnessed the siblings helping a wolf. Mira yelled, "Hold him down!" to her brother in the front yard of their veterinary clinic.

"I am!" Xander had snapped back. "Hold him tighter!" The wolf had yelped in pain but didn't growl. It didn't try to bite Xander as he freed its paw from a steel-jawed leg-hold trap with his bare hands.

"There you go," Mira had murmured into its ear.

Mira and Xander had a way with animals. They looked straight into their eyes and touched them without being attacked. Mira's whispers soothed the animals' emotions and Xander's strength eased their physical injuries. They rehabilitated foxes, raccoons, and mountain lions and sent them all back to the forest.

I empathized with their odd behaviour, as it resembled my own, and often questioned their abilities. Who else could hold down a wolf? Okay, a vampire probably could, but I preferred to pretend vampires didn't exist, and with the caramel skin, the siblings were definitely not vampires. Neither Mira nor Xander ever asked questions; they never treated me like an outcast. They accepted me and I them, and I wondered what would happen if they knew the truth.

I turned the key in the front door and smiled at the familiar squeak of the hinges that heralded my entrance into my oasis. The heavy scent of flowers greeted me, and I inhaled deeply as I stepped inside. The warm moisture hung in the air, settling on my bare skin. At first glance, the store looked like it melded into an infinite corridor of exotic trees, shrubs, and plants. It was a greenhouse with a small waterfall in its center, splashing into a pond where goldfish dreamt.

The greenhouse had transformed into my personal rainforest as the plants grew over the years. Yes, I'd overdone it, but I liked it that way.

I bent toward the counter to inhale the sweet aroma of my blue orchid. "I can sleep longer because of you." The velvet petals glistened.

Time passed quickly at work.

I closed the store at six o'clock but didn't go home. The stack of new requisitions for the weekend had grown taller, despite working through lunch. *Great! How can I keep my date with Mira now?* After I tackled the orders, the cushioned armchair in the back room looked too inviting to resist. The shot of my blue orchid serum into my thigh sent me on a high, and I nestled my head against the side of the chair, closing my eyes.

William was back, finally. He appeared behind a thin fog, his silhouette fading out of focus. Seeming close, I reached out to touch him, wanting to feel the warmth of his skin. I pushed my elbows into the chair to stand, but I couldn't rise. My thighs felt heavy, as if a boulder rested on top of them.

I was in the landscape of a kindling dream, halfway between waking and a true dream state.

"William," I said, surrendering to inertia and sinking back against the chair, "I know about my parents."

"You don't know everything, Sarah. You have to be careful." He kept his eyes focused on the tile floor.

"But Helen told me to find you. How do I find you?"

"I already found you."

He walked away, and the dream ended. There was no intensity, no certainty. It was just a dream.

Placing my hands under my cheek, I turned to my right side. My memory of William so clear, I imagined him here with me. *He didn't want to look at me.* Was it because he knew what I was?

"You can't leave me," I whispered. What if he won't come back? I needed him now more than ever.

My eyes were half open, the contours and angles of the back room blurred and vague. My eyelids heavy, I wasn't ready to wake up. *Fall asleep, Sarah. Maybe William will be back.*

A new dream began.

"Sarah!" William cried, running toward me, but stopped. William's gaze focused over my shoulder, and he growled, baring sharp teeth.

The distance between his eyebrows narrowed, his skin tightened, and the muscles underneath stiffened. He resembled a vampire. Red veins streaked his cheeks, his eyes sank into gray-shadowed hollows, and the contours of his cheekbones intensified. He growled again, warning something to back off.

This dream ended.

I jumped to my feet, certain the dream would find its way into my life.

I will meet William. And he's a vampire.

My heartbeat quickened as I struggled to inhale and fell to my knees. This was the first time I'd seen him as a vampire in my dreams. My insides felt solidified, like a rock, as hate for a man I already loved formed around my heart.

Could I accept him as a vampire?

I heard a shriek escape my throat.

Is that why he accepts me? He knows what I am.

If William was like me, perhaps he could help me, us, find an antidote to change us into humans. That had to be the reason Helen wanted me to find him. The rock crumbled into sand, letting my heart beat again.

The front door opening startled me. My head whipped at the sound of squeaking hinges. I thought I'd locked it for the night and inhaled instinctively, trying to identify who it was. Suppressing the urge to rush, I staggered to the front of the store, my foam-like knees almost buckling.

Relieved to see a familiar silhouette, I exhaled. Mira and Xander's mom had her face buried in a floral arrangement decorating the front window. She lifted her head, her mouth curving up in a kind smile. Her floor-length skirt swayed as she strode toward the counter where I leaned heavily. The bracelets around her left wrist rattled.

"I thought I'd find you here," she said, examining me with her wise brown eyes.

"Hello, Mrs. Gobert." Noting a slight tremble in my voice, I forced a smile.

"You look like you've just seen a ghost." She scanned my rigid body from the bottom up.

"Oh no, I'm all right. How can I help you?" I asked automatically, doubting my fib worked. My demeanour must have seemed odd to Mrs. G, plus I never called her by her full name.

"Is it too late? I saw the light on, and the door was open. Mira's having a guest over. I wanted to pick up some flowers to brighten up the house." Mrs. G hesitated and cocked her head. "Are you okay, Sarah?"

"Yes, of course," I lied. "Which ones would you like?"

"Tulips. Are they out of season?" She was still looking over my tense stance.

"Not in this store. It will take a few minutes." I drew a deep breath and strained to move my numb legs toward the back. *Breathe, just breathe. Tulips: third fridge to the left.* "Red or yellow, Mrs. Gobert?" I called out to the front.

"Your choice, hon," she replied.

The brighter ones were my favourite, and Mira's, too. We shared the same style of wardrobe, liked similar haircuts and simple designs. Mira and I were like sisters. "Mira didn't mention anyone visiting," I said loudly.

"She doesn't know yet."

"Hmm?" I murmured, picturing Mrs. G. smirking.

I pulled the sliding door of the fridge, lifting a bucket of half-opened tulips. It seemed lighter than usual. Hugging a clear vase under my arm, I strung a purple and yellow ribbon around my thumb on the way to the counter. The foam in my knees slowly began to stiffen and I welcomed the stability. I imagined if they buckled and I fell over, my unnaturally hardened legs would crumble on the tiled floor, shattering like a broken glass container. *Concentrate, Sarah, concentrate.*

"Sarah, are you sure you're all right?" Mrs. G asked, looking at me with worried eyes.

The air felt taut with tension. "Yes, Mrs. Gobert. Would you please tell Mira I won't make it to our dinner this Friday? I'll call to reschedule." I hoped to sound genuine, knowing Mira would question my motive. She was my only human confidant, at least, the kind of confidant I could allow.

"Yes, of course I will," she said. I doubted Mrs. G believed a word that came out of my mouth. She knew me too well. Sometimes I wondered if she knew my secret since she would ask me to take a dying squirrel or raccoon back to the forest even though we both knew they wouldn't survive. After all, I couldn't watch the animal just die. Any nonhuman blood was precious.

After I finished arranging the vase, I set it on the counter.

"Thank you so much. How much do I owe you?" She reached into the side pocket of her dress.

"Nothing—it's a gift." I forced another smile as I fisted my palms, trying to control the trembling in my hands.

"Thank you, Sarah. Take care of yourself. You look a little pale." She winked and turned back toward the door.

"You too—take care, that is," I managed to say.

For the first time in eight years, I gave in to my second nature and whizzed through the store, completing my final chores in record time. The current of air generated by my passage scattered the papers and photos I'd pulled from Helen's chest. I rushed to pick them up, then paused, staring at the print of Helen sitting in the wooden chair at the log cabin. A shadow cast by someone behind the camera fell forward into the photo. The well-built frame looked familiar.

"That's impossible," I whispered. This photo had been taken over twenty years ago. "There is no way this could be William."

It's my father. He's the other half I embrace.

"Who's there?" I jumped up, my eyes searching the room. Sensing a strong presence, I felt my heartbeat speed up, and then it skipped a beat. A sucked breath squeezed into my lungs. My knees softened again as his scent filled my nostrils.

"William, I need you." My lips quivered, wishing he was real. "Help me. What do I do? You're the only one who knows me."

Nothing.

"Will I ever meet you?" I sighed.

I leaned on the granite counter and scanned the room as if I had x-ray vision. William's cologne floated through the room. *How is this possible?* "William? Where are you?"

No one answered. The front door was still closed, the window in the back too small to climb through.

"I must be going crazy." I wondered if hearing voices could have me committed. *Maybe when I start seeing William's ghost, I'll commit myself. Could he be a ghost?*

I stood in a tornado-like vortex of confusion and helplessness. Senses I couldn't control roamed through my body. The store seemed to swirl. My upper lip twitched. The vampire in me grew in strength, waking—enraged, furious. The fridge cooler clicked on, its innocuous sound like a hammer blow to my heightened senses. My other half fought to emerge, to exist. The side of the counter felt like foam against my fingers as I dented its surface. The void under my palm cracked. *I'm going to ruin this store.*

I shut my eyes and exhaled slowly, the way they do in yoga, but I couldn't find peace. Unfamiliar anger crawled out from inside me. The tiny hairs on my arms straightened as newly excited cells danced in my bloodstream, cells that had been asleep for far too long.

Control it, Sarah, control it.

This time, I took in two short breaths and released them together, like a woman in labour trying to manage her pain. My laugh vibrated my chest. I opened my eyes, then crossed my fingers, trying to crack them. The joints didn't release a sound, and I let my head drop, admitting that any control I had was about to be lost. I took another shot of the serum.

CHAPTER 4

The incision burned. The slow oozing of blood felt like hot water. I swept my hand across my chest and licked the red goo off with my tongue. The bitterness tasted foreign.

"Ahh!" My body shot upright. "No!" Pushing my back against the armchair, I mangled the sweat-dampened blanket with my feet. I sprang into a crouch on the floor, warily scanning my store for intruders, poised for an attack. *It was a dream.*

I touched the middle of my ribcage—no wound. Lifting my shirt, I saw no scar, not even a white mark resembling one. *But I can't scar*, I thought in disbelief.

"What am I going to get myself into?" I hissed, grimacing. I pressed my right hand against my lips. *How soon will it happen?*

A hollow rumble came from the pit of my stomach, and it wasn't from hunger. My gut warned me. This dream was strong. It woke up suppressed instincts—the need to fight for my life. Still crouched, I listened for intruders. No one else was in the store. It wouldn't happen now.

I exhaled.

"It was a dream, just a dream," I whispered, but I was in denial, knowing I couldn't escape this nightmare. I ran my finger through the center of my chest, from five inches below the hollow of my throat down to the floating ribs. Smooth. But the memory of a small round ripple under the forefinger was too clear in my mind. Tracing over the invisible pattern, I moved my fingers back up, shaking my head. "No . . ." I moaned, no louder than a whisper.

Some predictions were out of this world. I'd dreamt of creatures with orange, purple, and white eyes; long, unrecognizable bodies burning in roaring fire pits; flowing rivers of lava, flying streams of fire, caves filled with glowing mists—I couldn't comprehend these.

Deep inside, I knew from this dream's intensity that it had sealed my fate. The only unanswered question was when would it happen?

The sunlight from the oval window in the back room shined on my face. The front door opened, and I gripped the armchair I'd slept in to stop myself from running across the store. Instead, I rose and casually strolled out to the front to see who it was. It didn't surprise me that Mira would be the first to enter the store this morning.

"Hi Sarah! I love the bouquet you made. Boy, you're a mess. Did you spend another night here?" She embraced me, squeezing as if she were saying goodbye.

"It's good to see you, too. How is Xander?" I asked, absently straightening my wrinkled shirt and brushing my fingers through my hair.

"He's asking about you. After my mom's rendition of her visit yesterday it's been hard to keep him away." Mira eyed me suspiciously. "You look awful!"

"Thanks!" I rolled my eyes. Of course—I'd forgotten Xander's morning routine. "I'm surprised you managed to keep him away."

"Why are you cancelling our plans through my mom? There is such a thing as a phone," she finished with a long huff.

"Yeah . . . I'm sorry about that." My eyes fell on the papers sitting on the front counter. "I'm just really busy. and I have new orders that came in." I swished a sheet of paper in the air.

"Orders smorders." She looked straight at me.

Turning away to hide guilt, I focused on adjusting a wedding arrangement. I lied to Mira too often, and the secret weighed more with each fable. "I'm fine. I'm just tired."

"Oh, don't give me that tired crap—we both know how hard it is to tire you out." Her voice softened, became almost pleading. "Talk to me."

I gave in. "I found a letter from Helen."

"What did it say?"

"She said she's my biological aunt. My mother was her sister. She died at birth." I avoided the gory details—the feeding, the blood, my father being a vampire—pretty much all the stuff that would scare off a human. Even so, I felt a pressure lift off my shoulders, and I finished plaintively, "Why didn't she tell me?"

"I'm not sure, hon." I didn't hear the surprise I'd expected in Mira's voice. She reached out and tucked a stray lock of my brown hair behind my ear, as casual as any other day.

"I'm not sure either." My throat tightened. I was ready to spill more secrets but didn't know where to begin.

"What else did it say?"

"Not much." I shrugged, again consumed with guilt and wondered whether Mira believed me and how much more I could lie without breaking down.

She took my face between her palms, and I knew she saw through me. "Have dinner with me, for my sake," she said slowly, emphasizing each word. "I need to talk to you, and there's someone I want you to meet."

Making me think the dinner was for her benefit hit a soft spot. "Okay," I agreed. "Saturday night."

"Fine; I'll see you Saturday night." She paused before adding, "No cancellations."

"No cancellations," I promised.

Mira dropped her hands and turned her head toward the window, then back to me. I read concern and anger in the lines of her tightened cheeks. She looked as if she were listening to someone I couldn't hear. Then her eyes grew distant, as though she were lost in her thoughts, and she nodded slightly, agreeing with unheard words. She tried to hide this, but there wasn't much a face could hide from me.

"I've got to run. There's some business I need to take care of," she said, the sudden change in her behaviour out of character. Lips tight, she dashed out the front door.

"See you soon," I called after her, and waved.

The door didn't get a chance to close before a young man stepped inside. Tall and clean-shaven, he wore a black shirt that clung to his toned abs; his brown hair, bleached by the sun, held a hint of red. Turquoise eyes pierced mine—eyes I knew well.

My eyes fell on the design on his left wrist, and I caught my breath with excitement. The tattoo confirmed it was him. Dark green leaves within clean black edges, petals purplish on the bottom, shimmering blue at the top identical to mine—it was the tattoo of our blue orchid.

My mouth dropped open so I covered it with my hand. Even so, I blinked rapidly and rubbed my eyes, then lowered my arm behind the counter to pinch my thigh to make sure I wasn't dreaming.

I tried to speak, but the words stuck in my throat, choking all sound. "Uhm . . . ahh . . ." I finally managed. My cheeks felt hot. My heart skipped a beat. His did the same.

For the first time in my life, I wasn't dreaming about William. He was actually here.

I smiled and shifted my gaze back to William's face. When my mouth opened, I hoped my vocal chords would cooperate, but as quickly as he'd come in, he turned and walked out again—and disappeared.

"William! Wait!" I yelled, an explosion of sound from my lungs releasing the tension in my throat. "Come back!" I rushed out of the store after him and starred.

His legs were long, and his steps too quick for me to catch up—not unless I wanted to use my other half, and I couldn't give into the vampire inside me. Not now . . . or maybe, not yet.

My legs fought my mind as I began to trot. The trot turned into a run, and soon my legs carried me at their will. I'd lost control, and buildings and cars swooshed past me as the wind pressed against my body. Still, William seemed faster. Pushing my feet to their limit, I didn't want to let William go out of my sight, yet he disappeared like a drop in an ocean. My feet stopped. I stood frozen, soles of my shoes cemented to the sidewalk.

"Ugh!" I snarled in frustration. *Why did he leave without saying a word?*

My reflection in the storefront window display reminded me of someone else. Sweaty shirt, cobwebbed hair and grey circles under the eyes weren't part of a fashion statement I wanted to make when meeting William.

My lungs filled with air, drawing his scent in. The smell of the stranger who'd picked up my hat three times in the past month, the scent penetrating dreams . . . the same fragrance as my blue orchid. How could someone who had so much power over my emotions just walk away?

I pressed my hand to my heart, over the anguish lingering in my chest—not the pain of hurt, but a heartache. Deep sorrow buried under my breastbone, the sorrow of having a part of me gone; grief and distress at being torn away from the handful of people I loved. It hurt so much I'd kill to get it back.

Feeling empty, I touched the middle of my chest and knew William would not be there when the nightmare became reality. The pain of the scar was bearable; knowing William would be nowhere near wasn't. He was the only one who could fill the emptiness in my heart.

* * *

By early afternoon, a storm hovered over Pinedale, mimicking my feelings. The murky weather had appeared out of nowhere. I stared out the store window, following the streaks of raindrops coursing down the glass. Each rivulet flowed on a specific path, then it connected to another bead on the way down, then another and another, until it became one broad stream that plunged toward the windowsill.

Two oval drops on opposite sides of the window trickled down at the same pace. One veered right, toward the center; the other one, left. They followed a ragged pattern across the glass, getting heavier on the way, collecting other droplets. Finally, they joined and danced down to the bottom as one.

I smiled, allowing determination to return to my body, recalling his heartbeat so clearly, it could be mine. William's flowery cologne settled in my store. As the scent filled my lungs and passed through me, time slowed, clearing my thoughts. This always happened around the blue orchid, my most potent flower. My senses intensified; everything happened in slow motion; tiny air particles circled in front of my eyes, dancing on the breeze from the heating vents; clusters of molecules created spiralling drawings, colourful swirls in front of my eyes.

The grandfather clock in the back room struck ten times; it was no longer daylight outside. As I cleaned the store, I abandoned the slow human motions; my movements were swift, my survival instincts strong. I'd never felt as free and didn't want to stop my other half as it stirred. The corners of my mouth stretched up as I thought of Sleeping Beauty waking, years after pricking her finger: her body frozen in time, life progressing, time passing around her as she lay there motionless, unable to live until awakened by Prince Charming . . . William was my prince, the blue orchid his kiss.

When I left the store, the streets were empty. I hesitated, looking over my shoulder, fearing this night welcomed someone other than the creature lurking in my skin. But the vampire in me wasn't afraid. With my back straightened, I confidently walked the familiar short path by the river toward my house. Tonight, not even a mugger would stand a chance.

I meandered, following my feet, letting them remember the way home. It was a bright night, the sidewalk showing as a light shade of gray, the white moonshine silvering parked cars and glittering in a nearby pond. The white oval in the sky made this night more complicated and difficult for me. My instincts grew stronger. The need to hunt surfaced like a hungry lion. Lust emerged as if I were a teenager wanting to explore another body. The needs of the other half were taking over.

The full moon above reflected in the front door of my home. It was the enemy I would be fighting tonight. When I stepped over the threshold, my gaze flew toward the dark corner of the living room, drawn by rustling wood chips and squeaking rats. The dryness in my throat increased.

My "pets" climbed one on top of another, trying to escape, as if knowing their minutes were numbered. I crouched by the third crate and picked up one of the rodents by the back of its neck. The hunger won, but I refused to drink from the source. I broke the rat's neck, sliced it open, and filled a glass with red fluid.

"At least it looks like red wine," I observed.

Plugging my nose out of habit, I gulped it before the blood cooled and became lethal. Its potency flew through me, expanding my veins. The pale skin on my hands flushed. I drank the blood of five more; each one tasted sweeter than the one before.

Sated, I shifted my gaze toward the kitchen, thinking of the clear syringe filled with blue fluid in the fridge. Like an addict needing her next fix, I jabbed the needle into my thigh. The serum spread through my body like hot water. Sweat beaded and dripped from my forehead. I crashed down on the couch in the living room, falling into the middle of a dream.

A fire engulfed a wooden building in a jungle. I'd seen the building before, but it was difficult to recognize it behind the red and blue flames. My need to put the blaze out overpowered any rational thoughts that I could get hurt, but I knew the logs of the cabin would crumble within minutes. Thunder sounded, not too far away. I let out a cry and wiped the tears with the ball of my palm. Rage flowed through my body, and it shook like I'd had a seizure, helpless against Earth's element. Fury rushed out of my mouth in the form of foam. Ash fell like snow, covering my hair. Rain began to pour, and the penny-sized drops sizzled on the scorching wood, releasing smoke to the top of the canopy.

I woke up screaming. Sweat turned into pearl-like drops as it slid down my arms onto the sofa. The smell of the smoke wrapped in my hair. The dream was not only intense, but sickening. It tore at me from the inside out. Sadness tightened around my heart in an unbearable ache. I hated when my dreams turned into nightmares that would become real, and lately that happened almost every night.

"Enough! Why is this happening?" I shoved the glass syringe from the side table to shatter on the floor. "I don't want to sleep anymore!"

The next two nights, I reduced the dose by half, as I always did when the nightmares returned. The lower amount of serum would allow me to stay awake without having to give in to the instincts.

Forced back to sleepless nights, I felt torn. I wanted to be mortal but couldn't silence the immortal. I could not find my place in the world. Unlike the raindrops on the window, I remained alone, unable to find my path.

CHAPTER 5

William focused on his feet, grimacing at the thick layer of mud on the shoelaces, residue from the crossing in the Amazon. The hideous disguise of a homeless man had become a nuisance. This was not the way he wanted to present himself to Sarah.

He wondered whether she'd go with him to his home. Two weeks had passed since he came to Pinedale, and he still hasn't worked up the courage to introduce himself. *Coward!* he berated himself. *I should have said something by now.*

William wanted to tell her he was here, that he was real and that he needed her. He wanted her to know he was the William from her dreams, and she wouldn't be alone anymore. The half-breed envisioned running across the street to the flower shop so many times, imagined being welcomed by her embrace. Then he'd take her face between his hands and press his lips firmly against hers instead of saying hello . . .

Each time William thought about Sarah, the urge to sweep her away grew stronger. He memorized the exact location of each freckle on her cheeks, the way her auburn hair bounced when she walked to work each morning, an aloe and vanilla fragrance wafting from it that he found hard to resist. Her beauty must have captivated more than one suitor, yet she seemed lonely. William watched her through the glass window as she arranged the flowers. She picked the dying petals off roses to unveil the fresh buds.

As the days passed, he became convinced she belonged with him. The need to touch her grew. But he had to listen to Atram, his father. He couldn't get close—not that way, but temptation charged the need into a compulsion. He wanted her like he had never wanted anything in his life . . . and they'd only exchanged two short sentences:

"Thank you. Have we met before?"

"No."

His heart had skipped a beat when her voice hit his eardrums. It took on a new rhythm, one more synchronized with hers. He'd wanted to say more, but feared he wouldn`t live up to the dreams she'd had of him.

Coward!

Sarah`s fresh scent had travelled from William`s nostrils straight into his bloodstream. He could recognize it from miles away. Smelling Sarah`s aroma overpowered his senses. She had control over his body, and she didn't know it. William wondered whether he'd be able to control his desires around her. After all, he was still a man, with needs like any other.

Every time he came closer, ready to take her, he'd hesitated. When he passed by the store to make sure she was still there, he wavered. How could he not? He had never met her. Sarah had just received confirmation from her aunt about who she was, and now he had to take her away before the seekers found her. They were getting closer; he sensed it. Their stench of rotten eggs and dirty socks circled nearby towns.

William feared her safety would soon be compromised. Who else could protect her the way he could? Mira and Xander had done a great job, but even the shifters could not shield her from the seekers indefinitely. He knew first hand, for the siblings had trained him. Once the seekers found Sarah, more would come. William hoped she'd trust him the way he'd been told by his parents. But doubt lingered as he knew he'd only inhabited Sarah's dreams.

Wednesday. I'll talk to her tomorrow.

William knocked on the wooden door of a wide bungalow marked *21 Front Street*. The door opened as soon as he lifted his fist. The aroma of freshly baked pumpkin pie made his stomach rumble. He smiled at the welcome in the lady's face.

The hostess eyed William from top to bottom, then called over her shoulder, "Mira! Xander! It's for you!" She looked back to her visitor. "Hello, William, we've been expecting you. Come on in."

"Thank you, Mrs. Gobert. I wasn't sure I'd be expected."

"Don't be silly, dear." She paused. "You're much wiser than many will give you credit for."

William had been cautioned that the witch spoke in riddles. Hesitant, he walked inside and hung his filthy coat on a hook by a wall mirror. He turned back to close the door, but she'd already locked it. The half-breed followed Mrs. Gobert down a long hallway, pausing as she stepped to one side to discreetly push the basement door shut; the rising fog escaped under the door. She gestured with her hand to come in, but William stopped at a hall table.

"Beautiful tulips. Yellow are my favourite," he said, admiring the arrangement.

"That's why they're here, William." Her mouth curved in a mysterious grin.

The sparkling aura around the tulips held his eyes. He touched the silk ribbon and leaned closer to smell the flowers. *Sarah!* Her scent overwhelmed the fragrance of the bouquet.

"Are you coming?" Mrs. Gobert smiled politely.

"Yes, of course." He pulled his hand away from the vase, almost knocking it over.

"Be careful, William. Wouldn't want those to end up on the floor," she teased. The hardwood flooring squeaked when she strode over the aged strips of oak.

William followed her into the kitchen, watching her long, navy-blue dress dance over the tiles as she swayed her hips and hummed under her breath. Her hair, wound into a thick brown braid that fell to the small of her back, swung in rhythm, and the collection of heavy bracelets on her left wrist chimed, occasionally revealing a small birthmark while rattling. She turned to face William and gestured for him to take a seat. He pulled the chair out; when he looked up again, Mira and Xander stood across the table.

"I'll let you three be. Holler if you need anything." Mrs. Gobert patted the siblings on their shoulders and then strolled down the hall, no doubt headed back to the basement and its thickening fog.

"Thanks, Mom!" Mira called. She immediately turned to William. "Has she seen you?"

"Yes, but she didn't know it was me." He tried to add certainty to his guess.

"I doubt that." Xander snorted and gripped the back of the chair in front of him, knuckles white. "You don't give Sarah enough credit. Oh, that's right—you don't really know her." He stood tall and straightened his shoulders. Xander was shorter than William by an inch or so, but the way he presented himself made him seem taller than anyone in his company.

The half-breed studied Xander's tense neck muscles, his flexed arms, his head tilted slightly to the side in challenge, and William knew it would be difficult to persuade the shifters to let Sarah go.

"Why are you here?" he asked William, suspicion covering his deep voice.

"I need to tell Sarah the truth. And I need you to be okay with—"

"Why are you here in Pinedale?" Xander's jaw tensed.

"Sarah's in danger. The seekers have sensed her. They're on their way here, about a week away. I've been able to divert them with her scent as a lure." Now came the hard part. William wanted to exhale, but there was no air left in his lungs. "I have to take Sarah away."

"No way!" Xander growled. His muscles hardened to solid rock, and he didn't bother hiding his sharp teeth.

"Play nice, kids," Mrs. Gobert called from the basement.

Xander hid his incisors behind his lips. William held his back.

"Xander, I'm sure you understand the severity of the situation." He tightened his fists under the table and tried reasoning. "The seekers will take her from you if she stays."

"And they won't from you?" he challenged.

Why am I better for her? William wished he could answer with his heart and what he felt. "I can take her to a place that's safe where she'll be protected."

"Where's that?" Mira asked. She'd been observing the men from the side, her eyes narrowed as if she was waiting for William to make a mistake she could argue against.

"I can't tell you."

And there it was.

"And we're supposed to let Sarah go to hell knows where?" she echoed her brother's tone with a sneer.

"Yes. It's the only way she'll be safe. And I know you'll do what's best for her—the way Ekim wanted." He drawled to make his voice more pleading, more believable.

"And what does Ekim say about it? Why isn't he with you?" she asked.

"You know he doesn't want Sarah to know her father is alive—not yet. And, she wouldn't trust him. She'll trust me because she knows me."

The siblings rolled their eyes. "We should still run it by him," Mira replied.

"It's not possible to reach him. He's on the run, diverting the seekers," William lied, hoping they'd believe it.

"William, you have to understand that our promise to protect Sarah binds us until we're released. It's not that simple. We can't just let her go," Mira explained.

"I understand, but this is what's best for Sarah." he countered, softening his voice. The only way Sarah's watchers and best friends would agree was through reason.

"I'm going with you." Xander stood taller.

"You have to stay here to cover our tracks. For Sarah's safety."

"William, you must know what our orders are, what we promised Ekim. Our nature will not allow us to break that promise. Mom!" Mira yelled toward the basement.

Mrs. Gobert came back upstairs. The smell of fresh herbs and spices followed her. She walked into a kitchen filled with tension and offered her opinion without having to be asked. "You have to let her go, darling." The witch brushed Mira's face with the back of her hand.

"Will she be safe?" Xander asked.

"She has to go with William. It's her destiny. The prophecy cannot be fulfilled if they are not together."

William smiled with respect, glad her magic agreed with his plans. The siblings would listen to her, not because she was their mother, but because she was a powerful witch.

"Will you update us?" The siblings spoke together.

"I can send you a message once every three days."

Mira's shoulders relaxed.

"Use our falcon," Xander offered unexpectedly.

"Thank you, Xander." William bowed his head in appreciation.

"When are you going to see her?" Mira asked.

"Tomorrow."

"I still don't think this is right," Xander said under his breath, gripping the chair in front of him. His knuckles were now bloodless. He was still wary. Sadness grew in his eyes.

"The seekers are close. I have to tell her the truth."

"Come to dinner with us on Friday night. We'll all tell her the truth," Mira offered.

"Saturday," Mrs. Gobert interrupted, winking at her daughter, innocently fluttering her eyelashes. Her personality did not always match the witch stereotype.

The siblings' nature must be rubbing off on her, William thought.

"Saturday," Mira corrected, not questioning her mother.

"And you think she can take it? My existence and your uniqueness?" William asked.

"We'll take our chances, dream-boy." Xander smirked.

"Fine, I'll wait until Saturday." He paused before adding, "Unless there's an emergency."

That settled, the siblings became more hospitable. William cleaned up and changed into new clothes Xander offered him. The shifter`s grin gave away his thoughts as he handed the jeans, shirt, and a sweater to William: *She'll smell they're mine.* William didn't correct him. Sarah would still know it was William, and once she saw him, Xander wouldn't cross her thoughts. Xander's smell could never overpower Sarah's senses.

CHAPTER 6

I strolled through Riverside Park, appreciating the unseasonable warmth of this autumn morning. The sun was still low, its light spreading up, illuminating the park from below. A few clouds lingered in the sky. Stopping in the middle of the path, I closed my eyes and tilted my head back. The sun's rays bathed my face.

The sharp tick of my watch counted down the twelve hours before I spilled my secrets to the siblings. *I hope they'll believe me. I don't want to have to show them.*

A cool breeze from the west caressed my hair. Without the warmth of the new sunlight, the air would be crisp. Ground fog hovered, not yet surrendering the position it had held all night. It rose toward the tips of the grass and dissipated as it crept up the bottoms of the bushes and the broader tree trunks. Centuries-old willow branches swayed above the ground, their ends tiptoeing gracefully through the fog.

A shadow at the park's entrance drew my gaze, nebulous in the fog drifting across the park. Hoping the man wouldn't disrupt my morning, I resumed my walk; needing to be alone. Today, I'd decided I would take charge, take control. I would tell the siblings the truth.

My gaze on the gravel crunching under my feet wandered toward the stranger every few seconds, who ran toward me. Heat radiated from his body, like a space heater. The wind shifted direction, and I inhaled, feeling my lungs expand—then held the breath as the scent paralyzed my limbs. *William!*

Instinctively, I veered toward him. My gaze caught and held his, telling him I wouldn't let him go this time, but he was already running toward me at great speed. The muscles around his neck tensed, his eyebrows puckered with concern. He rushed, suavely but swiftly, determined to reach me, looking behind him as if he feared someone had followed him.

"Sarah, I don't have much time to explain," he began when we were close, his voice soft. He turned to look behind him, and I drew another breath, allowing his sweet and musky scent to raid my nostrils.

Nothing he said mattered. He was here. Instead of me finding him, *he* found me. "William?"

"Yes, it's me." His smile was tender. Then his gaze roved across the park, from one side to the other. "There's no time to explain. You have to come with me. Helen wrote they may be getting closer."

When his eyes focused on mine again, happiness overwhelmed me. His body's warmth connected to mine, and his scent danced around me, pulling me closer and closer. I could almost see the sweet air form a finger and bend it repeatedly, beckoning me in. Leaning against him, I inhaled again, certain what he had to say wouldn't resonate for a while. The last time I'd felt this intoxicated was after a bottle of wine.

"Did you hear me? We have to go. Now!" He tugged at my arm.

William's words entered one ear and left through the other. "What's happening to me?" The words slurred out of my mouth. Everything seemed so blurry around him. My body felt limp and I swayed on rubbery legs.

"If you stay here, you'll die. You have to come with me." William's widened eyes hypnotized me even more.

My knees gave way. William caught me under my arms and held me up. "Die?" I pulled my limbs closer to his, dragging a hand up to stroke his biceps. All I'd wanted was to roam his body and ignore the urgency in his voice.

He pulled me toward the end of the park. I dragged my limp feet over the gravel.

"You changed your serum—it's not working as well as it should." William turned his head to look behind him again, sniffing the air. "The seekers are getting closer. You have to come with me now to the cabin. It will take us a few days to get there, but you'll be safe there."

"Okay." Part of me realized my words swayed along with my body, like a career drunk, but I couldn't understand why.

William kept walking.

"Who are 'the seekers'?" I placed my nose against his shirt and inhaled deeply, to feel the limpness of a high.

"The cabin is protected. We'll be safe there." He spoke like an automaton, as if he'd planned what he was going to say. William nudged me toward the far end of the park—the end closer to my home.

"But I have a date today." I tried to sound serious, but my response came in on a giggly laugh. "With Mira and Xander."

William placed his finger under my chin, lifting it, pulling my stare from his pecs up to his eyes. He smiled. "I'm sorry I'm making you feel all drugged up. It's the serum. You're not used to the mixture you smell on me. But please, try to concentrate."

"You can make me feel anything you want," I replied, shamelessly indulging in William's scented spell. He quickened his pace to a run, and I hurried to keep up.

"I'll explain everything later, but now we have to run before it's too late. You must trust me. Your father would have wanted you to come with me. He'd want you to be safe." He widened his eyes, care and passion camouflaged by pain and loneliness.

Your father would have wanted you to come with me. He'd want you to be safe, I repeated in my head. The reference to my father brought me back to reality. The high was gone, but the desire to be close to William dug deeper than Earth's core.

William stopped, took me by the shoulders, and I glimpsed a tattoo on his wrist. "I know you're confused, Sarah, but if you don't keep it together, we're doomed."

I trusted him and didn't want to fail him. Our eyes met and I took his hand. Time slowed. Palms pressed together, our fingers wove a familiar pattern. My heart begun to beat a new rhythm, yearning to be taken away from the loneliness and emptiness I'd been living in for the past few days—no, since birth. My heart was asking to be complete. After years of hope, William was finally here, with me.

William knew this. He knew how much I needed him, and the same yen shined in his eyes. William led, and I followed.

"Why are we not safe here? Where are we going? Who are the seekers? Why do you smell like Xander? And . . . you know my father?"

"In due time, Sarah, I'll explain everything. I need you to stay quiet for now. Can you do that for me?"

"Yes."

We ran in silence. Unlike mine, his footsteps made no sound.

"How do you move like a ghost?" I whispered, mesmerized by my escort.

"Years of practice. Shhh," he hushed.

We turned the corner to my street, and William tugged me behind a masonry wall. A black Mercedes was parked in front of my house; tinted windows hid its occupants. As we watched, a gray cloud appeared out of nowhere, its shadow hovering above the car and the house, and nowhere else, as if nature wanted to warn us.

"Don't speak, just follow me. Is the chest still at the house?" he whispered.

I shook my head.

"Can you take me to it?"

I nodded.

William removed a syringe filled with red liquid from his pocket. "Inject this. It will help us disappear before they figure out how close we are."

Twirling the syringe in my fingers, I hesitated. This shade of serum was new. Biting my lip, I squeezed William's hand so tightly that my knuckles, then my fingers, whitened. His breath warmed the side of my face as he bobbed his head in encouragement. I jabbed the needle without twitching. We understood one another's facial expressions without having to speak.

I pulled him by the hand, and we turned to walk to the store, allowing the wind to push at our backs. Time slowed again. The liquid rushed in my veins, spreading throughout my body. Our heart valves pumped blood in the same rhythm; they thumped a synchronized beat. Just as in my dreams. We took the same steps, moved our arms in unison, breathed in and out at the same time . . . as if we were dancing, as if we were that one big raindrop on the path down the window.

Without warning, the wind pulled us back, pushing at our chests. I sensed trouble; a low growl rose from the back of my throat. My hand flew to cover my mouth. My eyes went straight to William. The serum warmed, then cooled in my veins.

"It's working quickly, isn't it?" he whispered, then peeked between the buildings where the from of my house was still visible.

Two men stepped out on the front porch of my house. They inhaled and, like well-trained hounds, began sniffing the air, nostrils flared. Their heads turned, their gazes fixing in our direction. We round the corner before they saw us. William quickened his pace and seconds later, we were running. Buildings, cars, people flew past us in a blur. No one reacted. They couldn't see us.

Then another feeling, one not so new to me, surfaced—shame. This was exactly what I'd been trying to suppress. Was I sacrificing my mortality by doing this? Though I wasn't sure, I knew I could trust William—even Helen had said so. I concentrated more, feeling the acceleration of my feet.

William turned toward the park, and we ran through it in seconds. He veered around a tree near the park's edge and whacked at a branch to set it swaying; then we ran to another and climbed up—more like flew up—into the dense canopy of yellows and reds, the leaves barely swishing behind us.

"We can't outrun them, and for our sake, I hope the serum has spread." William pulled my body against his. His sweet breath warmed my ear and cheek.

"Was that what made me growl?" I whispered, barely audible.

"Shh . . ." William placed a finger on his full lips, inches away from mine.

The two men were approaching and stopped directly below us. Fear crawled up my spine. William's arm tightened around my shoulder. I peeked through the curtain of leaves at their odd, elongated postures.

Long black cloaks concealed much of them. Hoods over their heads revealed nothing of their faces but orange eyes, with neither pupils nor irises, that radiated hatred and determination. Their only mission was to find their target. Pale, bony hands resembling sticks protruded from the edges of the cloaks.

I've seen them before. I sucked in a quiet breath. Eight years ago. These were not vampires, but they were not men, either.

The creatures sniffed like well-trained terriers, glancing toward the branch William had slapped at earlier. They spoke words I didn't understand, interspersed with high-pitched shrieking; then they turned and followed the false trail. My body sagged against William's. He didn't object; his arms held me tightly.

"They're gone," he whispered. "The seekers are quick, but not that bright. They'll retrace their steps. We have to go."

I nodded.

We jumped down, landing on the soft ground below us, our legs acting as springs. I liked this new feeling of greater power and agility.

"Who exactly are the seekers?" I asked.

"They're demons," he hissed. "Where's the chest?"

"My store. I know a shortcut."

I took William's hand guiding him through the newer part of the park, closer to my flower shop. We flew over shrubs and dashed past Mrs. Fox's backyard, the wind of our passage blowing her freshly washed laundry on the clothesline. The last hurtle over the Gaples' hedge lead us to the parking lot at the back of my store.

I never got to work so quickly. I allowed a cautious smile.

"If they can follow your scent from the house to here, they'll come here next," William warned. He sniffed the air. "We have another minute."

I unlocked the back door of the flower shop with a spare key under the flower pot. William had no trouble finding the chest and seemed to know his way around this forest of green a little too well.

"You've been here before?" I said.

"Yes." William's eyes fixed on the chest.

"Other than that day I saw you?"

"Yes. I had to make sure you were all right after finding Helen's letter," he admitted, ducking his head. His innocent shame surprised me.

"You know about the letter?" I asked.

"I asked her to write it. Although I wish she hadn't been so dramatic about your father," he said. "Things are complicated, Sarah. You—I mean we—have to save everyone. We have to stop the extinction."

"Who's everyone?"

"The world."

I pulled my hand away from his and stepped back.

He peeked through the front window. "Sarah. Don't panic, please. After we get out of here, I'll explain everything, I promise. If the seekers catch us ,they'll kill us." William looked cautiously toward the window again as he picked up the chest in his other arm. His softened gaze returned to me, and I took his hand.

I followed him like a week-old pup, trusting his every move. My senses tuned, the same instinct guided me when the mist at the lake had carried my legs toward the blue orchid.

A green jeep was parked across the street. He led me to it, and we climbed inside. I rested my head against the elevated back of the cushioned passenger seat, still eyeing William. "Are we coming back?"

"Not for a while, hon. Not for a while." He exhaled.

I stared out the window as William pressed his foot on the gas pedal. We squealed away from the curb, and I saw in the mirror the tires leaving black streaks on the road. I leaned my head back. My eyes moistened as we passed the Thank *you for visiting Pinedale sign.*

CHAPTER 7

The road weaved. I didn't know where we were going or how long we'd be gone for, and it didn't matter—I wanted to get far away from the orange-eyed seekers, but at the same time, I couldn't help feeling homesick. This was the first time I'd left, since my camping trip. Pinedale had always felt as if it had a bubble wrapped dome around it. Somehow, I'd always felt safe, especially with Mira and Xander at my side. Now I may as well have left the country, because I felt like a foreigner. Would my friends panic when I didn't show up for dinner tonight? Would they notify the sheriff?

While keeping his gaze on the narrow road, William handed me another syringe.

"It will help you sleep," he said. "You need to rest."

I recognized the blue liquid inside, but hesitated. "Um, not really—"

"I know you think you're not tired, but the human part of your body needs rest. You can't feel the aching muscles, but if they don't rest, they won't perform well."

I gasped. William knew what I am. We'd both run with unnatural speed; his senses were as strong as mine; we understood each other without having to speak. In my dreams, he was always human, but subconsciously, I knew William was like me, I just never admitted it for fear I'd reject the vampire inside him, the same way I rejected myself.

After I injected the new dose, my eyelids grew heavy. My head tilted back against the seat, and I slept, free of nightmares, free of dreams.

When I woke, I didn't know where I was. With my eyes still shut, I rolled my head to rest on William's shoulder. Our closeness sent waves of warmth through my body. I couldn't remember the last time I'd felt such tingling in my stomach. Snuggling, I inhaled his sweet smell.

William was still driving. I opened my eyelids a crack to see dense forest whizzing by on my left and green rolling hills on the right. The square, yellowed fields near Pinedale were nowhere in sight. The sun was gently setting, casting its glowing spell on the horizon. I finally lifted my head.

"How did you sleep?" William asked.

First I smiled, wondering whether his scent would intoxicate me the same way it had in the park. I welcomed it into my lungs but maintained control over my body. "Unusually well." My knees hit the dashboard when I stretched. "Oops."

"It's all right. I apologize—this is not the most comfortable place to sleep." William smiled. "You were out for a while."

My stiff thighs lacked blood circulation, so I rubbed them. Out of nowhere, questions spilled from my mouth as if they were water spraying from a punctured hose. "What kind of serum was that in the park? How did you know Helen? Where did the creatures come from? Why were they here? Are they still chasing us? How did you find me?"

William laughed. "Slow down. Just relax and let me do some of the talking." He gave me a crooked smile, dangerous and strong, but inviting.

I licked my lips, sinking back in my seat. "All right."

"Here." He gave me a syringe filled with pink liquid. "Take this before we speak again."

I took the new serum and scanned the side of the road for orange eyes. "You think they'll follow us?"

"I know they will. We have to lose our scent."

I frowned. "How?"

"The serum you took helps, and so will a stopover at the motel. We're almost there." He glanced at the empty syringe I now held. "We should be safe until morning."

"We'll be staying overnight?"

"It would take too long to drive to where we're going without stopping."

I was going to ask him about the long drive when my gaze drifted ahead to a long, one-storey building illuminated by bright fluorescent lights. A blue-and-pink neon sign on its roof flashed *Quick top Motel*. The *S* was unlit. Brown paint peeled off the clapboard siding on the front office and revealed faded patches of beige.

Two women strolled the sidewalk and rounded the corner. Their loud conversation about working the north side of the motel made me shudder.

William opened my door. "Sarah, please excuse the accommodations, but it's unlikely they'll sense us here, since they'll be concentrating on the more luxurious hotels."

I didn't have enough courage to ask him about the luxurious hotel. Heck, I still couldn't get used to the way my name escaped his mouth and suppressed the uncontrollable giggles I felt bubbling inside me.

Smiling mirthfully, William placed his arm around me, and we walked across the parking lot. *What is he smiling about?* Why was I acting like a fourteen-year-old one minute and a scared cat the next?

"Everything will make sense soon. I promise. I'm glad we got out of town in time." He squeezed my shoulder.

A red-haired woman in her late forties sat behind the counter in the office. She sighed heavily, leaning her elbows on the countertop as if too tired to stand on her own.

William spoke first. "Good evening," he purred.

She smiled back at him and batted her fake lashes. "Good evening. A room for two?" The hostess leered at William but did not spare me a look.

"Yes please, for one night. And if anyone asks, there's only one person occupying it." William slid his hand across the counter and left a fat roll of bills in her palm. "I'm sure discretion is common here."

"Of course!" She stuffed William's gratuity into her cleavage, then winked at him. "I understand."

William rubbed my shoulder. His touch was calming, but it quickened my pulse. His heart sped up to match mine. The weight of his palm made me feel more secure, despite the confused rhythm in my chest.

The landlady handed him a key.

"Come on," he whispered, sliding his hand to my waist. Our hearts skipped a beat.

We walked quickly along the front of the building and passed closed doors. The stench of day-old cigar smoke—how did I know it was a day old?—wafted from under one door. William stopped at number 109 and turned the key in its lock, the click of the tumbler louder than normal in my ears. He pushed the door open, and I stepped inside.

The motel, a two star accommodation, wasn't much worse than the conditions I lived in back in Pinedale. The room was neat but outdated, the patterns on wallpaper and fabrics mismatched. Avocado green shag carpeting, flower-patterned curtains, and gold glass swag lights were holdovers from the seventies. Neon light shone through the large window to illuminate the interior in uneven flashes. William opened the window, which helped to flush the stale air from the room.

"There's one bed," I noted. My cheeks heated.

"I'll sleep on the chair." William stretched his arms out, and his shirt lifted above his navel, baring a defined pelvis above low-cut jeans.

Turning away, I felt the heat increase in my face. "I don't need to sleep, but you must be tired." I shut the door.

William dropped my backpack onto the chair. I had grabbed it when we rushed out of the store; it always contained a few useful toiletry items.

He gestured for me to sit down on the bed. "I'm not tired."

The phone in the motel office began ringing, and I jumped, frowning. "Why is my hearing so sensitive?"

"You're not used to the combination of so many serums. Your senses will adjust as your body learns to use their components in the right proportions."

"I don't understand."

"You and I—we're unique," he started.

"Really?" I said sarcastically, and William apologized with a smile. I bit my lip, regretting my rudeness.

He read my face. "You have nothing to be sorry about. Your hormones aren't dealing well with the serums."

"Is that what caused my reaction in the park? I was acting like one of those women street-walking on the corner."

"You inhaled the remains of my serum. I'm used to it, but you're not."

I lifted my brows. "What kind of serum did you take?"

"I . . . I was nervous to meet you and wanted to make sure you liked me, so you would listen to me."

"There's a difference between liking someone and wanting to jump their bones," I retorted, then slapped my hand to cover my mouth.

William laughed. "Maybe it's better if you let the serum wear off a bit."

I changed the subject. "Why are they chasing us? Who are they?"

"We're somewhat special." William raised a finger to stop my interruption. "We have to use the serum to protect ourselves from the bad guys. We are the only human-vampire offsprings in both this world and the underworld." He said this slowly to make sure I grasped every word.

"The underworld?" I asked. "You don't mean underground shopping malls in downtown Toronto, do you?"

"No, not that kind." William sighed. "You and I were similarly conceived. Our parents were best friends. Our fathers were vampires and our mothers human."

"You're the same as me?" The question was impulsive.

"Concentrate, Sarah. Haven't you thought there is more to the world?"

"Yes, but I tried to block that part out."

"Good, you were supposed to so the seekers couldn't find you. But you can't anymore. The sooner you embrace who you are, the better."

"Where are your parents?" I asked.

"All access to the underworld has been blocked. Two months ago, my parents went to berak through to get your father. They never came back." His eyes clouded. "I was told that if they didn't return, I should find you. You were my only hope for a future where we would not be hunted anymore."

An echoing knock vibrated the door.

"Shh," William skidded across the room. He closed his eyes, leaned against the frame and took a whiff before turning the knob. The door flew open, almost knocking him back.

I jumped up.

"Give it to me now!" A pale man trembled as he stepped inside. Even though I'd never seen a real vampire before, I couldn't mistake the hollow eyes and sharp fangs.

"Karl, you must stop following me. It's not safe for you. I've told you the seekers are looking for me." William said.

"You know him?" I asked, peeking from behind William.

"Yes, he's been stalking me for blood."

I used William's body like a shield, wondering if the vampire was here to drink our blood. There was no way I would let him touch me! Would the creature be stronger than the bear I'd faced eight years ago? Would he attack us? My thighs trembled and i felt my foot tapping on the soft carpet, jiggling my weight from side to side.

William glanced at me from the side. "Not your blood. Vampires have an agreement with humans that allows both to coexist. We supply blood in exchange for human protection from demons."

"I'm hungry." Karl snarled. His pale hands shook and cheekbones stretched the skin as he smoothed his tongue over the cracked lips. I wondered where he'd found the strength to push the door so forcefully. His eyes sunk deeper, and empty veins pulsed under the skin on his face as if they craved blood as well. Was that what I looked like when my other half stirred?

"I understand what you're going through. We'll get more supplies to you soon, but the agreement will be void if you hunt humans. You won't get any blood from us that way." William said.

"Fine." The vampire hid his fangs and stretched out his hand.

William pulled out a steel canister from his backpack. He opened the lid, and I smelled human blood. After he poured something else into it, the aroma made me lick my lips, but I'd never drink human blood.

"It will kill him. The blood is dead," I whispered, remembering Aunt Helen teaching me the most important rule of drinking blood: it had to be fresh.

William handed the flask to the vampire. "It should hold you over for a while."

Karl gulped it down, then disappeared before the container hit the floor.

I stood frozen. William just introduced me to a world outside of my bubbled Pinedale; one I tried to pretend didn't exist.

William closed the door.

"How did he drink that? Dead blood is lethal to vampires."

"Not anymore." He shook his head. "Are you hungry?"

"Yes." I nodded eagerly.

"What do you crave?"

Is this a trick question? My stomach grumbled.

"What do you crave?" he repeated.

"A burger. Fries perhaps—" I sat on the bed, still in shock.

"Yes that will fill you up, but what do you feel is missing in your veins?"

"Blood," I answered with more confidence. *Embrace your other half.* I squared my shoulders.

"There's a silver canister in your backpack. Open it."

"When did you—"

William raised his index finger to his lips.

I dragged my bag over and pulled out the container. Liquid contents swished inside. Centering the cylinder between my thighs, I turned and lifted the lid, then stuck my tongue out in disgust at the thick red fluid. "When did you drain it from a . . . " I took a whiff from the thermos.

"An elk," he finished.

I'd never had elk blood before—or blood that was dead and cold.

William waggled a finger at my backpack. "Pour the pink serum from that flask into the thermos. Here." He took the lid from my hand so I could comply and watched while I extracted the flask of serum. "Go on, pour it in," he challenged.

As instructed, I removed the cap and emptied the flask. As the serum flowed into the red goo, the mixture bubbled and simmered. Then it swirled, blending into the blood, diluting the viscosity. The canister warmed between my palms as the blood began to take on life. The smell of the burgundy fluid became more appetizing by the second. I held my nose so close small bubbles from the mixture fused around my nostrils, teasing my taste buds.

"The serum is waking up the dead cells," explained William. "You can drink it now. You'll be fine, I promise."

The liquid was homogeneous, with no sign of the pink serum. I took a hesitant sip. As soon as its sugary flavour ran along my tongue, I lost control and gulped it down in a deep swig. Much better than rat's blood. Much, much better. "Oh . . ." I sighed.

"Tasty, I presume?" William sat at my side.

"I guess I've been missing out a bit. *Erp*. Excuse me."

"Tasty" was a weak word to describe it, more like scrumptious, delicious, mouth-watering. What else have I been missing? The hunger I'd denied, the feelings I hadn't allowed, the senses I'd refused, experiences rejected, touches yearned for but never received . . . I was so used to living in my own world, isolated from everyone. Would being closer to William be as gratifying as it was in my dreams?

TWO HALVES

The dance floor was half empty. To us it didn't matter. No one stared at me in my dreams. I was not self-conscious and one everyone should fear to cross. The music was continuous. It didn't stop; we didn't stop. I slipped my hands over his abs and chest, then up to his neck. His remained on my hips, moving them to our own rhythm.

Lowering his head to my neck, William kissed it gently, swooshing his lips over the surface of my skin, teasing. It tickled. I mimicked the behaviour on his chest. He yelped with pleasure, and his face came up, moving to my ear and inhaling. "Vanilla and aloe—my favourite," he murmured.

"I know." I placed my finger on his lips to hush him.

"Ouch." William ground his teeth.

I pulled my hand away from his as the jolt of electricity from our touch brought me back. My palm stung. "Why does it hurt to touch you?"

"I'm not sure." He blushed. "It only hurts when we touch in a non-platonic way."

I felt elk blood rush to my cheeks. Could I love William as completely as I did in my dreams? Would I find the comfort of his body again? Would we be one? Could we be one?

We sat on the edge of the bed in silence, our thighs almost touching. William's warmth oozed toward me. I wondered how hot his leg would be if it twined with mine. The fluttering in my stomach returned. As I exhaled my lower lip pushed out to direct the breath over my face, but it didn't have the cooling effect I'd hoped for. William seemed just as lost. *Where do we go from here?*

I welcomed the light breeze from the open window that flapped the curtains. The crisp air reminded me of the forest I'd stood in eight years ago. Two doors down, someone was finishing a slice from a large vegetarian pizza. One of the two ladies on the corner sprayed cheap perfume over her neck. A small fox carried a rabbit in its mouth as she led two kits across the road.

William stood to close the window, eyeing my sniffs. "If you can sense what I think you can, you're much more in tune with your skills than I expected you to be." He smiled with pride and concern as he returned to the bed. The pressure of the mattress sprang me up. "We have to be careful."

"Because the seekers can sense me now?"

"Yes. If I can sense your feelings that much better, so can the underworld."

"Why don't they just let us be?" I groaned.

"We're a threat. We can't get caught."

He pulled a sapphire ring from his pocket. "Put this on."

I did, expecting the large ring to be loose, but it shrank to fit my finger. "How—"

"Just wait," William whispered. "It will show you what you need to know."

A light shot from the blue gem and struck the back wall of the room. A picture appeared as if played by a movie projector. The image jumped from dark rooms where figures fought one another in the gloom to brighter ones where people lived in peace. Then the darkness returned, illuminated only by firelight as rivers of hot lava burned walles into deep dungeons. The imagery unfolded silently, but inside my head it told me a story of the underworld as screams of tortured creatures, vibrated my ears. Agony filled their faces; death was a yearned-for dream as Aseret, a greedy warlock who became a demon lord tried to control vampires by starving them.

"Why are they doing this?" I focused on the orange-eyed seekers guarding their prisoners.

"Demons want to impose the laws of the underworld and rule all. They use spells to break creatures down before they have a chance to flex, stealing other's abilities and powers to make them stronger." William moved to the window and shut the flowery curtains. The irritating flashing from the motel sign no longer interrupted the flow of the image on the wall. "There's a constant battle in the underworld as demons seek to destroy," he continued. "Vampires are older and wiser. They haven't changed who they are, unlike the warlocks who turned into demons when they sought power. Now the vampires are limited in their whereabouts because of the demonic takeovers." William sat in the armchair. "They can no longer abide by the code established between them and humans. This world is no longer balanced." He gestured toward the wall projection.

"The code: Blood in exchange for protection." I recalled William's conversation with Karl.

William leaned forward and took my hand; he squeezed it and a rush of energy shot from him, through my body, and out my other hand, the one wearing the ring. The imagery changed. Institutions where criminals received a new kind of capital punishment for their crimes: death by draining provided the supply of blood vampires needed. And William distributed serums to revive the dead blood.

"Vampires and humans work together but now have a common enemy to fight," he added.

"The demons would kill a vampire." Anxiety rushed through me; I wanted to understand everything, and quickly. I wanted to know why I was created.

"Wouldn't even flinch," William shook his head.

I flinched. "How are demons different from warlocks?"

"Demons have powers; warlocks have spells. The virtuous warlocks fight to restore the balance disrupted by the demons. The demons have been blocking access to the penitentiaries, hoping the vampires will self-destruct without blood. You saw Karl. He looked like he hasn't fed in weeks. If the agreement between vampires and humans is broken, a new kind of war will be unleashed. The keepers guard the peace between humans, vampires, and warlocks. For humans, it's the angel Gabriel. Drake heads the vampires, and Castall is the highest-ranking warlock."

The window that had been slightly ajar flew open, and I jerked back. The flowery curtains fluttered into the room, and I leaned back to avoid them. The flashing light intruded again; I blinked in the same sequence. William rose and closed the curtains, this time so they overlapped.

"There's no demon keeper?" I asked.

"No. Demons are not natural."

The warmth from his body was gone. The chills that would normally run down my spine were gone. Cold passed through my back slower, teasing, thawing in some parts only to refreeze again.

"Some time ago, a high-ranking warlock became a demon. He wanted to take over the vampire and human world, using warlocks as his disposable minions. His name is Aseret."

The wind whistled outside, forcing itself through cracks and smaller openings.

"*Is?*"

William nodded.

I knew I wouldn't like this demon and pictured a giant monster with horns on his head and smoke spewing out of his nostrils, juggling little red spheres of molten rock from claw to claw while wild fires raged behind him, casting him into black silhouette.

"Sarah?"

"I'm listening." I shook the image off.

"The keepers created a prophecy to bring him down. We are part of that prophecy. He's now bound to the underworld and cannot escape to do more damage, but he has seekers and demons working for him. We're supposed to bring balance back to the underworld."

I looked at him incredulously. "You and me? But I don't have the muscles you were talking about."

"Didn't you listen? We don't need muscles."

"Because their orange eyes will fry us before we get a chance to flex," I quipped, and laughed, the sound tremulous. "Well, it's about time something made sense in my life. I can't believe I missed so much. I thought I was the only one—the only weirdo."

William let go of my hand. The picture on the wall disappeared.

"Don't say that." He brushed his fingers against my face. The electricity that trickled from their tips ignited my body. "You're special—we're special. You've suppressed your most natural vampire instincts and functioned on a different wavelength from me. That's why you couldn't sense me the way I always sensed you."

"You sensed me?" I bit my lower lip. "Since when?"

"Since you were taken away to live in Pinedale. Since I can remember." He took a deep breath and added, "Even before I knew about you, I had a memory of you."

A faint memory flowed through me. "I crawled behind you on a marble floor."

"That's right. We had to squeeze between the legs of a table." He took my hand again.

I closed my eyes. "The cookies in the garden room. I followed you, but my sun hat slid forward when I bopped and blocked my view."

"You were quick to push it up and grab the treats." William laughed.

"How old were we?" I asked.

"Almost ten months." William stared at me and I recognized the longing in his eyes. He missed me and needed me as much as I needed him.

"So we *are* connected, you and I." A rush of energy passed through my body, as if seeking to confirm the connection.

"The problem is . . . I can sense more than just our connection. I feel when trouble is brewing in the world. I hear whispers from far away if they have anything to do with me. I can feel the powers shifting as fears and desires change." William stared at one spot on the wall across the room as he spoke. He clenched the bedding and twisted it in his fists. Sweat beaded and dripped from his temples, as if he were reliving those fears and desires all at once.

"William?" I touched his shoulder, and he jumped. "Are you okay?"

"Yeah, nothing to worry about." He moved over to the chair.

The twenty-one years of my life that I had thought to be complicated seemed so simple now. Supposedly, I was to be part of a secret prophecy. I closed my eyes and shook my head like this was like another bad dream.

A growl escaped my mouth, as if arguing with someone of higher power. My throat tickled when I thought about the mammals lurking outside. Being part of something greater . . . I had no clue about that, but it was not at the top of my list. A few hours ago, I was worried about telling Mira and Xander my secrets and whether someone can fill in at the store for me, but now William made it sound like we had to save the world.

"I've been working with my parents on a serum to help us get through to the locked underworld. Aseret has sealed it off with magic," he said.

"While I've been trying to find a serum that could change me into a human," I said wryly.

We sat in ominous silence. William wanted a serum that had a different effect to the one I sought. Were we so different? One moment I wanted to explore the side I denied, the next I felt ashamed. But the pull toward a world I'd just been introduced to was getting stronger.

"Did you ever find a serum that could change us into mortals?" I asked.

"Would you really want that?"

My mind screamed, "Yes!" but I couldn't say it aloud.

"You don't want to admit it, but you answer is 'no.'"

"All I've ever wanted was to be a normal human being," I insisted.

"Sarah, you are normal. You're just a little different." He took a deep breath. "The serums that kept you hidden make it hard to accept yourself as a half-breed. It will take time for you to understand, but you will. And I'll be here with you for every step. I'll help you learn how wonderful it is to be who we are. I'll bring you back, Sarah, I promise."

William's gaze warmed my insides, melting anxiety and any logical arguments I might form against accepting my sadistic vampire side. There was no ice around my spine when he spoke that way. Still, freeing the emotions after twenty years of suppressing my instincts wasn't easy. *Could I really accept both our sides?*

"But what we are is—"

"Not what we are, Sarah *Who* we are." William smiled gently. "It hurts me to hear you refer to yourself that way. You are a person, not a monster. You're just like me." He took my hand and pressed the palm against his chest. His skin sizzled, but I didn't pull it away. My mind drifted off, coaxed by his warm touch.

We danced toward the bar, and William sat on a stool. Our lips never parted, our bodies never separated. The lights dimmed down to a romantic red, bouncing off the disco ball that hung from the ceiling to sparkle around us. The music was subtle and slow, changing to match our mood.

As much as we wanted each other, we took our time. "I love you," William breathed as he gently pulled his mouth away.

"I love you."

The tips of our noses touched. Our breathing became heavy and deep. My fingers moved deftly up William's white shirt, then to his shoulders to slide it off, revealing his muscled torso. His gaze fell to my halter dress, to the swell of my breasts. He grabbed my bottom to lift me onto his lap. My legs swung around his hips. We began our passionate kissing sequence once again.

The telephone in the lobby rang again and interrupted my daydreaming.

William jumped off the armchair and came to my side. He leaned forward and took my hand in his as if he'd sensed my distanced thoughts. "Are you all right, Sarah?"

"Yes. The serum in the park kept us hidden from the seekers. How?"

"The red one guided our dead cells to wrap themselves around the live ones and shield their existence. We cannot be sensed in a pure vampire form. They can only smell us, and I took care of that too—no heartbeat detected, no blood pulsing through our veins, no warmth. It's the best protection vampires have from demons—being lifeless. If they can hide their scent, they're almost undetectable. The serum lets us become comatose, but unless taken with a more potent one, it only works for a few minutes." Smiling, he showed the mark on his wrist.

"The blue orchid makes the serums potent," I said.

"Yes. And the pink serum gives life to the cells long enough to drink the blood. It took a long time to research the orchids. We used the discarded leaves and flowers to make rare wrinkle creams and perfumes for the human market. Our parents were the owners of Les Fleurs Exotique. Your Aunt Helen was part owner. She inherited your mom's share, and you inherited hers."

William was talking about the emerging company Helen had invested in. Of course I knew Les Fleurs Exotique. The company dominated the cosmetics industry and I was a share owner—a majority share owner, I presumed. This explained where Helen's funds came from and her continuous following of the stock market.

"How did I miss all this?" I asked, then suddenly yawned. Glancing at the clock on the bed table, I realized it was almost midnight and I'd missed my date with the siblings. They have to be worried since I never showed up.

"Human senses are weak. Vampire senses are strong. You were not told for your safety. The serums kept your senses asleep until now."

"Why did they separate us?"

He looked at me from under his brows. His breathing deepened as he moved his face closer to mine until it was inches away. I closed my eyes, ready to accept his kiss. Then he touched my hand.

"Ouch!" I jumped back, startled by the electric current that flew from him to me.

"That's one reason. The other is our safety. We're useless to them on our own." He shrugged. "But . . . I feel useless without you." His eyes held mine, and I knew what he meant. With William beside me, I could conquer the world. It didn't matter that I didn't believe it. As long as he was with me, everything made sense—even when it didn't.

"We are the only proof that vampires can be turned into 'weaker' humans. If the demons got their hands on us and the serums, they could use our research to weaken the vampires. There has to be more, though." William sighed deeply and his gaze fell on the diamond pattern on the wall. "Why both of us together? Why can't we touch without pain? Think how easy it would be to spike human drinks with the serum before a vampire's meal. A vampire feeds on polluted human blood; with resurrected cells, they could become defenceless. Demons would win."

Every time William mentioned the demons, my skin crawled, an unpleasant sensation, given that I feared anything that could crawl: the tiptoeing of tiny legs up my arms or torso, the slithering of mucus-like worms, the unpleasant tickle of waving centipede legs on my arms . . . Goose bumps formed on my skin, and I shivered.

William rose and walked toward the pattered wall where he stopped, rested his right elbow on his left hand, and chewed on his thumb. "There has to be more to us than just our serums," he mumbled around the digit.

I chuckled, but he continued chewing.

"Demons know that vampires need humans to survive. But ever since they began receiving blood donations from prisons, they no longer have to hunt. Vampires provide protection to humans. That's why the human species is safe with vampires in this world. But no humans, no vampires; no vampires, no humans."

I imagined a world without compassion and care, where fear and power ruled. Raging fires burned forests to ash, destroying any life, feeding on the energy released at death. I heard tortured screams, cries for help that would never come beneath a smoke-choked, lowering sky that blocked the sun and allowed darkness to suck any remaining life from the earth. These dreams hunted my nights. They were the ones I never spoke of. I didn't dare move. William's gaze was still fixed on the other side of the room, and for now, I wanted it to remain there.

His voice deepened. "If the demons overpower the vampires, their hunger would drive them to defeat everyone above ground. The keepers had to stop the destruction and created the prophecy. That's where we come in."

"But how? What are we supposed to do?" I asked.

"I don't know." William's lower lip quivered. His eyes emptied, as if they'd witnessed the death of millions at once. "Two species will become extinct unless we're able to save them."

I filled my lungs with a deep breath. My life was taking on a new meaning as I came to understand who I was. We understood both sides, William and I. We could save them.

CHAPTER 8

William caught my gaze, then looked away. "There are rumours in the underworld that your father was captured a few years ago. All these years, he's been leading the demons down false trails so you could be safe," he blurted.

"My father was captured?" I held my breath through five flashes of the outdoor sign, but it seemed like a dozen passed; I wanted to move, but my limbs wouldn't cooperate. *My father could still be alive.* How would I react when I met him? *Would* I meet him? Would I be able to move then?

A tear rolled down my cheek and I tasted its saltiness in the corner of my mouth. I had a relative, one who for all these years was closer than I'd thought. He meant more than I could ever imagine, this father I would have dismissed before today. *He's been struggling to keep me safe.*

I nodded to William to go on. The pressure built in my eyes. One blink would relieve the weight, like an overflowing dam.

"Ekim sacrificed himself to protect you and your mother. He kept the seekers distracted so Saraphine could return home safely. She made it back to the cabin just in time, where they could no longer find her. Ekim covered her trail and led them away." He drew a deep breath; his gaze shifted to the floor, then he squeezed his eyes shut and hunched his shoulders. Losing her hurt him as much as if he had lost his own mother.

How wrongly could I have perceived my father? I'd always blamed him for my deformation, but now that I'd heard the truth, a new space in my heart began to fill. It had been waiting to be completed all my life, waiting to understand where I came from and my purpose. Now I was loved. I'd been loved by more people than I could ever have hoped. The love of two unique beings could save the worlds of two species. Was I that wrong to refuse my other side? To vanquish any memory associated with my traits? To crush the gift from the one who had given up his freedom for me?

"Why did they allow me to..." I swallowed. "To feed on—"

"They didn't know what would happen after our birth. They had no idea we would share the traits of humans and vampires equally. And with all the running, you were born early. Our parents had no time to prepare. A child doesn't know any better in the beginning, and a vampire baby would be hungry. By the time Helen came back into the room, it was already too late. Saraphine lost too much blood. My mother told me your aunt has never let go of the guilt."

I quivered, remembering the tiny red palm prints on my mother's freckled, pallid face. I remembered more now: pin-sized dots in her bosom; red drops welling, collecting, and flowing down, a stream of blood getting wider and heavier. It wasn't a dream after all.

"Once you fed, Helen took you away, gave you the serum to control your thirst that Saraphine couldn't reach for, and followed her directions about your rearing."

"I'll never forgive myself for that," I whispered. The dam spilled over.

"No one blames you, Sarah." He wrapped his arms around me.

I rested my head on his shoulder. "Then why do I feel so guilty?"

"Because you're human."

"Human." I pulled away to look at his face and shook my head. "I didn't mean to. I didn't mean to—"

"I know, I know." He stroked my head.

I sobbed. William hushed my whimpers and brushed the tears away. After I finished crying, which took awhile, I wiped my cheeks with the ball of my palm. "They chased my parents because of Aseret?"

William nodded. Hatred for the demon lord trembled my heart, and the aching pain reminded me of the same throbs I'd felt in my nightmare a few days ago.

"Aseret figured a vampire and a mortal had become enamoured of each other and feared the union. Our conception caused chaos in the underworld." William squeezed my hand again and another image from the underworld appeared, pictures of seekers, pain and exhaustion in their orange eyes. "Punished by Aseret after failed missions to bring the half-breeds they searched for," he explained.

"And if they find us?"

He looked at me. "We'd be killed quickly, if we're lucky."

"I would never let that happen." I growled, then lifted my other hand to cover my mouth. The thought of someone hurting William was unbearable, yet somehow closer to a possibility than I wanted to imagine.

William smirked. "Your dead cells are fighting the live ones. They're trying to coexist, not be suppressed. Once you accept them as your own, it will be easier to control. Don't worry, no one will find us if we get to where we're going." He smiled and released my hand. The image winked out. "The seekers never found the lab, and they never will."

Never say never.

The air in the room became stale again. Outside, a motorbike passed with a throaty rumble, leaving exhaust fumes in its wake. It would be fruitless to open the window now.

"You're more like a half-breed than you think you are." William stretched his legs forward.

I fluttered my lashes like an experienced temptress. He weakened and curled back his stretched legs. I pouted. William liked that even more and came closer so I could feel the warmth of his breath.

He kissed the tip of my nose, then pulled back.

My gaze skidded away from his mouth as soon as I began imagining how juicy his lips would taste. I didn't want our bodies to interpret this as non-platonic and zap us. And there was nothing platonic in the way I would kiss William. Stepping away, I put my face in front of the ten-inch fan, feeling the need for air conditioning.

"Really? And I just wanted to be ordinary." I said, my voice breathless.

"There's nothing ordinary about you." The words rolled out of his mouth in a murmur. He moved his body closer.

I wasn't used to receiving compliments that stroked my needs and desires contained until now.

William carefully studied my response. "Your dreams—we've known about them. My parents knew you'd be expecting me. Your ability to dream about me came from a spell so you'd trust me." He sounded guilty.

"Did . . . did you know about them?"

"Yes," he said, lowering his voice. William looked away.

"So, what I dreamt wasn't real?" I pressed my hand to my throat to stop my vibrating vocal cords while William concentrated on the patterned wall.

"We don't know what you dreamt."

I exhaled.

William's sinful eyes held mine. "The dreams were meant to show our relationship the way it's supposed to be. What you know about me from your dreams will be true. I hope I've been good," he drawled and smiled, the turquoise gems of his eyes piercing my soul.

I allowed the double entendre of the lengthened "good" to hang there. "You've been my best friend, William. You've been my only confidant. We . . . We shared a *very* close bond." I bit my bottom lip.

William's smile was ingenuous. He stared at me, as if trying to read my thoughts. I wasn't sure how much of our dream affair I could reveal.

William touched my finger with his lips and kissed it, then a second one and a third. He continued playing with them until I wanted his lips to tease more than the fingers. The music was fast, but we moved to our own beat, following the rhythm of our hearts. The floor emptied. We were the only ones in the club. My face rested between his palms—

where it belonged. I tangled my fingers into his soft hair, and he placed his mouth over my swollen upper lip; I did the same to his lower lip. The gentle kiss rushed through me like a falling star, and I wondered what feelings a fiercer exchange would bring. How blissful could the pleasure of fully kissing William be? I arched my back toward him, signalling for more. His hands glided up my body and held me tight, his contours pressed full-length against mine. All the contours I longed for.

The headlights of a car parking in the motel lot brought me back. I tried to continue until I saw his face and realized I'd given away more than I'd wanted to. To hide my embarrassment, I cleared my throat. "You were someone I could rely upon and trust. I didn't have anyone like that, except Mira and Xander." My smile faded. "I miss them. They must be worried about me. Didn't you say you knew Mira? How? Why didn't she say anything?"

"Your friends will understand. It's not surprising you felt comfortable around them."

"What do you mean?"

"I've known Mira and Xander for a while now. They're your watchers. More precisely, they're shapeshifters assigned with the task of protecting you." William moved closer to my side.

"I knew they were hiding something!" I chewed my thumb.

"Just like you have been," he reminded me.

"Right."

"Mira and her brother are unique. They're stronger than many demons with exceptional skills. They can switch their appearance instantly. They change their looks to fit their surroundings."

So many incidents now made sense. Was that the only reason they became my friends? To protect me? I didn't want to believe Mira and Xander were only doing their job. How could I know someone so well and not know them at all?

Guilt swept through me. Did the siblings think I was dishonest with them, having never shared my secret? Despite our trust, I'd never let it slip.

"We've deceived each other when we were supposed to be best friends," I said aloud.

"Your well-being was their priority, and they do care about you." William took my hand.

"But she grew up with me! Her body changed like mine. She got older. I've known them since we were kids."

"Yes, because they're shapeshifters," William repeated, his voice patient. "All they have to do is think what or who they want to look like, and it happens. Their growth was just part of their shifting. They chose to look the way they did to help you. Mira and Xander needed to befriend you, to be close to you, but still keep your secret."

Wanting to groan, I leaned my head against his shoulder. "I wish I had known. There are so many things I could have told her."

"We can't control everything in our life. I'm surprised you've kept your secret so well. Watchers and shapeshifters can be persuasive."

"They're not like that. They're my friends." I sighed, gazing at William from the side.

"Yes, they are. Mira and Xander would not have done anything to make you feel uncomfortable."

"No, they wouldn't." My memory of the siblings seemed distant. So much had happened since I'd last seen them. I missed them and wondered where they were. Surely they would check up on me at the store What would they do when they found it destroyed? I cringed at the thought of all my flowers and shrubs lying dead and dried up on the store's floor. My life's work. Ruined. Destroyed.

"Perhaps it was for your own good, not to know. Your mind could not have been strong enough and you'd be giving away your thoughts about the siblings—it could have lead the seekers to your thoughts, and to you. They would have found you even quicker." William sighed.

It all made sense. I couldn't hold a grudge against my friends for long. "Do they have any other secret skills I'm not aware of?" I rolled my eyes.

"Animals." He chuckled. "They talk to animals and control their behaviour. They can use them to protect themselves, to fight with them, or avoid being hurt by the animal."

"Any animal?" I widened my eyes.

"Yes."

The camping incident when the bear was about to attack me and suddenly fled. *Xander! I'm going to get you for that!* The bees in the lunch room that swarmed around Chris after he taunted me in the woods. *Was Mira responsible for the mouse that ran up Carmen's pants after he threw the spit ball?* I chuckled.

I released the tension in my neck, and wondered whether the connection I had with Mira was one of true friendship or forced. No, I trusted the siblings. Our friendship was true. And perhaps our connection was strong because we weren't human, at least not completely.

I lifted my head off William's shoulder. His face came closer to mine and I did not move away. My hand was back on his chest. It didn't hurt this time. My intention was only to feel the heart that I knew. I didn't want to pull away—not that doing so would be easy since William's hand was still on top of mine, pressing gently.

"I feel I know you already. You were so real in my dreams. So many of my dreams actually become real, but I never questioned your presence there." I whispered. "I dream of future events—I just don't know when they will happen." I shifted my weight from side to side.

"Like I said before, those dreams were placed there so you could trust me—"

"No, I can foretell the future. My dreams become real—I know which ones will become reality." I widened my eyes and hoped he would understand what I said. Beside Hannah, William was the first person I'd ever told about my abilities.

"I believe you, Sarah. You have a gift." He stopped, as if unsure if he should continue. "I'm guessing it's the side effect of Castall's spell."

"So the warlock knew you'd come to see me one day."

"Yes. He did. There are only the two of us in the world. It's natural we'd be drawn to each other. The same way gravity keeps us grounded, we are pulled together to be complete."

William's voice was calming.

He was the same William from my dreams after all. I sighed, and my heart skipped a beat, and I heard his do the same. Our gazes met. "Did you feel that?" I whispered.

"Yes. I'm not sure how our hearts fit into everything, but their rhythm is connected." William placed my hand on my lap and stood to pace again.

"How much do you know about me? Did you dream of me? Is that how it works?"

"No, I only knew about you from my parents and Helen. They told me it would be dangerous for us to be close to each other."

"We're close now." I stepped into his path to make my point.

"A lot closer than now—without fabric between us." He tugged at my T-shirt.

I was getting used to the flirting and liked it. "Dangerous how?" I teased.

We leaned in. The heat from his body jumped to warm mine.

"Well, we're quite powerful by ourselves, although you probably don't know your true strength and potential. Think of what we could do together." William rested his hands on my hips and pulled me toward him. I drew a sharp breath and held it. "Think how you'd feel if you didn't have to take the serum to dream. If the spell allowed you to have premonitions when you felt comfortable, peaceful, and safe in your dreams, do you think you could have them when you're feeling the same kind of comfort without sleeping, without dreaming? If you embraced that other half you've been suppressing—without fear—I'm sure you'd be able to foresee the future." He tightened his grip.

It wasn't a question; it was a statement. William spoke with such assurance that I felt it could happen. Was he suggesting I could be a fortune teller? A psychic? How ironic that word seemed. *Eros' Psyche. William's Psych.*

He lifted his hands to my shoulders and gently pushed me down to sit on the bed again. "We are the offspring like no other: the best vampire traits, with additional qualities, and the best human traits. Almost flawless."

"And what exactly are the best human traits? From what you're saying, human beings are inferior to those in the underworld."

"But most humans value life—all kinds of life. If they found extraterrestrial life, they'd value that, too," William countered with softened eyes. "Look at you. How much did you want to be human? How hard did you work and what have you sacrificed to be mortal? That's not something you can learn or achieve by casting a spell. It's something within you." He patted his chest. "It can only be there already, and be intensified."

William spoke with passion and confidence. Being half human was just as important to him as half vampire. He understood his purpose, and I was part of his life now. I was the last puzzle piece he'd been looking for.

"Okay, but how can you say vampire traits are good? Look at what I did to my mother. And now you're in danger, because of me."

"No, it's not because of you. I found you because I need you. If they found you . . ." He hissed with anger. "If anything happened to you . . ." William walked to the other end of the room and leaned his fists against the wall, his head lowered between his arms. He shook his head from side to side. "I could not go on."

After a moment, he pushed back from the wall and turned toward me. "We can bring peace to both worlds. Demons create chaos every day to speed human extinction: the oil spill in the gulf, the financial crisis, wars, famine, tsunamis, hurricanes." He returned to take my hands in his. "They cast spells to create droughts, and nature has to balance it with floods. They're expecting humans to self-destruct. They're playing humans the same way they do vampires, hoping they'll become extinct, and you know what that means for vampires, right?"

I nodded reluctantly.

"The demons can sense everything about humankind, but it's harder for them to sense us as vampires, especially with the serums, which confuse them. The serums I've develop will help us approach their caves undetected."

"So, you want *us* to go to the underworld?"

"Yes, but not to fight the demons. It's not time for that yet." There was intensity in his voice as he sat by my side.

"For your parents. You want to find them."

He took my hands in his—where they naturally belonged. "Yes. I think they're still alive, and so is your father. It's the best leverage Aseret has."

I tensed. "He's expecting us to come."

"Yes, he is. We'll go prepared—once you're ready." He kissed my forehead.

A rush of new energy flew through me, as if I'd been connected to an electrical outlet. I straightened my back. He squeezed my hands and I tightened my fingers around his. "And I assume you'll get me ready."

"Yes, I will," William said firmly, and grinned. "Once we get to the cabin, you'll see how powerful you are. And I'm curious to see what we can do together." He winked.

I felt my mouth curve in a nervous smile. "This goes against everything I thought was true. Even Helen told me to suppress the dark instincts." My stomach gave a tug, belying the words that came out of my mouth. My pulse wanted to quicken, but I fought against a current of something new in my bloodstream that flowed in the other direction.

William moved closer. "Helen didn't know everything. She took her sister's death hard, but I wish she hadn't been so dramatic. Sometimes less information is more—you do less damage." His grip tightened as he leaned closer to whisper in my ear, "Do it for your parents, and their love. They fought to bring peace. They fought for a miracle that would define their love. You are that miracle, Sarah. You must know that."

"I think I do." I allowed his scent to flow into my lungs, hoping the drug would kick in the way it had in the park, but it didn't. He was so close. It made it difficult not to kiss him. "Are we mortal?"

"There's no pattern in the way we age. When I'm with you, when I feel my heartbeat change, time slows down. Anyone can be killed, including those in the underworld. It's all about the energy needed to kill them. But I will not allow that to happen to you—to us." His chin came up.

Us.

Inside, I promised myself not to be separated from William. I couldn't allow it; I couldn't allow my heart to go back to its normal beat. It would not feel right—it would not *be* right. Yet somehow, the pressure constantly pushed against my chest like the veins weren't thick enough to support the flow of blood into my heart.

The middle of my ribcage itched, as if healing from a wound. The feeling confused me—I'd never had a scar in my life and cuts healed in seconds so I never had the time to itch the injury.

I dismissed the ache and looked at him from under my eyelashes. "You said we are vampires with additional qualities. Is one of your qualities 'unbelievably handsome'?"

"I wish." William took a deep breath. "I had a spell cast on me, as well; one to make me fearless." He looked at me as if waiting for a reply, but his eyes glazed over, as if he was lost in thought. His jaw tightened.

"Here I thought you were my knight in shining armour, but you were getting magical help after all," I teased.

William half smiled. "The side effect of my spell was fiercer than yours. I'm able to sense people's—or demons', for that matter—worst fears and greatest desires." His eyes focused on me. Thinking about my own fears made me swallow. "But that isn't the worst part. I can manifest these fears into reality and make my victims live their nightmare. It can stop them in their tracks, break their concentration . . . and maybe make them lose their mind." William's eyes again grew distant again. I touched his face. He shivered and caught my hand, holding it in his.

"So if someone fears drowning in a swimming pool, you could make the pool appear?" I asked.

"Yes."

"What if it's an ocean? How do you do that?"

"No, I wouldn't have to make the ocean appear." He forced a laugh. "We would use a time vortex to travel to the ocean, and it would happen there."

I frowned. "Time vortex?"

"We would appear there as soon as I let the thought through," he explained.

"I don't believe it," I said, my voice flat.

"Do you want to find out?" His grin deepened the dimples in his cheeks.

My eyes widened. "You wouldn't dare!"

He laughed, but behind William's eyes, I noticed a spark.

"Why can't we use a time vortex now?"

"I can't make it happen unless the right amount of true fear or desire is present; it's hard to change your innermost feelings."

"Wow." I shook my shoulders, letting the shudder continue through my body. Then I remembered the orchid on his hand and showed my wrist with the identical flower. "How did you get your tattoo?"

"Helen sent me a picture of yours. I loved the idea of having the orchid so close to me, feeling its power and protection." William smiled.

"Copycat!" I joked

"I'll remove it if you'd like me to."

"No! I really like it." I sighed. "We must be connected somehow."

"Now you believe me?"

"I don't think I ever doubted you—after all, I've known you all my life." I smirked.

He showed a kind smile.

I yawned.

"You're tired." He lifted the covers beside me and plumped the pillow.

"I'm not tired." I yawned again.

"It's the serum. Your body's not used to so many injections. Lie down. If you don't want to sleep, you don't have to. Just relax."

I couldn't argue with William. Though I didn't need to sleep, he insisted I rest on the only bed in the room. He settled in the chair. As I thought about all I'd learned, I finally, involuntarily, doze off.

For the first time since her death, I dreamt a memory of Helen:

We were planting tomatoes in the backyard. She wore her favourite flower-printed dress, its skirt gracefully dancing in the wind.

"Are there others like me?" I asked.

Helen was quiet for a moment. "There are many beings in the world, all of whom must be respected. We all have a reason to be here, although that purpose does not always reveal itself when we want to know."

That hadn't answered my question. "What do you think my purpose is?" I pressed.

"You're the only one who can figure that out, dear. If you have trouble doing that, I'm sure you'll meet someone who'll be able to help you. Then you'll know it in your heart, the way I do, how special you are."

Helen had known this would happen. She knew I would meet William.

After two hours of sound sleep I awoke feeling a newfound peace. A set path I recognized had been unveiled in front of me and I knew what I had to do. It didn't matter who I was. What mattered was that I was created to bring peace. If I could change one life for the better, I'd have justified my existence. Maybe I could save my father, who had given up his freedom for me. Maybe I could honor my mother, who had given up her life for me. If that meant going to the underworld with William, then that's what I would do. Finally, I accepted who I was—both of my halves. With a sucked in breath, my heart skipped a beat.

William sat up with a puzzled face. His heart had skipped the same beat as mine. He inhaled as well. "What happened?"

"I don't know. I felt it too." I placed my hand in the middle of my chest. The throbbing pressure was gone.

"Yes, but yours skipped first, mine second. What changed?" he asked.

"I accepted who I am. My other half."

"That would explain why the beating went back to the way it was before I met you." He came to my side, leaning over so his ear was against my chest, separated only by my T-shirt. I used all the willpower I had to control my desire. The butterfly-like flutter in my stomach returned and I bit my lip. But William was a gentleman and went back to sit in the armchair. "I was certain of my path, and then when I saw you . . . when I saw how alike we were—the loneliness and isolation—I hesitated. I wasn't sure whether I could do this. But now my heartbeat is adjusting to yours. It always wanted to beat to the same rhythm but couldn't. Not until now." He looked up at me. "We're on the same path now."

"How exactly could you have been lonely at school? I mean, look at you."

"Now, is this a question for me or you?" He raised his eyebrows.

I bit my lower lip. "I just thought—"

"I was home-schooled," he interrupted.

"Why?"

"I'd lived with my parents in seclusion. I never had to keep the secret of being a vampire, and never wanted to. I don't think I would know how."

"I'm sorry. I didn't mean to assume you weren't lonely." I yawned.

"It's all right. You couldn't have known. Go back to sleep, Sarah." He came over and gently pushed at my shoulders until I sank into the mattress.

"Good night."

"Good night." He shuffled back to the chair.

I turned to lie on my right side, then on my left. Then I flipped on my back and stared at the ceiling. After a while, I looked back toward the window and the chair where William was resting.

The ticking of the alarm clock pounded in my ears. It was close to two in the morning and William was still sitting upright, snoring with his eyes open. I went to his side and brushed the back of my hand against his cheek. He didn't flinch. With my right arm behind his shoulders and my left under his knees, I braced to lift him. This would be the first time I'd used my strength since my run in with the bear.

When I held William a few inches above the chair, he murmured, "I'll find you, Sarah. I'll never let you go."

I carried William to the bed, where he stretched his long limbs, and lay down beside him, close enough to feel the heat radiating from his body. His warmth wrapped around me, just as it had in the park. It didn't seem to matter how far away he was; I was beginning to understand his presence and how to sense him. With my eyes closed, I listened to William's deep, rhythmic inhalations and loud exhalations.

I stared at the yellowing ceiling, noting my first night away from home. Would I ever retrun to Pinedale? My instinct told me I would, but it wouldn't be home anymore.

CHAPTER 9

After forty minutes of tossing, I turned to my right side, rubbing my stomach to settle its loud grumbling. It didn't help, but the whiteness of my hands distracted me; they were so pale they almost glowed in the dark. The last drop of saliva passed through my throat, scratching it, and I reached for a water bottle on the bed table. My stomach growled again.

Not wanting to wake William to ask for more blood, I scribbled a note, left it on my pillow, and crept toward the door, remembering a vending machine around the corner at the end of the long building and the Cheetos and bubble gum within it. When I turned the doorknob, it squeaked, but William's breathing remained deep and even. My foot nudged the door open, and the hinges squeaked even louder. William still slept. Sliding through the crevice, I slipped out and pulled the door shut behind me.

I fiddled with the coins in my pocket, but my stomach pulled me toward the end of the building. The alley was dark, only lit by a streetlight at the motel's entrance. As my eyes adjusted, my ears tuned in on rustling behind the garbage bin. My throat itched. Feeling a hook in my stomach, I was drawn toward the smelly bin to the discarded leftovers it held—and the rapid heartbeats of five rats. My mouth watered. Hunched lower, I focused on the prey, then leaped over the bin.

They had no chance. Four rodents wriggled in my grip while I fed on the first one. I concentrated on the warm, fresh blood flowing into me, into my veins, and contemplated what else I might find once the rats were done—the burning in my throat had eased, but my stomach wasn't satisfied.

My ears perked up. A raccoon across the road groomed itself in the bushes. Anticipating its blood, I turned toward the street—and froze.

About ten feet awa stood a tall man, observing me. His glowing purple eyes pierced mine. He wasn't just a man. If he had been, I would have run away already.

I squeezed my eyes shut, afraid he'd extract secrets from my brain. *Is he still there?* I peeked through thin slits in my eyes. He hadn't moved, but the glow in his eyes softened. The lump in my throat passed with more ease, and I opened my eyes, taken aback by the familiar shade of his purple pupils. Frozen, I was unsure whether to run or let the seeker do as he pleased, but again, he didn't move.

Is he a seeker? He looked like one, but he wasn't dressed like one. The plain jeans and a hooded vest were a far cry from a long cloak. Despite the casual clothes, his demonic mien was undeniable. Seekers' eyes were orange, his purple. Taller than the others I'd seen, his feet were planted in a wide stance. Long fingers clutched an object he held in his left hand, the blue streaks emanating from it were diluted by the light from the streetlight around the corner.

The man looked at me as if this wasn't the first time he'd seen me and I recognized something familiar about him. I noted the twitch of my right arm as I prepared to defend myself. My hips shifted, positioning my body to lunge while he scanned me from the bottom up as if to make sure he'd found the right person. His head cocked to the right, and I thought I saw a smile. I frowned. According to William, seekers could not show genuine emotions. So maybe he wasn't a seeker after all. I wasn't ready to fight one; at least, I didn't think so.

I moved my right foot back; he moved his foot forward. Could I outrun him? I hesitated, noting the outline of powerful thigh muscles under his jeans. Maybe I could outsmart him.

"Can I help you?" I tried to sound calm and untroubled, but my voice shook.

"I think I'm the one whose help you need," he said.

His comforting tone did not match his demeanour. I recognized it but couldn't remember from where. Was this a trick? "I don't understand."

A door slammed loudly in the motel; it didn't startle either of us.

"Are you Sarah?"

I knew I shouldn't reveal my identity to anyone and wished I'd stayed in the room with William. The gurgling of my stomach disagreed. I glanced toward the five carcasses piled in a small pyramid, wishing I'd had time for the racoon across the street.

A cloud floated away and allowed a few stars and the thin crescent moon overhead to light the alley. The neon sign flashed around the corner, sporadically splashing its brightness into the illumination from the streetlight and the blue glow in his palm. Only the rustle of leaves broke the quiet of the forest.

He cocked his head to the other side.

"Who are you?" I asked, trying to add some bravado to my tone. His stance seemed familiar, as did the purple eyes that held mine.

"I've been looking out for you for a while. It's never been the right time to formally meet."

I took another step back. My heartbeat quickened.

"Don't fear. My name is Eric."

The name sounded familiar. Could he be here to help us?

"I'm a demon, and I'm bound to you forever. They call me the evil-bender—"

In front of the garbage bin, a motel door slammed into the wall as it flew open. William dashed into the alley. His gaze darted to me, his eyes pleading for me to come to his side. I didn't move, remembering Eric's almost identical step earlier. Then William refocused on the demon. His eyes sunk in and contours of his cheekbones intensified. William's forehead wrinkled as the vampire instinct took over. Only then did I see a dozen fleshy spikes just below Eric's chin. I hadn't noticed those before; my gaze had been hypnotically fixated on the purple eyes.

William tore an iron bar from the railing along the side entrance. He came at the demon with speed I didn't think possible and swung the bar behind him, prepared to strike.

The evil-bender stretched out his hand. A bright light shot from his palm. It hit William in the center of his chest and lifted his feet off the ground. He flew backward and indented the asphalt when he landed, bones cracking and air gusting from his lungs on impact.

"No!" I ran to kneel beside his limp body. William lay on his side, unconscious.

The evil-bender smiled wickedly. Furious rage boiled in my veins. My muscles tightened, shoulders broadened. First I'd take care of this demon, then I'd tend to William. I let out a roar, turning back toward the attacker.

As I prepared to launch forward, a vision appeared of another world—a world I had not seen before. A long corridor stretched before me, its walls painted with landscapes more beautiful than any art I'd seen on earth. Candles in wall sconces burned smokeless and illuminated the hall. Silky plush carpeting covered the floor, patterned along the edges with gold stars. It smelled like home; it felt safe and peaceful.

It was unlike any dream I'd had and it lasted less than a second before I was back in the dark alley.

Eric's wicked smile hadn't faded, but now it didn't seem to be meant for me as his gaze skidded to the side. *Is it for William?* I wondered, holding his still body. When I stood, my rage was ready to explode from inside me. Stepping in front of William, my knees flexed, and I was ready to strike, ready to protect William.

I no longer wanted to know who this man was and I imagined ripping his throat like a savage beast in revenge for what he'd done to William. Any demon whose calling began with "evil" couldn't be good. I narrowed my eyes, knowing I wouldn't go down without a fight.

The evil-bender stood still, looking at me as if I were I child who needed to be taught too much in a short time. He opened his mouth to speak, then closed it and shook his head. Tension fuelled his purple gaze, which was no longer directed at me. An orange glow of another demon's eyes rushed at me from the corner of the building. *Those* eyes definitely belonged to a seeker.

He's a spy! Eric is a spy for the seekers! My insides twisted, but I didn't show it. I held my stare on the traitor, hating him for hurting William. Any hope I had vanished. Eric was here to find us and make sure we couldn't get away before others arrived.

Talons outstretched, the seeker flew straight at me. Eric, still facing me, seemed unfazed. I wanted to move, but my feet had been glued to the ground by a blue glow under my soles. Either my instincts had been asleep for too long, or Eric had more tricks up those long sleeves than I thought.

The seeker sprang toward me, but in the tenth of a second it took him to pass the evil-bender, Eric stuck his arm out and grabbed the seeker by his throat. The demon squeaked and released a high-pitched yelp. I slapped my hands over my ears. The demon squirmed, but Eric didn't let go. He winked at me, and I heard, *Don't worry, I'll find you again. We'll get through this.* Except Eric didn't move his lips.

He stepped back and disappeared with the seeker into a blue mist.

"William. William!" I hurried to his side, breathless.

William remained unconscious. I shook him by his shoulders, then pressed my ear against his chest, listening for air entering his lungs. His torso rose with a drawn breath, then fell on an exhale, and I took his face into my hands. "William, come back to me, please." My eyes blurred.

"It's okay, Sarah. I'm okay," he whispered, opening his eyes.

"Are you hurt?" I pulled him into an embrace.

"Nothing time can't heal. Where is he?" William sat up abruptly, and his heartbeat skipped. "Did he hurt you?" Grimacing, he lifted his hand to the side of his head and I assumed he was probing a bruise.

"No, he's gone. Don't move. Let me help you back inside."

He shivered but didn't pull away as I helped him to his feet. We staggered back into the room. I left him on the bed to get ice and rushed back with a bucket. William moaned when I pressed a handful of ice against his head, but he didn't argue.

"Who was he?" he asked, seated on the edge of the bed. "Where did he go?"

When I pulled the ice away, he closed his eyes and rubbed his temples. William reached in his backpack for a silver flask. Thunder sounded in the distance.

"He was a demon. An evil-bender." I told William of the meeting in the alley, including my vision and Eric's hold on the seeker. William tipped the container of blood to his mouth and after a few sips, the glow of his skin returned as if he'd had a magic potion. I placed my hand to the back of his head. I knew the bruise would soon be healed and the lump would shrink.

"Here." He took my hand and placed it on his third rib. "Push down and up by a fraction until you feel it locked. It will heal quicker."

I leaned into the bone and pressed my palms hard. The bone cracked.

William shut his eyes and tensed his jaw.

"I'm sorry." I pulled my hands away.

"No. That's good." He exhaled. "I don't know who this evil-bender is, but your vision . . . How did you do it? I thought you could only get premonitions in your dreams. The relaxation theory was just a theory—you weren't relaxed in the alley, were you?"

"No. I don't know why I got the vision. What was that place?"

"The high underworld."

"As opposed to the low one?"

William rolled his eyes, chuckling. "That's exactly what I would have said." He laughed again.

"You're making fun of me!" I accused.

"Never!" He smirked. "The high underworld is where the keepers maintain the balance between good and evil. Not many have seen it."

"You've been there," I guessed.

"Yes. The entrance is in Spain, behind the Caballo Falls in Monasterio de Piedra. I was eight. My parents took me."

Outside, a strong gust of wind whirled leaves into the air. When the rustle of settling leaves faded, another rumble of thunder roared, this time closer.

"Sarah, you shouldn't have gone out. When I saw you weren't here . . ." William tucked my hair behind my ear.

I read the fear he'd felt when he found himself alone. "I'm sorry. I just needed some fresh air and food. It won't happen again."

"We have to be more careful now. This is the second demon who found you; others can, too. A seeker has been here; others will follow his lead."

"Shouldn't we leave?" I looked toward the door.

"No, it's still safer here than the airport."

"I don't think Eric meant to hurt me. He took care of the seeker."

"I hope you're right." William sighed. He moved to double-check the window and found it locked. Droplets of rain began splattering against the glass. "But if he didn't want to hurt you, what did he want?"

"He said he's bound to me forever." I paused. "And that he'd find me again."

William frowned. "We have four hours of sleep left."

"You need to lie down. You hit your head pretty hard." I pushed lightly against his chest, urging him to sit down in the chair. There was no point in asking him to lie down on the bed. He was just as stubborn as I was.

"But—"

"I won't go anywhere, I promise." I bounced onto the bed.

He didn't argue. His face was lined with exhaustion, his eyelids drooping. Although his body did not need a break, his head did. The hum of rain soothed, and unlike earlier, William's eyes finally closed.

CHAPTER 10

William woke at six in the morning. The sun's rays had crept above the horizon. His eyes moved back and forth below his half-shut eyelids: then he patted the sheets on either side of him with his hands. Our arms touched. I heard his heartbeat speed up, but he calmed it almost immediately.

"Hi." He rolled over to hover above me.

"Hello." I controlled each breath as it left my lungs. William's lips had swollen during the night. Mine quivered when I thought of the certain pleasure I would feel if they touched his. "How's your head?"

"Okay now." His gaze found the chair, then came back to the bed. "I don't suppose I sleepwalked to the bed." The eyes holding mine twinkled.

"You didn't," I answered, striving to sound casual. "I figured there's enough space for both of us." I tried to forget I wore skimpy underwear and a T-shirt underneath the covers. My breathing quickened.

"Hmm. And how exactly did you manage to get me in bed with you?" he teased.

"Oh, stop it. You know I carried you." My stern tone melted as the heat from his body radiated to warm mine.

"You did?" William widened his eyes. "How could such a fragile little thing like you carry someone like me? I'll have to find a way to thank you. Perhaps—" He lowered his face closer to mine.

"William!" I feared what would happen if he came any closer. It took all the strength of will I had to keep my arms at my sides, hands gripping the sheets. The urge to throw them around his neck and crush his lips against mine made my mouth water. I wanted to feel their tenderness and taste their sweetness. To have them caress my face, my neck...

My right leg slid between his, and his right leg slipped between mine. The heat sizzled from our bodies, as fierce as our desire, our hunger undeniable. The music was faster, but we moved at our own pace, hearts beating in time. Our kisses deepened. He explored my mouth with passion. My lips fit against his naturally.

I pulled away for a moment to breathe, and his eyes pleaded for me to come back—an invitation I couldn't resist. This time, I pressed my body harder against his. He responded. I knew this night would end in ecstasy.

"I'm sorry," he said, interrupting my daydream. "Thank you. That was very thoughtful." He narrowed his eyes, curious, since my breathing was too heavy for William not to notice.

"What are the plans for today?" I said quickly, crawling from under him. I straightened my shirt and fixed my hair.

"We're going to the airport." William rose and stood by the bed.

Knowing I could soon lose control, my gaze darted away from his boxers as I recalled taking his pants off at night when he snored. I sagged with relief when he pulled up his jeans and began packing the few things we had.

He handed me a new syringe filled with pink liquid.

"We're going on a plane?" I asked, inserting the needle.

"No, we're going for a swim." He laughed.

"Ha-ha. You're so funny."

He grinned. "Yes, on a plane. I don't suppose you've been on a plane before. Are you scared?"

"Are you going with me?"

"Yes."

"Then no, I'm not scared."

"Here." He handed me a small book.

I opened one of the two passports. "We're crossing the border?"

This would be the first time I'd been so far away from Pinedale, my store and everything I ever knew about my life. I wondered where my friends and watchers were. Would they feel like they failed protecting me? It wasn't their fault and I hoped they'd forgive my sudden departure.

"Yes, but please don't think about it. Make your thoughts as blank as possible. Think of snow, white bunnies, igloos, and the ocean with many icebergs. The seekers shouldn't sense you, but just in case . . ."

"Okay." I found the page with my photo. "Willemina Jones," I read aloud. "Nice one. How long did it take you to come up with that one?" I wasn't trying to be rude, it was the kind of smart-ass remark we made in my dreams.

"I'm Sarphen Jones," he said.

Laughing, I threw my head back. "*Sarphen?*"

"I like to be unique."

"That you certainly are." I chuckled.

"Let's go. We don't have much time."

I brushed my teeth and hopped into my jeans while William waited with our luggage.

We walked toward the end of the motel, hand in hand, despite the sharp pains in our hearts. Most guests slept, but not all. Someone moaned as we passed the third door. My cheeks felt hot. William disregarded the whimpers and deep exhalations. He didn't let me carry anything, either. The backpack rested comfortably on his right shoulder.

When we passed the entrance, the red-haired receptionist looked up, waved, and dropped her head back on the front desk to sleep. William dropped a post card into a mailbox and I wondered who he sent it to. Then he tugged on my hand, pulling me in the opposite direction from the jeep.

"Wrong way," I whispered.

"We're switching cars."

"Are you stealing one?"

"No, just taking a more comfortable one. I borrowed the jeep." He grinned. I pictured William sneaking into a neighbour's garage in the middle of the night, to "borrow" the yellow Hummer that shone in the parking lot of the motel. Vanilla air freshener waffled in the air before we reached it.

"Well, that won't get any attention," I said, blocking the sunlight with my hand as it reflected off the bright yellow paint.

He smiled. "You get your sarcasm from your father. We're not driving far, and I really like this one. Looks almost like mine."

"You have another one?"

"Yes. We can't take this one on a plane. It's a rental—harder to trace."

"Now that one makes sense," I teased.

"It's important that you stay quiet for the rest of the way. They have spies everywhere." He widened his eyes.

"But we'd see them. Or you could sense them, couldn't you?" I asked as he opened the door on my side.

"Not all of them." He dashed around the car to get in. "There are several kinds of demons. The seeker demons can smell what they are focused on. They're fast and their only mission is to find what or who they're looking for. There are also fire demons, water demons, air demons, etcetera—they control the natural elements. And passers—they can pass through hundreds of miles in seconds through a time vortex. Movers use force to move objects—their power depends on how strong they are. Freezers stop you in your tracks. The different talents can be combined by more powerful demons."

I remembered the blue glow under my feet when I met Eric.

William continued, "Shapeshifters can look like anyone or anything they want—"

"Like Mira and Xander."

"Yes."

"And they can sense me?" I asked nervously as faces of my classmates and neighbours flashed through my mind. Could anyone else I'd known be a seeker or a freezer?

"Not all demons are bad. Most were good." William turned the key in the ignition. The car purred to life.

I wondered if this world would ever make sense to me. "If the demons were good, what happened?"

"They were stronger types of warlocks who used to balance the world. Warlocks stole demon qualities. The balance has shifted too much to call them warlocks anymore. It's easier to use a power than a precise spell. If there was drought, they'd make it rain. If there was enough pressure for an earthquake, they'd readjust the tectonic plates to ease the tension and minimize its intensity. Think of them as invisible fairies that made the world work. These are just the small examples."

"Small. Right." I nodded. "I can see why the frequency of hurricanes and floods has increased."

William turned onto the street. "Had they not interfered, the planet would look a lot different than it does today. In the past two hundred years, they've been helping our planet less and less. The numbers of good warlocks decreased when some of them wanted to use magic for their gain." William sounded disappointed. "They kill to take what others have. If a powerful demon were to kill me now—"

"Don't even think that!" I interrupted.

"They'd gain my fearless abilities," he finished.

I shivered as my heart trembled. "Could a demon use a spell to have our abilities?"

"I don't think so. What we have is a special gift from the keepers. I'd imagine such conjured abilities need a lot of magic and power, more than Aseret has at his disposal, for now. Sarah, I won't let anything happen to us. I promise."

"Pinky swear?" I hesitated, then held up my hand.

William didn't laugh and hooked his smallest finger around mine, left hand on the wheel. "Pinky swear."

He drove well above the speed limit, peeking back through the rear-view mirror more often than necessary. Goose bumps covered my arms as I imagined what he could be looking for. A gravel side road and stones broke under the Hummer's heavy wheels. I tried not to pay attention to our route when William swerved to avoid a squirrel darting across the road.

My head rested against the back of the seat and I closed my eyes. At first, white bunnies and icebergs flooded my thoughts. It felt like weeks had passed since I'd awakened from a nightmare I thought would end my life. With William at my side, the nightmare was fading. Curiosity and apprehension had replaced the ache in my chest. The new world I'd been introduced to made seem Pinedale more boring than before, and I wondered if I would ever return. Would I see Mira and Xander again? I missed my luscious green world and the humidity it produced that condensed on the glass fridge doors in my store.

When I opened my eyes, the sun was higher, the ruddy morning glow now pale, washing everything in white, life-giving light. I remembered the warmth of the sun's rays in Pinedale on the day William came for me. In the moment I looked at him, he made a sharp right turn that threw my head the other way. A city's silhouetted outlined the horizon.

He noticed my clenched hands, fingers curled into my palms. "Block any thoughts you can, Sarah. The serum will help you, but you need to give it the initial kick."

I turned on the radio, shut my eyes and thought of Iceland and snow.

"You have a nice voice," William complimented.

I realized I'd been humming.

"Thank you. I'm just trying to be thoughtless." I continued with a tune.

A few minutes later, William stopped the Hummer. "We're here."

"Already?" I opened my eyes. We were parked in an underground garage.

"We have an hour until the flight." He handed me an iPod and a large sun hat. "Put these on. Keep your eyes down. Don't speak. There could be a shapeshifter on patrol. Try to act natural, and don't be nervous. I'll be with you the entire time." He squeezed my hand.

Chills climbed my spine. Had I been too oblivious of the danger? My heartbeat quickened.

"Don't worry, they shouldn't sense us. I won't let anything bad happen. Let's go."

We got out of the car, and William took our luggage from the trunk, the two cases strapped together. I wasn't sure when he'd packed them, but he must had been in a hurry. The suitcases were uneven, and odd bulges stuck out in a couple of places. He held my hand tight as he led me toward the exit, pulling the wheeled luggage behind us. I heard it wobble and turned to see it weave from side to side like a bloated drunk.

I thought about everything other than the airport and flying. The iPod wasn't doing its job; even with the volume set high, I still heard the flight announcements. As I tried to focus on the iPod's songs, a shy-less woman behind the check-in counter flirted with William. It took all my will to keep looking at the floor, but even so, I glimpsed her hand brushing his when she handed him our boarding passes.

William led me toward Gate 3.

Just before we stepped through, someone blocked our way. "Where do you think you're going?"

The middle aged man didn't resemble a demon, but William's grip on my hand and the tightened curves of his cheeks told me otherwise. I removed the ear buds and let them hang over my shoulders.

"I'm sorry, but you must have confused us with someone else," William tried.

"You don't think I'm that stupid, do you, William? The underworld is searching for you and the girl. Surely you didn't think you could escape that easily." He was almost laughing. "Master will be pleased!" he shrieked, keeping his human eyes fixed on us.

I remembered that shriek too well. The cold began working its way up my back, but I controlled it.

William pressed his lips together. I forced heat toward my spine, striving to remain calm. Unsure how long I'd be able to keep my vertebrae thawed, I let more blood flow to my lower back to keep me strong. It circulated faster, without increasing my pulse. I allowed my other half to come to the fore.

Skeptical about the demon's powers, I sensed the tension in his hoarse voice. Each sentence ended with the sound of crackling fire. His body gave off heat. My instincts telling me to dig further, I inhaled—and smelled smoke. The demon's short blackened hair was dry with split ends, most likely from heat exposure. The face, although human, was free of wrinkles, unusually youthful. *That's what he wants to appear as,*

I told myself, noting fine lines crisscrossing his cheeks, invisible to the human eye, but reminding me of a pattern I'd seen on the floor of a dried-up lake. *He's lacking moisture.* All the details came together for me in a fraction of a second.

I realized I wasn't as afraid of him as I'd thought I would be as I examined him carefully, seeking a weakness, and found it.

I crossed my fingers behind my back and said to William, "It's okay, honey." Then I turned to the shifter. "So, you found us." I shrugged. William's jaw almost dropped. "Now what? You're going to make a scene in the middle of a busy airport?"

"Oh, you must be a stupid one. You don't know how easy it is to clean up human casualties," the demon drawled. "Just try to run, and the airport will be reduced to ashes." He laughed loudly.

I hadn't counted on that but I controlled the rage that I wouldn't have to use to complete my task. William maintained his grip on my hand. "Fine," I said. "We'll go quietly to prevent casualties." William widened his eyes even more but remained calm.

"Flight 103 to Paris is now boarding," the overhead speaker announced.

We didn't move.

"I just need a quick drink. We've had a long trip, as you can imagine." I pointed to a water fountain tucked in a corner on the side wall, close to the washrooms, concealed slightly from the rest of the airport. Its aura was identical to the blue orchid's in the mountains and drew me in. "You can come with us," I said to the demon as if granting a favour, secretly glad no one else was at the fountain.

"Don't try anything, stupid girl. I will kill with a touch," he hissed through his teeth. The demon tightened his jaw. The lines of his human face shifted, changing angles as his cheeks twitched with my mention of the fountain. The jaw line lengthened, then returned to its original shape. His nose seemed to shrink, for a moment, then lengthen. His open palm changed colour, from flesh-tone to orange, as a golf ball-sized sphere of fire formed in his hand. "Make it quick," the demon commanded.

The sphere grew larger as we came closer to the fountain. I placed my hand on the knob, then turned back toward William. "You must be thirsty, honey. Have a drink as well." I went first, holding the last mouthful in, letting my cheeks bulge as I turned my face so William saw them.

The demon stood three feet away, concentrating on the fountain, the fire ball continuously growing in his hand. The sphere was now the size of a baseball. It sizzled, spitting flares. I stepped away, and William moved to the fountain. The demon focused on William's big gulps.

When William released the knob on the fountain, I turned to face the demon and spat the water at the creature's face. It was like throwing acid on silk. Shrieking in anguish, the demon flung his hands to cover the damaged skin. When he tried to pull them away, they stuck to the melting flesh. William followed my lead, spitting at him with more force, scorching the beast further. The water bubbled over his hot skin, burning the flesh. The demon's palms stretched, thinned, and began to liquefy. Hardly any steam rose as the beast's dry skin absorbed the liquid.

I cranked the knob of the fountain, redirecting the water with my palm at the yelping creature. The demon no longer resembled a human. His body convulsed in pain, but I did not relent, too determined to finish it. He screeched and squirmed as he melted from the top down, slowly vanishing into nothingness, leaving behind a pile of wet clothes.

"And the witch is gone," I said to the puddle, releasing the knob.

"How did you know?" William took me by the shoulders.

"I don't know. He was so hot, and his hair and his skin were so dry . . . I thought demons must have a weakness of some sort, and then it all made sense. I figured he was a fire demon and that he'd be afraid of water," I rambled.

William held me tight. I closed my eyes, pressing my face against his chest. "I know, I know," he crooned. "It's all right, Sarah. We're all right. It didn't occur to me to read his fear until you mentioned the fountain. That was brave, Sarah, and smart!"

"Can we get out of here?" I asked, trying to take my gaze away from the pile of slime.

"Yeah. Here." He pulled a syringe of serum from a compartment in his carry-on bag. "Take this before the flight, just in case. By the time they figure out what happened, we'll be gone."

"I feel like an addict." I pushed the needle into my thigh.

"Soon you won't have to." William scanned the hall for further threats. I knew he didn't want to take the chance of crossing paths with another shapeshifter anymore than I did, especially one whose weakness might be more difficult to decipher. He tossed the empty syringe in a wastebasket, and we headed for the gate, leaving the pile of slime that resembled barf behind.

We passed through Security posing as honeymooners incapable of separation. I wrapped my arm around William's, brushing my cheek on his biceps. William controlled his pulse and kissed the top of my head.

"Now, I know it's not the serum making you behave this way," he teased as we stepped onto the plane.

"What do you mean?" I fluttered my lashes.

He laughed guiding me into the window seat. "I mean, I hope it's not just an act," he said softly.

"It's not," I said, eyes steady on the view beyond the oval window.

"Shh." He put his finger to my lips.

I sunk in my seat and kept my iPod on for most of the flight. William's face held the same expression I had: one of happiness and the sense of belonging we both craved.

Over twenty-four hours ago, I walked through Riverside Park to contemplate how to tell Mira and Xander my secrets. I guessed they'd realize what'd happened given the abilities William described they had. The more I thought about the siblings, the more I felt they belonged in my new life even more than they did in my old one, and I hoped it wouldn't be too long before I saw them again.

CHAPTER 11

After a two-hour flight, we stepped off the plane into a wall of air thick with moisture. The humidity slammed against my body like a tangible thing. I closed my eyes and took a deep breath, then exhaled to taste the exotic atmosphere. The intensity of new flavours excited me. Beads of sweat formed on my temples. The heat was strong and sweet at the same time. It curved around my arms like a winter blanket, the density of the warmth so high I could swim in it, like in the Dead Sea.

I shaded my eyes from the bright sunlight with my hand, looking for clues as to our location. The curved tops of green mountains in the distance rolled from left to right.

William took out the serum as soon as the suitcases arrived. I jabbed the needle into my thigh. He held my hand, pulling our luggage with his free hand as we hurried out of the airport. William's yellow Hummer was easy to spot in the parking lot.

"So, where are we?" I asked when we reached the car.

"Sao Luis."

I perked up. "Seriously?"

William grinned. "Yes."

I lost control and jumped up and down feverishly. "You're the best!" Suddenly my arms were wrapped around William's neck and my legs around his torso, and I was kissing his cheeks, his mouth, his forehead, his eyes—everything my lips could find—until a fine spark of electricity zapped us. I regained my balance. "Sorry."

"If I had known you'd be this happy, I would've figured out a way to tell you earlier." He lowered me to the ground.

"We're staying in Brazil!" I squeaked. "This is—was—my primary orchid exporter." I wondered what shape my flower store was in now, after the seekers most likely had their hands on it.

William saw my concerned frown and interrupted my worry with, "We're driving to the Amazon."

"William!" I almost leaped back into his arms. All I could picture in my mind was green. Green, green, green, and more green! "How could you have kept this from me?"

"For our safety," William said with a laugh.

"Is that where the cabin is?" I asked excitedly.

"Yes."

"Eeeee!" I shrieked, hopping from one foot to another.

William grinned as he made his way around the car.

"I *feel* like a three-year-old on Christmas morning!" I was still bouncing on my toes.

He opened the trunk and effortlessly lifted our luggage inside. "Well, enjoy the ride. We won't be coming back this way anytime soon."

"It doesn't matter, as long as we're far away from the demons."

William froze. "Stop," he whispered. I felt his skin tighten.

"What is it?"

"Shh. Did you feel that?"

"No."

"Don't move," he ordered as he closed his eyes.

"Is it a demon?" I breathed, almost afraid to open my mouth, but I had to ask.

"I don't think so." He kept his eyes closed. "There's something blocking my senses." When he opened them, confusion beamed through his eyes.

"William! Sarah!" a deep male voice called.

We froze, our heartbeats picking up their rhythm. Our eyes met. My first instinct was to run, but I didn't, remaining still and silent. Concern carved William's face with new lines; he didn't recognize who had called us, either. He slowly turned around, squeezing my hand.

An old man stood in front of us. He looked extremely familiar.

"I won't hurt you," he said like a teacher trying to compose an agitated class. With a posture of a seventy-year-old, he seemed unnaturally agile. Wrinkles covered most of his face and hands, but there was youthfulness in the creases I couldn't imagine. The wisdom in his eyes gathered from centuries of experience shined. He didn't look like a demon. His long gray hair and beard made me think of a wizard. It wasn't a mien you'd come by on Earth, so I guessed he wasn't from the upper world.

I took a deep breath. His lilac scent calmed my nerves. My gut told me we were safe, but I wasn't sure if I could trust this new instinct.

"My name is Castall." He smiled like an old friend.

We exhaled long-held breaths at the same time. William spoke first. "Castall? Of course. I'm sorry. You look much younger in person. How did you find us? I thought we were discreet."

"You have been discreet." He waved that line of conversation away and glanced around the parking lot before saying, "I cannot stay long. They're working to break my spell."

"Spell?" I asked.

"To hide my whereabouts." His tone softened. "It's a pleasure to finally meet you—both of you." His mouth curved up in a smile that seemed unfamiliar to him, as if he had kept it hidden for a long time, saved for a special occasion.

"Wait—how do we know it's you?" I cut in. "William, didn't you say there are shapeshifters all over?" I took a step back, the memory of orange glowing eyes of the fire demon still fresh.

"Here." He held out his wrinkled hand to display three wavy lines on his pale wrist. "Any warlock with this birthmark means you well. Fear those with the sphere—on demons, warlocks, and any other creatures you may come across. They are your enemies."

Still sceptical, I didn't move closer.

"Sarah, I'm the reason you're here." He stepped forward to touch his index finger to my forehead before I thought to retreat. "Close your eyes."

As if he'd cast a spell on me, I obeyed. Colours swirled in front of my eyes. A mix of centuries-old scents passed through my nostrils. Something told me I was now looking at 1856.

Two young women picked wildflowers in a field by a forest. In the shadow of the trees at its edge, two pairs of vampire eyes followed the maidens' movements. Instead of killing at the first pulse they heard, they stood like hunting beasts mesmerized under a spell.

A dome of colourful lights loomed over the valley. *Where did the light come from?*

Castall stood near the northern edge of the field, arms raised above his head. The bright rays spread outward and up from his hands.

I heard Castall's voice in my head: *"The spell was meant to counteract Aseret's curse to control vampires. They'd be able to live together."*

My mind's eye zoomed in on two couples standing in front of one another.

"The vampires could no longer hurt humans. Their appetites were under control; they now craved only animal blood. They fell in love with the maidens at first sight, and they became inseparable."

My gaze was drawn to one of the vampires.

"That's your father, Ekim," said Castall.

I gasped. This was the first time I'd seen him. My stare was directed to a female. A dozen or so freckles were scattered over her nose.

"That's your mother, Saraphine."

My eyes welled up, but I couldn't open them to release tears. I tightened my grip on William's hand. I knew the other pair of star-struck lovebirds were his parents.

I'd explained to William what I'd just seen. "Did you know about this?"

"Yes, my parents told me." Then he asked Castall, "Do you know anything about them? Where are they?"

"I can only show you the past, not the future. I do know your journey will be hard. You will have to let Sarah go, only to find her. Here." He handed William a shiny stone. "Squeeze this crystal when you think there's no hope." Turning to me, he held out a small wooden stick. "Thump the bottom of this stick twice when there is no way out, and you'll find an exit."

"How do we know we're using them at the right time?" I asked.

"You'll know. I must go now. I bid you well on your journey. Stay strong, and don't lose hope—your mission means more than you think." He looked around before whispering a warning, "Beware of Xela."

Castall hit the side of the Hummer with his cane. A rectangular doorway with edges that sizzled with a purple glow materialized. He walked into the opening, disappeared, and the portal closed behind him. I stared at the lavender mist that carried a lilac scent dissipating around it.

"Who's Xela?" William stared where Castall had disappeared.

"You're asking me, Mr. Know-it-all?"

William closed his eyes as if sensing underworld energy. "I don't think we should stick around here." He nudged me toward the car. "I certainly do wish I knew it all, though," he added, climbing in the driver's seat. He fastened his seatbelt, started the car, and floored the gas pedal.

An hour and a half later, the two-lane road turned to dirt. Another two hours passed as the dirt road narrowed into a track that wound its way between taller, older trees. It wasn't too long before the track shrank into a trail. Large fern fronds brushed against the Hummer's sides and roof, and I felt as if we were bouncing along in a buggy amongst the overgrown vegetation.

Deeper in the Amazon, the luscious greens reached higher toward the sky, and the forest floor began to clear. Three hours passed before we stopped at the edge of a river. We opened the car doors, and I stepped out, welcoming the hot but fresh air and its dampness. The thick warmth reminded me of my store, and I promised myself to one day return and fix the damage I imagined the seekers evoked.

I looked at the murky water. "Where to now?"

"Now we wait at the crossing." William pointed to the narrow path leading toward the riverbank. "For Agubab to bring the boat."

"Agu-who?" I shuffled my feet, eager to see the secret place William spoke of so obliquely.

"Agubab. He's an Amazon native and he knows this forest better than anyone." William tilted his head up to the sky, stretching his arms. "He's also a good friend of the family. He'll help us cross the river." He leaned forward to peek around an acai tree toward a curve in the river. As if summoned by his gaze, a wooden raft appeared, sliding through the muddy water.

"That's a boat?" I lifted an eyebrow and pointed an imperious finger at the wooden contraption. "We're getting on *that*?"

"Yes," he drawled, then laughed. "With the Hummer."

"But that's impossible. We'll sink," I said in a high-pitched voice.

"Don't underestimate the strength and precision of the Amazonians in constructing a raft. It's sturdier than many North American yachts."

I sniffed. "If this is anything close to a yacht, I think I'd rather swim." Even *though I can't swim.*

"Yeah, and the water bugs wouldn't bother you at all," William muttered as if to himself.

I wanted to believe William—that the thousand or so twined bamboo poles would hold us up—but it was difficult. The raft was steered by a long wooden stick. Agubab, an older man with dark skin and deep scars across the top of his arms, gripped the pole near its top, pushing the end back and forth in the river to gain momentum. Native jewellery decorated his neck, wrists, and ankles. Beside him stood a small boy, maybe seven, who seemed to stare, unblinking.

Only when it floated closer did I notice that the raft widened into a larger area at the back, almost large enough to load a car. At the rear of the raft, a wooden box covered something that resembled an engine. My gaze returned to Agubab.

"Panther," William supplied, following my gaze. He jerked his chin toward a thick white line smudged down the middle of Agubab's forehead. "Tribal marking."

"Stop reading my face." I punched his arm, laughing.

He laughed.

Agubab leaped on the shore. He and William pulled the front of the raft on the bank and secured it to the trees on either side. A small ripple of water touched the shore as they loaded the Hummer, but the raft didn't wobble under the vehicle's weight.

I tapped my toe on the bamboo deck before stepping aboard. It didn't budge. Adrenaline mixed with something else pumped through my veins. Whatever it was, it allowed my body to better absorb the natural elements around me.

We cruised through the jungle for over an hour. The raft turned into a narrower passage, then another. I ducked under long vines that hung from a lowering forest canopy while William crouched near Agubab, talking about the weather and activities in the forest. When he and his son Nats helped us off, William handed them a brown bag full of supplies. I smelled a mixture of chemicals and pharmaceuticals. The natives guided the raft farther down the river until they disappeared.

Soon I was enjoying the air-conditioned interior of the Hummer scented with the smells of the jungle. I ran my finger over my damp arm, then held it to my nose. Images of the jungle's wild denizens appeared in my mind, conjured by traces of odour each one had left in the droplets clinging to the hairs on my arm. It was impossible to block out the littlest creatures. Just thinking about them sent chills down my spine.

The dense canopy didn't let much light through. I looked around for the animals I sensed, but couldn't spot them. Everything melded into a green backdrop. The trees were as tall as the Eiffel Tower, their branches dense with foliage casting dark shadows over the landscape below. Branches of several trees intertwined, further knitted by vines and creeper plants that created snarled green nests and spidery lattices between the trunks. The shades of green ranged from blackish corbeau to the palest breath of verdure and eye-popping citreous tones; most I'd never seen before. High atop the canopy, where the sun still oozed amongst all the leaves, a rainbow of flowers bloomed.

Paradise. We are in paradise, I thought in awe, my eyes never stopping their perusal of the exotic vegetation. I opened the window and stuck my head out. Hot wind curled around my face.

"You like it?" William asked.

"I thought my store was a rain forest, but this . . . this is beyond beautiful." I pulled my head back in. "How much farther?"

"Another hour, no longer—I promise."

"How do you not get lost?" I asked.

"GPS," he answered.

Not seeing the typical device, I looked at William and noticed the digital watch on his right wrist displaying our coordinates. Which struck me as odd; he was right-handed.

"I don't like to cover up my tattoo," he said as if reading my thought.

I smiled and allowed nature to sink into my heart—the sounds, the smells, the changes in temperature, the fauna, the flora—everything worked so well together, one dependant on another. The same way I depended on William.

As we neared the end of the drive, a spot of bright pink slid past the corner of my eye. I craned my head to the right toward the dark forest floor, trying for a better view. "Was that an orchid?" I asked.

"Yes."

"It grows with so little light?" I knew these orchids existed; but had never imported them.

"Yes, it's a rare species."

"Look, another one!"

William laughed. "Turn and look out the other side."

I did and gasped. Dozens of flowers, bunched together, glowed amidst the greenery, so many I lost count. Their numbers grew to the thousands, their species into the hundreds. The explosion of colour was endless. How could something this magical be hidden from the rest of the world? I was sure the glow of this exotic paradise must be visible from space.

"We're almost there. Just . . . around . . . the corner . . ." William turned to the right, guided the Hummer down a steep hill and straight through a wall of bush, then onto a narrow track that magically appeared beyond it. At its end, a rustic log cabin sat nestled amongst the trees in the middle of a circular clearing of freshly mown grass. Given the amount of shade here, I was surprised the grass took so well. This was clearly not a natural floor for the rainforest. A dozen or so sunrays squeezed through the canopy in thin streaks to touch on the clearing, forming oval patches of light on the green carpeting. The long, ribbon-like rays seemed like a touch of heaven that watched over the hidden clearing.

The cabin had round trunks stacked horizontally, corners interlaced at the sides, and two wooden chairs and a small round table were on the front porch. The structure was old but well taken care of; someone had planted flowers in deep pots, and ivory sheers fluttered in the front window; two candle chandeliers hung at opposite ends of the porch. *I've seen this place before. Not in my dreams, though. I'm sure I would have remembered a dream this beautiful.*

"Helen was here," I said, remembering the photo of her sitting on the porch.

"Yes, just before you were born." William's voice was quiet. "And awhile after, to take care of you." I felt his intense eyes on me, watching my reaction.

"The shadow of a man in the photo—"

"My father."

He knew the contents of the chest, then—at least some of them.

We parked on the left side of the cabin.

"Agubab?" I didn't have to elaborate; William read my facial expressions all too well.

"Yes, he's the only one who knows about this place, maintains in when I'm gone. We can trust him."

Before I'd touched the handle, William was there to open my door. Stepping out on the soft grass comforted me, and I had the urge to take my shoes off to feel the blades tickling my feet. Agubab must have visited before picking us up; the smell of the freshly cut grass flowed in the air, blending with a bouquet of fragrances from the flowers blooming around the cabin.

The front door stood slightly jar. "Was someone here?"

"No. No one was here," he answered calmly.

Satisfied, I continued my inspection of the tranquil clearing. "It's beautiful." I was mesmerized; surely the kind of joy and bliss I felt must be too sinful for one person to experience all at once.

I stretched my arms and closed my eyes, and let one of the light streaks warm my face. Then I spun in a circle. When I stopped, I realized I would not miss my store too much. This was better—much, much better.

"I take it you like it?" asked William.

"Love it!"

"Let's go inside. I'm sure you'd like to freshen up."

William took one step and was standing at the front door of the cabin, hands on hips. He turned back, gesturing for me to do the same.

I lifted my foot, then set it back down again. Even if I knew I didn't need to be torn between my two halves, that I had to let them co-exist with no boundaries, the leap I had to take was difficult. My brows narrowed as I searched for an internal compromise, for a way that my two sides could cooperate.

My feet moved, and I took two human steps, then stopped again.

"Sarah, you don't have to hide anything here," he said in encouragement.

"I'm scared," I answered, feeling the vocal cords in my throat vibrating.

"Why?"

"What if I can't control it?"

"I'll be here to help you. Don't worry, you won't run into any walls," he said, smiling confidently. He held out his hand. "Come on. You can do it. Just like in the park—"

"Except without the serum, and through my own will," I finished. "Okay."

My next step was quick, and I stood at William's side. I simply thought about it, and my feet took me to where I'd wanted. Everything would have been perfect except for that stray stone lying at the top of the porch steps. It turned my foot; I lost my balance and fell. Strong arms caught me before I touched the wooden porch.

William lifted me and held me close, his arms tightening around my waist. The heat between us woke feelings that should have been awakened a long time ago. He looked into my eyes, his warm lips inches away, his breathing heavy but measured. I could feel our hearts underneath our shirts, pounding so hard. Mine started to hurt. William pulled his body away but held my shoulders, steadying me until I found my footing.

"Sarah, we can't." He drew a long, steady breath to slow his pulse. "We can't get close."

"I don't understand." I took his hand in mine. A small jolt of electricity shot between our palms.

"Me neither. But my parents warned me that we cannot be together —no matter how much we want to be." He gently moved my hand back to my side.

"That's not fair," I whined, not caring if I sounded like a little brat. "How are you going to teach me what I need to learn without us getting close? I know what I'm feeling; I can hear in your chest what you're feeling. Our hearts are ready to burst." I tried not to blink. If I did, the tears collecting in my eyes would roll down my cheeks.

"That's exactly it. Should our hearts be trying to escape our bodies to the point that it hurts? I'm sure you felt the pain."

"Maybe they're just trying to be together," I suggested, looking at him from beneath my lashes, hoping to convince him. It didn't work.

"I've always been told we cannot be together until we have the right serum to control it." He pressed his fist against the middle of his chest. "No one ever explained why. Then my parents disappeared, and I had no choice but to look for you." William looked away and pushed the suitcase closer to the door with his foot.

"You were left alone." I pulled his hand away from his chest and squeezed it.

"Yes, but that doesn't matter. When I first came to Pinedale, it took me a while to figure out how to approach you. When you reduced your dose, I sensed you'd be in trouble; even then I couldn't tell you. I wasn't sure whether you'd believe me, because I'd been warned against getting close to you." William waited for that information to sink in.

A few clouds passed overhead, stealing the streaks of light for a moment. When they shone again, I asked, "What's the correct serum? What's stopping us from making the mixture?"

"I don't think it has anything to do with the serum." He dropped my backpack off his shoulder. "It's something else—there must be another reason why this is happening."

I sighed, letting my shoulders droop. "And here I thought I could be happy and normal with you."

"At least we have half the puzzle solved." His smile was weak.

"What do you mean?" I asked.

"We know you're normal. Now what can I do to make you happy?" His smile widened, and he charmed me with his eyes. It made it that much more difficult to stay away. It made control almost impossible, and William irresistible.

"William!"

"I love it when you say my name," he hushed.

How exactly was he expecting me to stay away when he said stuff like that?

"I promise I'll do everything I can to figure this out. I've already been thinking about it on the way here," he added.

"You have?" I widened my eyes. We were so close to each other I could feel his breath on my face.

William cupped my cheeks in his hands. "Of course; you are my equal, my match, my other half." His voice was soft, but it carried a hint of sadness.

Closing my eyes, I waited for his kiss, but William's lips found my forehead, not my lips. I exhaled. It didn't matter. The man I'd been dreaming about was here, standing in front of me—professing his love for me in the only way he could without hurting me. William didn't need to get to know me; he already knew me. He didn't need time to fall in love; he was already in love. We both knew we were meant to be. We belonged together and could not live without each other. Our two hearts had been sealed together, and wherever we went or what we did, no one could tear that apart. Our hearts would continue their unique synchronized beat as one.

CHAPTER 12

"Come in, I'm curious to see if you like it." William pushed the front door open and stood aside so I could step into the main room first. I stopped five feet in, where the wooden floor changed to marble tiles, and peered down a short hallway into a large room—the laboratory William had mentioned.

One table held neatly stacked piles of papers and cup holders with sorted pens, markers, and coloured pencils. Books were arranged on a shelf to the right, from tallest to shortest. In the glass-fronted cupboard beside it, empty flasks reflected the fluorescent light, aligned according to size. The neatness was mildly intimidating, and I looked away.

Equipped with machines and gadgets, this room would be better than heaven to a molecular biologist or genetic engineer. A wide glass-topped table stretched the entire length of one wall, hinged to open every four feet. I moved closer to peek inside and saw hundreds of petri dishes and agar plates with culturing cells precisely positioned in three by five sequences. On the wall above the table, a magnetic whiteboard held photos of various orchid species, pinned with small magnets, labelled with dates and notes. Another area contained microscopes, two computers, and a wall filled with graphs, diagrams, and aerial pictures of the Amazon. My small laboratory at the flower shop seemed like a child's playroom in comparison.

"Where's the staircase?" I asked, remembering that William had mentioned a passage that led to the lower level when we were on the airplane.

"It's hidden for safety reasons. Only a few people have ever known about the apartments." He pointed to a pair of doors on the right. "There are two bedrooms on this floor that can be used as guestrooms."

"Let's go see." I examined the floor tiles, hoping to find a way to reveal the staircase.

"Hold on." He laughed. "We'll do that later. Let's freshen up first." William pulled me toward one of the bedroom doors. He opened the door and gestured for me to go me inside. "You take this one."

Simple in decor, the room felt warm and inviting and it smelled homey. White sheets on the queen-sized bed glowed in the soft light from a Tiffany lamp on the side table. The large window had the same ivory sheers as the front one and filtered in the jungle from the outside. Framed black and white photographs of the jungle decorated the walls. Even in two shades, the beauty of the Amazon shone through the glass.

I opened the closet to find my clothes tidily hung inside. "You've been getting ready," I said toward the other bedroom. *My cream shirt!* I pulled it off a hanger.

"I had to just in case our exit from Pinedale was sudden—which it was," he answered.

He could have been whispering and I still would have heard his voice. I also heard what I was too shy to hear: fingers unbuttoning his shirt, the soft metallic clank as he unbuckled his belt. Then William turned the knob on the shower and I imagined him standing without clothes, water cascading from the showerhead, to run over his body . . . I saw the outline of his masculinity behind the steam, knew where the drops fell on his arms and torso, the route they followed down his figure before splashing onto the floor.

The quiet rumbling in my stomach brought me back, and I rushed to get ready. It took less than five minutes, though I wanted to take longer. I wanted my shower to last forever, to see him there in the other room, linked through the water, but I also wanted more than anything to be back at William's side. I wondered if his thoughts were as sensual as mine.

We walked out of our rooms at the same time. William's hair was tussled and damp. He'd splashed a fresh layer of his woodsy, musky cologne on his chin. "Come on," he said, taking my hand and drawing me toward the rear of the cabin. "Let's get you acquainted with our new home."

"Home," I repeated, still mesmerized. It did feel oddly familiar. I liked the sound of it being our home.

At the back of the laboratory the room blended with the forest behind it. The glass walls curved overhead into a ceiling, mixing with the sea of green that stretched beyond them. Potted orchids surrounded two wicker lounge chairs, a loveseat, and a coffee table, the furniture arranged in the center of the room. It was the perfect sun room.

"I think I remember this room." I touched the top of the nearest chair with my fingertip. "It was my favourite."

"Look up."

I tilted my head to follow his finger. Thirty paces away from the house, almost touching the sky, a small wooden platform rested between the branches at the top of an old tree. If William had not shown it to me, it would have remained invisible, even at the brightest hours of daylight. Vines and epiphytes had grown over the bottom of the platform, leaving only inches of the wood exposed.

"What's that?" I squinted, trying to see more.

"A tree house." William grinned.

"Of course," I replied sarcastically.

"Well, it's a bit more than a tree house," he admitted. "It's our natural serum haven. You'll understand once we're there." William caught my hand and pulled me toward the kitchen. "There's some food ready in the fridge. Let's eat before we go up."

"Up there?" I pointed a finger at the sky.

He laughed. "Yeah."

I sat patiently as William prepared the food at vampire speed. The garden salad, fried chicken, and rice deliciously crammed into my mouth. The sun had set by the time we finished our meal; the remnants of its rays streaked upward. The chorus of crickets and other vocal night insects was getting steadily louder. Thinking of all those insects made goose-bumps rise on my arms. Shivers flew through me as I twitched and shuffled my feet.

"You okay?" William asked.

"Yeah, just a bit nervous," I fibbed, casually covering my head with a bandana I'd originally tied around my neck.

"You sure? You're fidgeting."

I nodded.

"Are you ready to go exploring?"

I sensed a double meaning but took his hand and felt no pain. William led me outside into air so laden with moisture it was difficult to breathe. The temperature had dropped a few degrees but provided little relief from the humidity.

We hiked toward the ceiba tree that propped the tree house in its crown. Massive buttress roots sprang from the ground around its base, supporting the enormous tree whose central trunk measured at least ten feet in diameter. Other roots dug into the loam of the jungle floor and intertwined with the roots from neighbouring trees to create a complex web of looped nests that made it easy to start our climb. Scaling the nearly 180 foot giant proved not as difficult as I thought it would be. I hugged the trunk, feeling the life energy that emanated from its center and used this energy, connecting to it. All I had to do was think that I could climb, and I did. My steps were slow at first but as my confidence grew, I moved quicker until I was joyfully scampering.

I went up into the canopy, passing enormous flowers that almost engulfed the branches and created a colourful community of pink, purple, and yellow orchids. Most I had seen before, and the sheer size of their blossoms surprised me. Even more dizzying, the palette of colours stretched for miles. We reached the top of the canopy where the pink petals of the ceiba were in full bloom, showing off their striking yellow centers.The scent was intoxicating. A thin layer of pollen from the flowers covered the trunk, and the feelings I had when I met William in the park returned; I tried to control them.

"How do you feel?" William asked.

"Like I just reached heaven." I rested my elbow on a branch, nostrils flaring, eyes closed, absorbing the splendour around me.

He was smiling when I opened my eyes. I focused on the center of the tree's crown. Below the point where the top of the forest touched the sky, I saw a hidden entrance to the tree house, obscured by a cluster of blooming flowers and foliage.

William watched me with fervor, wordlessly taking in my full transformation. I felt the corners of my mouth stretch upward, aware of the solitude painted on my face. My glee must had shone through my eyes and showed in my every movement. At last, my hunger was satisfied.

I pushed aside the branches over the door and entered the green aerie. The momentum of my heart picked up.

"Lie down," he whispered.

I obeyed, stretching on the wooden floor as first stars sparkled in a velvet-black sky through an opening in the canopy. Speechless, I stared. I could never have imagined a place this picturesque and couldn't have dreamt of anything more beautiful. The stars glittered in bliss, dancing in front of our eyes.

"Take a deep breath," William instructed.

I did, and a potent, sweet fragrance filled my lungs, touching each nerve. My exhale felt as if I'd lost strength.

William lay down beside me. "Another one, deep," he said again, almost whispering.

I submitted into the oasis and the dense air worked its way through my blood vessels straight into the veins, feeding each organ and each cell. I let my breath out with reluctance. "What was that? I can feel it working its way down to the smallest cell."

"You're getting all the serums at once, without chemicals." He clasped his hands under his head.

My brows pinched in a mild frown. "Isn't that dangerous?"

He shook his head. "Your body adjusts and learns to know which pollen to react to. You must have felt this before, working with the orchids."

I remembered the camping trip eight years ago and how the smell of jasmine, rose, and lilac nearly carried me to the pond's edge. "I think I did. The first time was when I found my blue orchid."

"How do you feel?" William propped himself on his elbow.

"I can feel the pollen inside me, like it's trying to work with each muscle and organ. It's heightening my senses." I curled my knees up.

"These orchids are pollinated by moths, so their smell is stronger at night."

"Did you plant them here?" My head lolled to the side. William's eyes reflected the full moon.

"Yes, with my parent's help." I heard a hint of sadness in his voice. "This is our oasis. The demons could never find it. To them it's as if we were invisible. It's our little paradise."

"But I thought the cabin was invisible to them. Isn't it?" I asked.

"It is, but if they knew about it, they could find it. *This* place is special. The flowers protect us and shield us, the same way the serum shields our living cells."

I let out a long, slow exhalation. *Amazing.*

William rolled onto his back, took my hand, and held it tightly, twining his fingers with mine. My thoughts flew toward my lustful dreams of him.

It was a long time before we stopped to catch our breath, breathing through slightly parted, engorged lips. William squeezed my hips tighter with his hands. "I could kiss you all night," he murmured.

"You just may have to," I replied.

His hands travelled up my bare back to untie the black bow of my dress. I took his hand before he pulled the knot apart. "Come with me." We walked toward the loveseat against the far wall of the club.

He smirked. "You know you're not leaving tonight without taking that dress off."

With his face so close to mine, I kissed the tip of his nose in acknowledgment. Our bodies never parted as we made our way to the sofa.

"You're lost in thought," William noted.

I turned my head toward him and tried to sound casual. "Do you think there is a difference in the way vampires and humans kiss?"

"I wouldn't know." He turned on his side, propping his head on his elbow.

I closed my eyes. "This place is absolutely sinful."

"You're reading my mind, Sarah." He wasn't referring to the forest. His voice fell to a whisper. "Sarah."

I turned to face him, and his eyes locked mine. Sparks of passion flew between us, and the lust I knew too well exploded inside me like fireworks.

"I don't know how long I can control myself around you."

"Then don't." I ached with a longing as deep as his.

"But . . . I've never . . . what if—"

"It's okay, William. I've never either. We're safe. We're protected here. You said it yourself. No one can—"

His lips pressed hard against mine, silencing me. All I heard was the synchronous thumping of our hearts.

Pum.

The warmth of his mouth invited me to open mine, letting him find me.

Pum-pum.

We explored each other, giving in to intuition. My body, firmly pressed against his, seemed to melt under his heat, like butter on fresh toast.

Pum-pum, pum—

At first his fingers tiptoed against my body and just as the pulse surged through my veins, his palms slid flat and he held me tighter, guiding my hips against his.

Pum-pum, pum-pum.

With a gasp, we pulled away from the long kiss to look at each other, our heartbeats building to thunder in our chests.

I won't be able to stop, I read on his face.

I won't try to stop you, I answered with my eyes.

William's enlarged irises, the sparks in his eyes, showed no doubt of his full desire and passion. Before I could take a breath I was in his arms, and this time, I did not want him to let go.

Pum-pum, pum-pum, pum—

William's lips heated, eager with excitement. His hands danced on my back toward my neck, his fingers gently tangling into my hair before sliding back down to my hips. The delight, my pleasure—they were excruciating. I wanted to taste more than just his lips.

Pum-pum, pum-pum, pum-pum.

"Arghhhhh!" we screamed, and pushed each other away.

I clenched my hands and crossed my arms over my chest, trying to stifle the pain in my heart. "What's happening!" My jaw tightened, and I squeezed my eyes. Tears streaked my cheeks. I prayed the throbbing would end, but it didn't.

William curled on the floor in a fetal position on the other end of the platform. I knew his agony was just as torturous as mine. "I don't know," he wheezed, squirming and rolling from side to side on his back. "It hurts more to know we have to keep away."

"William!" Sharp daggers of pain pierced me, as if cutting off each vein and artery that led to my heart. We were not meant to be together, yet we could not be separated.

My toes were still curled when the pain begun to ease off. We sat in tight balls of misery on the floor at opposite ends of the tree house.

"This is the reason we cannot be together," he said through gritted teeth. William tried to stand but fell down. "We . . . will . . . die. Our hearts will be torn from our chests. I'd rather stay away from you than know I'm the reason you died."

"We'll figure it out. You said we were created for a reason. We just need to find that reason, first. What if we can change the—" I stopped. *The spell. If the spell did not have any side effects, could we be together?*

Instantly, everything became clear. How could I have missed it before? Castall's spell was too powerful. It gave us gifts beyond what it was meant to give—powers that made us too strong. Our abilities unbalanced the equilibrium of the underworld. We could overpower the demons and warlocks. Even if we didn't want to, it could happen. And so we'd been cursed.

It made perfect sense. We were half human, half vampire. There was no warlock in us, so how could we have the skills we did? We were only meant to have two halves—there was no space for a third. This imbalance we created could not be allowed. Someone in the underworld had cast a curse to make sure we couldn't be together. Not that way. Not now.

No. Not yet.

I looked at the sapphire that circled my finger. William crossed the room toward me and I held my arm out. "This is the truth. Show me what I want to know."

On command, the ring displayed an image from the past—and it wasn't what I expected. We were not under a warlock's spell or a demon's curse. We were intoxicated by a potion, one that had been tampered with. Brewed underground in a witch's pot, the mixture that gave us our gifts came with a price of pain.

"Look at those herbs and how they shine. They shouldn't be there," I said.

"How do you know?" William asked.

"I can feel it. Sort of like you can sense stuff, I guess. Someone tampered with the potions meant to give you courage and me the dreams. Someone does not want us together." I nodded toward the image. "Look closely."

"I believe you." William sat on the floor behind me and stretched his legs out on either side of me.

I shook my hand and said to the ring, "Who did it? Show me who did it." Nothing happened.

"It won't show you."

I turned to him. "Why not?"

"They probably cast a protective spell."

"Of course." I lowered my hand, rolling my eyes. At that moment, I vowed I would figure out a way to counteract the cursed potions and bring the equilibrium back. We could not rest until we lived like a man and a woman should.

"It makes perfect sense. I told you we were stronger together." He smiled, trying to reassure me.

Someone wanted us apart, and their plan had worked until now. Now things were going to change, because I wasn't about to leave my other half.

William pulled me toward him and held me from behind, gently kissing the back of my head. Our hearts behaved, beating almost at their normal pace. We could bear the minimal zaps.

"You have to teach me everything you know," I said.

He nodded.

"I guess our rescue mission is becoming a quest."

"We'll figure it out," he said. "Let's get back to the cabin. We have a long day tomorrow."

I let him help me up, and we began climbing down. Near the base of the tree, William leaped from branch to branch to land on the ground.

"At least we don't turn into bats," I joked.

William's eyes filled with guilt.

I gaped at him. "We could?"

"Oh, come on, Sarah—you'd believe that?"

"You liar!" I laughed. "What about unicorns? Do those exist?"

"Well, I haven't seen one, but you never know," he teased. "Follow me."

My gaze flew back up at our tree house. I didn't want to leave. The pollen infused me with the confidence and power I lacked and now I needed it like drug. Finally, with a sigh, I turned to follow William—and froze. "I wouldn't go this way if I were you," I warned him.

"I always go this way. It's a shortcut," he answered over his shoulder.

"Well, I just got this funny feeling that you'd trip over a rock and—"

Thump. William plunged to the ground and landed hard, hitting the side of his head on a rock. He lay still, not moving.

My heart leaped into my throat. I rushed to him. Blood streaked the side of his head. "William! William! Are you okay?" I asked breathlessly, shaking him by the shoulders.

"Ouch." He grimaced. Rolling onto his back, he frowned up at me. "I wish your warning was more specific, like 'Watch out for the rock.'" He grinned to take any sting out of the complaint. The small gash on the side of his head had stopped bleeding and had almost healed.

"You've got to stop doing that!" I punched his arm in exasperation.

He threw a wounded expression up at me. "What?"

"Banging your head on rocks and asphalt!"

He ignored my concern and said, "You just had a premonition!"

"Is that what it was? I thought it was a gut feeling," I said, absently rubbing my stomach.

"Maybe that's what it's supposed to feel like. Was it the orchids?"

I shrugged.

"You're a tough nut to crack, Sarah," he teased, "but one I want to crack—soon." The sultry look he gave me made me shiver. "It's getting late. We'll sleep downstairs tonight."

I offered my hand. He took it, and I pulled him from the ground. It didn't take much effort. It still seemed funny to me, pulling a grown man to his feet without having to flex.

Skipping across the clearing toward the cabin, I imagined my parents' room. Warmth swept through my body as my blood bubbled with excitement. William unlocked the entrance to the chambers below by punching a four-digit code into a keypad embedded into the side wall. The marble at my feet cracked open, then dropped ten inches before sliding horizontally into the surrounding floor to reveal a staircase spiralling downward into darkness. The panel slowly moved aside. At full thickness of the floor and its supporting joists, the door to the basement was most likely bulletproof and fire resistant.

Light filtered up the entrance well as we descended. Sconce cones on the side walls illuminated enlarged photographs of bright orchids native to the rainforest outside.

"Does Agubab take care of all this when you're not here?" I asked, sliding my fingers across large pots of phalaenopsis orchids that decorated the chamber.

"Only when someone is scheduled to arrive—he'll see the larder is stocked and there's clean linen on the beds, things like that. The home itself is self-sustaining. Generators provide electricity, and timers turn the lights on and off for things like the plants." He gestured at the pots of orchids. "And water the plants. The cabin isn't vacant too often."

He led me to a set of double doors and swung one open. "You can sleep in your parents' room. I'll be a whisper away," he assured me. "Good night."

William remained on the threshold, leaning against doorframe. His eyes told me he didn't want to leave, but he kept his distance. I naturally glided toward him. He leaned in to kiss me on the cheek, and the blood raced in my veins.

William looked like he fought against an invisible force that kept him at my side to step away, but reluctantly, he did. His cheeks sagged.

"Good night," I whispered back.

"Don't let the bed bugs bite." He smirked.

Frost wrapped around my spine. *Does he know?*

CHAPTER 13

When I crossed the threshold into my parents' room, the stability in my knees disappeared. My heart sped up. It felt like they were still supposed to be there. I took a deep breath. After so many years, their scent still lingered in the air. With my eyes closed, I let my mind wander the past: seeing my mother sitting in the corner chair, reading a book: my father sliding his finger across the spines of magazines stacked under a Tiffany lamp on night tables. As I inhaled, more pictures flowed on the back of my eyelids, memories trying to imprint into my mind, and I finally opened my eyes. The pieces of furniture were positioned the same way.

On the back wall, draperies covered what I knew would be a faux window, framing black earth. I moved to the left wall and brushed my finger along one row of books. Most were science and genetics, but there were also romance novels, fiction, and magazines held in neat binders.

In the corner opposite the armchair where I'd pictured my mother, crystal figurines sparkled within a china cabinet, their reflected light casting tiny spots on the walls across the room. My attention shifted from those to the Tiffany lamps on either side of the bed. The room was cozy but sad.

I opened the drawer of the night table and unhooked the chain holding the ruby ring from my neck. The ring felt heavier than I remembered, as if resisting being apart from me. As I weighed it in my hand, it sparkled brighter, glowing with a new purplish hue that throbbed brighter, then dimmer. When I brought the ring closer to my eyes the stone faded to its original shade. Shrugging, I dropped it into the drawer. *It'd be a shame to lose you.*

Sleeping was out of the question. There was too much information I had to sift through. My body recuperated by sitting in one spot. The lack of movement relaxed the muscles. Tissues restored themselves. I had to admit I was exhausted from the massive dose of electrodes I'd absorbed from the orchids, and I was convinced the heavier scents could fry some nerves in my brain. With my eyes closed through the night, I shivered as memories of past dreams came back. One made me press my fist to the middle of my ribcage.

At five-thirty, William came to my room.

"Did we have to be in separate rooms?" I asked.

"Only until we get a grip on our emotions."

"Are you saying you're out of control?" I teased.

"Me? Out of control? Not possible!" His sarcastic tone vibrated throughout the room, and we laughed.

William looked better than the night before. The gash on his forehead from the fall had vanished. After a fresh shave, his natural scent blended with the smell of lavender and a spicy aftershave. The first whiff of him after being apart stimulated my senses. My body tried to absorb it without having to touch him. This time, the result of inhaling his aroma seemed to lift the fog that obscured my mind, and I thought with clarity. William was the cup of coffee I needed in the morning to wake up and function.

He wasn't dressed like the lab technician I pictured him to be, ready to mix potions and serums. William wore brown shorts, a white T-shirt, and Sketchers.

I looked down at my similar clothing choice. "Great minds think alike."

"They sure do." He eyed me. Then he cleared his throat. "Didn't you rest?"

"I'm not sure I want another night here," I confessed.

"Tonight I'll stay with you, if it makes you feel better," he offered, as if nothing had occurred between us the day before.

Was he that good at controlling his emotions?

William stepped back, then automatically took my hand. "Are you ready to go outside?"

"I thought we'd be mixing serums."

"I think it's more important for you to learn what you can do."

"Let's go." I eagerly pulled him toward the spiral staircase and skipped up every second step to the upper level.

After a liquid breakfast, William led me to the door and lifted a sun hat from the wooden hook beside it. "I think it should fit you."

Quizzically, I took it. "Why? There's shade everywhere."

"Shade doesn't protect your head from falling insects." He glanced at me, as if gauging my response.

I cringed. Does he know? Of course—he could read my worst fear. Beetles, crawlers, fliers, spiders—anything with more than four legs made the tiny hairs all over my body stand on end. I knew they couldn't hurt me, that I was the dangerous one, but still, the thought of one getting tangled in my hair made me shiver.

"I'll just wear my bandana." I pulled the fabric from my neck up to cover my head.

"What are we doing?"

"Flying!" He widened his eyes in delight.

My heartbeat quickened, and we climbed to the tree house where he opened a small cupboard in the corner.

"Put this on." He handed me a harness.

I accepted the mass of webbing and buckles. "Uh . . . some help?"

"Sorry—I thought you'd be able to foresee how to assemble it."

I wrinkled my nose at him. "Ha-ha."

Grinning, William knelt on the wood floor and began encasing me in the harness. I felt his breath on my inner thighs as he buckled the first strap into place. Blood rushed to my cheeks, and I secretly wished I'd worn Capris instead of the shorts that nearly exposed my bottom if I bent over.

"Control it, Sarah. Watch the beat," he whispered, slipping the second loop of harness around my other thigh.

My pulse raced. "Sorry." I looked down at the top of his head as he attached a third strap around my waist and double-checked the buckles. "While you're down there . . ." I covered my mouth with my hand.

"Yes?" William tilted his head up, a sparkle in his eyes.

"Can you please pull up my sock?" I said quickly.

"Anything else?" he drawled.

"No," I drawled back, but my heart screamed. "Yes!" I was sure he heard its plea.

William stood and pinned a yellow orchid in my hair. "And here I thought you had other needs you wanted me to tend to." He smiled crookedly.

My pulse will not get any rest around him, will it? I drew a deep breath to calm my heartbeat.

By the time it returned to normal, William finished assembling his harness, and we were attached. I wished we could be this close forever. We walked forward to an open platform at the end of the tree house where he connected the carabiner on our harnesses to the zip-line.

Above the canopy, the Amazon horizon was endless, an ocean of emerald treetops floating like green mushroom clouds, leaves and branches dancing under the wind's breeze. It felt as if we were in the middle of this paradise. I'd thought I was on top of the world, but in the distance, tree-carpeted mountains rose higher.

"What's that?" I pointed to a spot of blue glittering between the trees.

"The emerald pond," William answered. "It's spring-fed."

I imagined plunging into the fresh, cool water of the spring. It had to feel refreshing in this heat.

"You want to go for a swim later?" William asked.

"Uh, I don't know how to swim."

He looked at me incredulously. "You've never been in water?"

I squirmed. "Does a bathtub count?"

"No. It's a good thing you don't have to learn."

I cocked my head, confused. "What do you mean?"

"You'll see when you're in the water." He snickered. "You don't know what you've missed out on." His attention returned to the zip-line. "Are you ready?"

"Can you hold me?" I asked as we stepped to the edge of the platform.

"I will." He wrapped his arms around me from behind and pushed off.

My eyes closed at first. The warm wind brushed along my face, and I opened them. *How can I take all this in?* I gaped at the Amazon's bounteous beauty. My muscles relaxed, and I took a breath and held it, my head swinging, unsure which way to look. Everything seemed so clear. Raindrops of energy splashed on my skin, soaking my body. A natural force absorbed by my flesh became part of me. The jungle's magnificence bathed my muscles and invaded my organs, making them stronger. Aware of the smallest particles inside me, I felt them travelling through my veins and when they reached my heart, calmness settled over me, one born of confidence. I felt invincible.

We made our first stop on a nearby platform. William guided me to the edge, and we stepped off and were flying again. I laughed joyously. My cheeks hurt from smiling.

Out of nowhere, the smell of smoke slammed into me. A vision of fire engulfing a wooden building appeared. The vision wasn't clear, but my insides distressed as I recognized the building within the leaping flames.

"William!" I grabbed the harness with both hands. My legs went limp, and my body trembled. The tragedy I'd seen couldn't leave my lips.

My head shook violently, trying to get rid of the vision: then I opened my eyes wide, wanting desperately to concentrate on the jungle. It didn't work; I still saw the burning cabin.

William now bore most of my weight. I could feel him tense as my terror passed from me to him.

"What's the matter?" he asked when we stepped on the next platform. He turned my body to face his. "You're not afraid of the height, I know that. I can't sense—"

"No. The cabin, our home—it will burn. The laboratory will be reduced to ashes." My eyes welled up.

His eyes widened. "Did you have a premonition?"

I nodded. "Our home will be gone."

"That's impossible. No one knows about the cabin. Will it get struck by lightning? Will I leave the stove on?" he asked in disbelief.

"I don't know." Tears streamed down my cheeks, and I fell to the platform.

"Then how?" he whispered.

"I had the dream before, except I didn't recognize the cabin until now. And I don't know when." I started hyperventilating. It felt as if I was sucking air through a straw.

"Who's going to burn it?" He knelt in front of me.

"I don't know!" I threw my hands up.

"Sarah, think back to your vision. There must be a clue," he pleaded, holding my shoulders.

"I didn't see anyone in the vision . . . No, no, no . . ." I didn't remember them in my vision, but when I'd dreamt of the burning cabin, I'd seen brightly glowing, orange eyes; the memory of them had tormented me for years. I saw them in the center of every flower, in any oval shape nature could create. They were always there.

"Seeker demons?" William saw the fear on my face. "Are they the same ones that chased us in Pinedale?"

I nodded.

William wiped the wet streaks from my face. "When? How long do we have?"

His voice didn't shake, like mine did. "Less than three weeks. It's not exact, but I've been shown less than three weeks."

"We'll move everything to the basement," William said firmly. He unhooked the back harness so he could pace around the platform.

"We could stop them. We know they're coming. We can stop them," I begged. "They can't destroy our home!"

"Have you ever tried to change a premonition?" he asked.

"Yes. It didn't work." I slouched.

William began chewing on his thumb and finally let out a long breath. "We have to assume you can't change what you've seen. We can only minimize the damage. Do you know how many are coming? How do they know about this place?"

I closed my eyes trying to remember the vision, but the answers to William's questions weren't there.

"I don't know. I can't concentrate," I admitted with frustration. "I can only see things when I'm relaxed."

"Sarah." He took hold of my shoulders again. "You have to try. You're the only one who can help us now."

"Take me to the next platform," I demanded, concentrating on the energy I'd collected from the crown of the forest.

The click of a hook echoed in my ears. William turned us to face the rising sun. We zipped through a tunnel of trees, moving faster than before. The sun's rays warmed my body, soaked into my bones. I could feel and hear the heat build-up from the friction of the hook on the zip-line, and I saw orange circles. My lungs filled with the warm air as I let my head rest back on William's shoulder and gazed at the bright sky above us. The circles slowly turned into ovals. A grid, similar to that on a calendar, appeared in my mind. Concentrating, I saw the squares slowly fill with digits. *1, 2, 3* . . . I counted each one as a number was assigned to it.

"The seeker demons . . . they'll be here in nineteen days, just before sunset. Just before it rains," I said in a voice like a robot.

"That's amazing," William said as we jumped to the platform. He unhooked the harness and faced me. "Don't worry, we'll be safe. Now that we know they're coming, we can use them." He rubbed his hands together.

"You're planning to fight them?" I asked in disbelief, yet a moment ago, I'd felt brave enough to entertain the same idea. Learning about the new me was beginning to take its toll. I bounced from one extreme to another—one moment human, the next vampire—as I tried to master the world of a half-breed.

"Not exactly," William amended. He chewed his thumb again. "You've gained incredible strength and intuition. I have, too. In the next two weeks, we'll have even more control. They won't even know we're here. We'll follow them like ghosts, invisible shadows." He mimed a stealthy jump from one side of the platform to the other, and I couldn't help smiling. "Maybe they can lead us to the underworld, and our parents."

This was a side of him I had not seen. This was a much braver William, a man more dangerous than I thought. He was not the same William who'd taken every precaution to avoid the demons.

"You're kidding, right? They're going to burn down our home, and we're going to watch them do it?" He moved to pace again, but I blocked his way. "You can't do this!"

"Think about it. How else are we going to find the road to the underworld?"

"I don't know!" I wailed. "I'm not the underworld expert."

"Neither am I, but I have a feeling this is our chance. Remember what Castall said?"

"You have to let Sarah go to find her," I supplied.

"I hate the idea of you going to the underworld, but I think I have to let you go, for you to find your true self, to allow both of your halves to coexist."

A strong wind picked up the pollen and swirled it into funnels. <y bandana slid off at the back of my head, and I fixed it. As suddenly as it blew, the wind stopped, and the pollen settled.

William was right: this was our only chance. The danger of the unknown appealed to me more every minute. A quiet voice called out to me, joining whispers from my darkest dreams, dreams that already predicted I would end up underground.

"Aren't they going to sense us?" I asked.

William hesitated before he spoke, then he perked up as if he got a fresh injection of adrenaline into his heart. "We'll keep a safe distance and cover our scent."

I wasn't convinced and heard a jitter in his voice.

William stared toward the horizon, while my mind turned over suspicions. We must have missed something. It didn't make sense—the orchids protected us; their fragrance acted as a shield to disguise us, make us invisible. How would the demons find us? No one knew about the cabin. No one knew we were here.

William jumped up as if he'd been burnt. "Where's the stuff from the chest?"

"Downstairs, in my room."

"Let's go."

We hurried down the tree and toward our home, finally stopping in the underground apartment. After we returned to the porch, backpack in hand, William pulled out the chest and dumped everything out on the table.

"Sarah, look through the papers. Is anything missing?"

I knelt beside him. "I'm . . . I'm not sure." I scanned the scattered contents while and carefully moved things aside. "I never looked through everything."

"What did you see the first time?"

"Helen's letter, grad pictures . . ." I flipped papers and journals. "Log books, a birth certificate . . . the ruby ring I have in the night table . . . Helen's photos from when she was younger . . ." I stopped. Where was the photograph of Helen sitting on the porch that had so mesmerized me?

"What's wrong?" William asked.

My hands trembled as I shuffled through the papers again. "Helen's photo of the cabin is missing. It must have fallen on the floor at my store, the first time I saw you."

"That's how they'll find us, then." He slumped into one of the chairs and dropped the papers he still held in his hands.

Our fate was sealed. I slid from my knees to sit slouched on the porch, staring absently at a knot in the wooden plank. My lip quivered. *This is all my fault.*

William lifted me to the other patio chair. He took my hands between his and rubbed them.

How could I be the reason for the destruction of this magical home? I didn't have to cry to show my guilt. My heart gave everything away.

"You couldn't have known," William whispered. "Things happen for a reason. We'll brave the future together. We'll brave *our* future together. They will not hurt you."

My hands warmed. His touch did not send any pains toward my heart, not this time. He only meant to comfort me, nothing more.

"Perhaps that's our fate. They have to find us so we can get our parents. I will not let them harm you," he repeated firmly.

William was right. Self-pity would not help us. I refused to go back to the lonely and solitary life I'd once known. *Over my dead body.* Hope fuelled me that the side I already embraced would help me fight.

William lifted his chin. "Over my dead body."

He wasn't reading my mind. We were so in tune with each other we felt what the other was thinking. We read the patterns of our thoughts on our faces.

And we had nineteen days in which to prepare—to train and mix new serums, before this haven was lost to us, forever.

* * *

"Again." William's eyes focused on me.

Leaping higher than before, I landed a third of the way up the ceiba tree in one spring. I smiled. My abilities improved each day. I inhaled, intoxicating my body with the orchid pollen that whizzed through my lungs quicker with each breath. My legs sprang again, and I almost reached the base of the tree house.

"Nice." William joined me and fastened the harness.

Zipping through the canopy became a necessity. I borrowed the life of the jungle to increase my strength. As I discovered the more powerful muscles in my body, William collected more pollen. He combined its various species for our experimentation. Some mixtures made our sight as acute as a cougar's. Others made my hearing as sensitive as a bat's. A combination of some increased the strength of the muscles in my limbs without increasing their weight, allowing me to climb the highest trees with ease, yet be light enough to jump from one frail branch to another without breaking it. We worked so intuitively together we became one another's shadow.

Even with the sense of urgency hanging over us, we found time to relax. We spent the nights downstairs in Willow and Atram's room. When I walked in the first time, the love they had shared here was still present.

"One of them plays the guitar?" I pointed to the instrument propped in the corner.

"Yes, my father. Would you like to listen?"

From then on, I listened to William playing every night before we said good night. He'd written songs, a mixture of soft classical, rock, and jazz. I listened raptly to each hypnotizing melody, watching his fingers performing a dance across the strings, never wanting his songs to end. When he didn't play, we'd share stories of our childhoods.

Finishing each other's sentences soon became second nature. We recognized frustration and pain in each other's face, humour and happiness in each other's eyes. Somewhere between, I saw the lust we could not act on. But for the first time, I found balance between my two halves.

During training, the mixtures strengthened our vampire side. We preyed on animals, fed on them, absorbed their strength. Biting into a racing heart that still pulsed was like biting into a ripened watermelon—blood squirted and ran down my face. William taught me how to fight, how to deceive an opponent, how to predict their next move.

On a later afternoon we sat at the base of a tree, relaxing after a hunt.

"Open your hands," he said one day, holding his hands behind him.

I smiled, cupping my palms in front of me. "Have you found a new orchid?" I should have thought to read his eyes, study his face.

"Close your eyes."

Although I detected a hint of nervousness in his voice, I did what he asked.

Tiny, hairy legs dribbled over my flesh a moment later. I knew the eerie tickling too well and flung the spider to the ground. "Are you crazy?" I shrieked, skipping from one foot to another, in case the thing didn't have the sense to run away. Finally spent, I leaned my back against a tree, panting, hoping the tarantula had vacated into the underbrush. "How could you have—"

I stopped in mid-sentence. My eyes rolled back until they closed. "There are three of them . . . three pairs of orange, glowing eyes . . . They have a plan. They're on a mission. Three seekers will be here." I opened my eyes and stared into space. "Two of them by the burning cabin, the third one . . ." I swung my head slowly from side to side. "I can't see him. He will be here, though."

Watching us, I think. I didn't get a chance to voice that before William had my palm in his hand, rubbing where the insect had touched my skin.

"I'm sorry I did that." He smoothed my hair behind my ears and smiled sheepishly. "I wasn't sure if it would work, using your fear to foresee their next move."

I trembled, looking at nooks and holes where the spider could be hiding. My head whipped up, a retort on my lips, but then I relaxed. "I'm not sure I can concentrate on the fear. Everything is telling me to block it."

"Just remember it's something you can do—if you can control your fear."

I nodded. If this was a way to foresee what the seekers were up to, I was willing to try.

William figured I couldn't have my visions unless I felt one of two extremes—tranquil and calm or fearful and pumped with the adrenaline surge of perceived danger. But no matter how much I tried to feel fear, knowing William was by my side minimized it a hundredfold, negating my ability. Our only hope was to expect the orange glow in the seekers' eyes to scare me—or for a spider to appear out of nowhere in my palm. I preferred the orange eyes. Helen had always compared me to and elephant afraid of a mouse.

On the third to last evening before the seekers' anticipated arrival, we sat on the porch, drinking virgin Bloody Marys. A light breeze flickered the candles in the two chandeliers.

"Let's wait in the basement until they're gone," I said. My voice broke. I didn't want to leave. Surely we could rebuild our haven.

"You know we can't do that. We have to follow them to find the entrance to the underworld," William reminded me again, as patiently as the first ten times.

The frost around my spine refused to melt. "What if we get rid of our vampire side? They'll stop *seeking* us and hunting us. They won't be able to trace us! Then we could stay here. Just like Helen said. She was right; we should have listened to her." My hands shook.

William knelt in front of me. "Sarah, calm down—you'll go into shock. Helen didn't know they'd use our family against us. If we don't find them first, they *will* find us. We have to strike first. Do you want to find them as a weak human or as a strong half-breed?"

"You're making this too difficult to dispute." I crossed my arms.

He unfolded them and took my hands in his. "We can always go back to the research, once our family is safe and the curse is lifted." William's brows arched persuasively, and he leaned in closer. "And I'll always be with you. You must know that."

Burning heat radiated from his body, settling on mine. Being around him was beginning to tear my insides. I couldn't act on my desires and had to control my lust. My hunger drained my energy.

"I know," I whispered, then drew a quick breath as a sharp pain pinched the middle of my chest.

"What's the matter?"

"It's a promise you can't keep." Sadness overwhelmed me.

His brows drew down. "I don't understand."

"I can't explain it." I pressed my fist to my chest and looked down at the floor. "It would just be too good to be true, to always be together."

"I promise I will never leave you," he said solemnly, tipping my chin up with his finger.

Never say never.

"My heart would not beat the same way without you," he cooed.

William sat by my side and leaned toward me. My senses awoke, screaming for more, but I knew I couldn't. It would only lead to pain.

"All better?" He looked into my eyes, knowing what the rhythm of my heart was saying.

"Yes, I'm sorry. I just—"

"Panicked. It's okay. You're still part human. It's one of the many reasons why I love you."

I gasped, then held my breath.

William's words flowed into me like the air I needed in my lungs, spreading through my veins to fuel oxygen into my blood. How could I fight that? The way he spoke would make the Wicked Witch of the West melt.

"I love you too."

William embraced me until the zap pushed us apart.

A screech jerked our heads up. A large bird circled overhead.

"I didn't know falcons inhabited the Amazon," I pinched my brows.

"They don't." William laughed.

My gaze found his. "What are you not telling me?"

He grinned. "Do you recognize that falcon?"

I studied the bird for several moments. "Mira and Xander's falcon?"

"I think so."

The falcon weaved between the tree crowns. It's shadow froated on the ground just in front.

"What would it be doing here?"

"Your friends are checking up on us. They shouldn't have worried; I sent letters." William's forehead creased.

"They're looking for me?" I perked up. Xander's morning jogging routine didn't seem too annoying anymore, nor Mira's constant calls. I wished my friends were here to help us.

"I think so."

"Will they be upset we left without saying anything."

"I'm sure they will. Not with you, but me. I wasn't supposed to kidnap you." He arranged the memorabilia back into the chest.

"You didn't. You saved me," I argued.

"Try explaining that to shapeshifters. I think it's time to visit the emerald lake." He stood up, sniffing the air as if he were trying to find a specific scent.

"Now?" I asked. "It's almost night time."

"Exactly. It's the best time to swim in the lake." William smiled mysteriously, and I felt my pulse speed up and my stomach tingle. He nodded toward my drink. "Finish up. I'll get the towels."

"I don't have a bathing suit," I said as he got up to leave.

He laughed. "You won't need one."

Minutes later, fronds and leaves brushed against my arms and legs as we walked along a well-worn path through the jungle. By the time we reached the pond, the only illumination came from the light bugs dancing in front of the night sky. The underbrush had been cut back at the end of the path, and a bench carved out of a fallen tree stood to one side in the cleared area. A swath of large plants blocked the passage to the pond.

"Unless you want to get them wet, leave your clothes here." William pointed to the bench.

"I thought you said I don't need a bathing suit," I protested.

He smiled. "Don't worry, I've already pictured you naked."

"Picturing and seeing are two different!"

"Not in my head," he said shamelessly, and laughed. "All right, I'll turn around. You can leave your undergarments on if you'd like, but they won't make a difference." William nudged me toward the shrubbery that blocked our passage. "When you're ready, put your foot in this loop." He pointed to a hanging liana with a loop knotted into one end; the vine itself had been draped over a branch overhead. "It will take you over."

"Can't we just jump over?" I eyed the green barrier, guesstimating its height.

"You could, but I don't recommend it. The vine carries you precisely where you should land to avoid the poisonous plants. And since you wouldn't know where that is, this is the only way in." He paused. "I'm turning around now."

I sighed, capitulating. "No peeking!"

"Of course not; imagining is much better," he teased.

My clothes flew off in haste. I would have left my undergarments on, but the bra was built into my tank top and the g-string didn't count as good swimwear. William didn't look, although I could swear I heard the corners of his mouth curve up with a held breath.

Once ready, I gripped the liana and slid my right foot into the loop—then shrieked. As soon as I put pressure on the vine, it sprang up and forward, swinging me twelve feet over the shrubbery, high enough that I cleared the top of the green barrier by more than three feet. I shrieked again as I passed over the wall and soared higher through the air, then arced down toward what looked like the reflecting surface of a mirror, oddly lit with green and blue light from underneath.

I hit the water with a loud splash, at first mentally cursing William for not warning me, then welcoming the coolness that enfolded me as I plunged below the surface. Fortunately I'd held the last breath I'd taken before submerging, a breath that would last ten times longer for me than for a human. I'd always won bopping for apples in high school. Even so, panic crept in, and I had to concentrate on remaining calm.

I can do this. Don't you just move your limbs to swim? I looked toward the surface and swung my arms and kicked my legs like the swimmers I'd seen on television.

When I opened my eyes and saw the underwater world, I stilled my efforts. The grasses and plants at the bottom of the pond released a fluorescent glow that illuminated the water in predominantly blue and green colours, with fuchsias and yellows accenting the edges and hovering near the bottom. I opened my mouth in awe. *Crap! I'm out of air!*

Just as I was about to swallow my first gulp, strong arms gripped me from behind and lifted me toward the surface. I exploded above the water, hacking and coughing.

William faced me. "Are you okay?"

"Yes—arghh . . .hah!" I sputtered. "Thank you."

Once I recovered, I looked up. A million stars glittered in the black sky, their light sparkling in the moisture on the large leaves lining the tall bank of the pond. I smiled before returning my attention to my current predicament and lowered my gaze to William, silently asking what to do.

"Kick your feet. I'll hold you up."

I followed his instruction, circling my arms. The swirls beneath my arms and legs gave me lift. Swimming was easier than I'd originally thought. William was so close. The water dripping his face underlined a strong jaw, and I focused on his lips.

"I'm gonna let you go now," he cautioned. The sparkle in his eyes reflected his wicked thoughts.

"Wait! I can't swim!" I yelled.

"Concentrate on the water. Let it buoy you up. You were born a swimmer, just like me. That's why you're so attuned to water when it's needed most. Remember what you did at the airport with the fire demon? Feel the water. It will help you. You can do this." He let go of one of my arms, then the other.

I locked my eyes on his for reassurance and kicked my feet in a semicircular pattern, swirling my arms through the water—and stayed afloat! "Oh my gosh, I'm swimming!" I squeaked.

"You're not swimming." He laughed. "You're treading water. *This* is swimming!" He dove head first, and I realized we were naked when William's white behind popped out of the water before submerging.

Can he see me underwater? Nervous, I ducked under the surface to follow him. It was as bright as I'd thought. *He tricked me!* I should have worn my bathing suit.

A school of tropical fish swam by, each a different colour and pattern, their shades shifting as the swarm zigg-zagged in unison. They looked like a mass of twinkling lights. I was surprised they weren't afraid of me, an alien in their midst. For a moment, I thought they looked right at me as if expecting me to be there.

Where is he? I kicked myself in a circle but couldn't see him anywhere.

Then I felt something brush against my left leg. I almost screamed until William swam up in front of me. My hands flew to my front, and I instinctively cupped my hand over my crotch and threw my other arm over my breasts. He laughed underwater, and his bright teeth and turquoise eyes flashed.

That's when I realized why he'd said bathing suits were unnecessary. William's teeth and eyes were the *only* parts of his body I could see. The rest of him was almost transparent; only a shadow created by the water's current passing around him, bending to define his silhouette, made him visible at all.

My head emerged above the surface. "How is this possible?" I blurted as soon as my head poked above the water. I saw William's head and a third of his torso bobbing, but nothing underneath; it was as if he had been cut at the point of submersion.

"It's the plants. I think their light makes our bodies disappear."

"Wow, people would freak if they saw this."

"I said *our* bodies, not human bodies," William said.

"Oh. Oh!"

"This was the best hideout I had from my parents. Even my father couldn't find me when we played hide and seek."

"Cool!"

"I know, eh? Don't you feel special?"

I did. Swimming freely underwater, even as a beginner, liberated me. William had said my skills would develop within minutes if I let my senses take over, and he was right. For the first time since my horrible premonition, I felt at ease. Knowing no one else lived within miles, I imagined we were the only two beings on this planet, and this perfect body of water collected here, for us.

We returned to the cabin before dawn. I silently promised to visit the pond often, once we were back from the underworld.

Now, though, the time had come to face the seekers. We had two days left for final preparations. The plan was simple: seal the basement, inject enough serum to make ourselves undetectable, and hide out nearby. Once they were done searching the cabin, we'd follow them to the underworld.

Our plan was perfect.

Or so we thought.

CHAPTER 14

William had made a body cream that would mask our scent from the terrier-like noses of the seekers. and blend our smell with the jungle. We had to rub it on each other two nights in a row, and today would be the first session. Self-control was essential as William covered places I could not reach, and I returned the favour. Every inch of our skin had to be coated with the thick cream.

When William pressed his palms against my body, his touch electrified my skin, each cell responding wildly.

You're in a salon, getting a massage—that's all. It's just a massage—orange eyes—just a massage—orange eyes. Breathe, just breathe. Don't stop breathing. Ugh . . . I wish I could enjoy what's happening to my body!

My mind was too weak. It inevitably wandered back to one of my best dreams.

William gently lay me down and hovered over me, kissing my forehead, then my head, my nose, each cheek. Taking his time, he kissed each freckle. Shiveres of pleasure roamed my skin. My arms curved around his back, then slid up to his shoulders, and I yanked at his shirt tearing it off to reveal the hard, rippling muscles of his torso. I quivered, craving the pleasure of closer contact.

A new song began playing, this one with a calmer beat, a slower rhythm. It matched the movements of our bodies, deepened the intensity of our kisses . . .

William gently tapped my shoulder. "It's your turn, Sarah."

Guilt washed my face as I strained to remember where I was.

"Try to control your heartbeat, or I'll lose control myself." He winked.

I pushed up from the cot we'd set up in the sun room, feeling my cheeks heat as I realized what my daydreaming had done to my body. My breasts had perked, and the tingling just below my pelvis was unbearable as tiny tremors stimulated the area. With a sheet tied at my front like a bath towel, I sat up, wishing I could dress to cover the physical signs of my desire, but the layer of cream he'd applied was still being absorbed by my skin.

William watched me. "When this is all over, I'm taking you away for a month to a place where no curse will reach us."

"Oh? To do what?" I coaxed, hoping to hear his fantasies.

"Whatever you're thinking. We'll make it real." He took my place on the cot.

Scooping a handful of cream and smearing it over my palms, I pressed them against his shoulders and slowly dragged downward in a thin layer. When my hands ran past his waist, William's muscles tightened and firmed. I stroked his thighs and calves, then begun rubbing upward to his shoulders. William moaned, like a whimpering puppy, his heartbeats revealing that he too yearned for more.

"Not so easy, is it," I said.

"You could say that. Should I turn over?"

I mustered as much control as I could and said casually, "Sure." My heart betrayed me. My gaze concentrated on top of William's body when he rolled over and clasped his hands comfortably under his head as he closed his eyes. I wasn't sure whether that was to make it easier on me or so he could enjoy the moment. His body responded to my touch, and no towel or sheet could cover his needs.

After the massage, we took long showers. The lustful heat washed off the surface of my skin, but inside, it felt as if my hormones were throwing an out of control party.

When I entered the sunroom, William pointed to a plate on the table. "Sandwich?" His v-neck shirt stuck to his torso like cellophane.

I bit my lip. "Thank you."

He'd explained we had to consume only human food for a couple of days to avoid too much blood pumping through our veins so we could become undetectable. I found it ironic that we were trying to be dead vampires but had to eat human food to prevent our mortal forms from being detected.

By five o'clock on the nineteenth day, the gray clouds of the tropical storm I'd predicted had rolled in. It hadn't rained in my vision, so they had to be here before the heavens opened. We hid in the understory of the forest, ten feet above the ground, close enough to see the cabin's front porch.

"Are you ready?" William whispered.

"No, but it's too late for misgivings now." My voice cracked.

How could I possibly be ready to face these demons? Am I fast enough to follow them? Will I find the courage to look past the bright orange glow of their eyes? Did we forget anything? My gut told me we had—no, that *I* had, but I couldn't remember what it was.

"It will be all over soon," William assured me. He wrapped his arm around me.

I swept the vicinity with my gaze, expecting to see orange ovals between the shrubs as they approached.

Eventually they did come, moving with cautious excitement and purpose. All three had an odd pattern of sniffing and rotating their heads to all sides more freely than a human could. They were tall, thin, and grubby-looking. The tallest one moved with authority. He had broader shoulders than the others and more wrinkles puckered his translucent skin. His eyes shone the brightest orange. The one that seemed second-in-command was about four inches shorter; he followed the leader's every step and moved whenever the leader shrieked. The shortest one, although still over six feet tall, had a hump on his back. He yelped the most of the three, and it reminded me of a child complaining.

Hunched over so their hands almost touched the ground, they moved across the forest floor, their heads turned toward the cabin as they approached it, studying every inch. Then they spread out. There seemed to no pattern to their search as they moved around the structure.

They went inside. I saw them briefly through the front window as they searched the lab. Less than a minute later, they came back outside. They were still hunched over, sniffing. Again they wandered, covering a ten-foot perimeter around the building.

After three minutes, they stopped, faced one another, and begun a strange discussion. The tallest one shrieked something from the back of his throat that sounded almost like a gurgle. The other two hissed and went back inside. Through the window, I could see the seekers gather at the center of the room. They lowered their skeletal bodies close to the floor. The tops of their backs moved as they followed a circular pattern outward leaving the house, then re-entering to retrace their path.

On the second exit, they covered more ground outside, moving only a few inches clockwise at a time, like three hands of a clock, ticking off each second with precision, orange eyes flashing. At one point, I thought the eyes flashed at me, and chills ran through my body.

I looked at William. He tightened his hold on my shoulder. His eyes and face said everything I needed to know. He was worried and hoped this would all end soon.

When I turned my gaze back to the cabin, the seekers were touching the wood with their palms, and it ignited on contact. I shivered, remembering the shapeshifter at the airport. Seeing what he *could* have done with his fire ball frightened me. It would not be long before the cabin was consumed by flame. It hadn't rained in months; everything was dry. The approaching storm only added to the seeker's haste to burn it.

Sadness filled my heart, and I wanted to cry. All I could think of were the years of work that would be gone in ten minutes. We wouldn't be able to move back. Once we found William's parents and my father, we'd have to transfer the basement contents to a safer location and rebuild there.

The flames licked the walls of the cabin. Though there was never any doubt, I had hoped it wouldn't happen, that by some miracle the cabin would withstand the fire, but that hope burned away.

I'd already seen this—twice. William kept his gaze on the hypnotizing scene, but I took a small step back along the branch toward the trunk and briefly closed my eyes.

They flew open when a pair of hot hands grabbed my shoulders and yanked me back so fast I had no chance to react. William turned as I crashed on the forest floor. The seeker's comrade joined him to grab me and hold me tight.

My fangs sprung. I struggled, but the four clawed hands heated. Any attempt at escape would burn. As the third seeker arrived, I slumped in defeat. One, I could probably vanquish—but not three.

My head tipped up to look at William, who crouched on the branch above, regarding us with terror-filled eyes.

He jumped down, growling and flexing his knees. "Let her go!"

Flinging my hand out, I wiggled out of their grip and stepped toward William, but the leader stepped forward and drew a line in front of my foot with a wooden cane that flew out of his sleeve. I slammed into a mystical force radiating from the line. The energy travelled like an electric current through my veins, burning away all the serum, evaporating all residue of the cream from my skin. Throbbing pain made me crumple to the ground. When I stood, the seeker's hot paws returned to my shoulders, immobilizing me.

William rushed toward me but was hurtled backward by the same force that had decimated me.

"The shield won't let you through," the shortest seeker squeaked then snorted. He cackled. "Not now!"

The tallest one looked at him disapprovingly, then shrieked and squawked something in a high-pitched tone.

My gaze focused on William, who didn't hide his confusion. Our plan to follow the demons to the underworld had failed.

What's to become of us now?

"Sarah! Fight!" William pleaded.

"I'm trying." I twisted to free myself from their iron grip angered the seekers, but they increased the temperature of their palms, pressing their hands on my shoulders. My flesh sizzled with a sound like french fries immersed in hot oil, and I writhed in pain and gagged at the stench of burning flesh. As I flung my head back in agony, I half expected to glimpse my scorched skin smoking under their grip, but all I saw were the seekers' red palms hovering an inch above my shoulders.

William stood motionless, his eyes half closed, concentrating. I assumed he was trying to identify the seeker's fears and wondered what could scare such beings—water, flood, tsunamis? Expecting catastrophies to manifest, I gazed beyond the force field, but nothing appeared.

Energy left William's body; it flew toward the demons, then bounced back from the shield. It wouldn't let William *or* his powers through.

They're going to tear us apart! Did we underestimate their intelligence that much?

William sprang at the shield and was ejected backward. He flew at it again and again, trembling with exhaustion and agony of the torture he repeatedly subjected himself to.

As the thought of being away from William sank in, I realized there was no way out. My body began shaking. Uncontrollable tremors tormented my muscles. I could already see my future without having to close my eyes—seekers led me through a dark tunnel toward a dungeon. Huddled in my dank cell, I heard the moaning of other creatures and high-pitched demon discussions in a room close by. It ended with me seeing William beyond a green fog; he couldn't see me.

"I'll be in the third cell!" I yelled, no longer fighting against the hot palms.

Castall's words now made perfect sense: *You'll have to let Sarah go to find her.*

I'm so stupid.

Penny-sized raindrops suppressed the blaze consuming the cabin. Its logs simmered in the deluge, water evaporating and smoke billowing in a thick gray cloud up into the canopy. The acrid stench of smouldering wood filled the jungle. *Just like in my dream.*

I clenched my teeth at the pain throbbing in my chest. The life I wanted was disappearing. Knowing William would find me didn't help. It was difficult to imagine being away from him at all. *When* would he find me?

William's face turned into a vampire's, fangs stretched and brows raised. He threw himself at the shield and then collapsed to the ground. I looked at him, pleading with my eyes for him to stop, but William struggled up, bracing his right hand on his knee while he caught his breath. His left hand slipped into his pocket, and when my three kidnappers weren't looking, he winked, then focused on his left hand— reminding me of our gifts from Castall.

I acknowledged with the slightest nod, feeling the small wooden stick that pressed into my hip through the pocket in my jeans. William mouthed *"I love you,"* and I whispered the same back as the tallest seeker extended the boundary of the field around me and the three demons. The ache of William's heart in my chest throbbed; it hurt more than the hot palms gripping my arms and hovering over my shoulders. It stung like a bucher's knife.

The seekers pulled me backward with the pressure of their claws. Their hands had grown gaunt, almost colourless and translucent against even my pale complexion, their bones standing out under their skin. The redness had faded from their palms, along with the sizzling sound and the smell of burnt flesh.

I relaxed the tension in my body. The only way I knew to beat the seekers was to extinguish them with the rain that hit the impermeable dome of the force shield. From the way they squirmed, it was clear they wanted to get away quickly. Their power was waning.

The leader drew a smaller circle, and the seekers pulled me into its shape. The edge of the oval sparked, then flames spread toward the center. I imagined standing in a fire, but it didn't burn. A doorway opened beneath us, keeping us afloat on a plate of cool flames. Panic overwhelmed me, and I longed to free myself, but their claws were locked on my body. We began to sink in the quicksand-like ground, and the glowing circle lowered as if it were an elevator.

TWO HALVES

William yelled, "Sarah!" His hands splayed against the shield despite the bolts of electricity zapping his body.

I'll see you soon! I promised with my eyes, but something inside me whispered that it would be a long time before I saw William again. It was a gut feeling strangely centered in the future.

William fell to his knees and disappeared from view, and with him, my hope.

CHAPTER 15

The underworld was dark, the air cold and moist. Tree roots crisscrossed along the ceiling of the corridor. Some stems dangled freely, robbed of the soil they'd originally formed in: others simmered at their ends, releasing a smell of rotten eggs and dirty socks.

Every twelve feet, the tallest seeker drew a new circle in the wall with his cane and another fiery door materialized. Heat emanated from the opening, but it did not burn. After passing through each new entry, the seeker played his cane over the tunnel in front of him, leaving a glowing orange mist on the walls that illuminated the way.

The other two forced me to follow him. They concentrated more on shrieking at each other than on me; as the corridor narrowed, there was no longer a need to pay attention to me becase each passage sealed behind us. Every so often, they tugged and pulled me. From the tone of the yelps, I guessed they were arguing over who'd get to turn me in to whomever they were taking me to and I assuemed I would meet Aseret very soon. The tallest seeker always won the argument.

The slippery floor made it difficult to keep my balance. I wondered how uncomfortable it was for the seekers to walk through the narrow burrowed tunnels, bent over in half.

Above my head, I looked for little critters lurning in the underground snarl of roots and earth. I saw none and finally decided they had enough sense to stay away.

How long could I survive this torment without William?

My heart skipped a beat and I felt his do the same. *William* . . . The rhythm of his pulse revealed worry, pain, and urgency. William was still trying to get through the force field. I knew he would succeed somehow; after all, I'd already seen him arrive.

Every second that ticked by without him was like a small needle poking at my arteries. Unsure how long I could tolerate those little pricks, I tensed my jaw. I sensed him, just the way he told me I would. With William far away, my thoughts blurred and crumbled, as if they had to pass through a heavy fog to reach my consciousness.

William, please find me.

Again my heart skipped a beat, as if in response to my plea, and I knew William was thinking about me. The beat quickened slightly, pulsing hope.

We stepped into a high-ceilinged octagonal hall. The leading seeker used his cane to draw a new circle on the floor and pushed me into it, then pointed to the glowing ring. "The shield will not let you pass through. Bow your head when Master Aseret enters."

I felt as if I'd entered an underground stadium with no bleachers. Five doorways covered with red velvet drapes propped in front of me. The glowing tunnel we'd emerged from sealed behind us. The middleone was oddly shaped, its entrance higher on the face of the wall. A wide staircase descended from the opening, narrowing as it approached the floor. More than twenty demons stood in the hall around me, peering surreptitiously my way.

Hundreds of candles illuminating the hall from a chandelier suspended in the center of the natural granite ceiling. Four grand support pillars rose from floor to the top, like ranked monoliths. Below the light fixture, flames roared in an oversized fire pit. Fifteen massive candelabras, each holding more than fifty candles, were arranged around a room so expansive the multitude of candles did not overwhelm the space. The demons certainly liked their fire. I inhaled. The acidic odour burnt the sides of my mouth, but I took an even deeper breath, trying to taste the air.

Could William's parents be here? Could my father be here? New energy of excitement shifted across my body as the idea grew. Jitters of anticipation hidden beneath my skin. I scanned the room again. *Perhaps this is the way to get to them. Maybe all this isn't in vain.* The thought generated a smirk, but I kept it off my face.

A figure of impressive stature entered. He glided across the floor. The long robe that was customary for demons covered his feet, but there was a small gap between its hem and the floor, with nothing between them but air. He was levitating.

Aseret, the vicious warlock.

Unlinke the others, Aseret stood straight. His dark brown eyes did not glow. His face elongated, and the flesh sagged from ages of experience, knowledge, treachery, and pain, yet was still expressionless.

Each arm folded into the cuff of the other, hiding what I assumed were twig-like hands.

Aseret floated to stand three feet in front of me, but I did not bow.

The tallest one shrieked apologetically toward his master.

"That is all right. This one's new."

I didn't like that Aseret referred to me as an object, and I raised my chin.

"Sso you are the one Xela told me to fearrr." His speech was slow, each word delivered at the pace of a snail. Aseret did not speak directly to me. His stare, though piercing, seemed focused somewhere over my shoulder. I was glad; the intensity of his eyes suggested a direct look might cut into my brain.

The contours of his face changed from soft to hard as he scanned my body as if looking for strengths or weaknesses.

Who's Xela? I wondered, remembering Castall's warning. It couldn't be someone I'd like.

"Where is the other one?" he asked my captors.

They shrieked as the second in command one took a big swing at the shortest one, who ducked and returned the gesture successfully. The tallest one raised his palms, glowing as brightly as hot lava, and smashed both demons on their head, almost knocking them to the ground. They stopped fighting and stood still, as if nothing had happened.

"Hmm." Aseret sighed. He visibly tried to compose and hide his emotions, but I could read the anger and disappointment on his face as his cheeks twitched. I knew the seekers would be punished for their failed mission. "She's of no use to me by herself. I have no need for her without the other one. Find him!" He focused on two demons standing at the door. They were taller than the tallest of my captors, and their eyes glowed brighter, which I would not have imagined possible. They left as soon as he looked at them.

William, be careful. I allowed my heart's pace to change by a fraction to warn him about the dangerous creatures.

Aseret turned back to face me. "You do not look ssstrong. You're weak and confusssed." He paused. "You're herrre, but not all of you is *herrre.* Part of you is ssstill on Earth. Do you have ssspecial powersss?" The way he spoke reminded me of an ESL teacher addressing new students—slowly and calmly, using well thought-out words chosen deliberately to ensure they were understood.

"What do you want from me?" I spat. My saliva hit the protective circle, sizzled, and evaporated into nothing.

Aseret did not move, but his nose twitched. "I'm told you yelled that you'll be in the thirrrd cell. Hmm. How did you know?" His lips pulled back, then tightened, unveiling sharp, uneven teeth.

"I went to see a fortune teller two months ago. She told me to say it if anyone kidnapped me." I paused, hoping he would believe my fib. "I didn't know what to make of it then, but I remembered when your demons took hold of me."

"Hmm, a fortune teller, how old-fashioned." He sneered. "I don't believe you. No one will find you here. But let's play your game." He sneered. Though he spoke slowly, his decisions were quick and confident.

Would Aseret imprison me in the third cell to prove his strength or as bait? I had a feeling it'd be the latter.

I wondered what his actual weakness was. He had to have one. He was cautious when he looked at me and kept his distance.

"And the siblings, where are they?" he asked me.

He knows Mira and Xander?

"I don't know who you're talking about," I said quickly.

"Hmm . . . Is it customary to lie in the human world?" he shouted. A few rocks clattered down the high walls to the floor.

I jerked back, surprised at the sudden change in his tone. He'd lost control, overpowered by anger. *Could this be his weaknesses?*

"These shapeshifters concern me. I want them here, on my side, where they belong!" Aseret's speech picked up momentum, though he didn't seem to be speaking to anyone in particular.

"Master, Castall would not allow—"

"Do not ssspeak!" The demon at his side fell silent at Aseret's hiss.

"Place herrr in the third cell." His words were sluggish again.

The seekers hesitated, but did not question Aseret. I didn't think anyone would.

Aseret turned away, floating toward the central staircase. *"Asamu rata lipear."* The hushed whisper flowed out of his mouth in a thin, reddish stream of light which carried the strange words on a velvety cloud of steam that hit the force field around me, sizzled and dissipated its spell.

As soon as the shield was down, radiant heat of six new palms burned from above my shoulders and at the sides of my arms. They didn't need to touch for me to feel the pressure of their strength. The seekers guided me through the second curtained entrance too quickly for my liking—I was still not used to the slippery floor.

Their palms urged me downward to the circular stone stairs, which ended at an unsavoury dungeon. The corridor was dank and dim with countless openings in the walls. Their interiors were obscured by a green sheer curtain of energy that projected foreign words randomly across their surface.

We passed two cells and stopped at the third, its opening blocked by a stream of green brightness flowing from the stairway behind us. The demons stepped inside the cell and pushed me against the back wall. Behind them, the light—a spell, I realized—spread to cover the entrance like those on the far side of the corridor.

"Do not try to pass through this spell," the tallest of the seekers said, his voice a faint imitation of Aserets, but lower. "It will kill you." They passed through the green barrier unscathed and left the dungeon without looking back.

The barrier intrigued me, and I focused on the scattered words. Fifteen of them floated on the green fog, and none except one looked familiar—my name.

I sat on the stone floor with my back against the cold side wall and wondered how long I'd be here. My stomach grumbled. The hunger did not bother me, but my heart did. The little needles were still poking. They had not stopped since the last time I'd seen William. "Where are you?" I whispered.

"Hello?" a weak male voice answered.

I sat up in surprise. "Who's there?"

"I'm a prisoner in the fourth cell. Are you a prisoner as well?"

"Yes. They just brought me in."

"What did you do?"

I sighed. "I don't know. I think I was too happy for their liking." I forced out a chuckle, wondering how much I should share with the stranger. "Why are you here?"

"I'm a permanent resident." He laughed quietly. "It's been over two years now, I think." After a pause, he added, "Creatures normally stay here a day or two, then they disappear."

My hand went to my throat. "What do you mean disappear?" I felt the vibration of my voice under my fingers as I spoke.

"I mean they don't come back to this world, or the one above. Sometimes they scream when they're taken away. Sometimes, if Aseret is too bored to torture, he'll order it to be over quickly. That doesn't happen often."

I wasn't sure if I should ask my next question. "Are you a demon? You don't sound like one."

"I'm a vampire," he answered.

A vampire locked away for so many years in a demon dungeon? This couldn't be a normal occurrence; they must have had a good reason to keep him here. *Could William's parents be here? How many vampires had Aseret imprisoned?*

"You're a vampire too?"

I didn't hear doubt in his tone that I was one—he spoke like a well-mannered gentleman.

A polite vampire? "Yes, I am." I hoped our similarity would bring him comfort, lessen the pain I heard in his voice. It surprised me, how normal I imagined him to be—like me. The ease of a conversation with a purebred vampire was natural. Even locked up, this vampire seemed tamer than the one I met at the motel.

"But you have a heartbeat?" I imagined him raising his brows. There was a hint of hope, even compassion, in the way he asked the question. The serum must have completely worn off. I wasn't expecting my other half to be revealed so soon—especially to a real vampire.

"Yes." I hesitated, not wanting to shock him—or make him hungrier for human blood than he probably already was. Not that there was much blood left in me—just enough to survive; enough to keep my heart beating. "I'm a little different from a regular vampire."

"How different?" His voice was still quiet, full of anticipation.

"I'm also half human."

Tiny clatters as pebbles fell from the ceiling, the sound spreading like a tsunami through the barren cell. I heard earthworms working their way toward the surface and demonic footsteps crossing the main hall upstairs. The occupant of the second cell was motionless. I started to wonder if the stranger was still there.

"I'm sorry. I didn't want to upset you," I said.

"You didn't." He was clearly trying to make his tone as normal as possible, but I could hear the undercurrent of excitement. I imagined him smiling.

Is he really that hungry? Have they not fed him here? "Look, don't try to break through your cell to get to me," I blurted. "You'll die. Even if you could, I'm still a vicious vampire. I'm sure I'm stronger than you." My rambling most likely undermined my warning, but I did feel bad for the stranger and didn't want him to get hurt.

"It's okay, I don't want your blood," he assured me. "I'm just a little surprised. There've been different creatures imprisoned here, but none of them as interesting. What is your name?"

He thought I was interesting. Of course he would. There was only one other half-breed in the world.

"Sarah," I answered. "I haven't known exactly who I am for very long."

"What do you eat?" My sensitive ears heard the fifth disc in his neck crack as he cocked his head to the side.

"Any human food, and blood—but I stick to animals. No human blood for me." I shivered.

"What do you look like?" I heard the smile in his voice again. My story must be intriguing him.

"Well, I'm five-six; I have turquoise eyes, caramel skin and wavy auburn hair." I heard him sigh pleasantly. *What a weird way to talk about myself.* "I look pretty young for twenty-one, but I do age. I'm not sure how that works, exactly, but I do age." It was oddly comforting, talking to this neighbour I'd just met.

"Of course you would. You're half human."

My heart warmed unexpectedly. "Why are you here?" I asked, hoping he would be as generous with his answers as I was. "You said you've been here for a long time."

"I was captured by Aseret over two years ago." His voice was quiet now. "It was an ambush on one of our northern clans. Demons and vampires had an agreement that allowed them to coexist. Each stayed off the other's territory and respected boundaries. Vampires lived on the northern continents. Demons thrived in the warmer climates of the south, feeding on the heat and Earth's energy to grow stronger. But they thirsted for more and more power as they began eliminating vampires.

The attack was quick. There were so many of them. That's how I ended up here."

"Where's here?" I asked.

"We're under Yellowstone National Park."

Now my trip with the demons made sense. I should have recognized the heavy odour of sulphur. We must have travelled in a time vortex, going almost back to Pinedale.

"Before my time, when vampires and demons lived in harmony, Aseret was a good warlock taught by their leader, Castall," my neighbour continued. "Aseret decided to strike out on his own. He wanted power and knew how to get it. When he became a demon, he upset the balance in the underworld, a balance that has not been altered for thousands of years. Aseret recruited frail warlocks and created an army. The weak-minded warlocks who couldn't manage spells too well turned vicious. Aseret promised powers beyond their imagination, and they followed him. He wants to overcome the vampires; if he succeeds, overpowering other creatures will be easy." I heard another crack in his neck as he lowered his head.

"But good warlocks still exist. They can help." I tried to revive the vampire's spirit.

"Yes, some remained good, like Castall, serving Earth the way they were meant to." He drew a deep breath.

I liked this vampire. And the human virtues I heard in his story.

"Castall gave me the love of my life in exchange for a promise," he continued. "We fought alongside the keepers without realizing they had a grander plan for us."

The story sounded familiar and intriguing. It was striking a nerve inside my heart. My focus on the vampires' connection to Castall broke as a strange feeling developed that I was slowly becoming involved in the tale. I imagined the vampire sitting beside me.

"Go on," I encouraged my neighbour.

"We decided to split up. I'd run, making sure the seekers only followed me. I easily misled them—the young ones are not too smart. My wife went to a safe place, where she gave birth to our daughter. She . . . died. Her name was Saraphine. My name is Ekim."

CHAPTER 16

"Ekim," I repeated. A hush spread through the cell, so profound it bounced off the walls and came back to my ears. Shivers passed over my skin, then deepened to trembling. When I tried to speak again, I couldn't. My lips felt glued together. The sound built up in my throat, increasing in pressure but unable to escape. My heart raced; I feared I'd faint. The tiny cell seemed to shrink, the walls closing in.

When the first wave of shock wore off, I was overwhelmed with happiness, not only relieved that I wasn't alone, but that I had a better ally here than I'd thought. My breathing quickened, running wild until my lips finally parted to let out some air, releasing the mounting pressure.

My chest tightened, and my eyes welled up. Until now, I'd thought my heart was only composed of the two halves; mine and William's. But now there was a third part. How I wished William was as close as my father was; how I wished I could share this moment with him.

I wanted to say the first words to my father that I'd practiced so many times, but before I could, I saw a flash of bright beams centered between two figures standing at opposite ends of a large hall, their arms outstretched. Streams of light flowed from their palms, one fiery red, the other cold blue; their exerted power met in the center of the hall in a dazzling flash of energy, a beautiful but dangerous display of power. The energy fed me more information from the vision.

The flame-red palms shook as their owner, Aseret, shrieked in happiness. The other hands were steady, despite the frail appearance of the man. He was tall and thin, with long, silvery-gray hair and pale, wrinkled skin. The vision turned both men around, and now I saw eyes full of wisdom, concentration, and peace. There was no fierceness in the old man's expression as in Aseret's, only composure and certainty. He looked more like a warlock than a demon. Castall.

"Run, now!" he yelled—and I was back in my small and gloomy cell.

Unable to gather the pieces of this future, I concentrated on the present. I managed to release some words from the back of my throat. "Are you . . . my . . ." I hesitated; saying "father" felt foreign. I decided not to ask, but to say it, hoping it would be true. "You are my father."

I held my breath, praying no one was pulling a prank or casting a spell.

"Yes, Sarah." Ekim's voice was soft, though louder and happier than before. "I am. I was hoping we would meet one day, but under more pleasant circumstances," he added ruefully.

"Why are they holding you here?" I'd thought my first words to my father would include something like "I missed you" or "I'm sorry I judged you," but although he was biologically my father, he was still a stranger in my world. No, he was new in my life.

"I'm here as bait. Aseret wants power, and the only way for him to get it is through you and William."

"You know William?" I already knew the answer, but I couldn't pass up the opportunity to say his name out loud.

"I do."

"We were supposed to rescue you," I said, dejected.

"Good job. Did William come up with that brilliant plan?"

I chuckled, then covered my mouth for a second to regain my composure. "We both did."

"You shouldn't be here, Sarah." His voice sounded muffled, and I imagined him placing his head in his palms.

"It was the only way to find you, and William's parents." I leaned my elbows on my knees.

"It's too dangerous for you to be here." Ekim's frail voice fell by an octave.

"Aseret seems to think I'm useless." I lowered my head.

"He lied. If he thought you were useless, he would not have allowed you to live."

"How are we supposed to help the underworld if we're not here?" My hands flew up in the air.

"Is that what Castall told you? That you have to be here to save the underworld?"

"Not in those exact words."

"I see."

"Are you mocking me?" I tilted my head to the side.

"Do you want me to mock you?"

Our bickering seemed so natural. *Has he really been gone all my life?*

"I'm sorry," we said at the same time.

"I just wish you were back on Earth." His words were heartfelt and sad. His love was clear in every syllable. "You're in danger here."

I sighed. "I have so many questions. I don't know where to start."

"Let me explain," he offered.

I nodded. "Please."

A pause, then after a long exhale he continued. "Your life must have been confusing and lonely. I'm sorry for that, but it was for your protection. We did everything to make sure Aseret couldn't get his hands on you and William. The day I met your mother, there were spells and curses already cast that would change our fates forever." I heard defeat and loss in his voice. "I remember 1856 as if it were yesterday. William's father and I were not yet best friends when we saw two beauties out in the field picking flowers. We were merely hunting companions and, at that time, happy two victims had strolled by instead of one. Otherwise we would have fought over who'd get the kill."

My skin crawled at the word "kill." Before I accepted my other half, that was the side of vampire's nature I feared most.

"We stood at the edge of the forest, hearing the thump of two young, strong hearts. The warm blood flowing through their veins sounded like a stream of fresh water that would quench our week-long thirst."

I'd felt the kind of thirst he spoke of—but never for humans. It made my stomach grumble again, and I wondered how long it had been since Ekim fed.

"Before we could strike, a rainbow of colourful lights flowed toward us. The impact of the stream sent us flying back into the bushes." He laughed. "When we stood up, all we could smell was . . . serenity."

Castall's spell, I remembered.

"The women came to our aid thinking we were hurt. Our thirst wasn't gone, but . . . we couldn't. Their beauty overpowered our hunger, and the scent of their skin woke up urges we'd long forgotten. We wanted to protect them, to know them, to be with them in every way possible— we'd instantly fallen in love with the two humans." He paused. "The change was more than falling in love; we had transformed. Our perception of this world cleared. We were no longer the monsters people thought us to be." I heard his smile that the memory conjured in his voice.

"You became more mortal than many humans I'd met," I said. My father's passion and devotion for his new life wrapped around me like a hand-woven blanket.

"The four of us lived undercover but at peace with humans—we became vampires with human virtues. We had another chance at the life we'd lost so long ago."

I heard a thump and imagined him straighten his curled legs onto the floor as he probably recalled the life he'd lost. My father's sacrifice and devotion to protect me had cost him his life.

"You're a good vampire," I said quietly.

"Yes, you could say that, but I wasn't always that way. I hurt and killed many people. I could see how it frightened you when you found out about me being a vampire." His voice fell to a shameful whisper. Ekim's pain for what he had done would never go away. He would forever be filled with guilt over what he had done before the spell, haunted by unforgiving memories. I knew that pain too well.

Could I change the way he feels about himself? Will he ever forgive himself?

"I understand now." I spoke like a mother to a child whose wrong doing was justified.

The cells quieted, and I felt warmed by my father's story and the chance I had to relive my parents' lives through him.

After a while, Ekim resumed his story. "We stayed at a cabin in the Amazon, trying to remain off Aseret's radar, working on the serums. We learned how to survive on animal blood, how to contain the burning in our throats. Our wives helped us realize there was nothing wrong with being immortal. Differences are unique, essential for the world to function. If everyone were the same, there would be no inventions, no art, and no music. Life would not evolve, societies would not progress."

"I blamed you for making me different when all you wanted to do was protect me, for our family to survive." I lowered my head.

"You didn't know the truth, and I'm sorry for that," he answered modestly. I wanted to say it wasn't his fault, but he continued, "The war in the underworld continued. Saraphine, your mother and Willow, William's mother wanted families. So did Atram and I, but conception was impossible for vampires. We worked on the serums, but our dead cells were incompatible with human ones until we found the blue orchid." My father must have stood up as I'd heard him shuffle his feet from one end of the cell to the other.

"Its potency gave life to the dead cells," I realized. Human and vampire cells compromised, and two became one.

"You've done your homework." I pictured him grin. "We thought the serums controlled our appetite, not the spells, until Castall, a good warlock chosen to bring a prophecy to fruition, came to see us to explain we would help to restore the balance and bring peace to the underworld. He told us we had a mission to help save the human beings and the vampires from the demons. We felt obligated to help. If it hadn't been for him and the keepers, we'd never get a chance at love." I heard him swallow.

I swelled with pride. My father was braver than I could have imagined, even for a vampire.

"If you met in 1856, how did our mothers live so long?" I asked.

"The spell altered more than me and Atram; it slowed Saraphine's and Willow's aging process as well. That's why you seem so young as well, don't you."

"Yes," I whispered, mesmerised by my father's story and his hoarse voice. William and I are a part of this prophecy?" I asked to confirm what I knew and felt inside.

"Yes."

The scrambled words suddenly shifted on the sheer green force field.

"Why doesn't Aseret just kill us?" I asked.

"I'm not sure."

I sighed. "Everything is so complicated."

"It will all work out." I pictured him smiling. "You're more important than you think."

"I wish I had you in my life. All my life," I admitted.

"I'm sorry you didn't. I wanted to come back to raise you so you wouldn't have doubts. I wanted your life to be easier." His voice sounded so sorrowful. I envisioned him hunched on the cold floor, hugging his knees tightly, grieving for the years he'd been without his family. "When you were still an infant would have been a perfect time to come back" He sighed. "I went to a warlock stronghold I thought was still under Castall's control to ensure I wouldn't interfere with the prophecy. I wanted to ask if it was safe for me to come home, but Aseret turned out to be my welcoming party. The seekers captured me."

I covered my mouth with my hand at the thought of the seeker's scorching palms on my father's shoulders.

"I'm surprised your watchers couldn't keep you safe, as they promised," Ekim said, his voice carrying an undercurrent of disapproval.

"Mira and Xander?" I asked.

"Yes."

"It's not their fault. We fled too quickly. I didn't even know we were leaving Pinedale until we were doing so."

"Still, it was their job. How did the seekers find you?"

"I reduced my serum so my heartbeat gave me away. William came just in time. We thought we had escaped, but I accidentally left a photo of the cabin at work. That's how they found out where we'd gone—and here I am."

The disc in his neck cracked again when his head came up. "Seekers found the cabin? After you escaped?" He sounded anxious.

"Yes." I lowered my head.

"Why didn't you run again?"

"We didn't want to hide. We'd made preparations to follow them to the underworld to find you, and William's parents."

"You knew they were coming?"

My gaze instinctively roved around my cell. I dropped my voice. "I have visions. They seem to come and go when I'm either relaxed or frightened. We thought we could outsmart them."

I explained William's and my gifts and what it meant for us, as well as our connection. Ekim didn't speak, but I could feel his smile in the newfound energy radiating from his cell.

"You're in love?" he asked.

I jerked back, then exhaled. If I had enough blood in my body, I would have blushed. "Yes . . . but we can't be together."

"Have faith that it will work out," he assured me. "Things happen for a reason. Perhaps it will make you stronger. Maybe it's for the best— for now."

"For now," I repeated. It was easy to speak about William to my father—a father I'd just met, but who had so much wisdom and understanding. *How could I have judged him so poorly, before I even knew him?*

"That's how I know William will find me," I continued. "When he does, he'll get us out and we'll find his parents."

"That may not be easy," he warned. "William's parents are in the other two cells. The spell keeping them locked sealed our communication. Aseret must be slipping. He didn't cast the same spell for your cell. I believe his energy has weakened with you here." He paused and added thoughtfully, "Or maybe he *wants* us to think he's slipping."

"I had another vision." I explained my latest one to him.

"Castall . . . He'll face off against Aseret." My father's voice vibrated. "Things are going to get a lot more dangerous than I thought," my father finished in a grim tone.

"Why's that?"

"Castall has been trying to bring Aseret down for over a hundred years. Both are strong. Those beams you saw were raw energy; if anyone crosses them, they'll disintegrate. If the two streams remain connected too long, Castall and Aseret will be overpowered. Everyone close by will die." His voice quavered, and he drew a breath to calm it. "Whoever gives up first will die. If neither gives up, they'll both die."

"I will not let my family die!" I growled, feeling the contours of my face tighten to a vampire's. When my fangs ejected, I was ready and my lip did not bleed.

"I know you won't. You're as strong as your mother and so Aseret fears you."

At that moment, I wished I knew what our prophecy had in store for us. I rested my head against the stone wall again, feeling oddly comfortable. Like I belonged here, like it was my calling to be here, with William at my side.

Where is he?

CHAPTER 17

Night crept in. A grey cloud of smoke continued to drift from the cabin. William sat on the remains of the front porch steps. The crackling of the smouldering fire had died down, leaving ash, charred wood, and a blackened beam outline of the scorched cabin. The first wave of the tropical storm had passed.

The sound of footsteps approaching instantly alerted him.

William had hoped the siblings would find him and Sarah after they'd returned from the underworld—together. That was not to be the case.

"I was wondering when you'd get here," he called toward the forest in a low voice.

"Where's Sarah?" Xander snapped, stopping inches from William's face.

"They got her," he whispered, his voice heavy as failure tore through his body in ripples.

"You said you would protect her! That you'd let us know if there was danger!" Mira visibly struggled to be rational. Her anger surfaced, and muscles tensed, stiffening all joints.

"I did. I thought we'd be safe. We took precautions. Didn't you get my messages?" He quickly recapped the events of the past few weeks, and that he and Sarah wanted to save his captured parents.

"We left as soon as we discovered you were gone. The seekers were right behind you until the airport and then lost your trail. We had to rely on Harlow to find you," she explained.

The falcon overhead shrieked as if it understood that he was part of the conversation.

Mira wanted to seem calm, but had no control. Small spots sprinkled her face, and her skin took on a green colour. This would have normally amused William, but when Sarah was in danger, it sickened him. William let his shoulders droop, leaned forward, and ran his hands through his hair, wanting to pull it out in frustration. There was nothing he wouldn't do to have Sarah back.

"Safe?" Xander pointed his finger at William. "You were planning to take Sarah to the underworld to rescue your parents. Couldn't you have left this place? You knew they were coming!"

"She'd learned. She was stronger than Ekim and Atram combined." Saying his father's name meant more to William than simply calling him *father*.

The siblings fell quiet. The odd crackle of burnt wood echoed in the clearing. Each time William thought about Sarah's kidnapping it hurt more, and he ached with loss. He'd underestimated the seekers' cunning.

"It's all my fault." William dropped to his knees on the soft dirt and ash forest floor. He could hardly keep himself from breaking into uncontrollable moans again, but he needed to appear strong. The siblings were not cowards. "How could I have allowed it to happen?" he groaned.

"Hell, it is your fault!" Xander growled ,looming uncomfortably close to him. Hands on his hips, he straightened and sniffed the air. "How many were there?"

"Three."

"They're covering their tracks with something. Their stench is diluted."

"Ekim will not be happy with us," Mira said to her brother, swinging her arms up in defeat. "For twenty years, we've kept her safe—twenty years! You've known Sarah for a few weeks, and you act like you know what's best for her. I should have never left the store that day! I should have known you'd screw it up the minute you came to Pinedale."

William's lip quivered as he held back a growl.

"Ekim will be furious." Xander spoke with authority and purpose. He was the quieter of the two, but very intimidating. "Couldn't you have asked us to come with you?" He finally stepped back, scouring the forest with his gaze.

"There was no time. How do you think Sarah would feel after finding out that the two people she trusted were someone else?" William said.

Xander gaped at him. "You're underestimating Sarah's intelligence," he hissed through clenched teeth, turning a shade of green like his sister.

"Don't taunt me! I did what I had to protect her. Who knows what would have happened if I didn't get her in time."

"Boys, control your testosterone!" Mira snarled, shifting her stance and squaring her shoulders, reminding William of a grizzly preparing to rear. She glowered at him. "For your information, Sarah was ready to confide in me."

"After twenty¬ years—wow, you're good!" William sneered, distress overtaking his usual politeness.

"Watch your mouth!" Xander's said through his tightened jaw.

"Stop hissing and step away!" William growled back, showing his fangs.

Magic rippled through Xander's muscles.

He'd be fun to fight, but it wouldn't be an easy fight. William cocked his head to the side.

Xander mimicked the movement.

"Okay, stop it, you guys! There's no time for that now. Let's find Ekim. He'll know what to do," Mira ordered, sounding calmer. Her composure soothed her brother, whose muscles softened.

"Ekim is gone," William explained. "That's why we wanted to go to the underworld."

"Gone where?" asked Xander.

"We think he's been kidnapped by Aseret. Don't you think Ekim would have been here, sensing how your protection failed?" William purposely shifted the guilt but regretted his cowardice as soon as he said it. "I'm sorry. I didn't—"

"Go on," Mira interrupted as the downpour started again. The forest canopy didn't let much rain through, and the drumming of raindrops on the foliage relieved the tension. Black smoke rose from the skeleton of the cabin, fading to gray as it floated toward the tree house.

"My parents were working on a plan to rescue him, but they couldn't get through to the underworld."

"I told you the rumours were true," Mira said to her brother.

"What rumours?" William asked.

"That the underworld is sealed by a spell. Those who live there are supposed to stay there and those who live here are supposed to stay here. Only select seekers can pass through," Mira began to bite her nails.

"Was that the force field that kept me away from Sarah?" Every time William spoke her name, pain throbbed through his limbs. His heart changed its beat, and he sensed she thought about him as well.

"The force field is the protective layer between Earth and the underworld. It keeps Aseret bound to the underworld. His warlocks must have found a way to break through." Mira scratched her head.

"No, that wasn't it. They drew a line in front of me. I couldn't pass through its energy."

"Aseret's powers have grown." Xander looked at his sister with worry.

"You think?" William sneered, once again unable to contain his sarcasm.

"Did the seekers say anything?" Mira asked in a calmer voice. She was clearly trying to move the discussion forward and was right to do so. Bickering would not find Sarah any sooner.

William sensed her heartbeat diminishing; its beating almost resembled a hummingbird's.

Worried, he began pacing back and forth. "The only thing they said that we could understand was, 'The shield won't let you through. Not now,'" William repeated, not bothering to mimic the mockery in the seeker's voice.

"What did they mean by 'not now'? Would it let you through another time?" Mira was smarter than her Barbie-like appearance projected.

Not now . . . Not now that I know? What if I didn't know it was there, could I pass through it then?

"I'm sure the seekers did not drive here, and I'm sure they didn't run, either." Mira's brother chose his words carefully as he paced three steps one way, then back. He shifted for a moment to a wolf and sniffed the ground. Then, he changed into a squirrel, leaping through the canopy. Finally, he jumped down to the ground, denting the ashed footing. Xander's seamless ability to adapt to his surroundings astonished William. The shapeshifter removed his shoes and pulled his feet across the ashen grass that began to turn to paste. "They must have entered the forest through a different passage in the force field. The doors stay open for forty-eight hours after they're created. Nature won't allow them to be closed too quickly after such an alteration to the natural world." He scanned the forest, looking composed and calm. Suddenly, the corners of his mouth curved up to a grin. "If you could not pass through the force field when you knew about it, could you pass through one when you didn't know about it?"

"Perhaps." William straightened his back.

Xander continued pacing, gently rubbing his chin with his hand; he resembled Sherlock Holmes. "If there is another doorway the seekers used, we may have a chance. But we have to find it without knowing." He waved his index finger to emphasize his point. "All we have to do is walk into an invisible wall. And it has to be quick. If we're not too late already"

"It's the only chance we've got." Hope returned to William's eyes, aparkling at its rims.

"Let's go, then!" Mira squealed with enthusiasm. "I'm sure not gonna let our only door to the underworld expire, are you?"

Xander beamed with excitement.

Losing Sarah had robbed William of his strength. Now, he felt himself regain some, along with anticipation.

William gathered rope and harnesses from the tree house and securied it to himself and the siblings. They followed the same circular pattern the seekers had used to search the grounds, but in a wider perimeter around the cabin. For the plan to work, they had to stay together. If one of them accidentally hit the doorway, the others had to be pulled in without realizing it.

Coordinated, Mira and her brother followed William's footsteps like shadows. As soon as he lifted his right foot, Mira's left was in its place. When William lifted his left foot, her brothers' right one took the spot. Moving clockwise, they covered the ground quickly, searching a twenty-mile radius in the first ten minutes.

After the halfway point, as they passed the eighth mile at the river's edge, an overgrown cliff blocked their path. The vegetation made it almost invisible, making it appear as if the rainforest continued into its depth.

William tilted his head back and examined the steep rock face. "How well can you climb?" The siblings had great speed and with their upper body strength, William was confident they could scale rock walls as well.

"As fast as you can! You won't even notice we're following you," Xander insisted.

Anchoring his hand on the moss-covered rocks, William put his body weight on it and extended his leg to climb up—and fell forward. The siblings landed on top of him.

"Ouch!" Mira grunted, her elbow jabbing into William's ribcage as she tried to stand.

Xander struggled on the other side.

"Sorry. Let's try this again." William brushed the soil off his pants and looked up, realizing they were not longer in the rainforest.

They were in the underworld.

"That was unexpected." Mira examined the wall of the tunnel they fell through.

"That was the point." William smiled. They were one step closer to Sarah. He listened to the rhythm of her heart and heard her subtle warning; he also heard the sounds of footsteps headed toward them. Rushing to untie the harness, he added, "We have to hurry. Seekers are coming." But Mira and Xander were already on alert, their muscles ripened.

The low ceiling made it difficult to stand tall. The siblings shifted, adjusting their height for comfort. The dank, dim tunnel was claustrophobically narrow. Its uneven floor was slippery from moisture. The trio took a few wobbly steps, hands reaching for the earthen walls as they found their balance. The corridor had just enough space for two people to squeeze through at the same time. As they walked toward its end, a reddish-orange glow brightened into a shining doorway, and a hint of aloe and vanilla fragrance wafted.

Sarah, William's heart skipped a beat. "It hasn't been long. I can still smell her. They came back to this tunnel," he said with certainty as the distinctive bitter, dirty sock odour of the seekers melded with hers. He swished the saliva in his mouth as the smell settled on William's tongue.

"The glow must lead to the passage door." Xander stepped closer to the fiery opening. "It should lead us into Aseret's dungeons. That's where they've taken her; I can feel it."

They stood at the fiery door, mouths slightly open, staring at the glowing oval. The heat was intense and the blaze looked real—a perfect entrance into hell.

"It shouldn't burn you," Mira said.

William lifted his eyebrows. "Shouldn't?"

"It's the first time I've seen one too. Besides, you said Sarah passed through one, so we'll be fine too." Mira stood tall, almost looking confident. Her head bumped the low ceiling. She didn't twitch.

"What about the force field?" William asked, not wanting to bounce off one again.

"Underground, the doors remain open. There is no longer a need for a force field. It's only intended to keep out enemies."

"Couldn't a human fall into the doorway unknowingly?"

"I don't think so. You have to be mythical, or *different,* to pass through. And you can't get any more different than us!" Xander stepped forward. The closer he moved toward the glow, the wider his grin became. Being underground stimulated instincts he hadn't used in a long time. Living in an ordinary world was difficult for a shapeshifter. In the underworld you could meet anyone, face off against anyone. It wasn't hard to find adventure if you wanted it. Xander lifted his foot and thrust it forward; it disappeared into the fire. Then his arms and the rest of his torso vanished.

"Show off," Mira muttered.

"Let's go." William followed Xander through the doorway. There was no burning, no heat, no pain.

In the next few minutes, the trio passed through eighteen tunnels and doorways until William's shoulder heated painfully.

"There you are." The demon laughed, pressing his hot claw harder against his shoulder, dragging him down to his knees.

The siblings whirled and Mira disappeared.

"I wouldn't do that if I were you," Xander warned with a grin. His neck stiffened.

"I'll kill him before you can move. Where's the other one?" the demon demanded.

Xander didn't move.

Suddenly, the heat was gone from William's shoulder. He leaped to his feet, but the demon had vanished. Mira stood in his place, hands on her hips. She thrust her chin out as black ash remains settled on the floor. "We couldn't protect Sarah from the seekers, huh?"

"How'd you do that?" he asked.

"We're more than just watchers, William, remember that." For the first time, just for a moment, William noticed purple sparks in her eyes.

"Coming?" Xander called, still grinning.

They stepped through the next opening into a corridor. The orange glow vanished. A few more paces took them into a large hall with a fire blazing pit at its center.

Aseret's hall. Shivers passed through William's body. His heart fought his mind's strong urge to run. This was where nightmares were made: a place of tortured black souls. Traces of fear and pain of its victims still hovered in the hot air. The strongest vampire would cringe at the thought of fighting against Aseret or his army of demonically powered zombies.

The hall loomed with eerie silence. "Where is everyone?" William's quiet voice bounced off the high ceiling, echoing a few seconds later.

"Hold on." Mira closed her eyes. She reopened them and squinted. Her twitching nose was now pointy, and her mouth had shrunk as she locked her eyes with a mouse surreptitiously feeding on a moth. The vermin ran toward a staircase, veering past the steps to dart through a small hole in the wall. A minute later, it came back, twitching its nose in the same way Mira did. The mouse squeaked.

Mira looked at William. "They're collecting energy. We have a few minutes before the first seekers show up."

"Impressive. Can it lead us to Sarah?" he asked.

"Of course." She squeaked quietly, and the mouse set off; they followed it through the second entrance to the right. It scampered down a circular stone staircase which led to a dungeon. The hallway was unkempt and dank, with hundreds of openings on both sides, though all were without doors. Some of them were empty; others had a flowing green substance, like fog, sealing their entrances.

"I'll stay back to keep an eye out," Mira volunteered, then nodded toward the mouse. "She said there's no other exit." She twitched her nose at the mouse, and it skittered across the slimy floor, scampering up the stairs.

William and Xander moved closer to the cells. The fog-like coatings over the entries streamed in many directions, swirling with scrambled words they couldn't understand.

"You said she'd be in the third cell, right?" Xander asked.

William peered closely at the sheer green fields. "Yes. Look!" He pointed toward the words floating over the surface of the third doorway. "There's Sarah's name—she has to be in there."

His heart rate sped up. Adrenaline filled his veins. He closed his eyes and listened to the heart that had stolen his. When he heard a pattern of identical beating, William sprinted toward the third opening.

"Wait!" Xander threw his arm out in front of William whose nose nearly touched the green field. "Are you crazy?"

"There's no time to waste," William retorted.

"This green field is a protective spell. It could kill you!"

"What do you mean it could?" William cupped his hands around his face, trying to see through the barrier, but it may as well have been solid. "Sarah? Can you hear me?"

"Some can kill on touch, and others can't," Xander explained. "Do you want to find her only for her to see you dead?"

"No." William took a reluctant step back. "What do we do, then?"

"I don't know," Xander admitted.

"Hurry up, you two," Mira called from the entrance to the dungeon.

Frustrated, William glanced at the corridor, then back at the green field.

Concentrate, William, concentrate!

Jamming his hands into his pockets, he paced three steps one way, then back, fumbling absently with the shiny crystal from Castall when he remembered. "Sarah! Use your stick!"

Xander looked at him as if he were looking at a madman.

William just waited. Nothing happened. He pulled the crystal from his pocket and held it out in front of the fogged coating. He'd hoped it was transparent on the other side.

A deep sigh resonated from the inside of the cell, and Sarah's heartbeat quickened and grew louder with joy and happiness.

CHAPTER 18

The wait was over. William was here, only a few hours after I'd been taken. My eyes squeezed shut, and I rubbed them with my fists, then opened them, trying to focus. I had to make sure the pounding in my chest was true.

William and Xander stood side by side in front of my cell. The walls around me moved away, and the room was again merely small. I'd expected us to be apart much longer. *He's here, now!*

My pulse strained to survive on the few drops of blood in my veins. I couldn't wait to be held in William's arms and inhale his intoxicating musky fragrance, yet the vivid memory of the electric zap frustrated me.

"William's here," I said as loud as I dared to Ekim, not wanting the demons to hear. "With Xander!"

"I see," he answered, without enthusiasm. "That was quick. Too quick. Things don't come that easily in life. I wonder—"

"They're special. We're special. That's why they're quick!" I stared at William who waved his arms up and down and moved his lips in slow motion, as if he were trying to exaggerate what he was saying so I'd understand. "Ekim, can you read lips?"

"I wish I could."

"I can't hear what William is saying. How are they going to get us out?" I turned my head toward my father as if there weren't a wall between us.

"He's doing something. Look at his hand."

William pulled his crystal out of his pocket and held it up, pointing eagerly and lifting his eyebrows like a maniac.

"Use it—he's saying use it, Sarah!"

I knew exactly what to do and hit the bottom of my stick against the wall once, then a second time. A small orange glow materialized at its end.

"It will show you the way out when there is none," Castall had told me. I drew a five-foot oval on the wall of our adjoining cells, the same way the seekers had in the tunnels with their canes, then stepped through it.

Ekim pushed to his feet, arms open. "Sarah!" Tears probably would have rolled down his youthful but tired face, but there was no moisture left in his body.

"Father!" I nearly ran over the tall, frail man and embraced him. His bones pressed against my body as we hugged, his prominent cheekbones dug into my face, his ribs, his sharp elbows and bulging kneecaps all stuck out—he was malnourished. Two rat carcasses lay in the corner of the cell.

I closed my eyes. A rush of energy took me to a different place. A dark labyrinth of narrow corridors appeared in my mind—a maze. I followed a blonde woman freed from the first cell in the dungeon. She was an inch shorter than me. William walked behind me, and I heard the footsteps of others further back. The woman turned at some corners and walked past others, leading us out of the underworld. When she stopped, we faced two exits. One led up and was as bright as daylight; the other led downward, into darkness.

The vision ended, and I found myself in Ekim's embrace. We were too close for him to have noticed my closed eyes, and I was glad; I couldn't think about the vision now—I was hugging my *father*.

Pulling away slightly, I looked at him. His colourless flesh almost glowed. Even vampires, although pale, had some tinge of colour in their skin. Ekim was completely white, drained. I hid my concern when he took my face in his hands.

"Honey, you're so beautiful! You look just like your mother!" He hugged me again, squeezing me against his cold body. I'd never felt a vampire's hug, but this felt natural and, despite his painful thinness and sharp bones, unexpectedly comfortable. "I've waited so long to see you, to hold you." Guilt and remorse shook his words, a deep regret at missing all the years we could never get back.

I swallowed through my dry throat, feeling overwhelming shame. Besides Helen, he was the only relative I had ever known. *How could I have ever thought so wrongly of him?*

Unable to contain the tears flowing down my cheeks, I had to make a confession. "I'm sorry. I didn't mean to ki— She's gone because of me . . ." I broke down sobbing.

"It's okay. It's all right. You couldn't have known," he soothed, stroking the top of my head. Then he thumped his right fist against the middle of his chest.

The gesture was familiar. My mother had done the same before dying. "You will always be here," she'd said.

"Look at your freckles. They're just like Saraphine's." He brushed his fingers on my cheek.

Would I be a constant reminder of what he had lost?

"I've waited so long to see you. Your mother would have been proud of you."

I pushed my worry aside. I would be what he had gained . . . and vice versa.

He dropped his gaze and pointed at the glowing stick I held. "Now, that's one worthy gift you've got in your hand."

"Castall." I smiled.

"What do you say we get out of here? I think they're getting impatient."

I looked toward our rescuers. His eyes narrowed, William glanced from my old cell to my father's, his brows narrowing in confusion.

"You go ahead through my cell; I have a couple more people to free," I began drawing an oval on the next wall in Ekim's cell. "I'll join you in a sec."

"I'm not leaving your side for a moment." My father stepped beside me.

The new circle singed the rocky wall, and we crossed cautiously inside the adjoining room, where a man and a woman sat hunched on the floor. The man had his arms around his partner. They rubbed their eyes, blinking at the orange glow behind us. Crumbs and food scraps littered the floor inside their green barrier. My stomach growled, but I didn't have the appetite to eat. It seemed the woman had been fed well during her imprisonment, but the man—a vampire—was half-starved and almost as white as Ekim. I wondered how long a vampire could go on without food before becoming a comatose ghost.

That's when I realized Aseret hoped the vampire would give in to his hunger and attack his love. The warlock knew nothing of love, nothing about sacrifice and devotion.

"Atram . . . Willow," Ekim whispered.

"Ekim!" They struggled to their feet to embrace their friend.

After their reunion, Willow focused on me. It felt as if my body was melting under her gaze, and it took me a moment to recognize the care and love on her face—the love of a mother. "Sarah," she whispered, covering her mouth, as if her smile would somehow run away. Eyes moist, she moved tenderly toward me and placed her arms around me. She stroked my back as a mother would to comfort her child. My chin sank in her shoulder as we held each other. With Helen gone, Willow was now the closest person to a mother I would ever have.

When she pulled back, her fingers combed through my hair.

I spoke first. "Hello."

"How did you get here? You shouldn't be here," Atram whispered in concern as someone's footsteps crossed the hall above us.

Willow's hands moved up to cup my face. "We knew they'd come to save us. Oh, Sarah! You're more beautiful than I could have imagined." She spoke my name with care, her pulse becoming loud and vibrant.

We'd heard more seekers shuffling their feet in the hall upstairs.

"Willow, Atram, we need to leave before the demons realize what we're up to. Follow me. I'll see you on the outside." My father embraced me again, then led the family through my cell, the only exit all three could take, as I stepped out of theirs, unscathed.

William pressed his lips to mine before I could speak. "I thought you said you were in the third one." He kissed my forehead, cheeks, nose, and lips. Starved for his touch, I dug my fingers into his shirt, clenching the fabric, and held until the tips of my fingers cramped. My heart ached, but the sweetness, the warmth that I'd missed, was too compelling. The pain I felt when he was away from me was fiercer than the pain from touching him.

As the jolts of electricity became unbearable, William pulled away. Ekim, Atram, and Willow had finished their rushed greetings and stood beside us.

"I was in the third one but couldn't get out," I explained.

Someone grabbed my arm from behind. Instinctively, I pulled it away, fisted, ready to punch, but I stopped mid-swing. Tall and dark, Xander's bright grin stretched his face. This was the first time I'd felt his true strength.

"Xander!" I jumped, throwing my arms around his neck.

"Hey, stranger. We need to leave now." Xander hushed with urgency.

Mira crushed into us, almost knocking down the gathered family members.

"Mira, I can't believe you're a . . . what exactly are you?" I whispered.

"No time for it now. They're coming! I'm not human, but I am your friend," she said earnestly. "Follow me." She took my hand and pulled toward the staircase as seeker voices resonated from the top of the steps.

"It's blocked." Atram looked up toward the only exit we knew.

Then I remembered. "I need to get someone from the first cell. She'll help us."

"Sarah, how could you possibly know—" William stopped. "Oh . . ."

"I'll be right back."

William caught my hand. "You're not going anywhere by yourself."

The siblings joined me and William inside the empty second cell, where I drew a new oval on the side wall. As I'd expected, a blonde woman was the prisoner. She seemed timid, her head slightly lowered and face covered in springy curls. Her well-fitted floor-length dress reminded me of Mrs. G's. A delicate aroma of red roses danced around her.

Xander stepped boldly forward, smirking as he devoured the woman with his gaze.

"Your name?" he asked.

"Alexandra. You can call me Alex. I'm a witch. Aseret imprisoned me." The woman's voice flowed in a melodious hum, as if she were singing a song; it was almost too nice.

Like a spell . . .

Mira pushed Xander's chin up to close his mouth. "Can we trust her?" she asked me.

"She'll help us find the exit. Right?" I scanned her frail body.

"Follow me." Nodding, she brushed my arm when she slipped out of the cell. A slight tremor of nerves and chills passed through me.

"Sarah, you're sure about this?" William asked carefully.

"I've already seen her help us. There's no point in wasting time."

"Let me see your wrist!" Mira ordered, holding out her hand. The trademark leather straps my friend usually wore were untied; I noticed three wavy lines on her wrist.

Alex pulled her hands out of her long-sleeved dress; seven pairs of eyes fixated on the blank spot.

Someone began descending the steps into the dungeon.

"Where's your mark?" Xander asked.

"I don't have one. I was cursed at birth," Alex explained. "I will not be marked until my destiny is decided." She looked up at us from below her long lashes.

"Don't lie. Witches are always marked at birth." Mira's jaw tightened.

"But that's why Aseret imprisoned me. I'm a cursed witch. He wanted to sway me to his side so I could get the sphere. He didn't want me to have a choice in my marking."

Xander kept his eyes locked on Alex, while everyone else exhaled with relief. My nerves never let go; there was a tight knot in my stomach, and a sharp pain came back to my chest, reminding me of my nightmare when I scarred. Shivering, I shook my arms and shoulders. The familiar ache moved up higher. I tried to suppress the distress, but the soreness on my chest intensified. My breath became shallower as I tried to quell the panic, and I fell to my knees.

William helped me up. "What's the matter? Are you hurt?"

The inhales were insufficient. I squeezed my eyes shut, waiting for the pain to go away.

"What did you do?" William demanded of the witch.

I opened my eyes.

"Nothing. It's not me." She took a step back from us.

The ache started to fade. "It's okay, I'm better. She'll help us. Follow her," I whispered pointing to Alex, and everyone focused on the slim woman again.

"One wrong move and I won't hesitate to kill you," Xander warned, his smirk long vanished.

Alex lowered her head. "This way." She led us to an unoccupied room further down the dungeon hallway.

We followed her in as I heard seekers take the last step. I had a moment of déjà vu when I crossed its threshold. The cell did not look like an exit.

Alex pressed her hands against the wall with her full weight behind them. She glided her hand over a larger stone, stroking each edge and corner as if trying to memorize its precise shape. With one strong breath, she cleaned the dust off its edges with one strong breath, then her hand went to her dress and she pulled a dagger from a concealed pocket.

William placed his arm in front of me. The siblings moved closer to my side.

The blade was paper thin at its edge. Even in the dim room, its plate reflected light in a thin, dangerous line. A red gemstone in the pommel glistened. Alex used the dagger to draw a mark on the stone. The mark shone gold, getting brighter each second, before it abruptly disappeared.

My gaze locked with William's, then turned back when I heard a low grinding of rock against rock. The wall slid back and sideways, opening a passage.

We followed her in, the stone wall quietly closing behind us.

"How did you know about it?" I asked Alex.

"This is the way they brought me in," she answered.

I wanted to trust her because I knew she would lead us to an exit, but there was something peculiar about Alex. A frown embedded on my forehead while paying attention to the witch. William's pulse raced at the same speed as mine. It thumped with worry and suspicion and I bumped his arm for an answer.

"It's not the right time," he whispered. "We'll deal with it later."

Alex led forward, her blonde curly hair bouncing from left to right as she walked with confidence. Her petite figure didn't show any signs of cruelty or distress from her captivity.

She walked quickly, aware of every turn before we reached it. The narrow tunnels of the maze weaved, widening at few points. We veered right, then left, passing through rough openings, doorways, and small halls. Most paths led up, toward the surface. The smell of sulphur intensified. The air thickened with humidity, making it difficult to breathe. We were close to a geyser or a hot spring.

"Here, cover your mouth." Atram handed Willow a handkerchief. "It shouldn't be too far now."

We came to a sudden stop before two doorways. One led upward and was as bright as daylight; the other led downward into blackness. "This way," Alex said, taking a step toward the darker one.

"That's just going to take us back," William argued.

"This is the way out," the witch said. "I'd used it before."

"Like hell, it is!" Xander growled.

Alex took a step back, and I felt sorry for her. I didn't like Xander taunting her and I didn't want her to be an outcast the way I'd been most of my life.

Mira came to my side. "Sarah, what do you think? Which exit did we take in your vision?"

"I'm not sure, but I think we should listen to her."

Willow's soft voice resonated from the back. "Sarah, darling, are you sure? Look at these exits. One clearly shows the way up to the surface, and the other one goes down toward the underworld. Why would we go into the dark one?" Willow's argument was good, but my gut told me otherwise.

William frowned. "Xander, can't you ask a mouse or a rat to lead us?"

"I would if there were any around," he answered, scanning the tunnel floor. No vermin braved scavenging in air this toxic.

"Why don't we go toward the light? We can always turn back," Mira suggested.

Everyone murmured agreement. I had my doubts about going the way my family endorsed, but I didn't completely trust Alex either.

"Fine; we'll go the way you want, but this is not the way I came in. Don't say I didn't warn you," Alex said.

We walked up the rough slope toward the light. I followed Alex with William behind me, and the others at the back. The air was just as stale here as it had been underground; I couldn't detect the fresh air I expected to blow in from the outside.

Wihout warning, Alex stopped.

"What's wrong?" I asked.

"The light . . . it doesn't look right. It doesn't have the brightness of daylight."

I focused on the dancing light ahead. Though it sparkled almost like the sun, it seemed a little different. Sunlight did not shift between light orange and yellow in an unsteady pattern. The beam of light radiated from a flickering source. We should have listened to Alex; it wasn't the outside after all.

"Turn around! Now!" I ordered.

Atram, who was the last in line, suddenly disappeared beneath the earth. Then Willow, then Ekim, Mira and Xander . . . William would be next. "No!" I shouted, reaching out to catch him before he dropped, but as soon as I flung my arm out, he vanished. Soil receded under my feet and I scrabbled and slid, falling down a steep, muddy chute.

My vampire sight could not adjust to the darkness as I skidded on my behind. Rocks scraped against my thighs with bruising force. The sound of us plummeting through the tunnel resembled that of a rock slide. The curvature of the chute was unnatural, though man-made—or demon-made.

William's body broke my landing. Alex's fall just missed me. In the strange orange glow that illuminated the area, my family stood in a line, covered in dirt and mud, their faces motionless staring past us.

I turned around to see over two hundred pairs of orange glowing eyes. Aseret smiled slyly in their midst.

CHAPTER 19

I was back at the beginning, in the large hall I'd first entered, but now I'd dragged my family into hell with me. My stomach turned inside out. The tension inside me pushed upward, and I wanted to throw up, but there was nothing in my stomach.

I can't believe I did this.

"Silly, silly creaturesss." Aseret chuckled, his head thrown back. "You thought you could essscape the underworld? Hah!" he mocked. "And take my prisonersss as well?" His gaze focused on Alex, although he no doubt meant to include everyone.

Everyone, including the witch, stood poised defensively, knees slightly bent, muscles tensed, wary eyes darting, waiting for any movement from the hundreds of Aseret's minions who watched us with predatory eyes.

"There'sss no need to be afrrraid," Aseret cooed, his words annoyingly slow. "I'm sssure we can work together. Mira, Xander, have you decided to join me?"

"You need me to even out that beauty mark for you on the other side?" Xander laughed, nodding to a pink scar behind Aseret's left ear which stretched down and disappeared beyond the cloak. He crossed his arms over his chest. "You're more delirious than I thought."

"Hmm, I guesss Daddy wouldn't apprrrove, would he?" Aseret sneered. "I can deal with that, forrr now." The sagging flesh on his wrinkled face shifted with a twitch.

"What do you want?" William asked. I knew he'd sensed the change the same way I had.

Aseret focused on him. "You're taking my prisonersss," he scolded.

"They're no longer your prisoners. They should have never been." William's tone firmed, fists clenched. He and the siblings showed no sign of fear. I was afraid, but only for my family.

"Hmm . . . That, I cannot accept, but I am willing to compromissse." Aseret's cunning voice began to dance with persuasion.

I stiffened.

Aseret pointed to William and me. "You two, for them—all of them. Their safety isss in yourrr handsss."

It was not a request; there would be no bargain. No matter what was decided, I knew Aseret wouldn't spare our family. William and I could read body language and facial expressions better than anyone. Aseret's eyes and tone were clear. He mocked us for his amusement, to see whether we'd give in.

"Over my dead body!" William said.

"That can be arranged!" Aseret threw his hands out, launching a fiery red beam toward us. I jumped away in time to avoid falling through the hole the ray burned in the floor. A river of lava flowed within the opening.

Atram and Ekim stepped in front of Willow, who needed most protection.

"I don't missss often," Aseret warned. "Think about it—you can work with me, or die here. There'sss no otherrr choice. I will get what I want."

"And that is?" I stepped forward.

"You've been holding out on me, Ssarahhh," Aseret drawled. Each word swam hypnotically out of his mouth. It had no effect on me, though, and I saw the frustration on his face. "Silly, Sarah. I've known about your powersss for a long time; I just had to figure out how best to ussse them, how to make them mine."

I didn't like him calling me silly or wanting any more power than he already had. "Even if we could, there's no way we'd give them up—especially to you."

"There's alwaysss a way, Sarah! What makes you more human makesss you weak. All you have to do is agree and I'll extrrract them from you, and your friendsss will be safe." His nose twitched. He was lying.

Aseret gestured for the seekers to surround us. Those present spread, joined by more seekers who streamed through the other four entrances. There seemed no end to the line of orange glowing eyes in front of us.

How are we going to get out of here?

But he hadn't killed us yet. Aseret would not have missed unintentionally—he wanted to scare us, not kill us. He wanted the powers—or did he? He was already strong and had an army of demons with abilities greater than ours. What did he want?

What makes us more human makes us weak . . . the serums?

"We'll never give them up!" I said to Aseret.

"Neverrr say neverrr." He laughed, almost gurgling as he tilted his head back. The hood slid off his bald head.

"Sarah, take my hand," William whispered. I placed my palm in his and felt Castall's crystal. A rush of energy flowed from William to me and from me to him. A new force rejuvenated our bodies and transferred the strength and power we each had to the other, multiplying our abilities. Light from the crystal shone from between our palms, but everyone seemed oblivious to our glowing palms.

I took a breath in, felt new vigour, felt our power magnify. For the first time, I saw through William's eyes—the concealed pain and suffering—everyone's worst fears. The phobias varied for each demon, though some repeated. From burning alive, to being torched by Aseret's hands, to long hours in a dark cell full of rats slowly nibbling at their weak bodies, the terrors made me cringe. There were many, so many I couldn't think, and I wondered how William dealt with this all the time. It must have taken a toll on his mind. My fears of small critters seemed insignificant.

William's eyes rolled back, then he closed them, and I knew he saw my visions. No one was aware of the exchange between William and me, an exchange that took seconds to complete.

I heard William's thoughts as clearly as if he were speaking to me. *Just don't think about their fear. If you do, they'll manifest into reality.*

I forced my thoughts toward bugs and critters. I preferred those over the nightmares.

"What do you fear, Aseret?" William taunted. "Us taking over? Vampires ruling the world? Losing your powers? Death?"

Aseret's face twitched and trembled faintly as he fought to keep his fears hidden. We saw horrible things as he tried to weave past what really scared him. In one phobia, Aseret was imprisoned, guarded by vampires. Then he appeared, amongst human beings, lost, unable to find his way, unable to ask for help.

"What do you fear, Aseret?" William demanded again, the echo of his voice vibrated through the hall.

Aseret struggled, hissing when he failed to block the first image. The power of the crystal combined our abilities and wrestled a clear picture from him: William stood behind me, his arms wrapped around me.

He fears us?

Aseret still fought and the vision faded out of focus.

"You're afraid of us!" William taunted, and laughed.

The image of our figures slowly turned clockwise, and we saw the secret fear Aseret had been struggling to keep hidden. William was hugging me—a nearly nine months pregnant me.

He fears our child, William whispered in his mind.

My knees almost buckled. A child! Our child!

Sarah, don't think about it. It can't happen here. Not now, and not this way. His mental voice was clear and firm.

Not now, and not this way. Hiding my happiness became a task in itself. My eyes closed for a moment, and William and I privately shared a premonition of a little boy, playing in a sandbox. He looked just like

William. Blue overalls hung on his shoulders, over a white T-shirt. Giggling, he waved his hand in front of his, nose saying, "Thop, pheese." Then a girl! She wore pink overalls and a wide smile that split her freckled face and showed off two little white teeth. Laughing at her brother, she waved a yellow daisy in front of the boy's nose. Twins!

William, they're beautiful!

A sudden burst of adrenaline shot through my body as the need to protect my future family grew. I soaked in the energy from the hot lava below us, from the thousands of lit candles, from the strength the demons were preparing to use. William did the same. Together, we became one dominant force which, through the crystal's power, created a protective shield around us, one we knew could not be penetrated, at least for a while.

We have to help them, I said to William as our family prepared for the approaching demons.

He nodded, taking a step back to include them under our shield. *We can't stay here with them. We have to fight Aseret or he'll find a way to break through the shield.*

Aseret's gaze flew from our family to us, and back, probably setting up a plan to kill us, and I doubted the protective shield could stop him. *William, can we leave the shield here?*

We can try. Think of your biggest fear as not having the shield and walk forward.

I thought of what it would be like to face Aseret without the shield's protection. I thought how vulnerable our human bodies would be. I thought about my family sizzling under the hot paws of hundreds of demons and shivered. Could I ever survive if I lost them? Would my life be emptied? I was the reason they're here! I couldn't let them die.

William nudged me forward. *It's working. Let's go.*

We left the shield behind us. *I don't think it will hold for long, but it will help.*

"Last chance!" Aseret shrieked, beginning to sound like his frenzied demons.

"Aseret, you will never lay your hands on my family! You should fear us—all of us!" William threw his shoulders proudly back.

"Harum sei mola tum!" Aseret ordered.

The demons lunged forward, but bounced back just as quickly, repelled by the shield. Each attack weakened the barrier. They tried to break through, placing their hot palms against it and singing layer after layer. With each break they made in the shield, a red circle appeared on my body, stinging like a fresh mosquito bite. The stronger seekers who passed through fought against Ekim, Atram, Mira, Xander, and Alex, all protecting Willow in their midst.

Mira and Xander vanished, then reappeared behind a demon and tore its head off. They shifted lightning fast, the body of a hawk blending into a wolf, then a mountain lion, bear, and even a small rodent.

"You are mine!"Aseret's eyes glowed brighter as each demon lost a fight, shining with greater intensity than any of the demons' orange orbs.

"Let us go if you want to live!" I threatened with all the rage I could muster as my cheeks tightened and joints locked and ready. The disks in my neck cracked, and its tendons stiffened. The veins in my face pulsed as I felt it shifted to a vampire.

Aseret stretched his arms and shot a new stream of magical fire. This time it wasn't meant to miss. The blow flew at me and William, and we sprang in the air before it hit us. We seemed to glide up in slow motion, and the blast drilled a hole where we'd stood. Two things I knew for sure—we couldn't fly, and the only way back down was into the river of molten rock Aseret's blast had opened in the floor.

Sarah, grab the chandelier, William thought as we reached the apex of our jump.

Still gripping his hand, I reached for the light fixture with my right hand, trying not to think of the fiery magma below us or the intensifying fight as the shield weakened under the demons' powers. The red spots on our bodies continued to multiply as if we'd been exposed to a plague.

Mira and Xander shifted so quickly they couldn't be out manoeuvred by any demon. Their powerful blows grounded their attackers.

Look! I pointed to a grinning Aseret. He wiggled his fingers gathering energy into his palm. The electricity weaved around his hand. A new fire ball formed as he prepared to strike us again.

Swing the chandelier, Sarah. Maybe we can make it to the staircase.

We rocked our bodies and swung our legs forward, then back. The chandelier did not move. Hot wax dripped onto our shoulders.

Swing harder! Use your strength! There's much more in you, I can feel it! William encouraged.

My focus turned to the energy around us, especially on the warm crystal. The chandelier started to rock. I pushed forward. It swayed more. In seconds, we swung back and forth, as if hanging on to a large pendulum.

"I didn't want it to end this way. We could have worked together!" Aseret released another beam of energy toward us.

Let go! William yelled.

But Aseret had calculated our trajectory and sent another fire stream where we would touch down.

I braced to take the hit but landed on the ground. "What the—"

William stared and I followed his gaze to a new, blue stream of light, which came Castall's palms to intercept Aseret's. He stood at the opposite end of the hall, close to our family. The continuous flow of magical light from both the warlock and the demon connected in the middle. My earlier premonition was playing itself out.

A flash of bright light grew between them, just above the fire pit, as they shifted to direct the energy toward each other. Castall's blue stream radiated cold through the hall, but he controlled the power. The two ribbons of light created a dangerous display of fireworks where they connected. I fed on that energy, remembering what my father had said.

Palms trembling, Aseret shrieked, then threw his head back in laughter. Castall's hands maintained their dominating patience as he yelled. "Run, now!"

"We won't be able to get through all of them." William pointed to the demons blocking our way.

"Jump—it's quicker." I said.

"On three."

"One—two—three!" we counted in unison, then flexed our legs and leaped over the crater in the floor.

One of the seekers ripped a velvet curtain from a doorway and threw it in our path to block our jump before we reached the edge. We slammed into the cliff of the opening as the curtain fluttered down, bursting into flames before it touched the lava. Bits of black ash wafted up.

Gravity pulled me down. We were next! Sliding, I scrabbled vainly for a handhold.

William grabbed my wrist and squeezed it tight. He held onto the edge of the cavity with his other hand. The crystal had landed on the brink of the hole. "Hold on!" he yelled, then hurled me up to the floor with one arm. A moment later, he jolted himself up, and we scrambled to our feet.

Four seekers came at me, two from each side. Their orange eyes glowed with malice. With a hiss, I showed my fangs. I threw one punch, then another, and a third with such velocity I didn't see my arm move. The demons fell into the open lava pit, taking a few others with them.

William fought beside me and took three down with one swing.

More came my way, so many I couldn't count them. They blocked the second entrance to the dungeon as we tried to fight through.

"Hold my hand!" William yelled. "Let's make a way."

I reached for William and he swung me up; I kicked as I flew in a circle, sending more demons into the burning hole. They shrieked and yelped as the lava scorched and burst them into flames before they submerged. The seekers may have been used to heat, but fire defeated them.

When I landed on my feet, William arced over the demons as I had, and more attackers fell to their death. Together, we created a passage to the dungeon for our family. One by one, they escaped while we held back hundreds of demons.

Before I headed down the stairs, I looked back at the warlock. Castall swung one palm away from Aseret and pointed at the crystal still lying at the edge of the crater. The beam of blue light reflected from the crystal in countless directions, sending out a powerful sound wave that disintegrated the demons on contact.

Aseret fell to his knees. "You will not win! I will rebuild!" he yelled before throwing a fistful of dirt down to the floor like a ninja. He disappeared.

Castall focused on me. "Keep running! He may try to get you himself!" Then he vanished the same way as Aseret.

William pulled me forward, following our family and friends. The echo of a wicked laugh bounced off the walls. A laugh I hadn't heard before.

CHAPTER 20

A sunsetting world welcomed us. The long rays quickly warmed our bodies. I took a deep breath in, savouring the crisp evening air. *Pine and damp leaves.*

We were free. With my arms stretched out, I let out a long breath. The sky glowed in pinkish and orange tones. Birds sang their evening song, ruffling their feathers. A balmy November wind whistled between the trees.

Ekim and Atram had stolen demon robes to cover from the sun and stayed in the long shadows of the trees. No one spoke at first, all enjoying the freedom, the first breath of fresh air after coming face to face with death. I expanded my lungs with another deep inhalation of the forest's fragrance. The smell of sulphur hung in the air, not as strong as it had been underground.

Xander sniffed and looked to Mira and my father. "Grand Teton Mountains. We're close to the hill. We can seek shelter there."

The battle in the underworld and what I learned about the prophecy gave me new strength. The thought of a family with William vibrated my insides, but I also feared for the lives of our unborn children. Fighting against Aseret and combining my powers with William's opened new doorways that had been locked for a long time, doorways that would restore peace among three species. I liked the new me.

My existence was no longer in question. Those surrounding me were more than allies; they were a family who loved me dearly. Unwilling to release William's hand, I pressed my other fist to my chest.

"I hear a stream. Let me go see if the water is accessible," Willow volunteered.

"I'll go with you." Atram tottered toward his wife.

"No. Go hunt with Ekim and the kids," she replied.

"If it makes you feel better, I'll go with her, Atram." Alex timid voice shook as she moved her eyes warily from side to side, her shoulders hunched, hands folded across her ample chest.

"Yes, we'll be fine," Willow assured. "The stream is not far."

"And we'll gather some food for you." Mira said to Willow as she stepped between Xander and Alex.

"The hill is not far. Aseret may try to find you," Xander said to William and me, scanning the surrounding woods, then sniffing the air. "We shouldn't stay here."

"We won't be long." Alex took Willow's hand; their backs were already turned before anyone could protest.

We hunted in haste Ekim and Atram caught four rabbits and two mountain lions. Their hunger was stronger than any fear. Even at their weakest, it didn't take much effort to overpower the mammals. William and I took down a few deer.

"It's all right, Sarah." Xander, collecting berries for Willow and Alex nearby, watched as I carefully wiped excess blood from the corners of my mouth. "You don't have to feel ashamed."

"I'm not ashamed. I don't want to hurt your feelings, and I've never done this in front of anyone," I explained.

"It doesn't hurt us. We understand who you are."

Mira walked toward us. "What Xander means is that we hope you'll accept us the way we accept you."

I punched Xander in the arm.

"Ouch, what was that for?"

"You sent a bear after me? Seriously?"

"I didn't let him hurt you." He rubbed his arm.

"Oh please." I rolled my eyes.

"Hah. Told you she'd figure it out." Mira laughed.

"I wish—" A purple mist appeared, glowing and widening, within the branches of a pine beside Ekim and Atram. "Look out!" I warned as the lilac-smelling mist enveloped a tree.

Castall stepped out of the glow, and I sighed in relief.

"Are you all right?" He placed his hands on Ekim's and Atram's shoulders.

"Yes. Thank you for your help, my friend." Ekim patted him on the back.

"Willow?" Castall looked around.

"She went to get water," William answered.

Castall nodded. "You should be fine for a few days. Safe from Aseret, but there's a witch named Xela bearing the imprint of the sphere who wants Sarah."

Xander stiffened.

William placed his arm around me, pulling me closer to his side.

"What does she want from us?" I asked.

"She wants you, Sarah. Be careful. I have not seen her in some time and couldn't find her in the underworld. According to Hannah's reading, she wants to be you. Somehow she expects to control you and it could destroy the prophecy. Aseret would no longer have to fear the future."

I locked my eyes with William. Our children were supposed to save the three species.

"Hannah?" I felt my forehead wrinkle.

"Our mom," Mira whispered.

"I will not let Sarah out of my sight," William declared. "But there may be a problem. We think we've been cursed." He squeezed my arm. "We can't get close. Even at the touch of our hands, our hearts ache."

My family looked puzzled as we hadn't had a chance to share the vision of our future.

"If we are to fulfill the destiny Aseret fears, we will have to *get close*." William moved his brows up.

A rush of fresh blood made its way up into my cheeks.

Castall came closer. "I wonder if . . ." He placed one hand on each of our heads, saying, "Let it be cleared."

Energy left my chest. William slumped beside me. Then the current sank back into our bodies. Nothing had changed. My heart still throbbed at William's touch.

"I cannot remove the spell. It's blocked," Castall said. "I can't feel another spell on you. Something else must have been done. It's flowing through your veins. I'm afraid until we figure out who did it, there's not much we can do."

"We think it was a tampered potion," William suggested.

"Then Hannah can figure it out. Take them to the hill," Castall said to Xander, "then come and get your mother to join you. Build your strength. Our fight has just begun. I bid you well." He thumped Xander on the back and kissed Mira on her head, then disappeared into the purple mist in the tree.

"What's with the friendly goodbye?" I asked Mira.

"Oh, that's our father," she answered with a shrug.

"Right," I said, adding under my breath, "Just when I thought I had it figured out."

"You don't know the half of it!" Xander laughed. "Like, me having to have zits in high school and stretch my height two feet to be unlikable. I'm a likable guy, don't you think?" He winked at me and flashed his famous flirting smirk.

"She's no longer available, Xander," William said.

I never was. I smiled kindly at Xander, who chuckled at William's jealousy.

Willow and Alex returned from the stream with makeshift satchels trickling with water. I put my fist back up to my chest.

"It still hurts?" William asked, looking at Alex.

"Yes."

"We'll figure it out," he assured me.

"Drink, before it drips away." Willow handed me the first satchel. I didn't let a drop escape.

As our dehydrated bodies filled with liquid, Willow and Alex ate their berries. I drew more from the water than its moisture—I drew life. Ever since we touched the crystal, I realized I could borrow life from all living things and morph that life into energy. I'd felt it before but never understood it.

"Thank you," Alex said in her shy voice, "for saving my life."

"You're welcome," I replied.

"I'm sorry we didn't listen to you, Alex," Ekim said.

"And I'm sorry we didn't trust you," I added. "If it wasn't for you, we probably would not have made it out. How did you know the maze changes its shape and paths?"

"I'm a witch. I will always remember the way I've already travelled," she said.

William remained quiet, studying Alex. When she spoke, his neck stiffened. I wondered what he knew that I didn't. We had no reason to doubt the witch. After all, she helped us.

"Okay, let's get going before night sets in," Xander said, jumping down from a tree he'd climbed to scan the terrain. "The path is clear."

"Wait!" William turned his attention to Alex. "Why do you fear losing me?"

"It's not true!" Alex took a step back. "I only fear Sarah losing you." She paused. "I know about the spell that keeps the two of you apart."

"How do you even know about us?" he asked.

"The prophecy of half-breeds coming underground is well known in the underworld. Aseret took me in because he wanted me to take your powers away so he could use them for himself," she explained as she slowly glided toward us.

"Why you, and why didn't you help him?" asked William.

"Although it hasn't been determined yet, I know I'm a good witch. I wouldn't do anything to be marked by a sphere. My powers cannot be used for anything I don't feel is right. I couldn't do as he asked. Aseret thought I could remove the spell that prevented him from getting your powers because my marking hasn't been decided."

I heard Xander's shortened breaths as he stepped back, seeming to be lost in thought.

"What spell?" I asked.

"The spell that keeps you two apart. He thought his spell was blocking his ability to take your powers, and he wanted me to help him remove it."

Xela seemed to be standing closer to William each minute.

"I thought a cursed potion is keeping us apart," William suggested as the side of his arm brushed mine.

"It wouldn't matter whether he used a spell or a potion to curse you. The point is he did." Alex's voice grew in confidence each time she spoke.

"Why couldn't he take the curse off himself?" Ekim rose from his crouch and tossed the hare's carcass into the brushes.

Alex shrugged. "He didn't say. Aseret wouldn't entertain anyone with an explanation."

"That sounds like him," Mira murmured, crossing her arms.

"I don't understand why he cursed them." Willow said.

"So Sarah and William couldn't fulfill their prophecy where two unique beings are to overthrow Aseret and rule both worlds." Alex turned back to us.

William's gaze found mine.

"Aseret is the only one who can remove it," my father said.

"How do we get Aseret to remove it if he wouldn't for his own gain?" I asked.

"If he needed my help, it must mean something's stopping his to do so." Alex explained.

Two mocking jays began their morning songs above us.

"We should head to the hill." William did not look satisfied with the witch's explanations. He still focused on Alex as he added.

Atram's stomach grumbled. The small meal from the hunt hadn't appeased months of malnourishment.

"We'll eat there—I promise," William said to his father.

Xander frowned but said nothing. I've known for years now that he didn't like it when others took charge.

Six of us could travel at great speed with our superhuman powers. I welcomed the wind pressing against my face and limbs. It felt right to move at such speed. Atram carried Willow as he ran through the forest, jumping over downed trees and ducking under low branches. Ekim, despite his hunger, kept up with his friend's quick pace. Xander held Alex tightly in his arms—I thought his squeeze on the witch was too strong. The feeling of jealousy surprised me; after all, Xander was like a brother to me.

We arrived at the hill in less than ten minutes, slower than normal, but Xander insisted on stopping every few miles. He trusted Harlow, who had been overhead since we emerged from the underworld, but insisted on climbing the tallest tree to scout our passage from above, making sure Alex watched his every move.

Show off!

The sun dipped below the horizon, and we arrived at what looked more like a higher mound of shrubs and trees at twilight. I didn't expect much and wondered if "the hill" was a code word for another hidden cabin as Xander pressed his palm against the trunk of a tree and unveiled a concealed doorway. We followed the siblings through a gap in the yellowing grass, and I inhaled the aroma of fresh mint and rosemary, Mrs. G's signature scent—we had entered Mira and Xander's other home.

The turf-covered door opened into a large combination family room and dining area. Furniture made of wood and other materials from the forest blended with the organic space. Roots sprang out of the ceiling and snaked a few feet across its surface before pushing back into it. A hanging basket chair dangled from one of the ceiling roots to the left; others suspended candle chandeliers, dried herbs, baskets of berries, and cloths and towels hung to dry. Though organized for convenience, everything worked more as décor than utility.

The underground hill contained everything a home should have and even if this wasn't the Amazon, it felt cozy. I wondered whether I would return to the jungle and if anything remained of the cabin.

We spent a quiet evening at the hill. I stayed close to William, the sizzling electricity between us pulling us closer. As difficult as it was to be together, it was becoming harder to be apart. The vision we'd shared in the underworld showed a spark of a promise, enough to elevate hope. At least I knew we'd be together. I was grateful to no longer see the fears

William recognized and found it easier to concentrate. I imagined Willliam appreciated not having my visions.

We were closer to each other than before and shared more than our thoughts or visions; we shared our souls. Eagerness filled me, and I couldn't wait until our bodies connected without painful electric shocks.

I sat in the wicker chair that hung from the ceiling, watching William cook, wondering when he caught the extra rabbits on our way here. His eyes glowed as he whistled a tune from one of his songs under his nose. My gaze fell to the muscles flexing in his upper arms, exposed when he'd rolled the sleeves of the shirt he'd borrowed from Xander, and I recalled a favourite dream:

I sucked in a deep breath when his mouth made its way down the back of my neck, and with it came his scent of jasmine, rose, and lilac overlaying a woodsy musk. Taking the satin of my halter in his teeth, William pulled, ripping the thin material. Holding one of the torn ends in his mouth, he travelled downward, close to my skin, until the dress hung halfway on my body, exposing my perky breasts. He pressed his bare chest against me, still supporting most of his weight with his hands. I arched my back, pushing my torso toward him. His hard body dropped even closer. My eyes closed, and I listened as fabric split, then glided over the loveseat, down to the floor.

I returned to reality to see William staring at my smile with great interest. My jaw tensed and I tried to shift my thoughts to the critters that might be lurking in the earthen ceiling.

He came to kneel beside me. "There are no bugs here, Sarah. I asked Mira to talk to them," William whispered, then chuckled.

"Oh, after what I've seen, I'm not afraid of bugs anymore," I said.

"If you say so, but that's not what your aura tells me." He winked, "You don't have to fear that we'll never be together. Remember what we saw. There's only one way to do that." William gently kissed the inside of my palm, sending fire through my veins. The ache and frustration returned and I had to keep busy to keep my mind off the curse.

We made arrangements for the next day. Xander and Mira would leave in the morning to join Mrs. G in her journey to the hill. We were hoping she might have an answer to the problem of the spell. Atram and Ekim would hunt.

Willow wanted to make a family dinner to celebrate our reunion. Giggling, she'd hug William and me whenever she had a chance, and I welcomed the embrace each time. Alex volunteered to help with dinner. Willow and Alex behaved like best friends.

William observed Alex constantly, keeping his distance, brows drawn downward. "I don't like her here," he whispered to me.

"If it wasn't for her, we'd still be underground. Just bear with her for now, please?"

"For now," he grudgingly conceded.

That night, we lay on the mattress in the second bedroom, me on one side, William stretched far on the other side, hands under his head. My longing to touch him in the way I always dreamt of trembled my hands. The same fire and hunger shone in his eyes. Unable to act on my desire, I closed my eyes, remembering my dream again

William's lips tasted like raspberries. His eyes were closed. The lights were dimmed, and the soothing fragrance of vanilla candles hung in the air. I pulled the loveseat's white coverlet over William's naked back. I knew it was my dream and no one would walk in on us, but I needed this moment to be completely between us. I wanted to be enclosed as much as we could be.

"Are you cold?" he asked.

"No." I laughed quietly. "I couldn't be hotter." I placed my palms on his hips to guide him where we both knew he was ready to go.

"I know." He gazed into my eyes and smiled. My longing and desire blossomed. Taking this as a welcome, he came forward; I arched my pelvis toward him, unwilling to wait any longer. Joy and pleasure sparkled in the turquoise eyes still fixed on my face.

Being so close was everything we'd wanted. Our hearts and our bodies were truly one. We completed each other. I smiled at William, tasting blood as my fangs pierced my lower lip. Then the vampire inside me overpowered my human side, and I lost control.

The rest of the evening became a beautiful dance as our bodies connected fiercely, tumbling across the floor of a night club somewhere in New York City.

"What are you thinking about?" William asked.

"You."

"Have I been a good boy?" He peered at me from below his eyelashes. I knew he read the lust on my face, felt the small vibrations of my body no one else would have noticed.

"You've been good in a bad way." I bit my lower lip.

William moved closer, as if inexorably pulled by gravity. "Soon, Sarah. Soon." He srouched his lips to my forehead. "Get some rest."

"Good night."

"Don't let the bed bugs bite," William whispered.

The walls of the cave-like dwelling absorbed most sounds, except for Mira's and Xander's chuckles outside our room. I shook my head ruefully, then took a deep breath in and closed my eyes, falling asleep within minutes.

"Me and you getting ready to . . ." I gave him a meaningful look so I wouldn't have to be specific. Then I knelt to collect the pieces of broken plate to avoid everyone's stare.

"Oh." William raised his brows. "And you didn't want to?" He knelt beside me, taking the pieces of broken ceramic out of my hands.

"We'll leave you two alone," Willow said abruptly, taking Atram by his hand and waving for Ekim and Alex to follow her to the far side of the living area.

"I did—I do, but the way I saw us . . . I wasn't there. You were with someone else."

"You know I would never touch another woman. You are my true match. I would never hurt you." He brushed my cheek with the back of his hand.

"I know. It was me, but . . . I didn't *feel* like it was me." I huffed in frustration.

"Do you think your visions have changed because of the crystal?" William asked.

"I'm not sure." A tear streaked down my cheek. "William, I should be happy. . . you and I were together . . . but I'm afraid. I feel danger and loss of hope."

"Sarah, I promise you, I will never leave your side," he assured me. "I belong with you and only you. I could not live without you. I could not survive. You bring out the best in me. You give me strength."

"I feel the same way." I leaned over and rested my head on his shoulder. He rubbed my back. "Maybe I'm just mixing in the fears from the underworld." The flames in the fire pit suddenly rose higher, as if receiving more oxygen.

William held me tight. I didn't want him to let go, despite the pain. "William? Promise me you will not take me to a sunflower field."

"You know you can't change the vision."

"Promise me?" I insisted.

"All right," he said, "I promise."

"And if we happen to get there somehow, we will not get too close to each other."

"I promise. I may not be able to control where we are, but I can control what we do . . . or not do."

"Even if I persist? No matter what, it cannot be there. I want to be fully present for our first time, and somehow I didn't feel like I was there."

"I promise it will not happen in the sunflower field. I can guarantee it."

"Pinky-sware?" I asked

William hooked his smallest finger into mine and said, "Pinky-sware."

"Thank you."

He set aside the broken glass and did not let me go as he rubbed my arms. "You're trembling."

"I have a feeling something bad is about to happen, but I don't know what."

"We're safe here," William assured me. He covered my lips with his, then I pulled away squeezing my eyes shut.

"I'm sorry you're hurting."

"It's not your fault, William. We'll get these fixed." I pressed my hand against the left side of his chest.

"May I speak with you?" Alex interrupted, walking into the kitchen area.

A new wave of chills invaded my skin.

I sensed trouble, and I felt Alex's presence carve into my visions. Like she was part of a future I'd already seen. We turned and watched her approach with her typical small steps.

"I'm sorry, but I overheard you speaking of the spell that's keeping you apart." She straightened the drying cloth overhead. "I can help you. I want to help you, to thank you for taking me in."

"How can you help us?" I asked, straightening my shoulders.

William frowned. "Let's go to the family room."

I set the sweeper back in its corner and followed William.

Atram and Ekim sat on the couch, sharing a quiet conversation about the delivery of new serums. Their attention flew to us as soon as we walked in.

"I thought the spell or the curse can only be removed by the one who cast it," William said, his tone almost accusing.

"What you say is true, but I can erase the pain temporarily."

"Really?" I perked up.

"Will that not offset the balance?" Willow asked as she wiped her hands on her apron.

"Not if you give up your gifts, while the spell's in effect. This wouldn't work for long, perhaps twenty-four hours or so. My spell can paralyze the curse because it would be offset by something you gave up." Alex settled in the swinging chair.

Twenty-four hours is not long, but it's long enough. I saw my hope reflected in William's eyes. He wanted this more than he'd admit.

"What exactly does this spell involve?" he asked, crossing his arms, as if reluctant to reveal his interest.

"It's actually more invasive for me than you. I need my inner tissue to complete the spell," she said.

Everyone stared at Alex. Willow sat down on her husband's lap on the sofa. He wrapped his arms around her slender frame.

"The tissue—my tissue—can cover up the spell. You don't have to do anything, just sleep," Alex explained.

"I don't feel comfortable with this," William said. "What if something goes wrong?"

"Nothing can go wrong. It's a simple spell." The witch shrugged. "If you'd like, your family can stay with you the whole time."

No one objected. Alex's proposition became irresistible.

"William, what if this is the only chance we have to get close for a long time, without pain? Your parents will watch it being done. My father will, too." I looked at Ekim, who nodded and then made my puppy eyes at William.

He sighed. "All right. But I'm not tired; are you? How are we going to fall asleep?"

"Serum. There's some left in my backpack." My heart pounded as I rushed to retrieve it. "Here." I handed a syringe to William.

The blue liquid in William's hand became everyone's focal point. He stared at the aquatic glow in his palm, then his gaze came back to me. "Now? Sarah, don't rush this," he pleaded.

"I'm not rushing it. I just want to touch you without being zapped."

William's face tensed.

"I'm worried too," I whispered, brushing my fingers through his hair. "But everything will be back to normal in a day."

I wrapped my arms around his waist, resting my head on his chest. He kissed the top of my head and stroked my hair, but the electric shock pushed us apart. The need to be close again increased the pain. It was almost unbearable to hug.

"We're here, in the safest place possible." I pulled away.

"Okay. At least that's true." William sighed, "Only for you." He injected the serum.

I jabbed the needle in my thigh.

Willow took our hands. "Come. Lie down here. We will not leave your side," she promised, helping me settle on one of the mattresses at the end of the room.

The serum slowed my pulse, as if I'd been injected with barbiturate.

"We won't let anything happen to you," Atram added, bringing two pillows.

William lay as close to me as he could without it causing pain. I turned my head to him and cupped his face in my hand.

"What are you doing?" he smiled.

"Remembering you for my dreams." An odd tug pulled at my stomach. The same one I'd had when the seekers first took me to the underworld. The one that told me I would not see William for a long time. I ignored it, telling myself it was only butterflies of excitement.

"Are you afraid?" he asked.

"No, just excited."

"I should have known. I still see the tarantulas." He laughed quietly.

My eyelids dropped lower, then closed.

"Sarah?" William asked. With difficulty, I opened my eyes again. "I love you." He thumped his fist on his chest.

"I loved you before I met you," I replied, this time closing my eyes to fall asleep.

CHAPTER 22

I knew they wouldn't discover my secrets, after all, I was the most powerful witch in the world! The half breed vampires were too stupid and lost in their pathetic *love.*

Not for long.

Sarah would soon suspect her recurring chest pains warned her every time I came close. I had to act before it was too late, before the stupid girl smartened up. My jaw tightened, and I felt my lip curve up in a smirk. *Relax. They're almost asleep.* I looked at them and laughed inside. *You humans give in to your emotions so easily.*

The dimly lit room was silent. No one moved, no one spoke. All eyes were on the two bodies asleep on the mattress against the wall. Ekim and Atram stood over their children, looking at them with mildly worried expressions. Willow held her son's hand. Sarah's and William's mouths were curved into smiles.

If they only knew! I wanted to stick my tongue out in disgust but refrained.

"Are they ready?" Willow asked me.

"Yes. It will not take long. Here." I handed her a cloth. "It's soaked with an herbal infusion. I'm going to have to cut my chest. Can you wipe it down when I'm done? It's to prevent infection and help it heal," I lied in my new soft voice. In truth, the potent concoction soaking the cloth would wash the spell away. "It will also put me to sleep."

"Of course," Willow said, accepting the damp cloth.

This is much easier than I thought. The sibling demons are gone. The timing is perfect. My insides vibrated with gloating laughter I could not release. *Aseret was right to call them silly creatures. How would these stupid beings have enough sense to take over the underworld?* I let out a quiet snort. *It's thrilling to be so differently perceived and deceiving. Aseret's plan is brilliant, flawless. Such wisdom, to have me curse the couple with a potion to keep them apart.*

Sarah's eyes moved under her eyelids; she was dreaming.

Soon, their demonic powers will disappear. Soon, I will be on my way to ruling the witches. Soon, Sarah will live her short life in exile before rotting to death; if these morons don't kill her first. William won't know until it's too late, and Aseret will take his place. No one will know! I chuckled.

"Are you all right, Alex?" Willow asked.

"Yes; I'm sorry—just got something stuck in my throat." I glanced around the room, my eyes resting briefly on the two vampires. *They're too dumb to know who I am. And Willow—it makes me sick that the human thought she could live amongst the mystical!*

After I sat cross-legged on the floor above Sarah's and William's heads, I placed my palms on their foreheads. Closing my eyes, I whispered the requisite chant in its ancient language, backwards to the original curse. Then I opened my eyes. This was more for show than anything.

I pulled my dagger from the back pocket of my dress. Ekim and Atram growled and took a defensive stance over their kids. "I will not hurt them," I lied, using my new, mollifying voice. "It's to gather my tissue."

"Alex, please be careful," Willow whispered.

I nodded with innocence. It annoyed me to be so polite, so calm and pleasant. It would still be some time before I could show and use my true powers.

My fingers fiddled, unbuttoning the front of my dress and I slid the dagger down my bared chest, from the hollow at the base of my throat to the floating ribs. *Nice and easy, not too deep. They have to believe I'm hurt enough to die on my own, but not too quickly. I'll let her suffer before bleeding out, dying, and decaying, all alone, without her body.*

Blood dripped. "Amena cora si lamu pentubi," I said, marking Sarah's temples with my blood. No one noticed I only did this to Sarah. A sudden gust of dancing wind swirled outside, rustling the last of the autumn leaves noisily enough to be heard inside the hill-home's thick walls. Sarah and William did not move.

"It's done. You can wipe the cut now, Willow." I stretched out onto the floor and closed my eyes.

Willow gently slid the wet cloth across my chest. My body arched up, releasing my invisible soul. My soul looked down at the mark on Sarah's head, and I knew where to go. I crushed into Sarah, pushing her sleeping spirit out. The spirit awoke too late—Sarah's body no longer housed it. It took the next available body and went back to its dreams.

At the same time, the potion the cloth had been soaked in evaporated, releasing its spell into the air. It hovered over my body, then slowly sank through it, releasing Aseret's finery spell.

"Look!" Ekim pointed at me. "What's happening to her?"

"Alex is changing." Willow gasped, before covering her mouth with her hand.

If I could, I would have chuckled until I fell over. But I could only listen to their speeding heartbeats and imagined them staring as an invisible cloud of magic washed away the curly, golden-blond locks, changing them in to straight, tangled black hair; hardened the eyes and let dark circles to appear underneath. It marred formerly white teeth with dark-brown and yellow stains from years of neglect. The youthful face sagged; wrinkles and blemishes resurfaced.

"This cannot be!" Ekim and Atram blurted together.

"Who is she?" Willow's voice trembled.

"Xela," someone whispered in horror.

The door in the hillside flew open, and in one leap, I knew Mira was at my side; Xander flew after her to grab my old, limp body—Sarah's new body—with one arm and wrap his other arm around her neck in a choke hold.

The siblings must have been warned by their witch mother.

"What do you want from Sarah?" he growled ominously. "Why are you here, Xela? Talk, or I'll break your neck the way I should have done years ago." Four sets of eyes stared at Xander and the limp body he held.

My new body stirred at the commotion. I opened my eyes and looked toward the far end of the room, where Xander's arm was still around the neck of the dark-haired woman. "What's going on?" I asked.

It worked . . . of course it did.

"Xander, who is this? Let her go or you'll kill her," I said casually.

It's strange, seeing my old body in front of me; I can't let them kill it. Let her suffer! Let her know what it's like to be one of the "bad guys."

"This is Xela," he growled from the back of his throat.

"Alex is actually Xela from the underworld. She's a witch in league with Aseret," Mira explained. She still half crouched in front of me, ready to protect me from whatever might come.

They have no clue.

William awoke as well. "What's going on?" He sat up, rushing to my side. "Sarah, are you okay?"

"Yes, I'm fine. Xander, ease up or you'll kill her." Though I liked the way his muscles flexed all over his body.

"That's the idea," he replied.

"You can't kill her. She didn't do anything," I said.

"Are you sure? When we got here, you were unconscious. We thought she hurt you." Mira turned to face me—the body she thought contained her friend.

"No, you have it wrong. She did not hurt us. She paralyzed the spell that kept us apart," I explained. *And* she *put Aseret's plan into action.* I chuckled inside.

"Sarah, they're right. This is Xela. She's dangerous. We should be thankful she didn't hurt you." Ekim looked lovingly at his daughter—me.

I cannot let them kill her. She has to suffer. She has to know what it's like to writhe in pain. She has to know what it's like to not have a choice of who you are! "Okay, but she didn't hurt us. She helped us." I focused on the limp body. "She helped us out of the dungeons, and she took the spell off. I can feel it already. Can't you feel it?" My hand pressed into William's, the way I'd seen the half-breeds do.

William's apprehension eased. "You're right. It worked." The worry faded from his face. He took me into his strong embrace. His eyebrows went up when nothing happened. There was no pain.

"Sarah is right. We can't just kill her. Maybe she wanted a new life; maybe she wanted to turn it around," Willow interjected.

"Not Xela. She's all about cunning and pain," Atram held his wife in a tight embrace.

Xander's eyes sparked with hatred, the way I'd remembered. A shadow of green shade covered his face. If he only knew what I'd done, he'd kill me on the spot.

"Let's just leave her in the woods and let fate decide what should be done with her. She's lost a lot of blood anyway." Willow pointed to the red puddle on the dirt floor at Xander's feet. "It will be difficult enough for her to recover."

"Fine, I'll drop her off in the vampire territories. Let fate decide that way," Xander growled. The vengeance inside him warmed my black heart. No one paid attention to me. They kept staring at Sarah's new limp body.

"I'll go with you," Mira said to her brother.

As soon as they left, William picked me off my feet and swung around the room. "I hope this lasts more than twenty-four hours," he said before kissing me passionately.

Your wish is my command. I guess I'm going have to get used to being good.

CHAPTER 23

She appeared out of a fog and stood ten feet away from me.

"Mom, is that you?" I had to ask; after all, I had never seen my mother, other than in the dream where I murdered her and in Castall's projection. Uncertain what she'd look like, the physical similarities between us were too striking. She had familiar features to mine, but a little older. Her triangular face centered a small, pointy nose and a dozen or so freckles aligned almost like mine.

"Yes, sweetheart, it's me," she answered. Her smile softened.

I wanted to believe what I saw was real, but logic told me it wasn't possible. My mother died. *I must be dreaming.* But the urgency of her expression told me otherwise. She seemed authentic and not part of a dream which foretold my future. It felt as if she'd stepped into my mind on purpose, to tell me something. Glowing light shined behind her, casting her into silhouette which didn't help to convince me I didn't dream—yet, I could feel her presence.

I knew this was a dream even before she spoke, from the pattern of lines on her face and the slight squint of her eyes. Her face was as readable to me as anyone else's. She smiled. My head hurt trying to remember where I fell asleep; perhaps that would give me some answers. But it was hard to recall. Seeing my mom confused me.

"Sarah, you're in trouble. You have to remain strong to get through this." She turned for a moment to look behind her.

"What do you mean? Where did you come from? You're not alive." My voice rose hopefully, but I knew it was too much to ask for; seeing her was bittersweet, nothing more.

"No, I'm not alive. I don't have much time." She glanced behind her again. "You will soon wake up, Sarah, and you'll find yourself alone."

"What do you mean?" Again, I strained to remember where I'd fallen asleep, trying to identify where I'd wake up. It didn't work. The throbs in my head intensified.

"Saraphine, he's coming," I heard a hushed voice say. "Hurry!" Helen appeared beside my mother. Her silhouette was faint and ghostly.

I stopped doubting my dreaming state. "Helen?" I smiled, unsure why my aunt was there.

"Sarah, listen to your mother. We have to go back, Saraphine."

"Look where obeying the rules got us!" My mother rested her hand on her sister's shoulder, but Helen disappeared into a mist.

"Sarah, listen," my mother said hastily. She looked so wistful, as if there was so much she wanted to say, but time would not allow it. "You have to find the ruby ring. It's the only way he'll see you and leave Xela. She's not who she seems."

"How do you know about Xela? Who is she?" I asked.

"You, Sarah. Don't look for us; your safety is most important. Don't give up!" She checked over her shoulder again before adding, "I love you. I always have." She thumped her fist on her left breast and disappeared.

"Mom!" I reached out, but she was gone, faded into pink mist.

No dreams came to me after that one and I couldn't concentrate on any thought, either; it felt as if my mind wasn't connected to my body and its dreams. It was odd that my mind would wander off and disengage from me this way. I got nervous and expected cold chills to climb my spine, but they didn't. Cool wind curved around my face. Strong wind, as if I were riding a bicycle downhill at full speed.

Identical feelings swept through me when I'd run at my fastest, but I knew I wasn't running. Someone's strong arms carried me. I couldn't understand why I felt detached from my body while my thoughts were clear, recognizing what the body was going through.

"Let's go! No need to burn her. She's as good as dead here," a familiar voice said. I recognized it as Xander's, but these words would never leave his mouth. This voice was deeper, hoarser. I pictured sharp fangs and an elongated tongue.

As *good as dead? Urgh! Wake up, Sarah, wake up!*

THUMP!

Neither dreaming nor waking but perhaps semiconscious, I fell to the ground and I felt pain. Normally, a fall from a few feet high wouldn't register any pain, but this one did. It bent my limbs in peculiar ways, denting everywhere at once. The way the blood clot into tight, small balls in specific spots on my arms and legs, and the way they throbbed as they did, made me doubt the bruises would disappear quickly. I tried to move, feeling my body roll over marbles. Bruises and rocks. The pain didn't wake me, and I lost consciousness.

* * *

I inhaled the scent of sweet lilac, rose, and jasmine from the bubble bath. The scent was mine and William's, blended into one fragrance. It covered my body like an invisible silk scarf. The tub was set in the middle of a jungle. Flower petals floated on the suds. Orchids bloomed as far as I could see. The trees were wrapped in flowery blossoms, orchid shrubs grew around their bases, and the ground was covered in petals: pink, fuchsia, yellow, orange, purple, white, blue, and black.

The hot water penetrated my body, warming it. I couldn't get enough of the heat and wanted to stay there for as long as possible. My fear and anxiety gone. The atmosphere was serene and I wanted this dream to be real.

My feet rested on the end of the tub. Steam evaporated from the tips of my toes, illuminated by the glow from two multicoloured candles on either side of the tub, their ruddy wax dripping down their sides and dribbling in ever-building ridges toward the forest floor. I breathed slowly, trying to isolate the aroma of each flower. The pollen travelled through my body, strengthening my limbs. I was at peace, unafraid, ready for a new life with William.

It was a peaceful, but brief, dream. I woke too soon—to a living nightmare.

A nightmare I'd once dreamt and had always known it would become part of my life I'd avoided it, denied it and tried to forget it. I'd convinced myself I was confused—after all, I couldn't scar.

I was gone; dead, yet alive. When I reached out, I felt I would touch William, yet I couldn't. My eyes lied when I saw him with me because I knew he was nowhere near. I lived a reality that seemed more like a dream. William appeared too far, and too close, for my liking.

With a great cry, I opened my eyes to find myself in the middle of dark woods. The relief of being alive washed over me in sweat. Droplets of moisture rolled from my underarms, back, and forehead and soaked my strange new clothes.

"Where am I?" I mumbled.

No one replied.

Am I still dreaming? I hoped but knew I wasn't.

A hollow sound came from the pit of my stomach, and it wasn't from hunger. My gut warned me of something strange. With hesitation, I denied what I knew to be true, then quickly unbuttoned the top of my dress to touch the middle of my chest. I ran my finger along a path I remembered and leaped to my feet when I touched the cut.

No! It's not possible!

The incision burned. The slow oozing of blood felt like hot water. I swept my hand across my chest and licked the red goo with my tongue, tasted the bitter, irony tang. My breathing became heavy and uncontrolled. My heartbeat was unfamiliar. The changing rhythm didn't scare; the heart itself did. A foreign lump thumped inside my chest. I placed my other hand five inches below my throat and traced the incision down to the floating ribs. The small ripple of the score under my forefinger reminded me of sandpaper, covered with sticky blood that dripped from the cut. It smelled revolting. The scar hadn't formed yet, but I knew it would.

What happened to me?

Hyperventilating, I fought to control my breathing. The air wheezed from lungs. *Breathe, Sarah. This can't be real*, I lied to myself.

My knees weakened, and I knelt on the ground where I'd lain a moment before. My palms felt sticky where they touched the fallen leaves and dirt. *How much blood did I lose?*

"William? Are you here?" I called in a whisper, with no hope in my voice.

As quickly as the words left my mouth, my hand flew up. *What happened to my voice? It's not mine!* Fearing to speak again, I stood.

Dark shadows covered the forest, but morning neared and the sky had lightened enough for me to see my surroundings. Fog hovered above the ground; the night's frost still covered the surface of leaves, dried grasses, and moss. The air was crisp, signalling winter's nearness.

A stink of spoiled eggs, rotten potatoes, and old raw chicken drifted around me from the ragged clothes on my body, clothing I didn't recognize. Wet boots were laced to my knees. Long, unkempt hair stuck to the back of my neck and the front of my wounded chest. I ran my tongue along crooked teeth, feeling nicks and chips on some, a thick layer of tartar and plaque on all. I could almost taste the yellowish stain. *But I brush my teeth*, I thought in confusion.

What did she do to me?

My hands aged, wrinkled and painted with blemishes. Broken nails trapped dirt beneath them. I placed the palms on my head and slid them slowly along the thick, snarled hair. Long hair. *No!* I thought in disbelief—in denial.

I dragged my hands on their downward path to touch a wider nose, thick lips, and a pointy chin. My features were not my own. My face did not feel like mine. Down further, I cupped breasts that had enlarged two sizes.

Tears spilled from foreign eyes to roll down unknown cheeks. The droplets were not mine; the face was not mine. A painful throb passed through me—not my heart, for the heart, like this body, wasn't mine.

"Where is my body!" I screamed, terror and anguish driving me to my knees. Someone else's echo vibrated throughout the forest. The breathing I thought I had under control picked up momentum. I struggled will small, quick breaths. The inhales didn't satisfy the new lungs I owned. The threat of panic lingered. *How could I let this happen?*

I closed my eyes and saw what, at first, brought a smile to my face.

William and I sat with our family at a dinner table in the hill. Mira, Xander, and Mrs. G were there, too. We were all happily celebrating our reunion. I saw myself, smiling. William had his arm around my waist in a tight embrace. We did not twitch in pain as we usually would have.

Alex's spell worked.

The glint of a familiar shape in the back pocket of my jeans became visible when the long sweater I wore had shifted up as I sat. Alex's dagger.

Then I heard what I dreaded. I wasn't having a premonition or a vision of an event that would happen in the future. Some cruel joke allowed me to watch my stolen life unfold in front of my eyes.

Mrs. G looked to Xander. "Did you take Xela's body far away?"

"She's close to Drake's hideaway. Once the vampires get a whiff of a witch nearby, she's as good as dead." His laugh was harsh, cruel; I'd never heard him sound so cold.

"It's Xela you're talking about. Don't underestimate her." Mrs. G sounded disappointed that the witch was left alive.

"She's lost a lot of blood, Ma. I doubt she'll even wake up," said Mira.

"I still don't understand why you didn't burn her," Mrs. G said. "Then it would have been certain."

Mira and Xander looked doubtfully at each other, as if questioning their decision to leave the almost-dead body intact. Yet I also saw they *couldn't* do what they wanted to. Something inside them told them they shouldn't; they didn't want to protect the body, but they couldn't harm it, either.

A small flame of hope sparked in the new heart, but it was quickly extinguished.

I tried opening my eyes to stop the image playing before them, but every time I thought of William, he was there with Xela, in my stolen body. The head throbbed as I struggled to control the show in my mind.

William took Xela's hand and drew it close to his mouth to kiss each individual finger. Xela smiled at him with my turquoise eyes.

Doesn't he know it's not me?

He didn't. To him, it was the Sarah he had known and a body he had longed for—longing which he could now satisfy.

"No!" I cried instinctively, knowing where this could lead. *She stole everything I had!*

Pain struck my heart, a different ache than touching William. I could handle the physical ache but not the sorrow, distress, and grief. To have gained a family and their love, to have overcome Aseret and the seekers had meant nothing.

Now, I was worse off than when I lived in Pinedale. Alone, with no newfound senses to guide me, I had no friends to ask for help. Once again, I didn't know who or what I was.

My left wrist began throbbing, burning. I lifted my hand in what seemed like slow motion to look at the source and sank lower to the ground. *Where is my orchid?* The inside of my wrist was red, as if it had been scorched. A new shape was forming, the dark outline shone with blackness as it became more visible.

The sphere I'd been warned about. It almost glowed while imprinting on my hand.

But I'm good. I started to cry.

The sphere darkened even more, as if mocking me. I turned my hand away in disbelief.

Blood rushed to my head in waves. I wasn't familiar with such increased flow in my veins. Even at my fullest, I was sure I'd never had so much blood inside me. *Is this what humans feel all the time?*

My face warmed, but it wasn't from the bright glow of the morning star. My cheeks heated up and probably flushed pink under the wrinkled skin. The forest spun, blending the trees into mush. My eyes showed me a forest from behind a haze and under a glare. *Is this the way humans see this world?*

Small flakes of what looked like first snow fell from the sky. A drop of melted snow splattered on a leaf, then parted and each half found a new path down toward the ground.

My stomach contracted, forcing its contents up. I couldn't control this new body. It didn't respond well to my physical needs and emotions. Somehow, it didn't seem capable of having emotions at all. Suddenly dizzy, I looked up, wanting to see the sunrise on the horizon, but I only saw white light with two purplish ovals. The spots whispered in a familiar male voice, *What happened?*

The white light faded to gray, then to black. The two purple dots were the last to disappear. I collapsed face first to the ground. I did not dream.

Chapter 24

My chest rose as I drew in more air than I could before. The volume of blood in my veins swelled. My chest was sore, and it felt as if there were golf ball-sized bruises on my thighs, ribs, and buttocks. Then I remembered: my body was gone.

Wake up, Sarah. Wake up. I know you can hear me. I heard a familiar male voice in my mind, but couldn't open my eyes. It wasn't William, but as soon as I thought of him, I saw them.

"I have a surprise for you." Xela tightened her grip around William's arm. They sat in front of the fireplace at the hill.

"I love surprises." He nuzzled his nose into her neck.

She moved away to see his face. "Tomorrow, we'll have a picnic. Xander told me about a place south of here."

William narrowed his brows. "I'm not sure it's safe to go out."

"We've been stuck here for two weeks. There are no seekers nearby." Xela stood and paced the room with her hands on her hips.

"Don't you think it's odd the spell isn't temporary?" William asked.

"Would you prefer it was?" She pouted.

No, William, don't give in.

"Of course not, but not having our powers feels strange. Doesn't it?" I gasped.

"It feels exactly as it should." She fluttered her lashes.

I saw concern on William's face, a worry he did not hide from Xela, though she couldn't read his face the way I could. William wasn't convinced the new me was all right. He kept his distance. Our magnetic connection disappeared. A spark of hope ignited in my new heart.

"If Mira and Xander are willing to come with us, then we can go and see."

"I already asked. They will," Xela said, her tone cocky. "Xander won't let me out of his sight." She smiled.

William frowned. "I noticed."

"Are you jealous?" she asked.

"No." He pulled Xela to sit on his lap in the chair by the fireplace. "Sarah, don't you feel odd without your premonitions?"

"Nope. Don't miss them at all."

"I didn't think so," he said under his breath.

I don't want to see this.

Then wake up, Sarah. Wake up and they'll be gone, the male voice said.

Who are you?

Open your eyes. Don't be afraid. I'm here to help you, the voice said in a whisper that resembled the hum of bees.

The smell of fresh water nearby wafted, and I heard it splashing continuously. The smell of peppermint hit my nostrils. I opened my eyes to bright light and squinted, struggling to focus. Strong arms helped me sit up as I pressed my palm to my brow, blinking.

Then I saw purplish sparks in the eyes of a handsome man. "Eric?"

"Hi."

The last time I'd seen the evil-bender was in the dark alley. His face seemed to glow like an angel's and I couldn't find anything evil about it.

"Where am I? Do you recognize me like this?" I swallowed over a lump in my dry throat.

"Don't you remember? I'm bound to you forever." The curves of his mouth showed kindness I didn't expect.

"What does that mean?"

"Here. You've been out awhile." Eric handed me a cup of mint tea. "Sip slowly."

I touched my cracked lips to the rim of the cup, and as I sipped, I remembered dreaming for a long time—except they weren't dreams. They were images of my stolen life, of my family and friends. They were pictures of Xela lying to William, who kissed her; of Xela flirting with Xander, who became more and more uncomfortable each time she moved too close, thanking him for taking the witch's body away; of her scheming to get close to my family so she could ruin the prophecy.

"I've been out for two weeks, haven't I?" When he nodded, I added, "How did you know?" I wasn't sure whether I should thank him for finding me or for recognizing me inside this body. I didn't know where to begin—all I knew was that the stranger I'd once feared, cared.

"I can't interfere too much, but I can guide you to fix things. Enough is enough." He smiled with soft eyes. The purple glow was gone, but its spark still simmered. "Mira and Xander have done the best they could under the circumstances, and I can't blame them for what happened to you. Xela's been very sneaky. She and Aseret have disrupted the balance too much."

"Why couldn't you find me earlier?" I asked.

"There's only so much I can do at a time. I had to pay attention to the bodies. They were being moved." He ran his fingers through his hair and I saw guilt and confusion flash in his eyes.

"What bodies?" I cracked my stiff finger.

"Bodies of lost souls. Aseret and Xela did too much damage at once for me to keep track of you and your family. Things began to fall out of equilibrium. We decided it was time to meddle as well," he explained.

"Who is 'we'?" I asked.

"I'll show you once you've gained more strength." He shuffled his feet, seeming nervous.

"You've been watching out for me," I realized, remembering Eric in Pinedale when he first bumped into me. I recalled him in the reflection of my own eyes, when purple stars shone, and in my parents' room in the Amazon when violet light bounced off the crystal figurines. The whole time, it was him.

"I have, but I followed too many rules. Too many lives have been altered at once. Too many spells had been cast. I thought Mira and Xander could take care of you when I couldn't. Changes, changes . . . all the time, changes." He lifted a hand to push his hair back and left his fingers tangled in his brown strands as he walked in a circle. Eric lowered his head in disappointment, then as if coming out of a trance, he looked back at me with a determined expression. "It's time to fix things. It's time to help you fulfill your prophecy."

I smiled. Could I be so fortunate to have found a friend in a foe? "Pinch me?" I quipped.

"No need." He let out a sobering laugh and pointed at my alien body. "If any of them see you this way, they'll kill you before you get a chance to breathe."

"I could hold them off. I learned skills. I remember everything," I said.

"Yes, but not in this human body. Xela's body is frail compared to yours."

That's when I noticed the needle in my arm. A clear tube connected to an intravenous machine pumped fluid into me. The side of my ribcage jutted awkwardly, and bones stuck out from just beneath the skin. I felt weaker—although it was difficult to tell in this body; I wasn't sure what to compare my strength or health to. The gnarled limbs were pale. I touched the hair. It had been cut to shoulder length.

"Easier to keep," Eric explained.

"It's okay. It's not like I was used to it." I half smiled, pulling my hand away from my head. The effort to move any part of my body tired me. The new heartbeat was irregular. I only felt it sometimes. Not attuned to the new pulse, I listened but couldn't hear the rhythm in my chest, nor William's.

"Sarah." Eric shifted from one foot to the other. "I'm not sure how to get your body back. We can fix this one a bit, but I don't know if you can ever be who you were—back in your skin." He kept his gaze on the floor.

I held back the tears. "I'm still me, in here." My hand pressed to the middle of the chest where a pinkish scar was visible just above the collar of a cream shirt. I raised my chin. "No matter what happens, they have to believe it."

"They will." He smiled.

"Then what do we do?"

"You, rest. I'll get everything ready." Eric propped up my pillow and covered my legs with a fluffy blanket. It matched the baby-blue colour of his shirt.

I looked around the room. The few smokeless candles didn't illuminate the space, but it was bright. A two-storey opening in the wall, about twenty feet wide, provided enough light. It appeared as a white rippling sheer and I realized a waterfall flowed beyond the hole in the wall. We were behind a waterfall. I found it odd not to hear the rush of the falling water as clearly as I thought I should. My new ears were to be blamed for the unified sounds.

I swung my feet down to the plush red carpeting with its gold star border. "Eric? Why now? Why couldn't you help me in Pinedale? And why do they call you the evil-bender?"

"I change bad things into good things." He sighed. "I thought the siblings would be fine when I was needed elsewhere. When it became clear your fate had turned for the worse, it was too late. Not only did Aseret ruin the last institution the vampires had good relations with, but he also tampered with the prophecy that can save all kinds. He's gone too far."

"You said 'we' before. Who's 'we'?"

He took a deep breath, then paused to hand me a pea-sized pill. "It will calm your new pulse. You may feel dizzy."

I swallowed the white tablet. The swirling in my head reminded me of how intoxicated I was when I first met William. When I thought about William, I saw them again:

"Come. It's not far." Xela pulled William's arm. His eyes were closed.

"I smell flowers," he said, "sunflowers. Sarah, I thought you said—"

"There's no need to worry. Mira and Xander ran the perimeter. It's safe here." She smirked. She was about to ruin the prophecy. She didn't want William—she'd had her designs on Xander all the time, in all my visions. William was just an obstacle she had to deal with first.

William did not follow, standing frozen at the edge of the golden field. "It's not safety I'm worried about."

"What's the problem?"

"I pinky-swore," he answered.

"Don't let some silly, childish game ruin our day. It's the perfect spot. Look." She pointed to a small clearing in the field where a picnic basket was set on a blanket.

At the word "silly," his head jerked up. He stared at Xela, then at the blanket. "Sarah, you know I love you, but this is not the right place," he whispered.

Xela came back to his side. She stood on her toes to kiss him. The kiss increased in intensity, and she wrapped her arms around his neck to pull him closer. William closed his eyes again and followed her to the picnic blanket.

"No!" I screamed, shooting to my feet. The body I had dropped to the plush floor.

Eric picked me up, propping me down on the bed and sat at my side. "What you're seeing is not happening."

I felt my forehead crease. "What do you mean?"

"You've been having nightmares, talking in your sleep." He handed me the peppermint tea.

"They're not nightmares, Eric. They're real." I sipped.

"I know they're real, but their timing is off. I've been listening in."

Listening in?

Yes, listening in.

"How did you do that?" I placed the steaming cup on the side table.

"It's part of being bound to you. I can hear your thoughts and you can hear mine."

"All the time?" I asked.

"No, only when it's needed. What you're seeing is real, but it won't happen until a week from now."

"A week! We only have a week to stop them!" My hands trembled; their veins pulsed thicker.

"Sarah, calm down."

"This *is* calm. How do you calm down in this body? My family is gone, my friends are gone, my life has been stolen!"

"Take another one." He handed me a second pill.

I felt like a druggie—first the serums, now pills. Would I ever control my body through my own will? *Of course not—I don't even have my body!*

We'll help you fix things. I promise.

"Who is 'we'?" I demanded.

Eric cleared his throat. "Hold my hand and close your eyes."

I placed my hand into his.

Now concentrate. Think about your loved ones and open your eyes, he instructed.

I did as he asked. Then I brought the new hands to my eyes to wipe away the fog. I still wasn't used to this new blurred sight.

"Hello, Sarah." The familiar voice didn't resonate. I shook my head from side to side, in case I was dreaming. The hushed voice felt comforting. Mira's cat purred with love when its kitten suckled its milk. This voice purred. It was a voice I'd heard as an infant, then later in my dreams—or what I thought were my dreams.

"Mom," I said. The new body collapsed. Eric caught me from behind and supported my back. I was glad to remain sitting. The new legs were numb and weren't responding to my desire to run and hug the ghostly figure standing in the doorway.

My throat ached, not from thirst or hunger, which felt different now, but with the hoarseness I remembered after I'd cried all night, when I'd found out I was the reason she was gone: as if I'd swallowed sand. I realized how much I missed not having her in my life to share secrets, wipe my mouth when fresh blood dripped off a vermin I sucked, tell her about my dreams, cry and laugh at the same time.

I realized how much I loved her.

I wanted her to be alive, and hold me, brush my tears away and whisper that everything would be all right. I wanted her to place a band aid in the spot where I injected my first serum, even if it healed instantly, and kiss my forehead good night. I wanted to know that when I woke up, she'd be there in the morning—not dead.

My mother floated like a dandelion's parachute toward me. "Darling, I'm sorry you're in so much pain."

How?

She's a ghost for now, Eric answered.

For now?

I'll explain later. Just know that she's always with you. So is your Aunt Helen. He nodded to the woman behind my mom. She wore her favourite flower-printed dress.

"Hello, Sarah."

Happy for the first time in this body, I expected a premonition, but nothing happened. *I don't understand,* I said to Eric.

Stay still. Spirits are fragile, especially ones whose destiny has not been decided.

I didn't pretend to understand. Even if I wanted to, this body was too shocked to move. After sucking in a quick breath, I let it out slowly. The pills were working. The intoxicating feeling returned.

So did William and Xela.

"So, when do you plan to fulfill the prophecy?" Xela didn't bite her lip or blush the way I would have.

"I haven't seen you hunt in two days. You've lost your colour."

"I just like the human food better."

"But you're only half human. You need to hunt. You need to be you."

"I'll just take the serum." She shrugged, then winked, looking hungrily at William. The gesture reminded me of our motel hostess. "Prophecy?"

"Soon, I hope." William kissed her nose.

I don't want to see this, I thought.

Then stop thinking about him for a moment, Eric said, breaking my concentration. *Your mother's ghost cannot appear often. The spirit can only do so when it's safe in their realm.*

What do you mean she's a ghost for now? How is their destiny not decided?

Their bodies were stolen before their last breath sounded and are being held captive. Their spirits remain hovering between the now and hereafter.

My focus shifted from my own troubles to my family. *We need to find them*

That's what has kept me so busy, and away from you. I'm sorry. Looking for their bodies is not our priority now, Sarah. I thought I had to find them first to help you, but I've been wrong. We have to get you back first. We have to switch what's been wronged. Hence, the evil-bender. Eric squeezed my hand, most likely trying to ease the tension he must have seen on my face. I couldn't control this face as well as my old one.

What you say is impossible. I whispered in his mind.

Never say never.

Our conversation seemed like it lasted minutes, but the exchange of thoughts between us took seconds.

"Don't be afraid, darling," my mom said. "We cannot stay long in this form. It takes too much energy. We have to return to our realm."

"Where are you?" I asked, taking a step closer. Eric held me by the elbow.

"We don't know," they answered together.

"Then how can I find you?"

"You can't, not now. You have to get back to William first. Once you have him back and the witch is gone, you'll know how to find us. We'll deal with the witch then." My mother's spirit flickered, angered.

"How do I get back to William?"

"The ruby ring will show your true self. It's the only way you can get them to see the real you," Helen said, floating closer to my mother's side.

"You have to be quick. The two of you don't have a chance against the siblings and four vampires. Wear the ring and go see them, Sarah. They'll recognize the real you." My mom explained.

"We have to go, Saraphine." Helen placed her hand on my mom's shoulder.

"Not yet. Please!" I reached out, crying. "I need you."

"You will always be here." Mom pressed her hand to her chest.

"We believe in you," my aunt encouraged me. "Remember, everyone has a purpose in life. You're about to be tested."

"Will I see you again?" I asked.

"I hope so." My mother smiled and blew me a kiss. My forehead warmed.

Their ghostly figures disappeared like a fresh fog blown by the morning wind.

I sucked in a quick breath and plopped down on the bed. When my mother vanished I expected to feel empty, but I didn't. Instead, she gave me hope beyond what I'd imagined. I no longer felt alone.

CHAPTER 25

"Have you vortexed before?" Eric asked.

"No. I just heard about it." I lifted my head higher to seem brave, but nausea came to this body quicker than to my old one. The idea of travelling to another continent through a time hole sounded dangerous, but at least we were doing something to get my family back.

The past three days of resting, regaining strength, and learning how to use this body in its human form had been exhausting. I popped vitamins, gained five pounds, and fought the urge to use vampire skills I no longer had. It was like having a urinary tract infection: waking at night to pee, but when you tried, nothing came out. Only my infection was a human body I didn't understand. Even when I had tried to suppress my vampire instincts, I had unknowingly used them. They had been responsible for the clarity of a mockingbird's perfect pitch, the intense smell of Helen's pancakes, and the crisp shapes of flower petals, leaves, and stems at my store. And all of it was gone, stolen by the witch.

"It will only take seconds. Don't close your eyes or you'll vomit," Eric warned. "When the mist clears, we'll be in front of the cabin's remains. Don't waste time—find the ring. You said in your sleep last night that they're planning to visit the cabin to recover what they can. I'll guard the front. Put the ring on as soon as you can. Ready?"

"No." I snorted a laugh.

"That's good. Xela would have been snobbish, too ashamed to say she's afraid or nervous. Don't worry, they'll see the real you."

"I hope you're right." A long breath escaped my lungs.

Eric squeezed my hand. I strained to keep my eyes open as the waterfall room began to spin, the liquid blending with the walls, the tapestries swirling into new patterns, the ceiling mixing with the floor until everything spun together and I couldn't distinguish one piece of furniture from another. The blue and red tones of the room mingled into a purple mist that shifted toward green and gray.

The contours of our burned home came into view, with taller grass and ever-blooming orchids behind it. Seconds later, we stood on an overgrown lawn. The sun filtered through the canopy to speckle everything below with sunshine. *Beautiful.*

"Go," Eric ordered in a whisper.

I ran, wishing I could have my vampire speed—the ability I'd taken for granted when I had it. Every step took more effort, like running through solidifying tar.

Half-burnt stumps of the logs propped the remains of the cabin. Charred skeleton of our home cracked when a swift gust of wind blew. The smell of the smoke still overpowered the jungle's natural scents. Finally, I made my way to the foyer. Nothing was spared, but I knew the fireproof door to the underground apartments had protected my parent's room.

I punched in the four digit code, and the floor moved aside. Before going down the staircase, I looked at Eric, who stood still, his eyes half closed, listening to the sounds of the forest. No—he listened for any approach of two shapeshifters and two vampires.

Scampering down, I hit every second step in my rush to my parents' room—a room I didn't want to stay in when I first came here, and now I wished I could never leave. I leaned back against one of the walls and closed my eyes, inhaling, hoping to smell jasmine, rose, and lilac with a woodsy, musky undertone, but this new nose wasn't sensitive enough to pick out the few particles I was sure floated in the air.

The drawer opened quietly, though I knew the ears I had lied. "There you are." The ring shone, although not as brightly as I remembered. I pitied humans having to look at the world this way, missing its true beauty. Before I could put the ring on my finger, I heard voices. "Crap!" I tried to squeeze it on, but the band was too tight.

My gaze flew toward the stairs, and I ran.

Five steps before reaching the top, I froze and held my breath, afraid to release it.

"What are you doing here, Eric?" Mira's voice.

"I'm here to make right what's been wronged," he answered.

"You can't rebuild the cabin. Why would you? It's none of your concern."

"Not the cabin—Sarah."

"He's a shapeshifter. He could be working for Aseret," Xela suggested.

"Shut up, witch!" Eric answered.

"Witch?" Xander sniffed the air, then growled. "She's here."

"Great, Eric. You don't have time to make our relationship work, but you find the time to cozy up with the witch. How could you?"

"This has nothing to do with us, Mira. She's good," Eric answered.

"I loved you! I loved you, and you left me for a calling."

I didn't need my vampire abilities to hear the quaver in Mira's voice.

"Nothing has changed between us, sugar," Eric replied.

"There's your lover-boy." Xander laughed, then sniffed again. "A two-timing lover-boy hiding the witch in the basement." The pain in Xander's voice couldn't be camouflaged by the vibrating snicker.

"You let her go downstairs?" William spoke for the first time. My heart pounded faster as if responding to his voice by itself.

"Do not move, Xander!" Eric warned.

"We can't let her escape, not this time. I'll kill her myself," Mira growled.

"Put your feelings aside, Mira. Think about it. Why didn't you kill her before?" Eric asked. "You couldn't. Your oath to Ekim to protect his daughter was stronger than you could understand. That's why you left the body in the woods."

"Our oath has nothing to do with this, Eric. You should know." The tone of Mira's voice rose each time she spoke.

"Xander, listen to the memories of the past," Eric said.

I peeked from the lowest step that placed my sight even with the floor. Xander turned his head to the left where Xela, posing as me, stood by William's side.

"Don't even go there, lover-boy," he hissed with anguish.

I couldn't take it anymore. I had to see them. They would see beyond the flesh. William would know. He'd read my face. *I'm coming out.*

Stay there. They're quicker than you think!

"I have to tell them." I stepped out into a patch of sunlight shimmering on the footprints left in the ash on the marble floor.

"Keep her away from me!" Xela yelled. "She'll curse us again, William!" The siblings rushed to stand in front of her.

William was quiet. He stared at my face. My heart beat harder and all I struggled to concentrate on the breathing through lungs which felt smaller with each inhale.

"Is it on?" Eric asked.

"It won't fit," I whispered.

"What won't fit?" Xander asked.

I pulled out my fist and opened it. The ruby sparkled in the sun.

Don't show them, Eric said in my head.

Don't worry; I know what I'm doing.

"It's your ring." William squeezed Xela's hand. "I knew it had magic, just like this one." He picked up Xela's hand with the blue gem that had remained on my old hand. I assumed she wasn't aware of its power. "That's what the witch came for."

I saw my body standing next to William and wished it was *me* but not with that soul. I couldn't bear to look at the hate in my eyes.

Look at me, William. Look at my face. To hope we'd still have our connection from the underworld was too much, but he did cup his elbow in his hand to chew on his thumb. *That's right, William! You're smart, figure it out. She switched our souls. You've felt it.*

"Now you're getting rings for the witch?" Mira asked Eric. "You're not the jewellery kind of guy. What did you do to him?" she growled at me, looking as if she wanted to rip my heart through the freshly healed wound in my chest. I was sure she could do it—and that no one would stop her.

"Stand down, sugar. She will not harm you," Eric warned. He concentrated on Mira's eyes, as if communicating something. The tension in Mira's shoulders softened. Eric looked as if he was hypnotizing her.

"Not this again." Xander rolled his eyes, but he wasn't standing in front of Xela any longer. He'd disappeared from her side and reappeared beside Eric, who had a blue glow emanating from his palm. But the glow wasn't as bright in today's daylight as it had been that day in the alley by the motel. He smashed Xander in the middle of his chest, but Xander didn't move; he returned a blow.

Mira rolled her eyes. "Guys! This isn't the right time for your testosterone peak."

They moved so fast, I could only see a dust cloud speckle with shining blue lights flitting through it. I heard thunder, but there were no clouds. Each time Eric and Xander clashed, the roar of thunder became louder.

My eyes wandered back to William, who had released Xela's hand. The witch's gaze focused on my hands. She saw the magic in the ring that I had always seen; I saw lust for newfound power on her face. A strong wind blew my short hair. Ash swirled in the clearing, and when it settled, the ring was no longer in my palm.

"You will never get any power again!" Xela yelled.

Everyone stopped: Eric and Xander paused mid-swing, the dust drifting around their feet; William lowered his thumb from his mouth; Mira held impossibly still.

She put the ring on her finger as I knew she would.

Across the tall green grass, in the middle of the circular field where I first twirled with my head tipped up to the sky, stood a figure, identical to the body I wore.

Mira gasped. William's eyes never left my face, and I thought I heard his heart skip a beat, and mine did as well. The pull toward him increased.

Don't move, Sarah, Eric cautioned.

He knows. William knows it's me.

Not yet. He's still confused. Don't move. Let me do my job.

But—

"Why are you staring at me?" Xela asked. "Kill her! Kill her before she hurts us."

"Shut up," said William.

She needs to touch you, Sarah, Eric whispered in my mind. *When she does, I'll do my job.*

"You're so brave, come and get me yourself," I taunted Xela under my breath. I knew she'd hear me. So did Mira, Xander and William, but they were in shock. My expression told William to stay where he was. His heart skipped a beat—he understood.

Mira and Xander stared at the extended inch-long spikes of flesh around Eric's neck. "He's bending," Mira whispered with pride, covering her mouth.

Xela flew to my side, her arms reaching for me. Before she could tighten her choke hold, Eric froze us with his blue light. Gravity gave in, and I saw myself float above ground, except my feet still touched the ashed grass. Then I realized my soul hovered above the body. The body I'd just left had empty eyes. I remembered someone saying you can see a person's soul through their eyes. Was that why they were blank? Was it because the body no longer had a soul?

"No!" Xela screamed. "William, help me!"

But William didn't move. I felt his heartbeat quicken, getting louder with each second as my soul got closer to my body.

Sarah, you'll need to push her soul out of your body. You're on an even playing field. She cannot hurt you now, but she'll fight.

A silhouette shimmered beneath my skin, and I grabbed it. Xela's soul tightened its grip around the body's limbs, not letting go, but when I touched my true body, I felt the strength of the forest come back to me. I regained the strength of a vampire.

Xela squeezed my neck with her hands. She wasn't going to let me into either body. Her body stood limp.

You can do it, Sarah. I believe in you. It wasn't Eric's voice I heard; it was William's. It was exactly what I needed to pull Xela out of my body. The witch wasn't surprised when she'd left my body, like she had done this before, and her ghosts hands grabbed my see-through neck. Could a soul die?

Grinding my teeth I pushed her away, the way William had taught me, and slammed my hand into her face. She shook it off and flew for my head, but I remembered my vampire skills better than what she'd learned while in my body.

Xela screamed as I deflected her blow and threw her soul back into her own body.

As I nestled in my silky smooth skin, Xela's thumped to the ground. I fell into William's arms and lost consciousness.

* * *

Two weeks had passed since I found my temporary home in a tent, set up in the middle of the clearing in the Amazon. Two wonderful weeks since I had reclaimed my body, and my life.

"How much longer?" I asked William as he led me through a crowded street. My eyes were covered with a silk scarf, and I'd promised not to peek. The sound of honking cabs, the wind of passing buses, and the muttered "excuse me" every few seconds from businessmen trying get home during rush hour told me we were in the city.

"Almost there."

We turned right.

"There's a step in front of you."

I stepped over a threshold into one of the buildings. The sounds of the street dissolved behind us when a door closed. The reddish glow under my eyelids darkened. The sound of my footsteps on the tiled floor bounced off the walls. I smelled candles.

"How romantic," I said.

"Just let me surprise you. Please?" William asked. I imagined his pouting lips mocking a gesture I would have made.

"That's kind of hard to do. You've used more cologne than usual. And now . . ." I sniffed "I smell tomato juice." I sniffed again. "And orange juice."

"You know, sometimes you make me wish you never got your abilities back."

"And you'd be stuck with Xela."

"I knew who you were the minute you stepped out of the basement."

"I know." I squeezed his hand. There were no throbs of pain. And there never would be any ever again.

"It was just hard to believe. I'm sorry."

It was the thousandth time William had apologized; Mira and Xander had apologized just as many times. The siblings had the task of getting rid of Xela, but they didn't kill her—Eric had other plans for her. But they had to bind her so she could no longer be a threat. I didn't know what that meant, and I didn't want to know.

Mira and Eric could finally spend time together. Castall and Mrs. G took a vacation in the hill. Xander was on a mission to learn whether seekers were looking for us—but couldn't find any. Apparently, they hid fearing Aseret's wrath, and we were not in any danger for a while. He also kept himself busy interrogating Xela.

William and I set up a campsite in the Amazon clearing while we determined whether we could rebuild. No one in the underworld knew about our home, except those who'd perished in Castall's blow in the underworld.

"Something about this place seems familiar," I said to William.

"I'm not surprised. Here." He untied the silk scarf.

I looked around the room. The lights were dimmed, and soft music played on the speakers. The iridescent petals of a blue orchid shone from a pot set between Fuzzy Navel and Bloody Mary drinks on the bar. The room was lit by hundreds of candles, and a disco ball spun lazily above our heads.

"How did you do that?"

"I'm sorry. I should have been honest when it happened, but I didn't want to embarrass you."

"I thought you only saw my premonitions, not my dreams."

"Again, I'm sorry. But we're here because I want to make your dreams come true."

He led me toward a gift wrapped in white paper. "Go ahead," he whispered.

I hurried to untie the decorative black bow. When I opened the white box, I gasped. A black Marilyn Monroe halter top dress was folded inside.

William pulled me in closer and kissed me the way I had always wanted to be kissed. My lips swelled on first contact. I didn't get a chance to put the black dress on or to wrap my legs around his waist or to lead him to the white leather sofa in the corner. The vampire inside overpowered my human nature, and the rest of the evening became a beautiful dance of fiercely connected bodies tumbling across the floor of a nightclub somewhere in New York City.

Bonus Chapters

The following three chapters were written from the point of view of the secondary characters, originally included in the story but cut in editing. I loved the chapters too much to not share them. Enjoy!

Bonus Chapter 1

Aseret changes Xela into Alex.

Xela strolled through the corridors of the underworld whe she'd heard Aseret's shout.

"Ketrab!" The demon lord bellowed, and the servant ever at his right hand jumped forward. He didn't dare delay in responding to his master—no one did. "Fetch Xela, now!"

Xela was already entering the hall, the black satin of her dress swishing about her ankles, its lace overlay flowing. She wore her dark hair loose, draping over her shoulders to hang down to her waist. The aroma of black roses followed her in.

"Aseret." Xela held her head high as she replied in a haughty tone. Royalty herself in the underworld, she was not required to bow.

Aseret rose from the grand chair where he'd been lounging to greet his ally. "Xela, any news, my dear?" It wasn't customary for him to be this polite, not unless he wanted something. He took her hand into his and lifted it to his lips for a peck—a sign of respect.

Xela smiled, head still high. Only her eyes wandered lower to observe the gesture.

"Seekers are getting closer, but we won't catch them just yet." She closed her eyes, remembering what she had seen in the steaming cauldron, a prediction in the murky liquid: the couple retreating from the seekers.

"Hmm. Do you know where they'll escape to?" Aseret asked slowly, drawing the words out and pausing between each. His flat nose twitched impatiently in his wrinkled face.

"To a green forest." She smirked. Xela enjoyed knowing more than he did and only gave away little bits of her prediction.

Aseret's lips tightened.

"Any particular one?" His mouth stretched into a thin line, and he inhaled through flared nostrils.

He's restraining his anger, she thought. *He doesn't want to be harsh, not yet.*

"No," she said. "That part is too well protected to be disclosed. I don't know how they do it." She pressed her hands to her head.

"Could someone stronger than you be protecting them?" he mocked.

"How dare you!" she snapped, eyeing him from his toes up. "This is not a place protected by any spell. It's man-made." Xela frowned, perplexed, and licked the saliva in the corners of her mouth with her tongue. It didn't matter how hard she tried to be ladylike, it never worked. The dirt crusted under her fingernails, the mascara smeared under her eyes, the debris tangled in the long-uncombed hair—all were required to maintain her witch-like appearance, an appearance most feared. Underworld creatures stayed out of her way. One stare from Xela could determine someone's fate. No one dared to cross her path.

"Innnterrresssting," Aseret replied in his famous drawl. The nose twitched again. "But we will find them?"

"Yes, they'll all be here." She closed her eyes. "Soon," she added, opening them. "And I will not like my new hairdo. Why would you want me to change this?" Xela grabbed her black locks and held them out, then let them drop.

"Very good, Xela! You've seen your makeover!" Glee picked up the pace of his monotone. "It's to make you look more . . . human."

"I *am* human, Aseret!" She waved her hands from the top of her slim figure to her toes.

"Believe me, Xela, as beautiful as you look now, I would rather you kept your current appearance," he soothed. "But you have to admit, it would seem at odds with what is considered ideal up above."

"I just wish the change wasn't permanent," she sniffed, straightening her dress.

"It has to be, if you want your kingdom," he warned. "It's the only way I will help you control the witches. It's still what you want. Isn't it?"

"I. Will. Not. Fail," she said firmly. Her confidence almost made Aseret take a step back, but she saw him regain composure as he lifted his chin. "And you will share your knowledge and powers." What she'd gain from their deal outweighed any sacrifice she had to make. Xela would finally be recognized as the highest witch in the world. Her dominance would be known immediately. No one would ever betray her again.

Aseret would not break the pack they had made. A promise sealed with blood, had to be kept. Breaking it would cost him his life.

The demon lord smirked. "We will be released from this realm and will no longer be bound by these walls. And we will be younger! Indestructible! We will destroy all who dare disobey! Our glory will reverberate throughout the world!" His deep bellow echoed throughout the hall as he floated higher and higher through the speech, rebounding back and forth from the walls before it bounced down the long corridors. Aseret lifted his arms, before drifting back down. His dangling cuffs slid lower to reveal pallid, wrinkled flesh. He tipped his face up toward the roof, and the hood slipped off his head, baring a pink scar behind his left ear that stretched toward his shoulder. The scar glowed, and when Aseret drifted back down and his cloak touched the floor, the light faded from the scar. He pulled the hood back over his head, the movement as dawdling as his speech.

Satisfied, Xela squatted on the cave floor. "Sand," she ordered.

Aseret threw his right hand forward and released a red stream of light toward the floor that disintegrated a swath of rock. Xela picked up a fistful of the fine, gray-black sand and allowed it to slowly pass through her fingers, streaming like water onto the floor, where it turned to polished stone. She stared at it quietly, sometimes squinting, other times opening her eyes wide as the flow of information played out for her in the rock.

"What do you see?" Aseret asked, his voice controlled. His nose twitched.

"Castall has warned them about me."

He rubbed his chin. "He'll pay for that later. What else?"

"It will be a long journey," Xela replied, feeling the premonition flow through her body like ripples in water.

"Will we succeed?" Aseret raised his brows.

"She will be wary of us. It will be hard to keep her away from him." The witch stood.

"Will we succeed?" he hissed, his tongue slithering like a snakes.

"That is still uncertain. I will separate them before it's too late."

"For how long?" Aseret circled around Xela, like he was stalking prey.

"That is also uncertain." Xela`s gaze followed the demon lord.

"What *is* certain?" He stopped.

"They will take me in. He will be mine." She smiled crookedly.

"And the child?"

Xela's gaze met Aseret's. She knew her eyes were still swallowed by her black pupils as she recovered from the spell she'd just read. "Not before he's mine." She paused, turning to scan through her thoughts. "And once he's mine, I will not let her near him again."

"And this future is certain?" Aseret completed his circling and returned to his original spot.

"It can't be more certain, unless they're closer."

"Let's get you ready, then. Let's get them closer!" He cackled loudly. Pleasure vibrated in his throat, and Xela assumed their goal to stop the prophecy would be moved forward.

"Go now!" he ordered without turning to look at the seekers. Three zombie-like demons were out the door before the last echo of Aseret's command died.

Xela turned to face Aseret and bowed her head in understanding. It was time.

"Hand," he said.

She stretched out her arm. With the sharp nail on his forefinger, Aseret sliced the witch's hand open. The slit spat out a small but steady flow of blood. He sampled its iron tang, then intoned, "Akhana mura til nero sima fom."

His words released a two-toned stream of light which flowed toward Xela. The orange-yellow light gathered into a cloud and hovered over her head before it sank to almost touch the top of her hair—sampling its victim, ensuring this was the right person before its moisture condensed. Bright rain danced over Xela's body, each drop progressively changing her appearance. The streams altered paths, leaving coloured valleys, rifts and mounts, shaping a new body.

Xela glanced toward a demon, and without having to ask, he sped across the hall with a full length mirror.

Golden blonde streaks lightened the dark hair, now bouncy with thick curls and cleansed of dirt and scum. Her eyes softened to a light blue in a pure and naturally pale face, free of smeared makeup. Crooked teeth straightened into even rows of white veneers. As the droplets trickled down to her feet, they left behind a young maiden, free of wrinkles and blemishes. A long, flowery dress hugged Xela's trim figure.

She glared at Aseret's pleased expression. "If you even think to laugh, I will cease our arrangement," she warned. But the new look, though awkward, triggered memories of her past.

"And what will you do about this?" He pointed at the sphere mark on her wrist.

"I'll use a more 'human' technique to cover it up." She laughed. "Makeup!"

"Clever, but what if it rains or you have to wash?"

Xela felt her new nose twitch the way Aseret's did. She wasn't impressed with this addition.

"I suggest a more semi permanent solution," he said with a sly smile.

Xela frowned and took a deep breath before asking, "What do you propose?"

"Scarring it; removing it from your wrist. It will hurt quite a bit."

"It's not the pain I fear, Aseret. This is who I am." She pointed to the mark. "I was born with it. Without it, I will never be treated with the same respect in the underworld again!" Xela didn't want to admit he was right. She wanted to turn her back to him but knew better than that.

"Not to worry. It will reappear once you remove the spell. Besides, when we're successful, I'll gain more respect than the mark itself earns." He squared his bony shoulders, exuding confidence.

"*We* will gain," Xela corrected with a scowl.

Aseret's nose twitched and he handed her a moist piece of fabric. "Take this cloth. Once it's done, wash the scar and the imprint will find its body." He looked into her face. "Will you be able to heal it in time?"

Xela pulled a piece of paper from her pocket, walked to the fire crackling in the hearth in the center of the hall, and picked up a chunk of charcoal. She used it to write on the paper.

"Get these ingredients to my cell as soon as I'm there." She handed the list to Aseret. Then she extended her left wrist. "Do what you must."

Aseret held his hand up, palm toward her. A thin stream of red flame shot out to sizzle against her skin. It seared Xela's birthmark, leaving a reddened, bloody wound. She clenched her jaw, biting through her lower lip with her new teeth, but did not move. A tear rolled down her new face, though not from pain. That was over.

Aseret snapped his twig-like fingers. Two seekers were standing at his side before he let his hand drop. "Take her down to the first cell. Treat her as a prisoner." He paused before adding, "But make sure she's well fed."

The demons took Xela by her delicate arms and led her down to the dungeon. She didn't speak another word.

BONUS CHAPTER 2

Mira and Xander wait for Sarah and William at The Grill.

The siblings sat at a table set for four. The Grill was packed, as it was most Saturday nights, but Michael, its owner, squeezed them in at the last minute. Mira and Xander watched the Funky Boys set up their equipment on stage, preparing for an after-dinner performance. The blue and red floodlights that illuminated the band's equipment flickered once in a while.

Mira inhaled the spreading aroma of chicken wings and barbecue sauce. "They'll be done to perfection tonight."

"Not quite, but almost." Xander took a whiff. "Undercooked by a minute." If there was anyone who knew food better than the chef, it was Xander. He skimmed the crowd toward the front door and frowned

"Tone it down, Xander, or you'll shift," Mira whispered, glancing around the packed restaurant.

His gaze met hers. "I don't understand how you can remain so calm."

Someone dropped dinner plates back in the kitchen. The heads in the restaurant turned toward the crash of the shattering crockery, but the siblings didn't flinch.

"I think I'll add on a couple of years," Mira replied. "Once Sarah knows the truth, we'll be able to date again. Seriously date."

"You'd date a human?" Xander swung his head around, as if trying to find a suitor but Mira knew he was looking for their late company.

"Yes. Stop fidgeting."

"What about 'lover-boy'?" Xander asked.

"It's been too long." Mira picked up the spoon to check her lipstick in its reflection.

"You mean he can't sneak in to see you? Wow, surprise, surprise."

"Shut up. We're both under oath. He can't step away from his, and I can't ask him to."

"And you'd find time to date a human?" Xander grinned with doubt.

"If Ekim doesn't need us anymore, then yes, *I would date a human*. I can deal with a shorter life span."

Xander gave his sister a confused look. "Why?"

"Why not?" She leaned in, clenching her teeth. "We've been around them enough. I know how they work. They don't disappear at the flick of a finger." She sat back on a sigh. "Look at Michael." Mira pointed to the blond owner, wrapping a damaged extension cord with electrical tape. "He's pretty hot—"

"And gay." Xander laughed under his breath.

"If anyone could make him straight, I could," she said.

"How? By shifting into a man?"

"No, by using my charm. That's not the point. I don't want to go back to the forest alone. Besides, I see how you've always looked at Sarah." She winked. Xander had a secret crush on the half-breed since childhood, but their oath to Ekim and the prophecy negated any advances he could make. And he never got over his true love.

Ahh, star-crossed lovers, Mira thought.

"Sarah's not human. She'd understand." Xander shifted his focus to the younger of the band members tuning her guitar.

"Sarah's also spoken for."

Xander leaned in toward his sister. "We don't know that for sure."

"Oh, come on, Xander—he's just like her. And she knows him already, without *knowing* him. You're sunch a bonehead Xander." Mira turned her attention to the waitress who came for the drink order. "An iced tea, please."

"Very mature, Mira. Add about a decade to your behaviour as well, will you?" Xander sneered, then placed his order. "Perrier with lime, please."

Frowning, Mira gave him a dirty look. "This battle is taking its toll on father. I hope whatever Sarah and William can do to help happens soon."

"I know what you mean." Xander sighed, suddenly serious, until his eye slid to the blonde hostess who had greeted them at the door.

"Hypocrite," Mira muttered.

He dropped his gaze to the menu where they stayed. Almost nothing could break Xander's concentration where food was concerned.

Mira stared at the listed selection of dinner combinations, indecisive. Her nerves hadn't let her eat all day. She licked her lips.

Today she felt more human than ever. Once Sarah knew the truth, Mira hoped they could be the friends she had always wanted to be, without any secrets. She smiled, straightening her back. For Mira, this was the beginning of a new life: shared secrets and double-dates.

I can do this—I can really have a life.

Then, Mira slouched.

Who am I kidding?

Sarah was part of a larger plan of which she had no knowledge, a plan that had to come first. She had to stop the extinction. The siblings had to protect her.

Maybe we could take her to the forest for a while. Maybe we could go with William and her to their safe haven. We should go with them.

But then we'd be tracked. Ugh, I have to figure out a way!

"You know she didn't work today," her brother interrupted her thoughts.

"I know." She sighed.

"So, where is she?"

"Maybe she's home getting ready. I told her there's someone I'd like her to meet. Except she probably thinks it's someone for me, not her." Though Mira secretly hoped it could also be someone for her, she knew the siblings' promise was more important. Their oath to guard Sarah would last until she didn't need protection anymore.

"I don't know if she was home, Mira. I missed both my jogs because of you. Did you really need a new dress? Couldn't you have gone and picked it up yourself?" Xander moaned, obviously irritated by the change in his daily routine.

"I had to get my nails done—you know, the way humans get them done. Sometimes you worry too much."

"And you not enough," he growled quietly. At least he was smart enough to be discreet about their shape-shifting nature, which could instantly morph their personalities from loving "angels" to savage beasts.

"That's why we work well together." Mira smiled.

"So where is she now?" he asked again.

"She's probably running a little late." Familiar waves of instinct ran through Mira, and she put the menu down. Scanning the restaurant, she hoped to see Sarah weaving between the tables toward them, but she didn't. "Although Sarah's never late."

There was something strange about today: the clouds had suddenly covered the bright sunrise this morning, and an odd stench had overwhelmed the fresh air, a stench of mold and mildew so strong it became acidic.

"And where is William?" he asked.

Xander has a point. Perhaps I overlooked something I shouldn't have.

Her instincts once again took over. "Xander, I'm getting a funny feeling." She patted her belly just below the navel.

"I've had it since this morning. Call her," he ordered.

Mira speed-dialled Sarah's number and let the phone ring four times before closing it. "She's not picking up. She always picks up my calls."

"Let's go." Xander was up and heading for the door, moving quicker than he should have in a public place. People turned their heads, frowning at their sudden exit.

"I'm sorry, Mike, there's a family emergency." She pressed three one-hundred dollar bills into the palm of The Grill's owner to cover the dinner and the inconvenience.

The darkness hid the siblings as they ran faster than was humanly possible down the street, then ducked into side alleys to get to Sarah's house. The closer they got, the more potent the mouldy stench became.

Xander stopped in front of Sarah's house. "Look." He pointed to the glowing orange skid marks on the road. They confirmed the sibling's worst fears.

Mira almost threw up. They could only hope William had gotten Sarah out in time.

"They couldn't run far in daylight. They had to have taken a car." She inhaled deeply. Mira didn't relish taking in the stench from the underworld, but she'd smelled worse. And she was searching for another scent, one that they already knew: William's. "He wasn't here. He didn't help her!" She panted.

"Hold on, Mira." Xander's steady voice calmed her panic. "Then where is William? He would have told us if she was taken."

Their eyes met in understanding, and the shapeshifters took off, sprinting toward Sarah's store.

The evening cooled. The seeker's stench was more difficult to detect here, away from Sarah's house, but it still present. The siblings should have recognized; it should have registered, even though the memory of it was lost in their minds. They were born for this, after all, but they had not smelled the odour in more than twenty years and it had changed a little, which put them at a disadvantage. The filth left an extra layer of salt and bitterness on their tongues reminding them of socks that had been worn for over a week in wet shoes. As they got closer to the store, the smell intensified.

Xander pulled on the handle of the closed door and it opened. They tiptoed inside.

The interior had been turned upside down. Crushed plants, shredded papers, smashed vases were scattered everywhere; water collected in puddles around the ruin on the floor. Sarah would have fainted had she seen it. Even her favourite orchid lay limp on the floor by the counter. Mira picked it up and tucked it back in its pot.

The store's phone flashed two new messages. Xander pressed the play button.

"Sarah, it's Kirsten. I'm sorry, but I'm down with a fever. I can't make it today." A cough. "I'll call you later if it breaks."

Beep.

"Sarah, it's me again. I hope you're doing okay at the store. I'm really ill. Please call me."

The blinking light stopped. The siblings looked at each other, inhaling in tandem, their chests expanding to their deepest capacity. They let the particles still in the store flow into their lungs to give them a better sequence of time during the past day's events.

"Kirsten never showed up. Sarah was here this morning, with William. Her and William's scents are mixed, combined into one. He got her out."

A hint of relief covered Xander's voice. His sister sensed anger, panic translated into rage and she shared his pain, his fear for their friends.

"She's safe for now, but . . ." Xander trailed off.

"The seekers won't stop now. They got too close," Mira finished for him. "We have to follow—"

"The seekers have started concealing Sarah's and William's scent. It's—"

"Dissipating." Mira nodded. "It's slowly being taken over by the odour."

"We'll follow the seekers until we know Sarah and William are safe."

The siblings let their innermost instincts take over. The smells told a story they could use.

"We'll be a full day behind, at least." Xander's body vibrated with eagerness.

"We won't catch up in time, unless we're lucky. Maybe the seekers won't find her."

"We can take a shortcut. Get Harlow to take the lead."

The sibling's falcon usually kept close to the shapeshifters.

"Yuck!" Mira knew the odour would start burning their nostrils soon, but it couldn't stop them.

The siblings looked knowingly at each other. There would be no time for goodbyes, no time for rest. This was what they were born to do, and they couldn't fail.

Mira ripped her new dress from the hem up to her crotch and tied the ends at the knees. Then she searched the black sky for their beloved falcon. Harlow could follow the seekers and lead them in the same direction by a shorter path. He would communicate with others of his kind until the siblings found Sarah. They could only hope they were not too late.

* * *

The seekers lost Sarah's and William's scent and headed south. The siblings couldn't understand why William had led them toward the demon lands.

Harlow left signs. He sent word back through others, telling the shapeshifters where to go. It didn't look like it would be a quick search, especially not on foot.

Mira and Xander ran most of the night, when no one could see their supernatural speed of a vampire, the fastest creature on earth. They rested during the day. Once the siblings hit open, uninhabited land, they took the chance and didn't slow again. A week of nonstop running brought them to the border of Mexico. Crossing over wasn't a problem; no human could spot them when they moved at their fastest.

Sarah's and William's scent had disappeared a few days back. The shifters' one consolation was that the seekers couldn't find it either. Harlow had told the siblings they were using other means to find the half-breeds, which puzzled the shifters. They could only follow the smell of dirty socks—the seekers' trail.

BONUS CHAPTER 3

Mira and Xander go to the hill to pick up their mom, while Alex plots to steal Sarah's body.

"Ma! We're here!" Mira called, the first to step through the door at 21 Front Street.

"I know, I know." Ma bustled forward to hug her kids as if she had not seen them in years. "How are you?" she asked, kissing each on the forehead. "I heard you had quite an ordeal. Here." She took their jackets and hung them on the hallway hooks. Ma was the best kind of mother. She'd iron Mira's dresses, cook Xander's favourite food, and she would never use her magic to scold them. To her, they would always be her little "monsters."

"No big deal." Xander shrugged. "I knew we could handle them." He picked up one of the two glasses of orange juice Ma had waiting for them atop the hall table.

"Right, you against three hundred seekers—no big deal," Mira teased.

"Three hundred?" Hannah raised her eyebrows and frowned. "Your dad skipped that part."

"Is Dad still here?" Mira asked.

"No, he had to go to Spain to speak with Drake and Gabriel about a spell no one seems able to break through. He said you'd come to get me." She used her cuff to wipe the rings of condensation the glasses had left on the tabletop and muttered under her breath, "No easy task, to break someone else's spell. It's nearly impossible."

"Nearly?" Xander asked.

"Unless you have their permission, it's impossible. Now, what brings you two home?"

"We found Sarah and William. They're at the hill with their parents. You're coming back home, Ma!" Mira chirped, eagerly jumping up and down.

"But you guys love it here," Hannah protested. "I can't uproot you again."

"We're not children anymore," Mira said. "Besides, it's where we want to be—in the woods." She gulped her drink quicker than her brother, keeping her eye on him while the juice disappeared.

Laughing, Hannah handed Xander a tissue to wipe the orange juice from his chin. "Slow down or you'll choke."

"You're not safe here, Ma." Xander insisted. "It will be better if you come with us." His voice grew wheedling. "It will make us feel better. Please?"

"Sarah and William need your help with a spell," Mira added.

"I cannot take it off," Hannah explained.

"But you're a powerful witch," the siblings said together.

"If I interfere, an imbalance will occur. From what your father said, this could be Aseret's curse."

"But can't you lessen its effect?" Mira suggested. "Or paralyze it?" The hope that Sarah and William could get close to one another ignited her own heart. *At least two soul mates could be together.*

Hannah capitulated with a sigh. "I can try. Get your stuff—only the necessities. We'll leave as soon as we can. I'll check the pot." She headed down to the basement, most likely to stir her pot-full of magical ingredients and look for signs of danger. Mira knew it was something she did before any journey she took. Five minutes later, Hannah called up. "Come on down, it's ready!"

In their rush to be the first into the basement, Mira and Xander got stuck in the doorway. The door frame cracked.

"If you two break this house again, you'll regret it," Hannah threatened.

The siblings looked at each other.

"Rock, paper, scissors," Mira called.

They threw their fists out at the same time.

"Ha!" Mira covered Xander's "rock" fist with her flat "paper" hand.

Frowning, Xander let her go ahead.

Hannah had returned her concentration to the pot. "Our journey to the hill looks safe, but we will travel separately. That's odd." She frowned, then tightened her lips and stared into the steaming liquid. She pulled out her hand. "Now, do you have something of Sarah's?"

"Here." Mira handed her three strands of Sarah's hair.

"And William?" Hannah looked at Xander.

Xander passed her a few strands of William's hair.

"I taught you well, but I won't ask how you got these." Hannah smiled. She inhaled, then released the breath in a long, steady stream to scatter the steam over the cauldron, unveiling a swirling, clear broth. Hannah threw the strands into the liquid, scooped a fistful of dirt from beside the fire, and added that into the mixture. Next in went bottled herbs, petrified spiders, and dried moths. She used a big wooden spoon to stir the contents into the simmering, bubbling liquid. Each fizz released a different aroma that carried a distinct prediction.

Mira and Xander shuffled their feet with excitement; they liked it when she brewed her magic—something they couldn't do. Generations of witches' blood flowed in her veins, but they'd been foundlings, taken in by the childless Hannah and Castall, and had powers more physical in nature.

After the first few swirls, Hannah drew a dagger from a pocket in her dress, placed the sharp edge in her left palm, and closed it tight. The siblings bit their lip. Hannah pulled the dagger slowly from her closed left palm. Burgundy drops dripped into the pot, each one releasing a different sound as it struck the hot concoction, her blood the main ingredient to conjure pictures.

Hannah stirred the pot again.

"What do you see? Is Sarah with William?" Mira hunched over the steaming pot.

"Are they together?" Xander added. "Can you soften their spell?"

"It's . . . it's complicated, and odd," Hannah said. "Everything is backward."

"Oh . . ." She shook her head in surprise. "I don't have to remove the spell. It's gone."

"What?" The siblings spoke together.

"How could it not be there?" Mira asked.

"It's been removed," Hannah said.

"By whom?" they asked.

Hannah drew a deep breath. "I'm not sure," she finally said, then picked up one of the jars she'd emptied into the pot and sniffed its interior. "They're fresh. Could it be a disintegrating spell? No, hardly anyone uses that these days. If a spell was cast, it was done for a reason." She turned abruptly to face both kids. "Who else is in the hill?"

"Ekim, Atram, Willow, and Alex," Mira answered then bit her lip, looking from Xander to her mother.

"Who's Alex?" Hannah asked.

"She's a witch we rescued from the dungeon. She helped us escape. Sarah saw her help us in her vision," Xander explained.

They read the concern in her eyes, in her trembling hands and quivering lips.

"She's harmless, Ma," Mira said quietly, but her voice shook. "There's no mark on her."

"*No* mark?"

"None. We checked," said Xander.

"It's impossible for a witch not to have a mark," Hannah said.

"She was cursed, and the mark hasn't been decided yet," Xander said, his voice tremulous. "Just like it hadn't for us until the time came."

When Ma and Pop had found them at the tender age of eighteen months, Mira and Xander were already powerful. It took patience and devotion to keep their hearts on the good side until it was time for their markings. The memory of being left alone, then living between two worlds still haunted them; they'd promised each other: where life took one, the other would follow.

"Not for witches. Our marks are there at birth, because it's in our blood. It's an ancient curse from the dark ages, to punish females. We have no choice. A witch cannot be cursed not to have one. Are you sure you didn't see one?"

"Yes, Ma," they replied together.

Hannah turned back to the pot, murmuring an incantation as she plucked and added a strand of her hair to the mix. "She cannot hide from me this way," she declared, stirring the contents before blowing the rising steam away again.

A new image appeared.

"Everything is backward. They're walking backward, talking backward. Look!" She pointed, and the siblings leaned closer. "Now she's walking on the ceiling, upside down . . . Alex's backward is exaggerated." Perplexed, Hannah continued staring at the liquid. "Wait! William and Sarah are no longer backward!" She frowned. "Alex is still backward."

"A backward Alex?" Xander asked, "What does this mean?"

Sudden realization drained Hannah's face of blood. "It's not Alex," she gasped. "It's Xela!" The fire under the pot flared, and they had to lean back from the heat and step away as the pot's contents began bubbling over. Hannah's face went slack. "Of course—Alex spelled backward is Xela!"

"Xela!" Mira's hand flew up to cover her mouth.

"Aseret's Xela?" Xander asked in disbelief, the shade on his face paled with green.

Hannah nodded grimly. "Yes, Xela, the witch who's been trying to rule all witches."

"But, Ma, you know Xela; we know Xela; everyone knows Xela, even all the vampires. This is not her!" Mira hurled her forefinger toward the image in the liquid.

Xander leaned against the back wall. "I can't believe this is happening again." He fisted his palms.

"It is her, under Aseret's finery spell. I should have known. He changed her so she could get close to Sarah and William. They're in danger!"

She sprang to her feet.

"Run, Mira; run, Xander! Warn them before it's too late!" The house shook, vibrating her command.

And they were gone.

SNEAK PEAK AT BOOK THREE IN THE SERIES

TWO EQUALS

CHAPTER 1

He should have killed her.

I couldn't understand why Xander thought the witch ought to live—not when she'd stolen my body to use in her scheme to destroy the human and vampire races. The memory of her theft sent chills down my spine. She'd almost killed me.

After my soul had been switched with hers, I'd never felt the same, and for the past four years I'd been trying to figure out the reason. She was the only connection I had to the answers to my questions. She was the only one who could explain why I'd changed. Yes, I was a mother and a wife now, but that wasn't the source of the dissimilitude. I could separate those responsibilities from my duties as a half-breed vampire.

No, it went deeper; something in me wasn't the same. Part of me had never returned to my body, and I had to know why.

Today I waited on the porch, counting the minutes. Every day, after training with my children, my friend Xander went to a secret cave to see his witch. I was determined to find their hideout.

I sat on the front steps with my eyes closed, welcoming the cooler evening breeze. With spring ending, the summer heat wave loomed, ready to blast the Amazon and dry up its burgeoning rivers.

Four minutes since Xander left, I tapped out the seconds with my wiggling fingers. My right knee bobbed and heel thumped on the deck, sending dull wooden echoes through the clearing. I pressed my hand onto the knee to stop the habit.

I'd been planning this for a while, to ensure I overlooked no detail. This time I would succeed. I would find the witch's hideout without Xander catching me, the way he had each time I'd tried before.

I inhaled a woody musk and opened my eyes.

"He's going to catch you," William warned, handing me a glass of water. He must have put the twins to bed before coming out to join me.

"I haven't tried to follow him for a week now."

"And you think that will make him less suspicious?"

"I'll be careful." The breeze cooled my fingers around the glass.

He raised his brows. "You're trying to outsmart a shapeshifter."

"You think I can't?" I retorted.

"I'm not getting involved in your quarrels, but he's still your best friend. He trusts your promise."

He was trying to make me feel guilty, but I was determined to have my questions answered, so I couldn't give up. Plus I hadn't told William that I'd crossed my fingers behind my back when I made the promise to my best friend. Childish, yes; unwarranted, no.

"He's hiding a witch who wanted to kill me," I reminded him, trying to justify my betrayal.

"He must have a reason." William sat in the wicker chair behind me and leaned forward, cradling his glass in his hands. "Come on Sarah, it's Xander. He'd never hurt you." He paused to sip from his glass. "And I don't like you getting too close to her. It's as if you're still drawn to her."

I didn't realize my fingers had tightened around my glass until it shattered. I stared at the slit in my palm, reminded of the blood I'd lost when in Xela's body. She'd cut her chest to let her soul escape and push mine away. My spirit had taken over her empty host. I never felt I'd gotten my full self back when Eric bent the witch back to her own body, returning mine to me.

William had gone into the cabin. He came back within seconds. "Just be careful, Sarah, please," he said as he bandaged a slit that would heal in minutes.

"I will." I kissed him. "I'll say goodnight to the kids, then go."

"I'll be waiting."

William began sweeping up broken glass and I rose and went inside, pausing to inhale the lavender soap aroma that wrapped my children's bodies like a blanket. I'd never forget the scent that my own and William's scents conjured when mingled with their natural honey and lemon smell. The twins slept with their mouths slightly open, exhausted from their daily training. The tricks Xander and Mira taught them became more difficult to master each day.

I often wondered whether we were pushing the twins beyond what three-year-olds should be able to do. My children had a constant need for naps. I'd find them in the middle of the hall, sleeping; up in the trees, their limbs dangling off supporting branches, sleeping; even in the emerald pond, floating on their backs—sleeping. But Crystal and Ayer weren't regular twins. We didn't have a name for what they were, not yet. Another mystery I'd lost sleep over at night.

The kids were developing abilities I didn't understand. Mira and Eric were teaching the twins what they knew, as well—when they weren't gathering the lingering souls from the hereafter. They'd promised me that, once it was time, I would be reunited with my mom and my aunt before they passed on.

I looked at my watch. I'd given Xander a ten minute lead; it was time to follow him through the forest. His daily ritual of bringing food to the witch was as predictable as sunrise and sunset. He'd leave right after the training, and in the evening when the twins went to sleep, splitting his duties between watching over me (which I no longer needed), and uselessly talking to the witch.

Was she tricking him the way she had tricked me? What was the point of keeping her alive? Part of me didn't like the jealousy swirling though my body. After all, I had William and the twins. I was happy— happier than I'd ever imagined—raising my children, preparing them for a future I was sure would be nothing short of difficult.

Was William right to ask me to leave Xander and the witch alone? Perhaps, but I agreed with what he'd said. I was drawn to Xela more than I wanted to admit. I'd always thought a connection had lingered between us after the soul switch.

I missed the adventure, too. I longed for the day we could finally be rid of the warlock, no doubt in a battle fiercer than the one in the underworld against hundreds of seekers. But Aseret had made no attempt to attack for over a year. His efforts to locate us were futile. Each time he tried, Eric could twirl his finger and magically tie Aseret back to the underworld. The warlock had seekers he could send to capture us again, but they had no chance against us. Their fears weakened them and William could wring their necks before they even blinked their orange eyes. We were safe, but I didn't want to feel safe. I knew as soon as we relaxed our guard, Aseret would step in.

Xander's tracks on the forest floor had been difficult to follow, but I'd eventually closed on him, remaining far enough back that he wouldn't detect my presence. Now I saw Xander slow his jog and shift back from a wolf form. The sun hung behind stray clouds, high enough not to affect my sight. I inhaled his aroma.

He froze, scanning the forest. Was he hunting, too?

I stopped when my best friend disappeared. *Crap!* I ducked behind a bush. Did he sense me? My ears perked up, sensitive as a hare's. I couldn't hear his footfalls. I peeked through the branches but he wasn't there. I'd lost him.

I rose and followed his scent, letting my nose find the way. Then I jumped back, startled, as Xander leaped in front of me.

"What are you doing?" Xander stood with his hands on his hips, brow furrowed. He was controlling his anger; green hadn't infused his face yet.

"You're sneaking off to see her again," I accused, holding my chin higher, but shame for following after I'd promised not to burned my cheeks. Revenge, though new to me, brewed inside me when I thought about the witch; I couldn't help it.

"First, I'm not sneaking. Second, it's not your business, Sarah." Xander squared his shoulders.

"She tried to kill me." I widened my eyes for emphasis, and crossed my arms at my chest.

"It wasn't her."

"What?" I blurted as resentment burned in my veins. "Then who? Why are you keeping her locked away? She should be dead." She'd stolen my soul by exchanging hers for mine, and pretended William belonged to her!

"Like I said, it's not your business," Xander said stubbornly. Nothing would sway him.

"Xander," I said, my tone more reasonable, "I just want to understand. We're friends."

He relaxed as well, though his answer wasn't satisfying. "No one can understand, because I don't understand."

"Then let me help you figure out whatever you're trying to figure out," I pleaded.

He shook his head, the opportunity closing again. "It's not a good time. Go home, Sarah; be with William, be with the kids."

I lowered my head.

"You don't want to be with them?" he asked.

I looked at him. "No, it's not that."

"Then what is it?"

"I miss you, and Mira."

"We're still around."

"Not the way you used to be." I bit my lip; my complaint sounded so childish.

Xander sighed. "It's complicated. I thought William was everything you'd wanted."

"He was, and he is." I cleared my throat. "It's just a little hard to let the dreams I'd had about him wear off."

"Mr. Perfect isn't Mr. Perfect?" He chuckled.

"Stop it!" I showed my fangs. "You know he is, but I'm having a difficult time letting the kids explore their demonic side."

"You're lying. I know when you lie." Xander leaned against a tree. I was beginning to amuse him.

"Well, it's complicated for me, too," I said.

"Fine. Then why is it so difficult for you to accept the children's training?"

"Because I don't understand their demonic side," I exclaimed. "I know how to be human and a vampire, but the demons . . ."

"First off, they're not *demonic*." He rolled his eyes. "Besides, you know us."

"You're shapeshifters."

He raised his brows. "We're a little more than that, aren't we?"

"Yes," I admitted. "And that's what I want to understand. What would make a strong shapeshifter like you want to keep the enemy alive?"

"There are things in this world you still don't understand."

His dismissal angered me. "Bull! I do understand, Xander, but you're keeping a shield between us."

"Sarah, I have to keep a shield between us." He stepped forward until he stood only a foot away from me.

"Why?" I held the air in my lungs when a hint of his testosterone oozed toward me.

"Because if I don't, I'll do something we'll both regret."

I felt the lump in my throat clear with difficulty. This wasn't the first time in the past year that Xander had almost crossed the line of our friendship. At one point he and William had had a falling out and hadn't spoken to each other for a month. Xander apologized. Eric convinced us to let it go, that it wasn't Xander's fault. I trusted Eric—more than I trusted my own instincts.

"Xander, I'm with William."

"I know. Believe me, I know."

"Then why?"

"Because I'm a man."

"And that's supposed to make me feel better?"

"I can make you feel better." He lifted my chin, rubbing his thumb on the dimple below my lip.

"Xander . . ."

"I've known you all my life and you bear the closest resemblance to someone I'd known well. Your curves are identical, your smile, the way your eyes light up when you say my name." He brushed the back of his hand against my cheek.

"That's because you're my best friend. I trust you. I . . . I love you, but not in the way you'd want me to."

"I know, Sarah," he sighed. "I love you too; not in the way you think, but it's the closest thing to love I may ever have."

"Why? Why can't you find someone?"

His laugh was bitter. "I already found her, but we cannot be."

"Who?"

"It's complicated."

"You know you have a friend in me forever, right?" I leaned in to comfort him. I shouldn't have, but I did.

"I know," he whispered, burrowing his face in my shoulder, nestling his nose in my hair.

The cologne he wore today smelled more attractive than other days. There was a hint of the woody musk I loved to smell on William, along with a sweet aroma of raspberries and the tartness of a rose. I tried to remember what kind of rose could smell so intoxicating.

Xander lifted his head, bringing his face inches away from mine. I didn't want to move, because I'd never looked at his mouth the way I did today. The pull toward him was magnetic. I felt his lungs expand as his chest pressed into mine. His eyes mellowed; his lip swelled, inviting me. I didn't want to breathe, afraid that if I did, my next breath would be shared with his.

"Shit!" He pulled away.

I shook off the pheromones that pulled me closer to him, shivering like a wet dog. What had just happened?

"I'm sorry about this, Sarah."

"What was that?"

He held up his hand. "I'll fix things, I promise."

"What do you have to fix now?"

"Look, if I show you where Xela is, do you promise to keep your distance?"

I nodded like an eager kid.

"And you won't question why I'm keeping her?"

I nodded again, stepping from one foot to the other.

"Nor hurt her?"

"Yes, yes, yes. I agree to it all." I grinned, knowing my friend had changed his mind.

"Pinky swear?" He held out his hand, hesitant. I didn't laugh. To me, this was the most important promise Xander could make.

"Pinky swear." I hooked my finger into his.

"Close your eyes."

"Why?"

"Because even if I take you to her, I don't want you to see where she is."

"Fine." I shut my eyes.

I heard a ripping sound and opened my eyes only long enough to see that Xander had torn the sleeve off his shirt. I closed my eyes again as he tied the sleeve over my eyes.

"And don't use your senses. I'll be confusing you anyway."

"You know you don't have to do that," I said.

"You'd be surprised what kind of trouble acute senses can get you into."

I exhaled. "Fine." But I crossed my fingers behind my back. I don't know why I did that; instinct, I guess.

I felt fur against my leg—Xander had shifted into a wolf and sidled up beside me, indicating that I should sit on his back. I climbed aboard, and he carried me through the forest. The cool wind wrapped around my limbs. I burrowed my face in his fur, and tightened my grip. He sped between the trees at his fastest, sometimes circling back the way we'd come. I tried not to use my senses, but that was like asking a human not to breathe. My senses were part of me and not something I could turn off—he knew that.

He leapt over a creek, then a second one. At one point I thought he'd jumped over a gully; perhaps he did. After a while Xander's sprint turned into a trot, then a walk. He shook his torso, wriggling me off his back. He shifted back before taking off my blindfold, then we continued as two humans on foot.

Twenty minutes later we stood in a valley deeper in the Amazon than I'd ever ventured, only the familiar flora and fauna indicated we hadn't left the jungle I knew. I'd never been to the Grand Canyon before, but this place was exactly what I imagined that geographical wonder to be, except here, the forest didn't thin into pink rock cliffs. It expanded, the greenery as luscious it was by my cabin. I looked up, shielding my eyes from the sun directly above us. My stomach grumbled when I heard a stream of fresh water gurgling nearby.

"We'll get food on the way back," Xander told me as he stepped toward a rock the size of a minivan.

I nodded when he looked back at me.

"When you see her, don't listen," he continued. "She'll try to sway you, and if she does, I'll have to sedate her."

"Okay," I said cautiously.

"And wipe that smirk off your face. You look like you've just won a prize." He paused. "Trust me, you haven't."

Turning, Xander pushed aside the boulder, revealing the dark opening of a cave. We stepped into the darkness. Just as my sight adjusted, Xander lit the end of a branch he'd retrieved from beside the entrance. I smelled gasoline. The torch cast pervasive shadows on the walls. Chills ran up my spine—not from fear, but adrenaline. I felt the way I had four years ago, when I fought against Aseret, then tricked Xela to get my body back.

Xander led me ten steps down into the cave before stopping to push open a wooden door. Rusted hinges squeaked, sprinkling their copper-colored dust in an arc along the cave floor. We stepped into a room lined with shelves holding pots and clear jars filled with dried ingredients and gooey liquids; dried herbs hung from the ceiling. The burrow reminded me of Mrs. G's hill, but this one felt lonely. Even with the heat streaming from a fireplace, the chills never left my spine. Anyone living here was meant to be isolated from the world. In one corner of the misshapen room, black roses bloomed on a low bush, allowing one red flower in the midst of its leaves. The aroma from the blossoms hit me as soon as we entered; their intense scent reminded me of the rosy scent I'd smelled on Xander.

"This was her house?" I asked.

"No, this is a replica of where she lived in the underworld."

I looked at him. "Why?"

"I . . . I have my reasons," he stuttered. Xander's voice never shook. His eyes darted from me to a darker corner of the room. He was wary of me and probably feared I'd kill the witch.

"I promised I wouldn't do anything," I assured him.

"Sometimes promises are broken."

"Not mine."

He rolled his eyes, but didn't lecture; I wondered if he knew I'd crossed my fingers behind my back.

At the far end of the room, Xela sat in a wooden chair, her arms chained behind her. The shadow of a webbed root penetrating the ceiling in front of her concealed her body. Beside the chair sat a bowl filled with leftovers. Xela's head had fallen forward.

"She's sleeping," I said in a low voice.

"No, sedated."

"Why?"

"I can't explain everything, but I'm not hiding her to spite you." Xander turned to face me again, his eyes suddenly mellower and the tautness in his jaw softened.

The smell of black roses filled the cave. A new rush of endorphins swam through my veins. My sight blurred.

"I've never met another woman like you," Xander whispered.

I felt his breath on my face. I wanted to push him away and punch him in the face the way I'd normally do, but I couldn't. Something held me in this gloomy room, and part of me felt as if I'd travelled back in time. The Xander with me today wasn't from today; he was happier, with shining eyes. He looked like he was in love.

I wanted him to place his arms around me, and as if on command, he did. He pulled me in closer, tightening his hands on my hips before running them up both sides of me to my arms, and finally framing my face. My body felt glued to his, which responded to my rushing pulse. I leaned in, wanting him to do things to me that only William had done. Xander's lips nearly touched mine.

William, I thought.

"Take me back," I whispered, straining to pull away. "Take me back to William."

Xander's eyes bulged and he jumped back.

A cackling laugh echoed through the cave. Xela lifted her head, unable to contain her mirth.

"Stop that!" I yelled, feeling my ears press against my head.

"Ahh, what's the matter? William ain't enough for you?" she taunted.

I sprang forward, ready to rip her heart out, but Xander stopped me midway. I pounded on his chest to make him move aside, but I may as well have been hitting rock.

"You know you can't stop me, Xander," I hissed.

"You can't hurt her."

"Ooh, the poor boy misses his witch." She laughed again.

"What is she talking about?" I asked.

"I can't do this. You have to leave, Sarah. Please." His eyes pleaded more than his words, and I read the pain in them.

I had no heart not to listen. I stopped. Turning on my heel, I darted out of the cave. The witch's laugh followed us.

I stepped out in the sunlight. "What was that?"

He grinned. "Me trying to kiss you?"

"You've tried before; no big deal," I said, concentrating on the blooming daisy at my feet.

"No big deal?" he exclaimed.

"The problem was, I wanted to kiss you as well."

"Really? I hadn't noticed." He smirked.

"You knew this was going to happen?"

He nodded.

"Then why did you let it?"

"It was the only way for you to understand why I cannot let anyone come here. Xela's magic is powerful and we haven't been able to contain it."

"We?"

"Mira and me. She understands. You should have seen her face when I tried to kiss *her*." He laughed.

"Eww-ohh! Your sister? What's with the kissing, Xander?"

"Could you control your lips in there?"

"No." I felt blood rush to my cheeks.

"Maybe I shouldn't have stopped. That way it'd make your trip worthwhile." He grinned.

"Don't do that again," I warned.

"Fine, but you need to understand," he pushed the boulder back over the entrance, "it wasn't me in there. The closer you get to this cave, the more powerful she is. She is doing this, and you need to stay away."

"Why keep her?"

He shrugged. "It's complicated."

"You've said that."

"Because it is. Let it go."

"Fine."

"Pinky swear?"

"Pinky swear," I sighed, but crossed the fingers of my other hand behind me again. I didn't want to come here, but felt drawn to the witch more than I'd like to admit. Part of me craved the unknown. And the rush I felt when Xander came so close to me. I wanted him as much as I wanted William, and I couldn't forget it.

The witch's laugh roamed through the valley, circling back to our ears again.

"Don't pay attention to her." Xander lowered his head.

"You're asking a lot."

"I hope I can explain it one day."

"Me too. It seems that she's sucking the life out of you, and I don't like it." I stepped forward to take his hand. The contact flowed over my skin like satin, and I felt my pulse speed up. I took his other hand, and the feeling intensified. Every time I touched his hand, I felt his life vibrate with mine. I heard my heavy breathing and didn't want to control it. All I wanted was to give in to the warmth oozing from Xander and let him fulfill the tingling urges near the bottom of my pelvis.

Xander's lips hovered above mine, then he whispered, "We'd better go, before I get slapped for you kissing me."

I jumped back, straining to concentrate on something other than my hot best friend. Whirling, I sped through the trees toward the stream I'd heard earlier. I jumped in feet-first and sank below the cool water, letting it cool my heated body. I didn't know where the heat came from, but I had a pretty good idea.

Xander waded into the water up to ankle depth, his pants rolled to his knees. Smirking, he offered his hand. "Don't worry, I won't let it happen again," he said as he pulled me up, "if you promise not to come here."

"Fine." I shook the lust off my body. *That was some magic,* I thought.

"You're soaked."

"Really?" I said sarcastically.

"Hop on and close your eyes." He shifted.

I swung my leg over his back and gripped his fur, pressing my body along his back as he took off and let Xander's heat warm my limbs through my drenched clothes. I cheated. I kept my eyes open as he galloped through the forest, across fields, and over gullies, memorizing the way to the cave. If I knew Xander the way I thought I did, he'd know I broke my promise anyway. Did he want me to break it? Did he want me to come back to the cave, even when he said he didn't? Or was it just me justifying my coming back?

As we left the boundary of the valley, I heard Xela's laugh inside my head:

I'm still here, Sarah. I'm still here.

About the Author

Marta lives with her husband and two kids in Cambridge, Ontario. A great skier (in her kids eyes), she loves the outdoors and quiet mornings on the porch with a cup of coffee. She can often be found creating new worlds in front of her computer. She has a sarcastic sense of humor and those very close to her know that she can make a joke out of almost anything; but she would suck as a comedian. Her favourite colours can all be found in nature.

If you enjoyed Two Halves, please consider leaving a review. All authors depend on the support of their readers to find an audience.

Books by this Author in the Two Halves Series:

Book 1: Marked: A Two Halves Novella
Book 2: Two Halves
Book 3: Two Equals
Book 4: Evil-Bent: A Two Equals Novella

Connect with Me Online:

Twitter: http://twitter.com/martaszemik
My Blog: http://martaszemik.blogspot.com/

Acknowledgments

As always, I am grateful to be surrounded by many loving people who support me, my fantasies, and my writing.

First and foremost my family, without whom this novella would never be in the hands of my readers.

Each writer takes a different approach to their work. For me, I began writing because I wanted to, now I need to. And I wouldn't be able to do it without the help, encouragement and inspiration from other writers and my blogger friends. I am honoured to know all of you. Your words of wisdom, share of knowledge and enthusiasm for the written word astound me every day.

I am grateful to my editors Marg Gilks and Nicole Zoltack, and my reader and editor friends for their invaluable input, critique, support and love. A big thank you to Robin Ludwig Design Inc. for the beautiful book cover.

To anyone who ever wanted to write: all it takes is will, imagination and belief. I hope I can one day inspire others to do what they love, the same way authors have inspired me.

CPSIA information can be obtained at www.ICGtesting.com
Printed in the USA
LVOW080903220912

299816LV00002B/4/P

9 780987 877215